For my father, TAF, thank you for all your sacrifices and constant support.

For Fatoba Oluwaseyi, I wish you were here to see our childhood dreams come true. I hope you find peace and light wherever you are.

This is a work of fiction. Names, characters, businesses, places, events, locales, and incidents are either the products of the author's imagination or used in a fictitious manner. Any resemblance to actual persons, living or dead, or actual events is purely coincidental.

WARNING: This novel depicts complex financial crimes, including Business Email Compromise (BEC), credit card fraud, identity theft, and money laundering. These descriptions are strictly for entertainment and narrative atmosphere. They are not instructional and should not be relied upon for accuracy or attempted. The activities described herein are federal felonies carrying severe penalties, including long-term incarceration. The author and publisher disclaim any liability for any actions taken by readers based on the material contained in this book.

Copyright © 2021 by Nate Haliv.

All rights reserved. No part of this book may be reproduced, transmitted, or stored in an information retrieval system in any form or by any means—graphic, electronic, or mechanical, including photocopying, taping, and recording—without prior written permission from the author.

For inquiries: natehaliv@gmail.com

Part 1

The American Dream

CHAPTER ONE

Just like every other country in the world, Nigeria has two sides.

If you've ever seen Nigeria on Western news, you already know the first side. That is the Nigeria they love to show. The overcrowded streets. The brown water in open gutters. The children with bare feet and sharp ribs. The crying mothers. The police checkpoint where a man in uniform holds an AK-47 like it's part of his body. The shaky video clips of burning tires, shouting crowds, and "breaking news" captions.

That is the Nigeria the world recognizes, because that is the Nigeria the camera always chases. And yes, that Nigeria is real. But it is not the only Nigeria.

There is also another part, a Nigeria most people outside the country barely see. The Nigeria of Abuja's wide roads and quiet estates. The Nigeria of Lagos Island where streetlights work and the air smells like perfume instead of smoke. The Nigeria of Port Harcourt neighborhoods with manicured lawns, private security, and gates that slide open like something from a movie.

In those places, you meet foreigners who came to make money and decided to stay. Europeans who own oil companies. Chinese businesspeople building projects. Indians running factories and supermarkets. Wealthy Arabs moving like they have no fear of tomorrow.

In that Nigeria, luxury is not rare. It is routine. You can see a car that costs more than an entire street back in my town.

You can see tall buildings with glass windows that catch the sun and throw it back like a mirror. You can see people eating in restaurants where one plate of food can feed a whole family for a week in the Nigeria that makes Western headlines.

Both Nigerias exist at the same time, inside the same borders. Most people just never get to choose which one they live in.

The Nigeria the Westerners see in their textbooks is where over eighty percent of the 230 million people live.

In these places, the air is thick with the noise of struggle. It is the sound of shouting bus conductors, crying babies, and the constant prayer of people begging God for a miracle that rarely comes.

I was born in the type of Nigeria Westerners see in textbooks. The underdeveloped part with limited or no electricity, and lots of ugly houses.

The Europeans call these places ghettos. We just called them home.

I was born in Ado-Ekiti into what people called the middle class. But you have to understand that the middle class in Nigeria is a very funny thing.

To an American, my family was poor. We were barely surviving. But in Nigeria, my father earned the equivalent of $48 monthly and owned a thirty-year-old Toyota Corolla with over one million miles on the dashboard.

He owned a small bungalow in Ado-Ekiti that had not been painted in ten years. Because we had a roof and a car, we were considered successful.

We were kings among the twenty million people who had no homes at all. We were royalty compared to the rest of the population.

According to the National Deposit Insurance Corporation (NDIC), **99.4% of the Nigerian population had less than five hundred thousand naira ($347) in their bank accounts as of 2024.**

My father was a proud man. He was a civil servant. In Nigeria, that means you go to work every day, but the government pays you whenever they feel like it.

Sometimes you get paid at the end of the month. Sometimes you wait three months for a single paycheck.

I remember the Sundays the most.

In a Nigerian home, Sunday is not for resting. Sunday is for show. It is the day you put on your best lace fabric. You shine your shoes with polish until you can see your face in the leather. You scrub your face until it hurts.

My father would wake us up at six in the morning. The house would be chaotic with the sound of my mother shouting instructions from the kitchen.

"Josh! Have you polished your father's shoes? Don't let me come in there and break your head!"

"Yes, Ma! I am doing it now!" I would yell back.

We would pile into the Toyota Corolla. The car was a fading shade of blue, scarred by scratches and dents. The engine did not hum. It coughed. It sounded like an old man dying of tuberculosis.

The church was only twenty minutes away. It should have been a quick drive.

But every Sunday, without fail, the car would die. It usually happened at the busiest intersection. The engine would sputter, shake violently, and then go silent.

My father would grip the steering wheel. I could see the veins popping out on his dark forehead. He would mutter curses under his breath, careful not to let us hear, but we knew.

"Everybody out," he would say. His voice was tired.

My siblings and I would climb out of the car in our Sunday best. The sun was already hot at eight in the morning. It pricked our skin like tiny needles. We would go to the back of the car and place our hands on the hot metal trunk.

"*Oya*! Push!" my father would command from the driver's seat.

We pushed. We sweated. The dust from the road coated our shiny shoes. Passersby would look at us. Some would laugh. Some would shake their heads in pity. I hated it. I hated the car. I hated the poverty that made us treat this piece of junk like it was gold.

"Daddy," I said one day. My hands were black with grease from the trunk. "Why don't we just walk? It is faster. The car is embarrassing."

The slap came before I saw his hand move. It was not a hard slap, but it stung.

"You are ungrateful," he shouted. His eyes were wide. "Do you know how many people are walking barefoot on this road? Do you know how many people cannot afford a bicycle? You are pushing a car, and you are complaining? Beg God for forgiveness so that he will not punish you for your ungratefulness!"

He was right, of course. In Nigeria, half a loaf of bread is better than none. But I did not want half a loaf. I wanted the whole bakery.

My parents worked hard. They worked from eight in the morning until four in the evening. They worked one hundred and sixty hours a month. And for all that work, the government paid them the minimum wage peanuts. As of 2024, the national minimum wage in Nigeria was 70,000 naira, which was around $48.

Imagine that. Working all month long, sweating, dealing with bosses who scream at you, just to take home forty-eight dollars at the end of the month. In America, you can make that money flipping burgers for three hours.

That kind of poverty kills you. I do not mean it kills your spirit. I mean it physically kills you.

I had four siblings once. My older brother was six when he started coughing. It was a dry, hacking cough that kept us awake at night.

My parents bought cough syrup from the chemist down the street. They prayed over him. They anointed his head with oil. But the cough got worse. He grew thin. His ribs poked through his skin like the wires of a birdcage.

It was tuberculosis. By the time my parents gathered enough money to take him to a real hospital, his lungs were gone.

He died in his sleep. He was so small in the coffin.

Then there was my younger sister. It was malaria. Just a mosquito bite. In America, a mosquito bite is annoying. In Nigeria, it is a death sentence if you do not have money for medical bills.

She burned with fever for three days. My mother used cold towels to cool her down. We did not have the money for the hospital admission deposit.

In Nigeria, the doctors do not care if you are dying. If you are bleeding out on the floor, they will ask for the deposit first. No money, no treatment. The rule is absolute.

I watched her die. I was holding her hand. Her skin was burning hot, and then, suddenly, it went cold.

I was eight years old.

That was the day I decided I would not be poor. I made a vow to the universe. I would make money. I did not care how. I would not be a noble man with empty pockets like my father.

I would never stand in a hospital room and watch my loved ones die because I could not afford to pay their medical bills.

To hell with having a good name.

I had a gift. My teachers called it a prodigy mind. I called it survival. Numbers made sense to me in a way people did not. When I was three, I could calculate change better than the market women.

By seven, I was solving quadratic equations for the secondary school students in my neighborhood.

I saw the world in codes and patterns. I looked at a building and I saw geometry. I looked at a business and I saw profit margins.

My father used to tap my head. "*I sabi say you go use dat your big brain bring money come,*" he would say in Pidgin. I know your intelligence will bring wealth.

He was right. He just did not know how I would get it.

Years later, before the FBI kicked down my door, I had twelve million dollars in Bitcoin.

I had seven million dollars in offshore accounts in the Cayman Islands. I had a mansion in Dominica. I bought them all with strings of code and other people's greed. But that was later.

The escape happened in 2019. I was fourteen years old, three weeks to my fifteenth birthday.

My mother's younger sister, Aunt Moji, lived in America. She was a legend in our family. She had married an American man and gained citizenship. In our culture, if one person makes it out, they must pull everyone else up. It is the law of the family.

She filed papers claiming I was her son from a previous marriage. It was a lie. A big, federal crime lie. But in Nigeria, the truth is flexible if it helps you survive.

The day we left for the airport, the air was heavy with rain. My mother held me for a long time. She smelled of curry spice and comfort. She was crying.

"*Ranti omo eni ti o je,*" she whispered into my ear. Her voice trembled. "*Ma kegbekegbe kan kan. Je ki nnkan ti o ni te e lorun.*"

Remember whose child you are. Do not join any bad gangs. Be satisfied with what you have.

I nodded. I promised her. But I think she knew. A mother always knows when her child is walking toward a cliff.

I had never been on a plane. The airport in Lagos was cold.

I wore my best jeans and a shirt that was slightly too big for me. I clutched my small bag like it contained diamonds.

We boarded the plane to Detroit. Aunt Moji sat in the row behind me because of a booking error. I found my seat next to a window.

Next to me sat a girl.

She looked to be about my age, maybe fourteen or fifteen. She had long braids that fell over her shoulder, woven with gold beads that clicked when she moved.

She wore headphones around her neck and was tapping furiously on an iPhone that looked newer than my father's car.

She looked up as I sat down. Her eyes were light brown, the color of honey.

"Hi," she said. Her accent was pure American. It sounded like music.

"Good afternoon," I said stiffly. I gripped the armrests.

She laughed. "You don't have to be so formal. I'm Jada."

"I am Joshua," I said. "But people call me Josh."

"Nice to meet you, Josh. You live in Lagos?"

"Yes," I said. "I am moving to America."

"Lucky you," she said, popping a piece of gum into her mouth. "I just spent two weeks there. My mom wanted to 'trace our roots.' It was... intense."

"You did not like it?" I asked.

She shrugged. "It's not that. It's just... everyone says Africa is my home, right? Because I'm Black.

"But I got there, and I felt like an alien. The food was too spicy. The traffic was crazy. I always repeat myself a million times before anyone can understand what I say. And I don't even understand any of their languages. I don't feel connected to it. Does that make sense?"

I looked at her. She smelled like vanilla and expensive lotion. She had smooth skin that had never known the bite of a mosquito or the rash of heat.

"It makes sense," I said. "You are American."

"Yeah," she sighed.

"I guess I am. Sadly, white Americans don't think I am American enough either. So, I neither belong here nor there."

We talked for hours. Or rather, she talked, and I listened. I was mesmerizingly silent, mostly because I was terrified the plane would fall out of the sky. She told me about Detroit. She told me about her school. She told me about music I had never heard of.

When the pilot announced we were landing, my heart hammered against my ribs.

"Can I have your number? Let's keep in touch," Jada asked.

"I don't have a phone," I lied.

I had an old Infinix with broken screen. The phone was once my father's, which he passed down to my mother, and she gave me when I was traveling so that we could keep in touch. However, I was too ashamed to bring it out when this girl was using the latest iPhone.

She reached into her bag and pulled out a pen. She grabbed my boarding pass and scribbled a number on the back.

"Call me," she said. "When you get a phone. You're going to need a friend who knows the ropes."

I looked at the number. Jada. It was the first American thing I owned.

We landed on July 8, 2019. I expected America to look like the movies. I expected gold streets and tall buildings that touched the clouds. I expected everyone to be smiling.

What I got was Detroit. It was gray. The sky was a flat, slate color. The air was not hot like Lagos; it was dry and had a bite to it, even in summer. We took a taxi to my aunt's house.

I stared out the window. "Where are the white people?" I asked Aunt Moji. Almost everyone I saw was black. It looked like we were in an upgraded version of Lagos.

She laughed, a bitter sound. "This is Detroit, Josh. You won't see many white folks in this neighborhood unless they are police."

My aunt's apartment was not a mansion. It was a small unit in a crumbling brick building. The hallway smelled of old frying oil and damp carpet. We walked in, and I saw a cockroach scuttle under the sofa.

There were five of us living there. Aunt Moji, her husband Dave, their two sons, and now me. It was tight.

That first night, I slept on the floor of the living room. I lay awake, listening to the sirens wailing outside. They sounded different from Nigerian sirens. More urgent. Angrier.

I saw a rat the size of a kitten run across the room. It stopped and looked at me with beady black eyes before vanishing into a hole in the wall.

This was America? This was the promised land?

The next morning, I went to take a shower. I stood under the hot water for ten minutes, just letting it wash away the travel dust. It felt like a miracle. Hot water flowing from a wall.

Suddenly, the door banged open. Aunt Moji stood there, her face twisted in rage.

"Josh! What are you doing?" she screamed.

I covered myself, terrified. "I am bathing, *ma*."

"Do you think this is Nigeria?" she yelled. "Do you think water falls from the sky? Do you know the water bill in this country? Get out! You are wasting my money!"

I turned off the tap, shaking. That was my first lesson. In America, nothing is free. In Nigeria, we had a well. Water was a gift from the earth.

Here, water was a product. Air was a product. Heat was a product. If you could not pay, you did not survive.

My aunt's husband, Uncle Dave, was an African American man.

He was big, with broad shoulders and hands that looked like they could crush a stone. He worked at a car factory.

He sat me down the second day. He looked serious.

"Listen to me, young blood," he said. His voice was deep. "You're in America now. And you're a Black boy in America. That means you got a target on your back."

I frowned. "But I have done nothing wrong."

"Doesn't matter," Dave said. "When the police stop you, and they will stop you, you don't argue. You don't talk back. You say 'Yes, sir' and 'No, sir.' You keep your hands where they can see them. You don't make no sudden moves. You understand?"

"Why?" I asked. "Are the police bad here?"

He sighed, rubbing his face. "White cops... they get scared of us. And when they get scared, they shoot. And if you're dead, it don't matter if you were right."

I nodded. In Nigeria, the police were corrupt. They wanted bribes. You gave them 500 naira, and they let you go. Here, Uncle Dave was telling me the police wanted my life.

But the most important lesson came from my cousin.

His name was Tunde-Sean.

It was a war of names. Aunt Moji wanted to name him Babatunde. In Yoruba land, if a pregnant woman loses her father while pregnant, the child has to be named Babatunde, which means 'Father has returned.'

On the other hand, Uncle Dave wanted to name him Sean, after Diddy, his favorite rapper. They compromised.

Tunde-Sean was sixteen. He wore his pants low, sagging below his waist. He wore oversized hoodies and walked with a limp that I later learned was fake. It was just 'swag.'

I was unpacking my bag in the room I was to share with him and his younger brother. I reached under the bed to retrieve a sock and my hand touched something cold and metallic.

I pulled it out.

It was a gun. A black pistol. Heavy. Real.

My heart stopped. In Nigeria, only armed robbers and mobile police carried guns.

The door clicked shut behind me.

I spun around. Tunde-Sean was standing there. His eyes were cold. He did not look like my cousin anymore. He looked like a predator.

"Put it down," he said softly.

"I... I found it," I stammered. "Is it... is it a toy?"

He walked over to me, grabbed the gun from my hand, and shoved me against the wall. He pressed his forearm against my throat.

"You ain't in Africa no more, jungle boy," he hissed. "Here, everybody keeps a strap. For protection."

"I won't tell," I gasped.

"You better not," he said. "If you tell my mom or my pops, I'm gonna put a bullet in your skull and send your body back to the village in a box. You hear me?"

I nodded frantically.

He released me. He tucked the gun into his waistband and smiled. It was a terrifying smile. "Good. Welcome to Detroit, cuz."

Over the next few weeks, Tunde-Sean became my guide. He showed me the neighborhood. He taught me the language of the streets.

"That over there?" He pointed to a group of boys wearing red bandanas on the corner. "That's fam. We run this block."

"Who are they?" I asked.

"Bloods," he said. "I'm a Blood."

I was confused. "Like... red blood cells?"

He looked at me with pure disgust. "Man, you really are fresh off the boat. Bloods. The gang. We used to have Crips here, but we smoked them out. Now we run the streets."

He showed me a hand sign. He twisted his fingers in a knot. "This is the set. You see an opp, that's an enemy, you let me know."

"You have killed people?" I asked, my voice small.

He looked at me, and for a second, I saw a flicker of sadness in his eyes, but he covered it with bravado. "I caught three bodies," he said. "Three."

He said it like he was talking about winning a video game. But these were human beings.

"Why?" I asked.

"Respect," he said. "Money. Power. *In this hood, you either the wolf or you the sheep. And I ain't no sheep.*"

He used words I had never heard. *Weed* for marijuana. *Lean* for cough syrup mixed with soda. *Strap* for gun. And the word *Nigga*.

"Why do you say that word?" I asked him one day as we walked past a liquor store. "I thought it was a bad word."

"We can say it," Tunde-Sean said. "Black folks. It's ours. But if a white boy says it? We beat his ass."

"But why can Black people call each other 'niggers' and get angry when white people call them that?"

"Shut up, Josh," he snapped. "Stop asking stupid questions. You think too much."

I noticed the tension between African Americans and Africans. The kids at the basketball court laughed at my accent. They called me "African booty scratcher." They asked if I lived in a tree.

They did not know that Lagos was a city of twenty million people.

They thought Africa was a jungle.

It hurt. But I remembered Jada's number.

I had convinced Aunt Moji to buy me a cheap phone from Walmart. I dialed the number.

"Hello?"

"Jada? It is Josh. From the plane."

"Josh!" Her voice was warm. "I thought you forgot about me."

"No," I said. "I could never forget."

We started talking every night. She became my anchor. She explained the things Tunde-Sean wouldn't. She explained why people were angry. She explained the history of slavery and Jim Crow that I had never learned in Nigerian schools.

We started dating a few weeks later. I was fifteen and she was fourteen, so dating just meant talking on the phone for hours and meeting at the mall to hold hands and take pictures. But she made me feel like I belonged.

School started in September. I was terrified, but I quickly realized something: American school was easy. In Nigeria, the teachers beat you if you failed. The curriculum was rigorous.

Here, the math they were doing in the ninth grade was math I had done when I was ten. I became a star. I got A-plus in everything. The teachers loved me. The students stopped making fun of my accent when they realized I could help them with their homework.

I even joined the football team. Not real football, soccer, but American football. I was fast, and I could calculate the trajectory of the ball better than anyone. I became a wide receiver.

Apart from the fact that Americans use iMessage to communicate instead of WhatsApp like Europe, Africa, and the rest of the world, my second biggest shock was the culture.

In Nigeria, if you are gay, you hide it. You bury it deep. If you come out, the law says you can go to jail for fourteen years. The mob might kill you in the street.

Here, I saw boys holding hands in the hallway. I saw a rainbow flag in the principal's office.

"It is... allowed?" I asked Jada one day.

"Of course," she said. "Love is love, Josh."

It took me a long time to understand that. To unlearn the hate that had been taught to me. But I saw how happy they were. I realized that the hate was just another form of control, just like the poverty.

I was assimilating. I was becoming American. I wore Jordans. I learned to speak with a slight Detroit drawl.

I learned to nod at the police and keep my hands visible. I listened to Kendrick Lamar and Taylor Swift.

I always avoided using the n-word though. I preferred saying 'bro' instead of 'nigga' when talking to another Black person.

But inside, the hunger was still there. The hunger I felt when I watched my sister die. The hunger to be rich. To have enough money to take care of my loved ones' medical bills. To buy a good car for my father.

I looked at Tunde-Sean, selling drugs on the corner to buy sneakers, and I knew I didn't want that. That was small money. That was dangerous money.

I wanted real money.

In 2021, I got a scholarship to a private school called Kingsley University. It's where my life changed.

CHAPTER TWO

Kingsley University is not just a school. It is a fortress. It sits on the hills of Los Angeles like a golden crown looking down on the peasants below.

It is a place built by old money and sustained by new greed. If Harvard is a classic suit, Kingsley is a bespoke tuxedo sewn with threads of gold. It makes the Ivy League look like a community college.

The air around Kingsley smells different. It does not smell like the exhaust fumes of Detroit or the dust of Lagos. It smells like manicured lawns and ocean breeze and money. Serious money. The kind of money that buys silence.

The university was started in the early nineteenth century by a group of white men who wanted to make sure their sons only spoke to other sons of importance.

For a hundred years, it was a closed circle. But money needs to grow. So, by the end of the nineteenth century, they opened the gates just a crack. They let in the sons of oil barons and the daughters of shipping magnates. They did not care about grades. They cared about net worth.

In the year 2000, the board of directors decided they needed a new image. They could not just be a club for rich kids anymore. They needed to look benevolent.

They created a quota for families of war veterans. And then, to show the world how generous they were, they created the Kingsley University Foundation Scholarship. Five slots. Just five. For the smartest, most brilliant poor kids they could find. It was a lottery ticket. A golden ticket.

I first heard about it on a Tuesday morning in Detroit. The radiator in our classroom was clanking loudly. The room smelled of wet wool and floor wax.

Ms. Carrington walked in. She looked like she had taken a wrong turn on her way to a country club. Her suit was sharp.

Her heels clicked against the linoleum floor with a sound that demanded attention.

She stood at the front of the class and smiled. It was a practiced smile. It did not reach her eyes.

"Good morning, students," she said. Her voice was crisp. "I am here to offer you a key. A key to a door you didn't even know existed."

She talked about Kingsley University. She showed us slides of the campus. It looked like a resort. The library had marble floors. The dorms looked like five-star hotel suites.

"Will we get jobs?" a boy named Damian asked from the back row. "I mean, real jobs?"

Ms. Carrington nodded. "A degree from Kingsley is not just a piece of paper. It is a passport. We are known for exclusivity. Any company in the world would fight to hire a Kingsley graduate. But more than that," she paused for effect. "You will make connections. You will meet the people who run the world."

I looked out the window. It was raining gray slush outside. I did not care about her pitch. I had a plan. I was going to go to Howard University.

I wanted to be around Black excellence. I wanted to be around people who understood the struggle.

Later that afternoon, I sat in the cafeteria with Jada. She was eating a slice of pizza that looked rubbery. I had a book open on the table. It was *The Wolf of Wall Street* by Jordan Belfort.

Jada chewed her pizza and looked at the cover. She shook her head. Her braids swayed.

"You've read that book a million times," she said. "Why do you keep reading it?"

I touched the cover. "He inspires me. The man is a genius."

"He's a criminal, Josh," she said.

"He started with nothing," I argued. "He used his brain. He became a millionaire. He flew private jets. Fucked expensive hookers. Wore expensive clothes. He lived the good life."

Jada put her pizza down. She looked worried. "I should be scared of you sometimes. Look at the people you worship. Jordan Belfort. Ross Ulbricht. Pablo Escobar. Ray Hushpuppi. The only thing they have in common is that they broke the law."

"They were smart," I said. My voice was low. "They refused to be poor. They used their intelligence to change their reality. Belfort made money out of thin air."

"And he went to prison," Jada said. "Ulbricht is never getting out. Is that the life you want? To be rich in a cage?"

"At least they lived," I said. "Most people in this neighborhood are in a cage too. But their cage is poverty. And they never even get to taste the lobster."

Jada rolled her eyes. She reached across the table and took my hand. Her skin was warm.

"It is pointless arguing with you. You are stubborn. Just like an African man."

I smiled. "It is in the blood."

"Are you going to apply for that scholarship?" she asked. "The fancy white school?"

"I am not sure," I said.

"You should," she said. "You are the smartest person in this school. You are smarter than the teachers."

"It is a waste of time," I said. "They don't give those scholarships to people like me. They give them to white kids or Jewish kids. No Black student has ever won. Why would they start now?"

"Because you are undeniable," she said.

She convinced me. I applied. I took the SATs. I sat in the exam hall and the numbers danced for me.

I saw the patterns. I saw the answers before I even finished reading the questions. I scored 1580 out of 1600.

Aunt Moji went crazy when she saw the score. She pasted the result on the refrigerator. She told my younger cousin, Devante, to look at it every morning.

"You see this?" she yelled at him. "This is your road map! Do not end up like Tunde-Sean. Do not die on these streets over a pair of sneakers. Be like Josh!"

Then the waiting began. Two weeks of silence. I pretended I did not care. I hung out with Jada. She had done poorly on her SATs.

She had decided college was not for her. She wanted to go to cosmetology school.

"I wish I had your brain," she said one evening at Pizza Hut.

I laughed. "Yoruba people are the smartest people on earth. It is a fact. Don't worry. When we get married, our kids will have my genes. They will be geniuses."

We laughed. It felt good to laugh.

Then my phone buzzed in my pocket.

I pulled it out. It was an email. The subject line made my heart stop: Kingsley University Foundation.

I opened it.

Dear Mr. Joshua Balogun,

On behalf of the Kingsley University Foundation, I would like to inform you that you have been invited to the next phase of your scholarship application...

I stopped reading. I handed the phone to Jada. My hands were shaking.

She read it out loud.

Her eyes got wide. "*Yo!* They are flying you out? They booked you at The Ritz-Carlton? Josh! These people are loaded!"

The email included a gift card for United Airlines. It said a driver would pick me up. It was happening.

I arrived in Los Angeles a day before the interview. The air was warm and dry. The Ritz-Carlton was a tower of glass and steel.

I walked into the lobby and felt small. The floor was polished marble. The ceiling was so high it felt like a cathedral. Men in suits whispered into phones. Women in expensive dresses walked small dogs.

I went to my room. It was bigger than Aunt Moji's entire apartment. The bed was like a cloud. I stood at the window and looked out at the city lights. I felt a hunger in my belly. Not for food. For this. For the soft sheets and the silence.

The next morning, I went down to the parking area.

It was like a car show for billionaires. There were ten limousines lined up. Drivers in black suits stood like statues holding placards.

"Damn," a voice whispered behind me.

I turned. A white boy in a navy suit stood there. He looked nervous. There were about fifteen of us. We were the finalists. We looked at each other with suspicion. We were at war. Only five of us would survive.

I scanned the line until I saw it. A placard with Mr. Joshua Balogun written in elegant script.

The driver was an older white man with gray hair. I walked up to him. I showed him my ID.

He bowed.

He actually bowed his head. "Good morning, sir," he said. He opened the door for me.

I sat in the back of the limousine. The leather smelled rich. I felt a surge of pride. A white man had bowed to me.

In Nigeria, the white men were the bosses. Here, for a moment, I was the king.

We drove to the campus.

If the hotel was impressive, the campus was a paradise. The buildings were ancient stone covered in ivy.

The lawns were impossibly green. There were fountains shooting water into the air.

And then I saw the helipad.

My jaw dropped. There were more than fifteen helicopters parked there. Students were getting out of them, carrying designer bags.

The driver pulled into a vast parking lot. I looked out the window and felt sick. There were no Toyotas here. There were Ferraris. Lamborghinis. Rolls-Royce Wraiths. Bentleys.

"Who owns these cars?" I asked the driver. My voice sounded weak.

He smiled in the rearview mirror. "The students, sir. Staff members park in the back."

I swallowed hard. The cars in this lot were worth more than the GDP of some African countries. How was I supposed to survive here? I was a boy who pushed a broken Corolla with over one million miles in mileage to church every Sunday. These kids flew to class in helicopters.

I walked into the interview room. It was a library with books that reached the ceiling. Two people sat behind a mahogany desk. A bald man and a pretty woman. They were white. They looked like they had never known a day of hunger in their lives.

"What is your future ambition, Mr. Ba... Ba..." The man struggled with my surname.

"Please call me Josh," I said.

He looked relieved. "Okay, Mr. Josh. What is your future ambition?"

"I would like to become an accounting officer, sir."

He nodded. He looked at my file. He saw the SAT score. He took a sharp breath. "I see you are a brilliant student."

"Yoruba people are the most intelligent people in the world," I said. It slipped out. It was something my father always said.

"Pardon?" the man asked.

"Oh, nothing, sir," I said quickly.

The lady smiled. She had perfect teeth. "Tell me, Mr. Josh. Where do you see yourself in ten years?"

I closed my eyes. I thought about the limousines. I thought about the rats in Detroit. I thought about Tunde-Sean bleeding out on the pavement.

I opened my eyes.

"I see two versions of myself in ten years," I said.

They looked confused.

"The first version," I continued, my voice steady, "won this scholarship. I see myself graduating from Kingsley. I see myself working at Apple or Google. I see myself managing portfolios. I see success."

The lady nodded. She liked that answer.

"But," I said, "I also see the other version. The version that did not get this scholarship. That version returned to the slums of Detroit. That version had to make a choice. To live in poverty or to survive."

The room went very quiet.

"I see myself joining a gang," I said. "Not because I want to.

"But because I refuse to be poor. I see myself selling drugs on the corner. I see myself blaming the system. I see myself angry. I see myself holding a gun. I see myself going to prison. And when I come out, no one will hire a Black ex-convict. So, I go back to crime. I see myself having kids who grow up hating the world because their father has nothing to give them."

I paused. I looked them in the eye.

"Those are the two versions. The only difference between the CEO and the criminal is this scholarship. You hold the pen that writes my history."

The interviewers were frozen. The lady's mouth was slightly open. The man looked pale. I had scared them.

I had brought the reality of the ghetto into their ivory tower.

"Thank you, Mr. Josh," the man said finally. His voice was tight. "You have made your point very clear."

I walked out. I knew I had taken a gamble.

When I got back to Detroit, I told Aunt Moji what I said.

She screamed. She threw her hands in the air. "What is wrong with you? Are you mad? Why would you tell white people you are going to kill people?"

"I was being honest," I said.

"Honesty does not pay bills!" she shouted. "They will think you are a terrorist! They will call the FBI! You have ruined it!"

She called my mother in Nigeria immediately. She put it on speaker.

"Sister!" Aunt Moji wailed in Yoruba.

"Your son has killed us. He told the white people he wants to be an armed robber!"

If Yoruba women had anything in common, it was their ability to make a mountain out of a molehill.

They could exaggerate in ways that even the good Lord would be shocked. I kid you not.

If a Yoruba mother is beating you with a stick or a belt and you raise your hands to avoid a strike or protect your face during the beating, she would start screaming that you tried to kill her.

My mother started crying on the other end. "Yeh! *Mogbe*! *Olorun maje*!" I am finished! God forbid! Josh, why?" my mother sobbed. "Did I not raise you well? Why do you want to join a gang? Have you joined a cult?"

"Mom, I did not join a cult," I tried to explain. "It was a metaphor."

"Meta-fire?" she cried. "Is that a new gun? Josh, please, I beg you in the name of God. Come back home. Let us wash your head with special soap. The devil has entered you in America."

"Mom, stop crying," I said. But she cried for an hour.

Two weeks later, the email came.

I won.

I was the first Black student in the history of Kingsley University to gain admission from the streets.

Aunt Moji fell to her knees in the living room. She started speaking in tongues. "Thank you, Jesus! My enemy has been put to shame! We are going up!"

That same day, a letter came from Howard University. I had been accepted there too.

I sat on my bed with the two letters. One was from a Historically Black College. It felt like home. It felt safe. The other was from a place where people owned helicopters.

"I don't know which one to pick," I told Aunt Moji.

She looked at me like I was insane. She hissed long and loud. "Are you crazy? Is your brain paining you? Howard? What is at Howard?"

"My people," I said.

"Your people are poor!" she said brutally. "Josh, listen to me. In this America, there are two ways to climb the ladder. You either have money, or you know people who have money. At Howard, you will meet nice people. But they will be middle class. They will be struggling like you. At Kingsley? You will meet the owners of the world."

She sat next to me. Her voice softened. "You want to help your family? You want to buy your father a new car? You go where the money is. You go to Kingsley."

Her words that night sealed my fate.

If I had gone to Howard, maybe I would be an accountant right now. Maybe I would be living in a small house in Maryland with a dog. Maybe I would not be wearing an orange jumpsuit. But the allure of the elite was too strong.

I went to Jada's house to tell her. We sat on her porch. The sun was setting, casting long shadows on the cracked pavement.

"I got in," I said.

She did not smile. She looked down at her hands. "I knew you would."

"I also got into Howard," I said.

"But you are not going there," she said. It was not a question.

"Kingsley is... it is a once-in-a-lifetime chance, Jada. The connections."

"I know," she said. She looked at me, and her eyes were sad. "I'm just worried."

"About what?"

"When Black people get that kind of money," she said, "they change. They forget where they came from. They start looking at us like we are the problem. You're gonna be surrounded by rich white girls who look like models."

"I don't care about them," I said. "You are my girl."

"What if you fall in love with one of them?" she whispered.

I grabbed her face gently. "Jada. You have my heart. I will never look at a white girl. I promise you. I love you. Black excellence or nothing."

I kissed her. We went to her room. We made love with a desperation I had never felt before. It felt like we were saying goodbye, even though I swore we weren't.

I lied to her. I lied to myself.

Just like she predicted, the world of Kingsley would swallow me whole. I would fall for the wealth. I would fall for the lifestyle. And I would fall for a white girl who would help lead me to my destruction.

CHAPTER THREE

Life at Kingsley University was not just different. It was a different planet entirely. As a scholarship student, I did not have to pay tuition.

The college also provided me with a monthly stipend of $500. To a boy who once pushed a broken Toyota Corolla to church, five hundred dollars was a fortune. It was enough to feed a family of six in Nigeria for two months.

But here at Kingsley, I would soon learn that five hundred dollars was what some students spent on lunch.

I was assigned to a dormitory. I use the word dormitory because that is what the school called it. But back in Lagos, or even in Detroit, we would call this a palace.

The building looked like a massive manor house from a British period drama. It stood tall with red bricks and white pillars that looked like they were carved by angels. It did not smell like a school. It smelled like lavender and expensive floor wax.

I opened the door to my room for the first time and almost dropped my bag. It looked like the suites at the InterContinental Hotel in Hong Kong. I know this because, in the future, I would stay in the presidential suite there for a month.

That suite cost me over twelve thousand dollars a night. A drug cartel paid for that trip. We were making millions every week by then.

But standing in that dorm room as a freshman, I was just Josh. And I was overwhelmed.

Everything was fancy. Two people shared a room.

We had cleaners who came in to scrub the floors and change the sheets. There was an eighty-five-inch Samsung television on the wall.

It was so clear it looked like a window into another world. We had a Jacuzzi in the bathroom. A Jacuzzi for students!

I sat on the edge of the bed. The mattress was soft. It felt like it was hugging me. I thought about my bed in Detroit. I thought about the thin mattress on the floor in Lagos where the springs would poke my ribs.

My roommate was already there.

His name was Eric Walters. There was a poster on the wall next to his bed. It was a framed cover of Forbes magazine from 2011. The face on the cover was Eric.

The caption read: *The Richest Teenager in the World. Net Worth: $2.6 Billion.*

I stared at the poster. Then I stared at the boy sitting on the bed.

He did not look like a billionaire. He wore a t-shirt with a coffee stain on the collar. His hair looked like a bird's nest. He was holding a fork with a piece of sausage in one hand and a thick book in the other. He was reading and chewing at the same time. He did not look up when I walked in.

Eric was a legend. He developed his own operating system when he was thirteen. It was so good that Microsoft got scared. They bought his company before he could put them out of business. He got one billion dollars in cash and shares worth another billion.

He was what they called New Money. His father was a schoolteacher. His mother was a cleaner.

He was a regular guy who had a brain that worked like a supercomputer.

"Hello," I said. "I am Josh."

He looked up. His eyes were unfocused behind thick glasses. He blinked twice. Then he smiled. It was a warm smile.

"Hi," he said. "I'm Eric."

Then he went back to his book.

That was Eric. He was obsessed with information. He took books to the bathroom.

He murmured about IP addresses in his sleep. He only acted like a normal human being for about thirty minutes a day.

During those thirty minutes, he would ask me how I was doing. He would talk about the weather. But then his brain would reboot, and he would go back to being a genius robot.

My first night was splendid. I filled the Jacuzzi with hot water. I lay there for an hour. I closed my eyes and listened to the silence. In Detroit, there were always sirens.

In Ado-Ekiti, there were generators and shouting neighbors. Here, there was only the hum of the air conditioner.

I woke up the next morning feeling refreshed. Eric was already awake. He was typing furiously on a laptop. His fingers moved so fast they were a blur.

"Good morning," I said.

He did not answer. He was in the zone.

There was a knock on the door. I opened it. A tall guy with blonde hair stood there. He had perfect teeth and wore a Zegna polo shirt that probably cost more than my entire wardrobe.

He stared at me for a full minute. He looked me up and down like I was a delivery boy who had walked into the wrong house.

"Hi," he finally said.

"Hi," I replied.

"My name is Craig. I am the head of this dorm. I heard you moved in two days ago."

"Yeah. That is right. My name is Josh. Balogun Joshua."

Craig frowned. "Bal... Bal-goon?"

I smiled. "Never mind. It is an African name. I am from Nigeria."

Craig's eyes lit up. "Ha! That is good. Are you a Nigerian prince?"

"No," I said.

"Are you the son of a politician? I heard African politicians are wealthy. They have oil money, right?"

I shrugged. "I am not related to any politicians."

Craig's face fell. The smile vanished. "Are you a New Money student then? Like Eric?"

"I am a scholarship student," I said.

The silence that followed was heavy. Craig's jaw dropped. Behind me, the sound of Eric's typing stopped.

A dark-haired guy was walking down the hallway. He heard me. He stopped dead in his tracks.

He looked at me with eyes that were cold and hard.

"You are a student in need?" Craig asked. His voice was a whisper.

I nodded. "Yes. I guess that is the term."

The dark-haired guy swore loudly. It sounded Russian. He stepped forward. His face was red.

"I don't understand why we keep bending the rules for Black people all the time," he shouted. "We pay a huge tuition fee to study here! And the college allows him to study here without paying a dime just because of his skin color? They talk about white privilege all the time but look at this! Black people are being treated better than us! Fuck!"

He stormed off, still swearing in Russian.

My heart was beating fast. I felt a cold knot in my stomach. In Nigeria, everyone is black. We have tribalism, yes. A Fulani man might not like an Igbo man. But nobody hates you just for your skin. This was different. This was hate. Pure and simple.

Craig recovered from his shock. He forced a smile, but it looked painful. "Ignore Viktor. He is quite conservative."

He handed me some flyers about the dorm rules. I took them, but my hands were shaking slightly.

Craig left quickly, like he did not want to catch a disease from me. I closed the door.

Eric was looking at me. "Don't worry," he said. "Viktor does not like anybody. He hates anyone that isn't Russian."

"I think he is going to make my life hell," I said.

I sat on my bed. I felt small.

"Just ignore him," Eric said. "He is not even that rich. He is only worth fifty-six million dollars. The only reason he is considered an Elite is because of his family line. They are old Russian aristocracy. But many Elites don't like him because he is broke."

I swallowed hard. "Broke? He is worth fifty-six million?"

"Yeah," Eric said casually. "That is pocket change here."

"I have $700 in my bank account," I said. "And some cents."

"Oh," Eric said. "Damn."

He spun his chair around. For the first time, he looked at me with full attention. He explained the world of Kingsley to me.

There was a hierarchy. A caste system.

At the top were the **Elites**. These were kids born into dynasties. Their grandparents were billionaires. They had names like Rockefeller or Vanderbilt or Rothschild. They ruled the school. There were school buildings in their family name.

In the middle was **New Money**. That was Eric. Self-made billionaires.

The Elites tolerated them because they had cash, but they looked down on them because they didn't have "breeding." They considered new money "lucky."

At the bottom were the **Students in Need**. The scholarship kids. The children of war veterans. We were the peasants. We were the charity cases.

"We are just here to make them feel good about themselves," I thought. "We are their project."

The next day was Sunday. I stayed in the room. I was afraid to go out. I was afraid to see Viktor or Craig again.

My phone rang. It was Jada.

I felt a pang of guilt. I had been so busy surviving that I had forgotten to call her.

"I guess you don't have time for your black friends anymore," she said. Her voice was sharp. "Now that you attend a college filled with rich white kids."

"Good morning to you too, Jada," I said.

"I miss you, Josh. This is the first time we haven't talked for two days."

"I am sorry," I said. "I am trying to get used to this place. It is overwhelming."

"Tell me about it," she said.

I told her about the room. I told her about the Jacuzzi. I told her about the cleaning ladies.

"Is it easy to make friends?" she asked.

I sighed. "No. It is hard. The people in my dorm... they aren't friendly. They are racist, Jada. They don't like poor people. And they definitely don't like poor Black people."

"Don't let them get to you," Jada said fiercely. "You are a genius, Josh. You are smarter than all of them. Who is your roommate?"

"His name is Eric Walters," I said. "He is worth two billion dollars."

Jada screamed. "What! You mean that famous tech kid?"

"Yeah. He was on the cover of Forbes," I said. "And the guy who yelled at me yesterday? The 'broke' one? He is worth over fifty million."

"Holy Moly," Jada whispered. "These white people have all the money."

"I don't know if I can cope," I admitted. "I feel alone. Eric talks to his computer more than me. Nobody wants to be seen with me. It is like I have leprosy."

"You will cope," she said. "You are a survivor. Remember who you are."

We talked for a few more minutes. When I hung up, I felt a little better. But also sadder.

She was in Detroit. I was here. The distance felt bigger than just miles.

I was hungry. I went to the pantry in our suite. It was stocked with snacks. Free food. I took a bottle of Pepsi and a bag of chips. I sat in front of the window and watched students walking below.

They looked so confident. They walked like they owned the earth.

Monday morning came. I dressed carefully. I wore my best shirt. It was clean, but it was cheap. I knew that now.

I walked to the lecture hall. The campus was beautiful, but I felt like an intruder. I saw the parking lot again. The sun glinted off the Ferraris and Rolls-Royces. It was a museum of wealth.

I entered the classroom. It looked like a boardroom at Apple.

Glass walls. Sleek tables. Leather chairs.

I walked to the front row. In my high school in Detroit, I always sat in the front. I wanted to hear everything. I sat down next to a blonde guy who was staring at the ceiling.

"You are not meant to sit here, scholarship student," a voice growled behind me.

I froze. The room went silent. I turned around.

It was Viktor.

"Come on," I said, trying to smile. "It is only a seat."

"No," another student said. He was wearing a suit. "The front row is for Elites. Scholarship students sit at the back."

I looked around. The back row was filled with kids who looked like me. Not black, necessarily. But poor and scared. Their clothes were simple. Their shoulders were slumped. It was the high school cafeteria all over again. The cool kids in the front. The rejects in the back.

"Go," Viktor said. "Know your place. The college did you a favor letting you in. Don't push your luck. Let those who actually pay tuition sit in front."

I felt the anger rising in my chest. In Yoruba culture, respect is everything. To be spoken to like a dog is the ultimate insult. I wanted to curse him. *Oponu. Oloriburuku.*

But I didn't. I picked up my bag. I walked to the back. It was the longest walk of my life. I could feel their eyes on me.

I could hear their snickers. I sat down next to a guy with kind eyes.

"Don't worry," he whispered. "You get used to it."

"I hate it here," I muttered. "I hate it."

"I tried to quit last semester," the guy said. "My dad wouldn't let me. He is a war veteran. He thinks this is heaven."

"My name is Josh," I said.

"David Lewinson," he replied.

David became my guide. He explained the seating chart. Front row: Elites. Middle row: New Money. Back row: Us. The untouchables.

"There is an exception though." He pointed to the blonde guy in the front row. "That is Dmitri. He used to sit back here with us. He was broke. Then suddenly, last semester, he showed up in Chrome Hearts and Gucci from head to toe. He bought a Rolls-Royce. Now he sits with them."

"How?" I asked. "How did he get rich?"

David shrugged. "Nobody knows. Rumors say he won the lottery."

He pointed to two other guys. One was Asian, the other white. "That is Wang and Harry. They are friends with Dmitri. They used to look like us. Now look at them."

I looked. Wang was wearing a watch that sparkled with diamonds. As in VVS diamonds.

Wang wore a pair of Christian Louboutin sneakers while Harry wore Giuseppe Zanotti. Those sneakers cost more than my stipend. Nothing less than $900 for those sneakers. My good Lord!

The money they spent on those sneakers could've saved my siblings' lives.

Over one million *naira*. On sneakers. As in sneakers for the feet.

"The Elites still don't let Wang and Harry sit in the front," David noted. "Only Dmitri made the cut."

"Interesting," I said. I filed that information away.

A man walked into the room. He wore a tweed jacket. The room went silent.

"I am Dr. Kennedy," he said. "Principles of Marketing."

He asked us to introduce ourselves.

"Use your phone," David whispered. "Google them."

"Why?"

"Just do it."

The first guy stood up. "My name is Edward Morrison."

I typed his name. Wikipedia popped up. Son of Donald Morrison. 52nd richest man in the world.

Edward Morrison: Investor. Net Worth: $5.2 billion.

He was eighteen. And he was worth five billion dollars.

"Holy shit," I whispered.

"Welcome to Kingsley," David said.

Then a girl stood up.

"My name is Melina Dervishi," she said.

Her voice was soft. It sounded like water flowing over smooth stones. I turned my head.

My breath caught in my throat.

She was not just beautiful. She was art.

She had dark hair that fell like silk down her back.

Her eyes were gray, sparkling like diamonds. Her skin was flawless. She wore a shirt with a double-C logo. It looked like a royal robe on her.

In Nigeria, we say a woman is *arewa*. Beautiful. But Melina was more than that. She was the kind of woman wars are fought over.

And her ass. My good Lord! Her ass could make a monk recant his vows. Hell, that ass could turn a random John Doe to Shakespeare.

"Looks like somebody is in love," David teased.

I showed him my middle finger, but I could not look away. I Googled her. Her father owned a winery worth a billion. Her mother owned a fashion empire. She was an heiress. A princess.

Then a boy from the back row stood up. He was skinny. He looked malnourished. "Hi," he said. His voice shook. "My name is Oliver."

"Is he wearing a GUGGI shirt?" Viktor shouted.

The class erupted. I looked closely. Oliver was wearing a t-shirt that tried to look like Gucci, but the spelling was wrong. It said GUGGI.

"You should have stuck to Primark!" another Elite shouted. "Stop trying to be us, you peasant! Wear Zara or H&M. Stick to your budget."

They laughed. Cruel, hard laughter. Oliver sat down. Tears streamed down his face. He looked like he wanted to die. I felt a burning rage.

These people had everything, yet they found joy in crushing someone who had nothing.

Then it was my turn.

I stood up. My legs felt heavy. "My name is Josh. Joshua Balogun."

"Oooo oooo ahhh ahhh." Someone made monkey noises from the front.

"Go back to the jungle!" someone else shouted.

Dr. Kennedy looked down at his papers. He pretended he did not hear. He was a coward. He knew who paid his salary.

I sat down. My face burned. David patted my shoulder. "Ignore them," he said.

The lecture began. I tried to focus. I was the smart kid. I was the genius from Detroit. But as they started talking, I realized I was lost.

They talked about stocks. They talked about mergers. They talked about hostile takeovers. The Elites and the New Money kids jumped in.

They spoke a language I did not know. I knew math. I knew code. I did not know how to buy a company. Before I left Nigeria, my father earned less than $50 in a month.

In Detroit, Aunt Moji spent her life paying bills. How would I know anything about buying stocks?

"Quick question," Dr. Kennedy asked. "Which strategy would you use to convince investors to save a company on the verge of bankruptcy?"

This was my chance. I knew the textbook answer.

I pressed the button on my desk.

"Yes, Josh," Dr. Kennedy said.

"I think the best solution is to sell the company at a low price," I said. "To minimize loss."

Silence. Then laughter.

"What does a scholarship student know about owning a company?" Viktor sneered.

Dr. Kennedy smiled condescendingly. "That is a... safe answer, Josh. But if we sold every company that was in trouble, we would have no economy."

I felt stupid. I felt small.

Edward Morrison pressed his button.

"Yes, Edward," Dr. Kennedy said. His voice changed. It became respectful.

"I suggest an illegal approach," Edward said smoothly.

"Explain," the professor said.

Edward leaned back. He looked like a king on his throne. "One of my companies makes women's clothing. Two years ago, we were crashing. Marketing costs were too high. We were going to go bankrupt."

"So, what did you do?"

"I falsified the annual report," Edward said. He said it casually, like he was talking about what he had for breakfast. "I made it look like we had a fourteen percent profit instead of a loss. I showed the fake report to investors. They put in more money. We used that money to fix the problem.

"By the end of last year, we made an eighty-eight percent profit. If I hadn't lied, the company would be dead.

"White-collar crime is just a tool. As long as everyone makes money in the end, nobody cares."

The class erupted in applause. They clapped! They clapped for fraud.

Dr. Kennedy nodded. "Bold. Risky. But effective."

I sat there, frozen.

In my neighborhood, if you stole a loaf of bread, the police would beat you. If you sold a little weed, you went to jail. But here? Here you could lie about millions of dollars, and they called it "bold."

"I feel dumb," I whispered to David after class. "I embarrassed myself."

"You are not dumb," David said. "You are just theoretical. You learned from books. These guys? They learned from their fathers. They own the companies. They play by different rules."

"Edward went to *Le Rosey* in Switzerland," David added. "Tuition is one hundred thousand dollars a year for a sixth grader. You went to public school in Detroit. Don't compare yourself to them."

He was right. But it didn't make me feel better.

I walked back to the dorm. I looked at the beautiful buildings. I looked at the luxury cars.

I realized something that day. Intelligence was not enough. Being smart was not enough.

To survive here, I needed something else. I needed power. I needed to be rich. I needed to make them accept me. And looking at Dmitri, the boy who went from the back row to the front row in one semester, I wondered what he had done to get it.

CHAPTER FOUR

Sometimes I forgot I was in a university. There were moments when the lecture halls of Kingsley University felt more like the runways of Paris or Milan.

The air did not smell like old books or whiteboard markers. It smelled of Chanel No. 5 and crisp, new money. It smelled like leather that had never seen a drop of rain.

Every morning was a fashion show. The hallway was the catwalk.

My classmates did not just wear clothes. They wore investments. They draped themselves in fabrics that cost more than my father's entire house in Nigeria. I saw girls walking in Valentino dresses that flowed like liquid silk.

I saw boys in bespoke Giorgio Armani suits that fit them so perfectly it looked like a second skin. They treated Prada, Dior, and Burberry like everyday wear.

I lost count of the number of Hermès Kelly and Goyard bags I saw on campus. And please, let's not talk about the Van Cleef & Arpels bracelets on their wrists. It was a sin to wear just one, so they wore multiple bracelets on each hand.

And then there was me.

My wardrobe was filled with clothes from thrift stores. My shirts were faded. My jeans had lost their stiffness years ago. I washed them by hand in the sink to save money on laundry.

In Nigeria, we have a saying. *Aso nla ko ni eniyan nla.* Expensive clothes do not make a big person. But at Kingsley University, that proverb was a lie.

Here, the clothes made the person. If you did not wear the right label, you were invisible. If you wore Zara instead of Valentino or Dsquared2, you would be treated like a pig. Worse still, you would be invisible.

I noticed the rules quickly. The Elites and the New Money students never wore the same outfit twice. It was a cardinal sin. To repeat a dress was to admit failure. It was a silent signal that maybe, just maybe, your trust fund was running low.

I repeated my outfits three times a week. I had no choice. The mathematics of my life was depressing. The college gave me a stipend of $500 a month. In my head, I broke it down like an accountant.

$140 went to my parents in Lagos. That money kept the generator running so that they would have electricity. The money also put food on the table.

$100 went to Aunt Moji in Detroit as a thank you for housing me. That left me with $250.

$250 to survive in a city where a bottle of water cost five dollars. Then there was Melina.

Melina Dervishi wore shoes that cost more than my entire life savings. I watched her from a distance. She was always surrounded by wealth. Her bag was Hermès. Her jewelry was Cartier. She shined so brightly that it hurt my eyes to look at her directly.

In my head, we were already lovers. I created a whole life for us in the quiet moments before sleep took me.

In my imagination, we lived in a mansion in Ikoyi. We had five children who spoke perfect Yoruba and perfect English. We were happy.

But in reality, I could not even say hello to her.

It was fear. It was the paralyzing fear of the poor standing before the rich. In Yoruba culture, you do not look a king in the eye. Melina was royalty. And I was a peasant with holes in his socks.

"You should talk to her," David said.

We were sitting in the lecture hall waiting for Professor Muller. I had been staring at the back of Melina's neck. Even her neck was perfect.

"I can't," I whispered.

"Why?" David asked. He was cleaning his glasses with the hem of his shirt.

"She is rich, David. I am poor. Look at us. It is only in Hollywood movies that the princess falls for the pauper. In real life, the princess calls security."

David chuckled softly. "It is better to try and fail than to never try. What is the worst she can do? Spit on you?"

I shifted in my seat. The chair was comfortable, but I felt restless. "Look around the room, David. Look at the couples. Look at Shannon."

I pointed to a girl in the back row. Shannon was a scholarship student. She was dating Taylor, another student on financial aid. They shared textbooks. They ate cheap noodles together.

"Then look at Edward," I continued.

"He is an Elite. He is dating Samantha. She is an Elite. They stick to their own kind. It is like a caste system. The lions date the lions. The gazelles date the gazelles. And we are the grass."

David shrugged. "What about Harry? He is dating Alicia. She is New Money. He is a Student in Need."

I rolled my eyes so hard it hurt. "Please. Does Harry look like a student in need to you? The guy drives a Bugatti. A Bugatti, David! That car costs millions."

I had stalked Harry's Instagram page the night before. It was a gallery of excess. Harry on a yacht in Monaco. Harry popping champagne in Dubai. Harry shopping in Tokyo. He was listed as a financial aid student, but he lived like a Saudi prince.

"He sits in the back row," David argued.

"He sits there for fun," I said. "He is mocking us. He is not one of us."

David sighed. "Maybe you are right. But I still believe love is blind. You can love anyone. Race, class, it shouldn't matter."

"That is a nice fairy tale," I muttered.

Just then, Melina threw her head back and laughed. It was a beautiful, melodic sound. I looked over. Viktor was whispering something in her ear. He looked smug. He looked like he owned her. He placed a hand on her shoulder, his heavy class ring glinting in the light.

A dark heat rose in my chest. Yoruba people call it *Owu*. Jealousy. But it was more than that. I wanted to walk over there and rip his tongue out. I wanted to be the one making her laugh.

"You are torturing yourself," David whispered. "Let it go, Josh."

But I couldn't let it go. The hunger for her was just another part of the hunger I felt for everything in this place.

The fun and games ended two weeks later. The darkness of Kingsley University revealed itself on a Tuesday afternoon.

It was Oliver.

Everyone called him "Guggi" now. The nickname stuck to him like tar. Every time he walked into a room, someone would whisper it. *Hey, look, it's Guggi. Nice shirt, Guggi.*

The poor boy had stopped eating. His skin looked gray. His eyes were hollow, like two burnt-out holes in a piece of paper. He walked with his head down, trying to make himself small, trying to disappear.

We were in the lecture hall on the third floor. The windows were open to let in the breeze. Professor Muller was droning on about market segmentation.

"Find a partner for discussion," the professor said. She checked her watch. She looked bored.

I turned to David immediately. We were a team. The two outcasts.

I looked over at Oliver. He was standing alone. He looked around the room with desperate eyes. He just wanted one person to acknowledge his humanity. Just one person to look at him and not see a joke.

He walked up to Viktor.

"Can I be your partner?" Oliver asked. His voice was a thin, trembling thread.

Viktor looked at him. He didn't just look at him. He looked through him. He looked at Oliver like he was a stain on the carpet.

"No, Guggi," Viktor said. His voice was loud enough for the whole class to hear. "Don't you get it? Nobody wants you. You mean nothing. You are zero. You shouldn't have been here in the first place."

The room went silent. I held my breath.

Oliver stood there. His face twisted. It was a mix of agony and rage. I thought he was going to hit Viktor. Viktor was twice his size, but grief and anger could make anyone strong.

I was wrong.

"Fuck you!" Oliver screamed.

The sound tore through the room. It was raw. It was the sound of a soul breaking.

"Fuck all of you!" he yelled. Tears streamed down his face. "I should never have come here! I thought this was a school! I thought I could make my parents proud! But you are just devils! You are arrogant, rich devils! You're only lucky because of the family you were born into. Yet, you belittle everyone else."

He spun around and pointed a shaking finger at Professor Muller.

"And you!" Oliver shouted. "You see it! You see them bullying us! And you say nothing! Because you are a coward! You are scared of their daddies!"

The Professor opened her mouth, but no words came out.

Oliver turned.

He ran.

He didn't run out the door. He ran toward the open window.

"Oliver, no!" someone screamed.

It happened in slow motion. I saw his sneakers hit the ledge. I saw the desperate flutter of his fake Gucci shirt. I saw his body tilt forward into the blue sky.

And then he was gone.

There was a sickening silence. Then, a dull thud from the concrete courtyard below. It was a sound I will never forget. It sounded like a heavy sack of rice hitting the floor.

Chaos erupted. Girls screamed. Professor Muller dropped her coffee mug. It shattered, brown liquid spreading across the floor like blood.

I ran to the window. I looked down.

Oliver was lying on the pavement. His limbs were twisted at impossible angles. He looked like a broken doll. A small pool of red was spreading around his head.

"*Oluwa o*," I whispered. Oh God.

David pulled me back. His hands were shaking. "Don't look, Josh. Don't look."

Oliver was dead. But the machine of Kingsley University did not stop. Within hours, the narrative changed. The police came. The ambulances came. And then the lawyers came.

We learned later that Oliver was the third scholarship student to die in five years. Three boys. Three suicides. But you never read about it in the news.

The college had a media team that could bury a story faster than an undertaker buries a body. They paid the parents. They silenced the press. They called it an "accidental fall" or a "pre-existing mental condition."

Oliver became a ghost. His seat in the back row was empty. And the Elites? They went back to talking about their vacations. They went back to laughing.

That was the day I learned the most important lesson of Kingsley University. Poor people are disposable. We are firewood for their fire.

My life pivoted during Financial Decision-Making.

David had not registered for the class. For the first time, I was truly alone. I walked into the room, feeling the weight of the stares.

I kept my head down. I clutched my bag tight. I walked to the back row, to the designated ghetto of the classroom.

Only two other scholarship students were there. They sat far apart, terrified of drawing attention. I sat in the corner.

"Can I sit next to you?"

The voice was confident. Smooth.

I looked up. It was Dmitri.

I froze. I blinked. Was this a prank? Dmitri Yahontov was a legend. He drove a Rolls-Royce Wraith. He wore watches that cost more than a kidney.

He sat in the front row with the gods.

"Sure," I stammered. "You... sure."

He smiled and sat down. He placed a leather notebook on the desk.

The air in the room changed. The other scholarship students gasped. The Elites in the front row turned around. Melina looked back, her eyebrows raised in surprise.

Viktor hissed like a snake. "What is wrong with Dmitri?" he whispered loudly. "You can take a pig out of the swamp, but you can never take the swamp out of the pig. He will always be a peasant. No matter how much he pretends to be one of us."

Dmitri heard him. His back went rigid.

His hands balled into fists on the desk. His knuckles turned white. For a second, I thought violence was about to erupt again. I thought about Oliver.

But Dmitri breathed out. He unclenched his hands.

"Ignore him," Dmitri said to me. His voice was calm, but his eyes were cold ice.

"I hear that all the time," I said. "I am not surprised. He is Russian."

Dmitri looked at me. "Not all Russians are racists, Josh. Some of us judge a man by his character, not his skin. My name is Dmitri Yahontov."

"I am Josh Balogun," I said.

We shook hands. His grip was firm.

If I had known that this handshake was the beginning of the end, would I have pulled away?

If I had known that this boy with the charming smile would lead me to a federal prison cell, would I have run?

Probably not. Even though I got caught. I enjoyed the lifestyle while it lasted.

I cannot change the past. I am stuck in the present, counting the bricks in my cell. But back then, I saw a lifeline. I saw a friend.

We listened to Professor Barkley. He talked about CEOs making tough calls. I covertly searched Dmitri's name on my phone under the desk.

Nothing.

There were no results for a "Dmitri Yahontov" who attended Kingsley. But there were hundreds of results for "Albert Yahontov."

Albert Yahontov. Fifty-six years old. Russian arms dealer. Net worth: one billion dollars. Rumored to supply weapons to rogue states. Rumored to be building nuclear components for the Kremlin.

I looked at Dmitri. Was this his father? The resemblance was there in the sharp nose and the cold blue eyes. But there was no official link.

"Can you tell us the answer, Josh?"

Professor Barkley's voice snapped me back to reality. He was looking right at me. He knew I wasn't paying attention.

He wanted to embarrass me.

I froze. My mind was blank.

"I think Steve Jobs was the true game-changer," Dmitri said instantly. He didn't even look up from his notes. Apple leads the market today because of his singular vision.

"Without his specific brand of innovation, the tech landscape would be stagnant. Though Samsung has been taking giant strides lately."

Professor Barkley blinked. He nodded slowly. "Correct. Very good."

I let out a breath I didn't know I was holding. Dmitri winked at me.

After class, he stood up. "Want to grab lunch? My treat."

I hesitated. "I can't, man. I went to the Royal Restaurant once. A salad costs thirty-five dollars. My father would faint."

Dmitri laughed. It was a genuine sound. "Don't worry about it. I'm paying."

I accepted. I was hungry. I was always hungry. The free snacks in the dorm pantry were keeping me alive, but I craved real food.

We walked to the restaurant. It was elegant, with white tablecloths and crystal glasses. We sat down.

"Order whatever you want," Dmitri said.

I ordered the Beef Wellington. Dmitri ordered the Aged Bresse Duck.

As we waited, the door opened.

Melina walked in.

She was not alone. Viktor was with her. They were holding hands. He was guiding her to a table by the window.

I felt my appetite vanish. I watched them. Viktor pulled out her chair.

He kissed her hand. It looked perfect. It looked like a romance novel.

"You like her?" Dmitri asked. He was watching me.

"Yeah," I admitted.

"Stop staring at her like a serial killer," he said. "Talk to her."

"I can't," I said bitterly. "Look at her, Dmitri. She is a goddess. I am a black man in America. And I am poor. She would never date me. How would I take her out? We could split a Happy Meal at McDonald's? That is all I can afford."

Dmitri swirled his water glass. "I don't think Viktor is right for her."

He pulled out his phone. He tapped the screen and slid it across the table to me.

"Watch this."

I looked. It was a video. It was dark, flashing lights, heavy bass music. A club.

There was Viktor. He was shirtless. He was sweating. And he was having sex with a girl on a sofa in the middle of the VIP section. Other guys, Elites from our class, were cheering him on, pouring champagne on them.

I felt sick. "If he loves Melina, why would he do that?"

"He doesn't love her," Dmitri said. "He loves owning her."

I looked over at Viktor. He was spoon-feeding Melina a piece of cake. She was smiling at him with total trust. "How did you get this?" I asked.

"I was there," Dmitri said. "Mark recorded it. He posted it on the group chat."

"Group chat?"

"The BBC," Dmitri said.

"Billionaire Boys' Club. It is a group chat for the top guys. They post everything there. Their conquests. Their crimes."

"Why doesn't anyone tell her?" I asked, outraged. "Those guys are her friends!"

"It is a cult, Josh," Dmitri said darkly. "They protect their own. And they all have dirt on each other. Mutually Assured Destruction. If Mark tells on Viktor, Viktor tells the police about the girl Mark raped in Cancun. Silence is the currency."

The food arrived. It smelled divine. For a moment, the Beef Wellington made me forget the ugliness of the world.

We ate and talked. Dmitri was curious about Africa.

"Is it true?" he asked, leaning in. "About the Nigerian Princes?"

I laughed. "You mean the email scams?"

"Yeah. I get five emails a week. Some guy named Prince Abacha wants to give me ten million dollars. I just need to send five thousand for legal fees."

"Don't send it," I warned him. "There is no prince. Just a guy in a cybercafé in Lagos smoking weed and hoping you are stupid."

He laughed. "Is it true about... you know? The anatomy?"

"Anatomy?"

"Black guys," he whispered. "Long dicks."

I choked on my water. "Seriously?"

"I need to know. For science."

I grinned. "Well, I saw Eric Walters naked once. His dick is twice the size of mine. So, the stereotype is not always true."

Dmitri roared with laughter. People turned to look at us. For the first time at Kingsley, I felt like I was just hanging out with a friend.

Then the bill came.

I glanced at the total. $189.78.

I felt a cold sweat. That was nearly my entire monthly budget.

"This is insane," I whispered. "This is four months of salary for some people in Nigeria." My father included.

"Relax," Dmitri said.

He pulled out a wallet. It was thick. He opened it, and I saw a rainbow of black cards. The Centurion. The Palladium. Cards that invite-only people possess.

He shuffled through them like a deck of playing cards. He pulled one out and placed it on the silver tray.

I saw the name embossed on the card.

ALEXANDER BROWN.

I froze. I looked at Dmitri. He was smiling at the waiter. Why did Dmitri Yahontov have a card belonging to Alexander Brown?

The waiter took the card. He walked away. A minute later, he returned. He looked apologetic.

"I am sorry, sir," the waiter said. "The card was declined."

Dmitri's smile didn't waver, but his eyes hardened. He cursed softly in Russian. *Suka.*

He reached into his wallet again. He pulled out a second card.

I looked closely.

JOSEPH ROSENBERG.

My heart started thumping against my ribs. In Nigeria, we know what this is. We call it *yahoo yahoo*. Internet fraud.

Dmitri Yahontov was not just a student in need who got rich. He was a fraudster.

The waiter took the second card.

"Who is Joseph Rosenberg?" I asked. My voice was low.

Dmitri stiffened. He looked at me. The warmth was gone from his eyes. He looked dangerous.

"He is a friend," Dmitri said. "Why do you ask?"

"I saw the name," I said. "On the card."

Dmitri leaned in. He looked around the restaurant to make sure no one was listening.

"He is just a friend, Josh," he said firmly.

The waiter came back. "Approved, sir. Thank you."

Dmitri took the receipt. He stood up. "Ready?"

I nodded. I followed him out of the restaurant. I looked at his expensive watch. I looked at his Rolls-Royce parked outside.

CHAPTER FIVE

Nigerians act funny sometimes. We are a people of logic when it comes to business, but when it comes to the events of life, logic often jumps out of the window.

The Yoruba people, my people, are particularly superstitious. We do not believe in accidents. If a bird cries at night and a baby dies in the morning, we do not blame sudden infant death syndrome. We blame the bird. We blame the old woman in the village with the red eyes. We connect dots that do not exist because it is easier to blame a witch than to blame biology.

I grew up laughing at these things. I was a boy of science. I was a boy of numbers. But you can take the boy out of Nigeria, yet you can never fully scrub the Nigeria out of the boy. The fear is always there, sleeping in your blood.

I knew something was wrong the moment I woke up.

It was a Tuesday. The air conditioner in our dorm suite was humming its low, expensive hum. I swung my legs out of bed, my mind still half-trapped in a dream about falling from a skyscraper. My feet hit the floor, and I stood up to walk to the bathroom.

Thud.

I slammed my big toe against the leg of the oak dresser.

Pain shot up my leg like a lightning bolt. I hopped on one foot, biting my lip to keep from screaming.

In Yoruba culture, hitting your left toe against a stone or a surface first thing in the morning is not just an accident.

It is an omen. It is the universe telling you to go back to bed.

It is a sign that the road ahead is filled with thorns.

I shook it off. I told myself I was in Beverly Hills. I was in America. The village witches could not cross the Atlantic Ocean. Their GPS did not work here.

I limped toward the closet to get dressed. I reached for my favorite shirt, a plain white tee I had bought from a thrift store in Detroit. As I pulled it out, my foot caught the edge of the rug.

Thud.

I hit the same toe against the wall.

I froze. Twice. I had struck my left toe twice in five minutes. My heart did a slow, heavy thud in my chest. This was bad. This was the universe screaming at me.

I looked over at Eric. He was asleep, but he was not peaceful. He was snoring loud enough to rattle the windows.

His face was buried in his pillow, and his laptop was still open on his chest, the screen glowing soft blue in the dim room.

Eric had been working like a madman lately. He was building an app. He told me it was going to kill Instagram. He called it "The Mirror."

He wanted to create a social media platform that did not use filters. He wanted people to see themselves as they really were. It sounded like a terrible idea to me.

Who wants to see reality? Reality is ugly. Reality is poverty. Everyone wants a filter. But Eric was the billionaire genius, so I kept my mouth shut.

I walked to the pantry. My stomach was growling.

I grabbed a bag of Cheetos and a can of Pepsi. It was the breakfast of champions, or at least the breakfast of scholarship students who were too scared to go to the cafeteria.

I sat on the edge of my bed and opened the soda.

Pop. Fizz.

And then, disaster.

The can slipped from my fingers. It did not fall on the floor. It did not fall on the bedspread. It fell right onto the white shirt I had just laid out. The dark liquid spread across the fabric like a gunshot wound.

Three signs. The toe. The wall. The spill.

I sat there, staring at the ruined shirt. I felt a cold dread settle in my stomach. The Cheetos tasted like dust in my mouth.

Then, my phone rang. The sound cut through the silence like a knife. It was a harsh, jarring ringtone I had set for international calls. Eric groaned in his sleep and pulled the pillow over his head.

"Fuck," he mumbled. "Is it morning already?"

I ignored him. I looked at the screen.

Mom.

My mother never called. Calling from Nigeria to America cost a fortune. She usually sent WhatsApp voice notes or long texts filled with prayer emojis. If she was calling, it meant the world was ending.

I picked up the phone. My hand was trembling.

"*E ka ro*, ma," I said. Good morning, ma.

My voice was low. I used the respectful tone. In my culture, you could be a king, but you still bowed to your mother. You still lowered your voice.

"Joshua," she said.

Her voice sounded thin. It sounded like it was coming from a very far away place, stretched tight over thousands of miles of ocean. I could hear the static of the connection. I could hear the sound of a generator humming in the background.

"Mom? What is it?"

"I am calling to tell you about your father," she said. She did not waste time with pleasantries. "He is very sick."

I sat down on the floor. "Sick? Sick with what? Malaria?"

"No," she said. She took a ragged breath. "He has been sick for a while. We did not want to tell you. We did not want to distract you from your studies. You know how your father is. He did not want you to worry."

"Tell me," I whispered.

"His kidneys," she said. "They are failing. Both of them. We rushed him to Afe Babalola Teaching Hospital yesterday. His body was swollen, Josh. He looked like he was filled with water. The doctor did the tests. They say he needs a transplant."

The word hung in the air. Transplant.

It was a rich man's word. It was a word for people who had insurance. It was a word for people in Beverly Hills, not for a civil servant in Ado-Ekiti who drove a thirty-year-old car and earned less than $50 monthly.

"How much?" I asked. I closed my eyes.

"The doctor said seventy-four million naira," she whispered. She started to cry. It was a soft, broken sound. "We have sold the land in the village. We have sold the car. It is not enough. It is not even close."

I did the math in my head. I was good at math. Numbers were my friends. But these numbers were enemies.

Seventy-four million naira. That was about $52,000.

$52,000!

I had $573 in my account.

"Mom," I said. "Is there... is there dialysis?"

"Dialysis is expensive too," she cried. "And the doctor said his body is too weak. He needs the kidney, Josh. Or he will die. They gave him a month. Maybe less."

I felt the room spinning. I looked at the eighty-five-inch television on the wall. I looked at the Jacuzzi in the bathroom. I was surrounded by millions of dollars of luxury, but I could not save my father.

I thought about my brother. I saw his small coffin being lowered into the red earth.

I thought about my sister. I remembered the heat of her skin before she went cold.

Not again.

I could not let it happen again. I was the one who made it out. I was the hope of the family.

If I could not save him, then what was the point of all this?

What was the point of the scholarship? What was the point of the struggle?

Why was money my enemy? Why was poverty my friend?

"I will get the money," I said.

The lie tasted like ash on my tongue.

"Josh," my mother sobbed. "How? It is too much money."

"I am in America, mom," I said. I tried to make my voice sound strong. I tried to sound like the man she thought I was. "I have friends here. Rich friends. The people in my school are billionaires. $52,000 is nothing to them. It is like fifty naira. I will talk to them. I will ask them to help."

"Are you sure?" she asked. Hope is a cruel thing. I could hear the hope in her voice, and it broke my heart.

"I am sure," I said. "I will send the money before the end of the month. Tell the doctor to prepare. Tell daddy... tell him to hold on."

"Thank you, my son," she said. "God will bless you. God will bless your friends. I knew you were our savior. I knew it."

We hung up.

I sat on the floor, staring at the phone. The screen went black. I could see my own reflection in the glass. I looked terrified.

I called my sister, Abisola.

"Hello, Brother Josh," she answered. She sounded scared.

"Abisola," I said in Yoruba. "Listen to me carefully. Hide the knives. Hide the pills. Watch mommy. Do not let her be alone. Do you understand?"

"Yes, bro," she whispered. "Is daddy going to die?"

"No," I said fiercely. "He is not going to die."

I ended the call.

"Hey, man."

I looked up. Eric was sitting up in bed. His hair was a mess. He was looking at me with concern. He could not understand Yoruba, but grief is a universal language.

"You okay?" he asked.

I stood up. My knees cracked. "Yeah. I am fine."

"You don't look fine," Eric said. "You look like you saw a ghost."

"I said I am fine," I snapped.

I walked into the bathroom and locked the door. It was soundproof. I turned on the shower so the noise would cover me. And then I sank to the floor and buried my face in my hands.

I needed fifty-two thousand dollars in twenty-seven days. I checked my bank app again. $573.11. I was drowning.

I called Jada.

She answered on the first ring. "Josh? Everything okay?"

"My father is dying," I choked out. The tears finally came. Hot, angry tears. "He is in the hospital. His kidneys are gone, Jada. They are gone."

"Oh my God," she said.

"They need $52,000," I cried.

"I don't have it. I don't have anything. I am going to watch him die, just like the others. I am useless, Jada."

"Breathe, Josh," she said firmly. "Breathe. We will figure this out."

"How?" I shouted. "I can't ask these people. They look at me like I am dirt. If I ask them for money, they will laugh. They will think I am just another African scammer."

"Don't do anything stupid," she said. "Promise me. Don't go to a loan shark. Don't do anything illegal. Just hold on."

"I have to go," I said. I couldn't talk anymore. I felt like I was going to vomit.

I washed my face with cold water. I looked in the mirror. My eyes were red. I looked like a desperate man.

I went to class.

It was *Global Business Issues*. I walked in like a zombie. David was there, sitting in our usual spot in the back row. He took one look at me and put his book down.

"What happened?" David asked.

I sat down heavily. "My dad. Kidney failure. He needs surgery. Fifty-two thousand dollars."

David's face fell. He looked genuinely pained. He reached out and squeezed my shoulder.

"Josh... I am so sorry."

"I told my mom I would get the money," I whispered. "I lied to her, David. I gave her hope when I have none."

David bit his lip. He looked down at his cheap sneakers.

"I have some savings," he said quietly. "From my summer job at the warehouse. I have $1,200. I know it isn't much. But you can have it."

I looked at him. $1,200 was a lot of money for people like us. It was his safety net.

"David, I can't," I said.

"Take it," he insisted. "We are friends. Friends help each other."

"Thank you," I said. My voice cracked.

I did the math again. I had $573. David had $1,200. I was still short by over $50,000. It was like trying to empty the ocean with a teaspoon.

The next day, I dragged myself back to the dorm after lectures. I felt heavy. Every step was an effort. I just wanted to sleep. I wanted to sleep and wake up and find out this was all a nightmare.

I reached my door. I heard voices inside. One was Eric's. He was talking about coding, his voice fast and excited.

The other voice was a lady's. She was laughing.

I frowned. Eric never had girls over. Eric was terrified of girls. I opened the door. I dropped my bag.

Jada was sitting on Eric's bed. She looked up. Her face lit up like the sun.

"Josh!"

She jumped up and ran to me. She threw her arms around my neck. She smelled of vanilla and home. I buried my face in her neck and held her tight. I was afraid she was a hallucination.

"How?" I asked, pulling back. "How are you here?"

"You told me the address once," she said, smiling. "I took the first flight."

Eric cleared his throat. He looked awkward. "I... uh... I am going to go to the library. Give you guys some space."

He grabbed his laptop and scurried out of the room.

"Jada," I said. "Why?"

She reached into her bag. She pulled out a thick brown envelope. She pressed it into my chest.

"Open it," she said.

I opened the flap. Inside, there was a stack of hundred-dollar bills. Thick. Heavy.

"What is this?" I asked. My hands were shaking.

"It is $17,210," she said.

I stared at her. "Where did you get seventeen grand?"

She looked down. "I sold the car."

"The Honda?" I gasped. "Jada... your dad gave you that car. It was his last gift to you before he died."

"I know," she said softly. "And I pawned my necklace. And the earrings my grandma gave me."

"No," I said. "No, Jada. I can't take this. That car... it is your heart."

She grabbed my face with both hands. Her eyes were fierce.

"Your father is dying, Josh. A car is just metal. A necklace is just gold. You can't replace a father. I know. I lost mine. I won't let you lose yours."

"But..."

"Take it," she commanded. "You said you were alone here. You said you had no friends. Well, I am here. And I am not letting you drown."

I broke down. I fell to my knees and wept. She held me. She rocked me like a baby.

For three days, Jada stayed. She was a light in the darkness. She met David. They hit it off immediately.

"She is a queen," David told me when he was leaving one evening. "She sold her car for you? Josh, listen to me. I don't care about Melina or whoever you are staring at in class. This girl? She is the one. Do not break her heart."

"I won't," I promised.

Then she had to leave. She had work. She kissed me goodbye at the airport.

"You will find the rest," she said. "I believe in you."

I watched her walk away. I had almost twenty thousand dollars now. It was a miracle. But it was not enough. I was still thirty thousand short. And the clock was ticking.

I went to class the next day. It was *Global Business Issues* again. I sat next to David. I felt empty without Jada.

The door opened. Dmitri walked in.

He was followed by his usual entourage of Elites. Mark, Viktor, the guys who owned the school. They were laughing.

Dmitri stopped. He looked at the empty seat next to Mark. Then he looked at me. He said something to Mark. Mark looked confused. Dmitri walked up the stairs.

The whole class went quiet. The stratification of the room was sacred. Elites in front. Peasants in back.

Dmitri walked right past the middle row. He came to the back. He sat in the empty seat on my other side.

David's mouth fell open.

"Hey," Dmitri said casually. "How are you?"

"I am fine," I lied. "How are you?"

Professor Muller stormed into the room. She looked furious. Her hair was pulled back so tight it looked painful. She slammed her books on the desk.

"What is wrong with her?" Dmitri whispered.

"She looks moody," I said.

"Mark dumped her last night," Dmitri said. He had a mischievous glint in his eyes.

I choked on air. "Mark? The student Mark?"

"Yup," Dmitri chuckled.

"But... she hates men," I whispered. "She spends half the class yelling about patriarchy."

"It was a bet," Dmitri explained. "Mark and Viktor bet a thousand dollars. Mark said he could bang her. Viktor said it was impossible. Mark seduced her. He slept with her. He recorded it. Then he dumped her. He posted the video on the BBC group chat last night."

"Holy shit," I said.

Professor Muller looked up. She zeroed in on us.

"Dmitri! Josh!" she screamed. "Get out! Get out of my class right now!"

"But we didn't do anything!" I protested.

"Out!" she shrieked.

Dmitri laughed. He stood up, grabbed his bag, and stuck his tongue out at her.

I grabbed my stuff and followed him, feeling the heat of embarrassment on my neck.

Outside in the hallway, Dmitri was still laughing. He pulled out his phone.

"You want to see it?"

He showed me the video. It was grainy, but it was definitely Professor Muller.

And it was definitely Mark. He was ramming into her from behind and calling her his slut while she kept calling him "daddy."

"That woman misses Mark's dick," Dmitri laughed.

I laughed too, but it was hollow. I had just been kicked out of class. My dad was dying. I was losing my mind.

"You want to get food?" Dmitri asked.

"Sure," I said.

We went to a cafe near the library. It was quieter there. We ordered tea.

Dmitri looked at me over the rim of his cup. His blue eyes were sharp. They saw too much.

"Tell me," he said. "What is really wrong? You look like you are carrying the weight of the world. Did you lose your dick overnight?"

I looked at him. I looked at the guy who drove a Rolls-Royce but sat in the back row.

"It is my family," I said. The dam broke. "My dad needs a kidney transplant. I need $52,000. I have raised some, but I am still thirty thousand short. I have twenty days left. If I don't get it, he dies."

I told him about my siblings. I told him about the tuberculosis. I told him about the malaria. I told him about the poverty that tasted like bile in my throat.

"I am tired of watching them die, Dmitri," I said, tears leaking out again. "I am tired of being helpless."

Dmitri put his cup down. He didn't offer pity. He didn't say sorry.

"How desperate are you?" he asked.

"I will do anything," I said. "Anything."

"I can help you," he said. His voice dropped an octave. "I won't lend you money. I don't believe in handouts. But I can teach you how to make it."

The air around us seemed to get colder.

"I am listening," I said.

"Are you good at keeping secrets?"

"Yes."

"Good." He leaned forward. "How do you think I make my money, Josh? You think my daddy sends me checks?"

"I don't know," I said. "David said you were a student in need. But you drive a Rolls-Royce Wraith. I assumed you had a secret billionaire father."

"My father is a billionaire," Dmitri said. "But the only thing he gave me was his last name. He doesn't acknowledge me. To him, and to his lawyers, I am a bastard."

"Oh," I said.

"I made my own money," he said.

He reached into his jacket and pulled out a leather cardholder. He opened it and fanned out a dozen cards on the table.

They weren't flimsy plastic. They were heavy. Metal. Titanium. They caught the light like obsidian blades.

I read the names. Jacob Grey. Edward Peterson. Michael Vance. Not a single Russian name. Not a single Dmitri.

"Why do you have these?" I asked. "Are you a thief?"

"I am an arbitrator," he corrected. "The modern-day Robinhood who takes from the rich to build a generational legacy so that my children and grandchildren don't suffer."

"You are stealing," I said. "You are stealing from people."

"Keep your voice down," he hissed. "Every wealthy family out there had someone, a great great great grandfather, who got his hands dirty to build family wealth."

He looked me in the eye. "Josh, look around you. Look at this school. Look at Edward Morrison. He bragged in class about falsifying reports to deceive investors. Samantha often talks about her parents optimizing their company's supply chain, which meant using child labor in Bangladesh to save four cents a shirt. They committed moral fraud to save their companies. Are they in jail? No. They are heroes. They are both Elites."

"That is different," I argued weakly.

"It is not different," Dmitri said. "It is the same game. The rich steal with pens, lobbyists, and shell companies. They steal labor. They steal tax money. And they get applauded on the cover of Forbes. I steal from people who have so much money they don't even notice the leak. These cards? They belong to 'Whales.' People with unlimited limits. If I take ten thousand dollars, it is like taking a penny from under your couch cushion."

He picked up the card labeled Michael Vance. "This system is rigged, Josh. If you work a job, paying taxes, saving pennies, you will die poor. You will work until your back breaks, and you still won't be able to pay for a kidney transplant."

Dmitri smiled. A sad hollow smile. "Jeff Bezos makes one hundred and fifty thousand dollars a minute. A minute! You think he works harder than your father? No. He just knows how to exploit the code. How long do you have to work before you get 1% of Elon Musk's wealth? A thousand lifetimes."

I looked at the cards. I thought about my father lying in a hospital bed in Lagos, his body swollen, his breath shallow. I thought about Jada selling her car.

I thought about the indignity of begging doctors for time. I had lost two siblings because of poverty. I wouldn't lose my father. No!

"How does it work?" I asked.

"It used to be simple in the past when you could easily clone a card and swipe the plastic. Let it take the hit. But technology has advanced now. A lot of places decline cloned plastics," Dmitri said, tapping the metal card. "These days, using a physical fake is suicide. Cashiers check the signature, the chip fails, the magstripe is weak. No. We use the data."

"The data?"

"We buy 'Fullz' on the dark web," he explained. "Full identities. Name, SSN, date of birth, mother's maiden name. Then, we don't just clone the card; we hijack the digital identity. Wang is a god when it comes to hacking. He uses that data to provision a digital wallet. He puts Michael Vance's Black Card onto an iPhone or a rooted Android."

"So, you shop with a phone?"

"Exactly. But you have to shop smart," he said. "You have to match the 'MCC,' Merchant Category Code. If Michael Vance buys crypto, the bank blocks it. But if he buys watches? Handbags? Fine art? The bank sleepwalks through it. That is his lifestyle. That is the job, Josh. We convert digital credit into physical assets. We buy a Patek Philippe for three hundred thousand on the card."

He leaned in. "Then we walk it down the street to a fence, a guy named Amir, and we sell it for cash. Sixty cents on the dollar. Dirty credit becomes clean cash. No paper trail. Everyone wins."

My heart was hammering. It was illegal. It was sophisticated. It was exactly what my mother warned me against.

Ranti omo eni ti o je. Remember whose son you are.

But whose son was I? I was the son of a dying man. A dying man who spent his lifetime playing by the rules, only to be crushed by them. The son of a man earning $48 monthly. What good is having a good name and watching your family die in penury?

No, I didn't want to be like my father. I wanted to be rich. Eat good food. Wear good clothes. Build companies.

And like my idols, Jordan Belfort and Ray Hushpuppi, I wanted to fuck the best-looking girls. The ones you only see on magazine covers and TV.

"Why hotels in Africa?" I asked, remembering his earlier ambition.

"Legacy," Dmitri said. "I want to build something real. Something my children can inherit. Your kids can't inherit your job at Google or Amazon. They can't inherit your employee ID. But they can inherit your hotel. They can inherit the deed to the land. I can't tell people I am a fraudster. So, I tell them I am an angel investor. And one day, the lie becomes the truth."

He was smart. He was terrifyingly smart. He wasn't just grabbing cash; he was building an empire on a foundation of smoke and mirrors.

"Can I make fifty-two thousand dollars?" I asked.

"You can make that in a single run," Dmitri said. "If you are good. If you are cold."

He gathered the black cards, sliding them back into the leather wallet like sheathing a knife.

"I am not alone, Josh," he said. "I have partners."

I knew that Wang and Harry were definitely among his partners.

"I am in," I said.

"Are you sure?" Dmitri asked. "Once you start, there is no going back to being a terrified scholarship student. You cross the line, and the line disappears behind you."

I thought about the doctor's deadline for my father's medical bills. October 31st.

"I am sure," I said.

"Why are you helping me?" I asked.

Dmitri smiled. It was a sad smile.

"Because we are both bastards, Josh. America treats you like a bastard because you are black. My father treats me like a bastard because I was a mistake. We bastards have to stick together."

He stood up, buttoning his jacket. "Meet me tonight. I will text you the address."

I watched him walk away. I sat there for a long time, staring at the empty teacup

CHAPTER SIX

Kingsley University has the finest dormitories in the world. It is a fact. But even paradise has its limits. Some students prefer the privacy of penthouses in downtown LA.

Others, the ones who truly operate in the stratosphere, commute from mansions in the hills. That is why there is a helipad on campus. Every morning, the sky above Kingsley buzzes with the sound of rotor blades as students arrive in private helicopters, their hair barely ruffled by the wind.

As Dmitri drove through the winding roads of Beverly Hills, I pressed my face against the glass like a child at an aquarium. I had seen houses like these on *Keeping Up with the Kardashians* or in movies about drug lords. In real life, they were even more intimidating. They sat behind high walls covered in ivy, their gates wrought from iron that looked like lace.

I thought about my neighborhood in Detroit. I thought about the boarded-up windows, the weeds growing through cracks in the sidewalk, the sound of sirens that was our lullaby.

Here, the only sound was the purr of expensive engines. A Lamborghini Urus zoomed past us. A moment later, a Bentley Bentayga glided by in the other direction.

"This is insane," I whispered.

"This is just Tuesday," Dmitri said, his eyes on the road.

"I will not remain poor," I said to myself. It was a vow. "I will not let my children suffer like I did."

Poverty is a tricky thing. When everyone around you is poor, you don't really notice it. You are just normal.

But when you are poor in the midst of wealth, poverty becomes a physical weight. It sits on your chest. It burns your skin. Driving a Toyota Corolla in a neighborhood of Kias is fine. Driving a Toyota in a land of Bugattis is humiliation.

"Rich folks live differently," I muttered.

Dmitri chuckled. "I told you, Josh. Working at KFC will never get you this. Hard work is a lie they tell poor people to keep them working. Smart work is the truth. You need to make money while you sleep. If you don't find a way to make money while you sleep, you will work until you die. You can't change your skin color, but you can change your financial situation."

He pulled up to a massive white gate. It swung open silently.

We drove up a long driveway lined with palm trees. At the end stood a mansion. It was modern, all sharp angles and glass, glowing white in the California sun.

"Please don't tell me you own this," I said.

Dmitri smiled as he maneuvered the car into a garage that looked more like a showroom. "I do."

"How much?" I choked out.

"Thirteen million," he said casually.

Thirteen million dollars. He said it like it was the price of a sandwich. I wanted to punch something. I wanted to scream.

"You made all that from credit cards?"

He killed the engine. "Not just cards. We do other things. Legal. Illegal. Gray area. My hotels are doing well. Diversification, my friend."

I looked around the garage. My breath caught in my throat. It was a collection of automotive pornography. A Bugatti Chiron in two-tone blue. A McLaren P1. A Ferrari LaFerrari.

"Are these all yours?"

"No," Dmitri said, stepping out. "The Wraith, the Porsche Panamera, and the Maybach are mine. The other cars belong to my partners."

I swallowed hard. My father was dying in a hospital bed because we didn't have $52,000. And here, in this garage, there was probably ten million dollars worth of metal sitting on polished concrete.

"Why don't you drive the Bugatti to school?" I asked, feeling a surge of envy so strong it tasted like bile.

Dmitri locked the car. "I don't like unnecessary attention. And the Elites? They are snobs. They would rather die than be friends with someone who drives a Toyota, but if you drive a Bugatti, they start asking questions about your lineage. The Rolls-Royce is... understated enough."

Understated. A Rolls-Royce Wraith. *May God punish poverty!*

We walked into the house. The front door was massive, made of dark wood and glass. Inside, the air was cool and smelled of expensive cologne and ozone.

The floor was marble, polished to a mirror shine. I felt dirty walking on it. My thrift store sneakers squeaked.

The living room was vast. One wall was entirely glass, looking out over an infinity pool that seemed to drop off the edge of the world into the city below. The furniture was white leather, sleek and terrifyingly clean.

I stood there, paralyzed by the luxury.

"It is not a sin to be born poor," Dmitri said softly from behind me. "But it is a sin to choose to remain poor."

Those words hit me like a bullet. They killed whatever hesitation I had left. I looked at the view. I looked at the pool. I wanted this. I wanted it more than I wanted to be good.

"Welcome to the headquarters," Dmitri said.

Voices drifted from the hallway. Three people walked in. I recognized two of them instantly. Harry and Wang.

But the third person... I blinked. It was Alicia.

Alicia, the New Money girl. Alicia, who wore Chanel to class and looked down her nose at everyone. She was wearing an oversized hoodie that came down to her thighs, her legs bare and smooth. Harry had his arm wrapped possessively around her waist.

Then, a fourth person entered. A girl I didn't know.

She was stunning. She looked Blasian—Black and Asian mixed. She had curly hair pulled back in a messy bun and almond-shaped eyes that sparkled with mischief. She reminded me of Karrueche Tran.

"I am sure you know Harry, Wang, and Alicia," Dmitri said. He pointed to the new girl. "This is Naomi."

Naomi looked at me and winked. It was quick, like a camera shutter, but I saw it.

I also saw Wang. He was staring at Naomi like she was water in a desert. He looked like a puppy waiting for a treat.

"Everyone here knows?" I asked, looking at Alicia.

"We are all partners," Dmitri said.

"But Alicia is rich," I blurted out. "Why is she—"

Harry stepped forward. His face was dark with anger. "Watch your mouth, scholarship boy."

"We all have our stories," Dmitri interrupted calmly.

"Wait," Harry said, turning on Dmitri. "How does he know we are partners? Why is he here?"

"I brought him because he is going to be our new team member," Dmitri said.

The room went silent. You could hear the hum of the refrigerator in the kitchen.

"Do I need to remind you of the rule?" Harry hissed. "No outsiders."

"You broke the rule first when you brought her," Dmitri shot back, pointing at Alicia.

Harry pulled Alicia tighter. "Alicia is the reason we are rich! Before her, we were making pennies. She brought the connections. She brought the big cards."

"I am not discrediting her," Dmitri said. "I am just saying, rules are flexible."

"He is Nigerian!" Harry shouted. "Nigerians are religious freaks! What if he wakes up tomorrow and Jesus tells him to confess? What if he goes to the FBI? We all go down!"

It was a fair point. Nigerians love God almost as much as we love jollof rice. But Harry didn't know my God was currently asleep while my father was dying.

"I will never do that," I said, stepping forward. "My father is dying. He needs a kidney transplant. I need money. I am not a snitch."

Harry stared at me. He let go of Alicia. He marched out of the room. He came back a minute later holding a duffel bag. He unzipped it and grabbed handfuls of cash. Bundles of hundred-dollar bills.

He threw them at me. They hit my chest and fell to the floor.

"How much do you need?" Harry yelled. "Fifty thousand? Here! Take it! Take sixty! Take a hundred! Just take it and get the fuck out!"

I looked at the money on the floor. It was right there. Salvation.

Dmitri grabbed Harry by the collar.

"Are you crazy?" Dmitri shouted. "Think, Harry! After he pays the bill, then what? He goes back to being poor? He goes back to struggling? He watches his next family member die? Is that what you want?"

"I don't care!" Harry screamed. "I don't care about him!"

"Stop it!" Alicia yelled, stepping between them.

The room was tense. Wang was still staring at Naomi. Naomi was watching me with a curious little smile. I looked at the money on the floor. I should have taken it.

If I were a smart man, I would have picked up those bundles, thanked Harry, and ran to the hospital. I would have paid for the surgery. I would have saved my father. And I would have walked away from this life.

But I had seen the garage. I had seen the pool. I had seen the way Alicia looked at Harry with respect and admiration.

I didn't just want to survive. I wanted to live. I wanted to be one of them.

"I don't want your charity," I said quietly.

Harry looked stunned. Dmitri let go of Harry's collar. He smoothed his shirt.

"He reminds me of myself," Dmitri said. His voice was lower now. "I watched my mom die of cancer. I couldn't do anything. I know what poverty tastes like. We all do."

He turned to the others. "Wang, remember when you had two shirts? Remember when people laughed at you? Harry, remember when you slept in your car after your dad kicked you out of his house? Naomi, remember the grocery store? Minimum wage? Have you forgotten?"

"It's none of my business," Harry muttered, wiping blood from his lip. "Rule is no outsiders."

"Fuck the rule," Dmitri said.

"Why don't we vote?" Naomi suggested. Her voice was cool, like water.

Everyone looked at her.

"Democracy," she said, shrugging. "If you don't want him, raise your hand."

Harry's hand shot up instantly. Alicia raised hers slowly, looking at Harry. Two against three.

"If you want Josh to join," Naomi said, "raise your hand."

She raised her hand. Dmitri raised his.

It was a tie. It all came down to Wang.

Wang blinked. He looked at Harry. He looked at Dmitri. Then he looked at Naomi. She was looking at him, her eyebrows raised slightly.

Slowly, painfully slowly, Wang raised his hand.

"Yes!" I screamed inside my head.

Harry sighed. He looked at me, then at Dmitri. The anger drained out of him.

"Fine," Harry said. "He stays. But if he screws up, Dmitri, it's on you."

"He won't screw up," Dmitri said.

Harry walked over to me. He held out his hand. "Welcome to the team, Josh. Sorry about the lip."

I shook his hand. "Sorry about the yelling."

In Nigeria, grudges can last for generations. But here, in this house of secrets, anger was a luxury they couldn't afford.

"So," Naomi said, hopping onto the kitchen counter. "Now that we are all friends... who is hungry?"

And just like that, I was in.

CHAPTER SEVEN

After the adrenaline of the fight had faded, the house settled into a quiet hum. Dmitri gestured for me to follow him. We walked up a floating staircase made of glass and steel. It felt like walking on air. His bedroom was at the end of the hall. It was not just a room. It was a command center.

One wall was covered in monitors. Screens glowed with lines of code, stock market tickers, and live feeds from security cameras. The room was freezing cold.

The air conditioner was blasting to keep the servers from overheating. It smelled of ozone and expensive cologne. Dmitri sat in a leather chair that looked like it belonged on a spaceship. He spun around to face me.

"Sit," he said. He pointed to a beanbag chair in the corner.

I sat. I felt small in this room. I felt like a child who had wandered into a wizard's tower.

"You need to understand how this machine works," Dmitri said. His voice was low and serious. "We are not just lucky. We are a system."

He told me the history. It started with him and Naomi. They were the Adam and Eve of this garden of sin.

"I was broke," Dmitri said. "I was eating instant noodles and hiding from my landlord. Naomi was worse. She was working three jobs. She was scanning groceries at Whole Foods during the day and stripping at night. She wanted to go to the Beverly Hills Design Institute. It was her dream. But dreams cost money."

"How did you know she would join you?" I asked.

Dmitri smiled. It was a cold smile. "I saw her eyes, Josh. I met her at the grocery store. I saw the flyer for the design school taped to her register. I saw the way she looked at the rich women buying organic kale and expensive wine. It was a look of hunger. Not for food. For life."

He waited until her shift ended. He approached her in the parking lot.

In Nigeria, if a stranger approaches you in a parking lot at night, you run. But in America, desperation makes you stay.

"I told her I had a plan," Dmitri said. "I told her she could have tuition money in three months. She didn't even ask if it was legal. She just asked when we start."

Dmitri had done his homework. He knew that the old ways, magnetic strip skimmers, were dead. The chips killed them. So, he bought a Shimmer.

"It's a wafer-thin circuit board," Dmitri explained, shaping his hands like he was holding a microchip. "You slide it inside the card reader at the register. It sits there, invisible, intercepting the data between the chip and the bank. I taught Naomi how to insert it in two seconds while pretending to clean the terminal."

He paused, pouring a drink. "But the shimmer only gives you the track data. To shop online, you need the CVV, which is the three digits on the back. That is where the art comes in. I taught her the 'fumble.' She drops the card. She picks it up. In that half-second, she memorizes the three numbers. Data plus code equals a digital clone."

"We hit a hundred cards in the first month," Dmitri said. "But it was small fish. People with credit limits of two thousand dollars. The problem with poor people, Josh, is that the bank watches them. If a poor man buys a TV, the bank calls him. We needed whales. We needed the kind of people who can lose fifty thousand dollars and assume their assistant bought a jet ski."

He needed more access. He needed more soldiers.

He turned to his computer. He typed a few keys, and a file opened. It was a list of names.

"I didn't hack the school," he said, tapping the screen. "I phishing-attacked the Financial Aid director at Kingsley. Stole his login session. That gave me access to the 'At-Risk' student database. That is how I found Wang."

Wang. The silent one.

"Wang had applied for every emergency grant in existence," Dmitri explained. "He was drowning. I got close to him. I bought him a beer. He cracked. He told me about his brother."

"What about his brother?" I asked.

"His brother stole from a Triad," Dmitri said. "A local heavy. He took the money and ran back to China. The Triad didn't care. They went to Wang. They told him the debt was hereditary. Wang wasn't looking for tuition money. He was looking for blood money."

It made sense now. The silence. The intensity. Wang was a man with a gun to his head.

"And Harry?" I asked.

Dmitri laughed. "Harry was easy. Harry is a junkie. His father is a war hero who got tired of bailing him out. He cut Harry off. A junkie without money is a liability, but a junkie bartender? That is a goldmine. In a club, the customer hands the card over. Harry has 'The Walk.' The thirty seconds between the table and the register. That is an eternity. He photographs the front and back. High definition. Perfect capture."

So, they built the team. Harry harvested the physical cards at the club. Wang managed the hardware and the encryption. Naomi worked the retail registers. They were a net, catching data from the unsuspecting rich.

"We buy luxury goods," Dmitri said. "Watches. Handbags. Jewelry. We focus on items with high resale velocity. We sell them to a fence named Amir. He pays sixty cents on the dollar. Crypto or cash. Clean. Untraceable."

I nodded. It was smart. In Nigeria, the *Yahoo boys* (internet fraudsters) often got caught because they tried to move money through wire transfers.

Banks track wires. But a Rolex? A Rolex is just metal until you sell it.

"But what about the AI?" I asked. "Banks have algorithms. Neural networks that detect spending spikes. If you buy five Rolexes on a stolen card, the system freezes it in seconds."

Dmitri leaned back, a gleam in his eye. "That is the problem. The Fraud Prevention Algorithm. It is the dragon we cannot slay."

He pointed a finger at the ceiling. "Unless you have someone who can put the dragon to sleep. That is Alicia."

"Alicia?"

"Alicia is our golden goose. Have you heard of StarCred?"

"The credit card issuer?"

"Yes. Alicia's stepfather is the CEO."

My jaw dropped. "You are robbing her stepfather?"

"We are," Dmitri said. "And she holds the keys. Every October, StarCred throws the StarCred Ball. But that is not the point. The point is access. Alicia has his administrative override codes."

He leaned in closer. "Before we hit a card, a 'whale' card, we text Alicia. She logs into the backend. She sets a 'Travel Advisory' on that account. She tells the bank's computer that Mr. Smith is currently vacationing in Los Angeles and plans to make large luxury purchases. She whitelists the fraud. We aren't just stealing, Josh. We are authorized users."

"But why?" I asked, stunned. "Why would she do that to her own family? She risks federal prison."

"Because he deserves it."

The voice came from the doorway.

I spun around. Alicia was standing there. She was leaning against the doorframe, her arms crossed. She had changed out of the oversized hoodie into a silk robe. She looked like a queen who had just ordered an execution.

"I figured he was giving you the orientation," Alicia said. Her voice was flat, devoid of warmth. "I don't want him telling my story."

Dmitri nodded respectfully. He stood up. "I will give you two a minute."

He walked out. The door clicked shut.

I shifted in the beanbag chair. I felt uncomfortable. I did not want to be alone with Harry's girlfriend. Harry was a powder keg, and I did not want to be the spark.

"Relax," Alicia said. She walked over and sat on the edge of the desk. "I don't bite. Unless Harry asks me to."

She let out a dry laugh, but her eyes were not laughing. They were dead.

"I am not scared of you," I lied. "I am scared of the federal indictment you are carrying."

"Good," she said. "Fear keeps you sharp."

She looked at her fingernails. They were painted a deep, blood red.

"My mother divorced my dad when I was five," she began. "Two years later, she met Liam. He was Wall Street royalty. He bought her diamonds. He took us on yachts. They got married fast."

She paused. She looked at the wall of monitors.

"Liam liked little girls," she whispered.

The air in the room seemed to vanish. I felt a cold chill run down my spine.

"He never raped me," she said quickly, as if she had rehearsed this defense a thousand times. "He was too smart for that. He knew doctors check for tears. He knew about hymens. So, he didn't penetrate. He just... touched. He made me watch things.

"He made me do things with my mouth."

She was shaking. Just a little. Like a leaf in a gentle wind.

"I was seven," she said. "He made sure the cameras were off. He made sure my mother was at the spa or the country club. I told her, you know? I told her what he was doing."

"What did she do?" I asked. My voice was thick with anger.

"She screamed at me," Alicia said. A tear slipped down her cheek. "She called me a liar. She said I was trying to ruin her happiness. She loved the money, Josh. She loved the lifestyle more than she loved me. She took me to a doctor to prove I was lying. The doctor said I was intact. So, she said I was crazy."

I stood up. I couldn't sit anymore. I walked over to her and hesitated. Then, I put a hand on her shoulder. It was risky, but I could not leave her alone in that memory.

"I am sorry," I said. "That is... that is evil."

"He stopped when I was twelve," she said, wiping her face. "I started fighting back. I started screaming. But the hate... the hate grew in me like a cancer. When I met Harry, when I found out what he did... I saw a way to hurt Liam. I saw a way to bleed him dry."

She looked at me. Her eyes were fierce now.

"The StarCred Ball is next week," she said. "You joined at the right time. We are going to rob him blind, Josh. We are going to take everything."

She smiled. It was a terrifying smile. It was the smile of a woman who would burn the world down to warm her hands.

"You are lucky," she said. "We are going to make you rich."

That night, I stayed at the mansion.

We ordered pizza. It was strange. We sat in living room worth millions, eating greasy pepperoni pizza from a cardboard box.

I watched them. I analyzed them. In Nigeria, we say you must know the person who cooks your food before you eat it. I needed to know who these people were.

Dmitri was the head. He was the strategist. He was calm, calculated. He saw people as chess pieces.

Naomi was the heart. She laughed loud. She made jokes. She was the one who made sure everyone had a slice of pizza. But I saw the way she looked at expensive things. She looked at them with a hunger that could never be satisfied.

Harry was the volatile element. He was always high. I could tell. His pupils were pinned. He couldn't sit still. He touched Alicia constantly. Touched her hair, her hand, her knee. He needed her to breathe.

And then there was Wang.

Wang was the shadow. He sat in the corner, eating his pizza silently. He watched everything. He watched Naomi specifically. His eyes followed her movement like a camera.

Wang scared me. He was too quiet. He had too much to lose. A man who is fighting for his family's life is a man who will do anything to survive. Even betray his friends.

I should have listened to my gut. I should have seen the way he looked at us not as friends, but as tools. But I was distracted by the luxury. I was distracted by the promise of fifty thousand dollars.

Later, when the others had gone to sleep or passed out, Dmitri poured two glasses of whiskey. He handed one to me.

"Rules," he said.

"Rules?"

"We have rules," Dmitri said. "If you are in, you follow them. Rule number one: No outsiders. Nobody knows what we do. Not your girlfriend. Not your priest. Nobody."

"Okay," I said.

"Rule number two: We share equally. Even if you bring in the card, the money goes into the pot. We split it five ways. Now six ways."

"Fair," I agreed.

"Rule number three," he continued. "When we do a big job, like the BEC, Business Email Compromise, we live together. Under this roof. Nobody leaves until the money is clean."

"Okay."

"And rule number four," Dmitri said. "The contingency."

He walked over to the server rack tucked in the corner of the living room. He pointed to a small black box wired directly into the main network hub.

"This is the hardware trigger," he said. "And Wang... Wang wears the remote."

"What does it do?"

"If the Feds come," Dmitri said, "if they kick down that door... Wang taps his watch. Or one of us hits this box."

"And then?"

"And then, the Cryptographic Erasure protocol executes,"

Dmitri said, his voice dropping to a lecture tone. "Movies tell you to drill the hard drives or melt them with thermite. That's amateur hour. It's messy and it smells. This script targets the **LUKS encryption headers** on every device in the house."

He tapped his temple.

"Think of our data like a vault," Dmitri continued, doing the explaining now. "The password is the key. But the header? The header is the keyhole itself. If Wang presses that button, the keyhole vanishes. The vault is still there, sealed forever. The data inside becomes random static. Mathematical noise. Even the NSA can't decrypt noise."

"Why does Wang have the watch?" I asked. "Why not you?"

"Harry is a junkie," Dmitri said, glancing at Harry who was nodding off on the couch.

"He might press it by accident when he is high. Naomi and Alicia might panic. I might be busy stalling the police. But Wang... Wang is a robot."

Dmitri looked at Wang. "He is calm. He is cautious," Dmitri said. "He will wait until the very last second. And then he will save us."

I looked at the black box. It looked innocent, but it was a digital guillotine.

"The FBI has supercomputers," Dmitri added. "If they get our laptops with the headers intact, they can brute-force the passwords eventually. It might take them ten years, but they will get in. We cannot take that risk. If we go down, the logic dies first."

I nodded. It seemed smart. It seemed foolproof.

CHAPTER EIGHT

The transition from a regular student to a criminal does not happen with a bang. It happens in the quiet moments. It happens in the choices you make when you think no one is watching.

For the next few days, Kingsley University felt the same, yet everything had changed.

The Elites still walked the halls like they owned the oxygen we breathed. But I was different. I carried a secret in my chest that felt heavier than my textbooks.

The first sign of my corruption was betrayal. It happened on a Wednesday morning in our *Global Business Issues* class. I walked into the lecture hall. I saw David sitting in our usual spot in the back row.

He had saved a seat for me. He had his notebook open and a spare pen ready. He looked up and smiled, waving me over.

David was the only person who had been kind to me when I was nobody. He was the one who offered me his savings when my father was dying.

But David was safe. David was a scholarship student who would graduate, get a mid-level job, and live a decent, quiet life.

Dmitri, Wang, and Harry? They were the ticket to the stratosphere. They were the ones who could save my father.

In Yoruba culture, we have a saying. *Aguntan ti o ba n ba aja rin, yio je igbe.* The sheep that walks with dogs will eventually eat feces.

I looked at David. Then I looked at the middle row where Harry and Wang were sitting. They were whispering, looking sharp and dangerous. I walked past David.

I saw the confusion cloud his eyes. I saw the hurt. It felt like I had slapped him. I didn't stop. I walked to the middle row and sat down next to Wang.

"Welcome to the dark side," Harry whispered, smirking.

I didn't look back at David. I couldn't. If I looked back, I might remember that I was supposed to be a good person.

By Friday, I was fully integrated. I went to Dmitri's mansion every evening. We didn't just hang out; we planned. The StarCred Ball was approaching like a storm front. It was the weekend that would determine if my father lived or died.

"You look like a waiter," Dmitri said to me after classes on Friday. He was looking at my clothes. My best shirt was a button-down from Goodwill that had a small fray on the collar.

"It is all I have," I said defensively.

"Not anymore," Dmitri said. He twirled his car keys. "Get in the car. We are going shopping."

We took the Maybach. The interior smelled of leather and success. We drove into the heart of Beverly Hills, to the streets where the tourists walked slowly and the rich walked quickly.

Dmitri pulled up in front of a store. It wasn't just a store. It was a temple. The windows were tall sheets of glass. There were no price tags on the mannequins. If you have to ask the price, you cannot afford it.

The sign above the door read DERVISHI in gold letters.

I froze.

"Dmitri," I said. "This is..."

"Get out of the car, Josh."

I stepped onto the sidewalk. My legs felt weak. This was Melina's family store. This was the kingdom of the girl I dreamed about.

We walked in. The air inside was cool and smelled of jasmine and money. It was quiet. The kind of quiet that commands respect.

"Good afternoon," a voice said. "How may I help you?"

I knew that voice. It was the voice that narrated my daydreams.

I raised my eyes slowly.

Melina stood there. She was dressed in a sleek black pantsuit that fit her perfectly. Her hair was pulled back, showing off her high cheekbones.

She looked professional. She looked intimidating. She looked like a queen in her castle. I couldn't speak. My tongue felt like it was glued to the roof of my mouth.

Dmitri stepped forward, smooth as oil. "Hi, Melina. We are here to buy a suit."

Melina looked at him, then at me. Her expression didn't change. She was working.

"Of course," she said. "Follow me, please."

She turned to a sales assistant who was hovering nearby. "Jacqueline, please prepare an espresso for Mr. Yahontov and his friend."

His friend. She didn't say my name. I felt a pinch of disappointment.

Jacqueline scurried away. We followed Melina to the men's section. It was a sanctuary of wool and silk.

"Why are we here?" I hissed at Dmitri when Melina walked ahead to check a rack. "You set me up."

"I am giving you a chance," Dmitri whispered back, grinning. "Don't mess it up."

"I can't afford a button in this store," I whispered furiously. "This is torture."

"Relax. You are with me."

Melina returned with three suits. She laid them out on a velvet table.

"What is the occasion?" she asked. She looked at me directly. Her gray eyes were piercing.

"A ball," I squeaked. I cleared my throat and tried to deepen my voice. "A ball. Black tie."

She nodded. She held up a navy blue suit. "Try this one."

I went into the fitting room. It was bigger than my dorm room. I put on the suit. It felt different from the stiff, scratchy material of Tunde-Sean's old suit I had worn to prom. This fabric felt like water. It moved with me.

I stepped out. I stood in front of the three-way mirror. For the first time in a long time, I didn't look like a poor refugee boy. I looked tall. I looked strong.

"Too boxy," Dmitri said from the sofa, sipping his espresso. "He is going to a party, not a court hearing."

I went back and changed. I tried a notch lapel suit.

"No," Dmitri said. "Boring."

Melina didn't say anything. She just watched, her face unreadable. Then she handed me a fitted silhouette suit. It was black, midnight black. The fabric seemed to absorb the light.

I put it on. I buttoned the jacket. It hugged my waist and flared slightly at the hips. It made my posture straighter. I felt powerful. I walked out.

Dmitri put his coffee cup down. He nodded slowly. "That is the one."

I looked at Melina. She was studying me. Her eyes traveled from my shoes up to my face. She tilted her head slightly.

"This looks good on you," she said softly. "It highlights your broad shoulders. And your muscles."

Time stopped. Did she just say muscles? Broad shoulders?

It is hard for a Black person to blush. But I felt the heat rise up my neck and burn my cheeks. My crush, the billionaire heiress, was checking me out.

"Thank you," I stammered.

"It fits your frame perfectly," she added, smoothing the lapel with her hand.

Her fingers brushed my chest. I almost stopped breathing. "You carry it well."

"How much?" Dmitri asked, breaking the spell.

"$4,597," Melina said. She said the number like it was nothing. Like she was telling us the time.

My heart plummeted. Four thousand dollars. That would go a long way for my father's treatment. It was a fortune.

I started to take the jacket off. "I think maybe..."

Dmitri stood up. He pulled out a black card. "We will take it."

He didn't blink. He handed the card to Melina.

I watched her face. I waited for her to ask why a scholarship student was letting another man buy him a four-thousand-dollar suit. I waited for the judgment.

But she just took the card. "Excellent choice."

She processed the payment. Jacqueline wrapped the suit in layers of tissue paper and placed it in a heavy bag with the name DERVISHI embossed in silver.

Dmitri took the bag. "Thanks, Melina."

"You are welcome," she said.

We turned to leave. I was halfway to the door when she spoke again.

"Bye, Dmitri," she said. Then she looked at me. "See you in class on Monday, Josh."

I froze. She knew my name.

We had never spoken in class. I sat in the back; she sat in the front. But she knew my name. I walked out of the store on floating legs. The sun seemed brighter. The air seemed sweeter.

"See?" Dmitri said as we got into the car. "That wasn't so hard."

"She knows my name," I whispered. I turned to him, grinning like a fool. "Dmitri! She called me Josh! Melina Dervishi knows my name!"

Dmitri laughed and started the engine. "You are hopeless, my friend. Absolutely hopeless."

I spent the ride back to the mansion screaming in ecstasy inside my head. For a few minutes, I forgot about the fraud. I forgot about the kidney failure. I was just a boy who had been noticed by the prettiest girl in the world.

The euphoria died the moment we walked into Dmitri's mansion.

The mood in the living room was tense. The team was gathered around the large dining table. It looked like a war council.

Alicia, Harry, Naomi, and Wang were hunched over a large sheet of paper. They looked up as we entered.

"We have been waiting all day," Alicia snapped. She looked tired. There were dark circles under her eyes, but she still looked sharp.

"Sorry," Dmitri said, tossing the shopping bag onto a chair. "I had to take the new recruit shopping."

Harry looked at the bag. He saw the logo. He smirked. "You took him to his crush's store? You are a sick bastard, Dmitri."

"What!" Naomi squealed, clapping her hands. "He has a crush on the Dervishi girl?"

"He is in love," Dmitri announced, grabbing a bottle of water. "But he has no balls."

"I have balls," I muttered, sitting down. "Two big black balls."

Wang rolled his eyes. He looked impatient. He tapped the table with a pen. "Can we focus?"

Alicia smoothed out the paper on the table. It was a poster-sized printout. It contained names, faces, and bios. It was a hit list.

"This is the guest list for the StarCred Ball," Alicia said. Her voice was all business. "These are the whales. We have identified the ones with the highest limits and the lowest security awareness."

She picked up a red marker. "We need to split up. Each of us has two primary targets. You need to get close. You need to get into the three-foot range for the scanner to work. Or you need to distract them while someone else does it."

She looked at me. "Josh, you are the new face. Nobody knows you. That is an advantage."

She pointed to a picture of a woman on the chart.

"This is your target," Alicia said. "Mia Hudson."

I looked at the picture. I blinked.

"She looks... young," I said.

The woman in the photo was stunning. She had blonde hair and big blue eyes. She didn't look like the other targets, who were mostly wrinkled men in their sixties. She looked like she should be in a sorority.

"Is she a daughter of a target?" I asked.

Alicia chuckled darkly. "No. She is the cardholder. Credit limit: five million dollars. She is the wife of Jonathan Hudson."

"Jonathan Hudson?" I asked. "The oil guy? Isn't he like... ancient?"

"He is seventy-four," Alicia said. "Mia is nineteen."

"Nineteen?" I gasped. "She is so young. And she is married to a fossil?"

"She was a maid on his private island in the Caribbean," Alicia explained. "He liked the view. She liked the wallet. It is a business transaction, Josh. He gets a trophy to show off to his geriatric friends, and she gets to pull her family out of the slums. He put her in his will last month. Fifty percent of his assets."

"Damn," I whispered. "That is cold."

"That is life," Alicia said. "Now, listen to the plan. You need to charm her. Mia is bored. She is surrounded by old people all day. She craves youth."

She smiled a little. "You are going to be the mysterious son of a Nigerian diplomat. You are going to flirt with her."

"Flirt?" I asked nervously. "I can barely talk to girls."

"You better learn," Harry said, leaning forward. "You are going to convince her to leave the ballroom for a bit. Get some fresh air. Maybe grab a late-night bite. There is a Chinese restaurant nearby called Yang Chow. We have a waiter there on the payroll."

"And then?"

"You eat. You laugh. When the bill comes, you check your pockets," Alicia acted it out, patting her silk robe. "Oh no! You left your wallet in your other jacket. You are so embarrassed."

"Mia will step in," Dmitri added. "She is polite. She won't let you wash dishes. She will hand her Platinum StarCred to the waiter. And here is where the game changes," Dmitri said. "Ten years ago, the waiter would just swipe it through a skimmer. But chips defeated skimmers. Now, we need the eyes. Our waiter will take the card. He will insert it into the tableside wireless terminal. He will stare at the screen, frown, and pull the card out. Then he will look at Mia and apologize."

"Apologize for what?"

"He will say the signal is weak in that corner," Dmitri said smoothly. "He will say the handheld isn't connecting to the Wi-Fi. He will ask, very politely, if he can run the card at the main register up front."

"And she will say yes," Alicia said. "Because she trusts the uniform."

"Once he walks away, he has thirty seconds behind the server station," Dmitri explained.

"He pulls out his phone. He'll snap a photo of the front. He needs the sixteen digits and the expiration. He'll also snap a photo of the back to get the three-digit CVV security code. That is the holy grail. The magnetic strip doesn't have the CVV. Only the physical card does."

"And with those photos?" I asked.

"With those photos, Wang can input the data into the burner phone," Dmitri said.

"He initiates the Apple Pay setup. We trigger the bank's verification SMS, Wang intercepts it, and boom, we have a digital clone of her card before she even signs the receipt."

"It sounds... high risk," I said. "What if she watches him?"

"It relies on human nature," Dmitri said. "She will be looking at you. She will be wanting to impress you. She won't be watching the waiter near the kitchen."

"Who is my second target?" I asked.

Alicia pointed to another picture. "Ruth Campbell. Middle-aged. Recently divorced. Bitter. She loves literature. You are going to be a literature student who loves her favorite authors."

"We need to know everything about them," Wang said from the corner. "The data on the card is useless if we do not know the zip code and the mother's maiden name to verify the wallet. We cannot go in blind."

Fraud is not just about technology. It is about psychology. It is about knowing your victim better than their spouse knows them.

We sat around the living room with our laptops. The air was thick with the click-clack of keyboards.

Wang hacked into their social media accounts. He bypassed the privacy settings like they were cardboard gates.

"Here is Mia's Facebook," Wang said, sending a link to my computer. "Read everything."

I opened the file. It felt invasive. It felt dirty. I was looking at private messages, photos, group chats. I started reading. Mia Hudson was not just a gold digger. She was lonely.

I read a chat between her and a friend named Sarah.

Mia: *He is asleep again. It is only 8 PM. I feel like I am living in a nursing home.*

Sarah: *At least the nursing home has a pool and a butler. LOL.*

Mia: *I am serious, Sarah. And when he is awake... it is worse. He is so weak. He doesn't last a minute. I don't even know what an orgasm feels like anymore.*

Sarah: *Girl, get a vibrator. What did you expect when you married a grandpa?*

I felt a flush of embarrassment. I shouldn't be reading this. This was her private pain. But I kept reading.

I found a group she was in: *Wives of Wealth*. It was a venting space. Mia posted often. She complained that Jonathan was sleeping with the maids—the irony was not lost on her—and that he treated her like a doll.

He makes me wear pink, she wrote. *He says it makes my skin look fresh. I hate pink. I look like a stick of gum.*

I noted that down. She hates pink. But she wears it for him. If I complimented her on a pink dress, she would hate it. But if I told her she looked trapped, she might listen.

Then I moved to Ruth Campbell. Her feed was different. It was filled with quotes from books. She was obsessed with vampire romance novels. J.R. Ward. Stephenie Meyer.

She wanted to be swept off her feet by a dangerous, dark stranger. I need a hero who isn't afraid of the dark, she posted. I looked at my reflection in the dark screen of my laptop. I was becoming that stranger. I was becoming the thing they needed, just so I could take what I needed.

"How is it going?" Dmitri asked, coming up behind me.

"I feel like a stalker," I admitted.

"You are an intelligence officer," Dmitri corrected. "Information is power. Use it."

I looked at the photo of Mia Hudson again. She was nineteen. Just like me. She had sold her youth for security.

I was selling my morality for my father's life. We were not so different, Mia and I. We were both prostitutes to circumstance.

"I'm ready," I said.

I closed the laptop. The data was in my head. Mia's loneliness. Ruth's fantasies. I knew which buttons to press.

CHAPTER NINE

The Chevy Express van Naomi drove was a beast. From the outside, it looked like a plumber's van. But inside? It was a spaceship. Plush leather seats that swiveled, LED mood lighting, a flat-screen TV, and a mini-fridge stocked with expensive vodka.

It looked more like a VIP lounge than a vehicle.

I ran my hand over the leather upholstery. "This is insane," I whispered. I made a silent vow right there. One day, I would be rich enough to buy toys like this without blinking. I would not just survive; I would conquer.

We looked the part. I was wearing the midnight-black suit from Melina's store. It fit me like armor. Dmitri looked like a Russian prince in gray wool. Harry and Wang were sharp in tuxedos. But the women? They were on another level.

Alicia wore a silver gown that shimmered like mercury. It clung to her curves and pooled at her feet. Naomi was in deep emerald green, with a slit up her thigh that could stop traffic.

We looked like money. We looked like trouble.

We pulled up to the gates of Liam Miller's mansion. It was a twenty-nine-million-dollar fortress. The iron gates were taller than giraffes. Security guards with earpieces stood watch like stone gargoyles.

Alicia rolled down the window. She didn't say a word. She just gave them a look, a look of pure, entitled boredom.

The guard stiffened. "Miss Alicia," he said, nodding. The gates swung open.

We drove up the winding driveway. The mansion loomed ahead, a sprawling monster of limestone and glass.

"This place is huge," I said, staring out the window. "Your stepdad is loaded."

"He can rot in hell for all I care," Alicia spat. She was picking lint off Harry's lapel, her touch gentle despite her words.

"How many rooms?" I asked.

"Twenty-one," she said.

I tried to picture it. Twenty-one rooms. My aunt's entire apartment in Detroit could fit into the foyer. Rich people didn't just have more money; they had more space. They bought air and light. Naomi parked the van next to a Lamborghini Huracán that looked like a jagged piece of lime candy.

I stepped out and almost tripped over my own awe. The driveway was a car show. Ferraris, Bentleys, Rolls-Royces. It was obscene. It was beautiful.

"The worst thing that can happen to someone in America," I muttered, "is to be black and poor."

Dmitri walked up beside me, adjusting his cuffs. "You can't change your skin color, Josh. But you can change your bank account."

Before Kingsley, I was simple. I wanted good grades. I wanted a job. I wanted Jada and a Toyota Camry and a small house with a porch. That was the dream.

But Kingsley was a virus. It infected you with ambition. Why dream of a Toyota when Mark arrived at school in a helicopter? Why dream of a porch when Edward had a private island?

"Oh my God," I gasped. "Is that a 1961 Ferrari 250 GT California SWB Spider?"

Alicia glanced at the red convertible. "Yeah. It belongs to one of Liam's friends. Fourteen million at auction."

Fourteen million dollars. For a car. My poverty felt like a physical weight, pressing down on my chest.

"Focus," Dmitri hissed in my ear. "Stop drooling. Remember why we are here."

We walked toward the entrance. The music drifted out. There was a live band and expensive laughter.

We slipped into the ballroom. It was a cavern of crystal chandeliers and gold leaf. The guests were the people you saw on CNN and in Forbes. Titans of industry. Wives with faces pulled tight by surgeons.

I pulled out my phone to take a picture.

"Stop," Alicia hissed, slapping my arm. "You look like a tourist. Blend in. Act like you belong."

She was right. I put the phone away. I straightened my spine. I was Josh Balogun, son of a diplomat. I belonged here.

A waiter materialized with a tray of champagne. I grabbed a flute. I held it like a beer bottle, my whole hand wrapped around the bowl. The waiter gave me a look. A tiny, split-second sneer.

"Why did he look at me like that?" I asked.

Harry sighed. "You are holding it wrong. Pinch the stem. Like this."

He demonstrated. Thumb and fingers on the thin glass stem.

I adjusted my grip. "This feels stupid. Who made this rule?"

"Rich people," Alicia said. "To separate us from them. Haven't you ever been to a champagne party?"

"We don't have champagne parties in Detroit," I muttered. "We have survival parties. We celebrate not getting shot in high school."

Suddenly, Alicia froze. Her face went pale.

A man was walking toward us. He was in his late fifties, handsome in a predatory way, with silver hair and a tan that cost thousands.

Liam Miller.

He stopped in front of us. His eyes were cold blue chips of ice.

"I don't recall inviting this... circus," he said, looking at us.

Harry tensed. His fists clenched at his sides. He looked ready to kill. Alicia squeezed his hand hard, anchoring him.

"They are my friends, Dad," Alicia said. Her voice was steady, but I saw the tremor in her neck.

"Whatever." Liam waved a hand dismissively. "Come with me. Your mother is waiting for the photo. Now."

Alicia hesitated. She looked at Dmitri. Dmitri nodded imperceptibly. Go. Distract him.

"I hate him," Harry growled as she walked away.

"Ignore him," Dmitri said. "Work."

I scanned the room. My targets. I spotted her instantly. Mia Hudson.

She stood out like a diamond in a coal mine. She was young, blonde, and devastatingly beautiful. She was standing alone, sipping champagne, looking bored and lonely amidst a sea of wrinkles.

"I'm going in," I said.

I walked over to her. My heart hammered against my ribs. Three feet. Get within three feet.

I stood behind her. "The dress looks good on you."

She jumped. She spun around, her hand jerking. Champagne sloshed out of her glass and splashed onto my lapel.

"Oh shit!" she gasped. "I am so sorry!"

I looked at the stain. It was annoying, but it was an opening.

"It's okay." I smiled charmingly. "It is the first time a beautiful woman has thrown a drink at me. Usually, they just slap me."

She laughed, flustered. She lowered her eyes. "I am just... nervous. I hate these things."

"Me too," I lied. "Are you here with anyone?"

She nodded toward a group of men. "My husband. Jonathan."

I looked. Jonathan Hudson was seventy-four. He looked like a raisin in a tuxedo. His hand was resting heavily on the bottom of a younger woman.

I looked back at Mia. I saw the flash of resentment in her eyes.

"You make the other women here look like ugly toads," I whispered.

She giggled. She twirled a strand of hair. "Thanks."

"Want to get some fresh air?" I asked.

"I don't even know your name."

I winked. "Meet me outside in ten minutes. I'll tell you then."

She bit her lip. She nodded. I walked away. I went outside to the terrace. The air smelled of jasmine.

Ten minutes later, she appeared.

"I must be crazy," she said.

"Just adventurous," I said. "I am Josh."

"I am Mia."

I bowed theatrically. "A perfect name."

I didn't waste time. I knew what she needed. She didn't need conversation. She needed to feel desired. She needed to feel young.

I moved closer. I touched her arm. The electricity was palpable.

"You are unhappy," I said softly.

She looked at me, surprised. "What?"

"I see it. You are bored. You are lonely."

Her eyes filled with tears. "You have no idea."

I kissed her.

It was frantic. It was desperate. We stumbled into the shadows of the garden, behind a tall hedge.

She pulled me down onto a stone bench. Her hands were everywhere. She was starving.

We had sex right there, under the moonlight, with the sound of the orchestra drifting from the ballroom. It was quick. It was raw.

Suddenly, footsteps crunched on the gravel. We froze.

But it wasn't security. It was another couple. A man and a woman, drunk and horny, stumbling into the bushes nearby.

Within seconds, the woman started moaning. Mia and I looked at each other and stifled a laugh. We continued. Ten minutes later, it was over. I pulled up my pants. Mia was flushed, her hair messy, her eyes bright.

"That was... amazing," she breathed. "I haven't felt like that in years."

"There is more where that came from," I promised.

We exchanged numbers. She went back inside first. I waited, straightening my tie. I walked back toward the ballroom.

"Josh!"

I stopped. My blood ran cold. Melina stood on the terrace. She looked like a vision in white silk.

"Melina," I choked out. "What are you doing here?"

"My parents are here," she said, walking over. "I got bored and decided to get some air. What about you?"

"Alicia invited me," I said. "We are friends."

"Oh," she said. She seemed relieved. "Why are you out here?"

"I felt uncomfortable," I said truthfully. "A waiter looked at me like I was trash because I held a glass wrong."

Melina laughed. It was a warm, genuine sound.

"Screw the waiter. You look great in that suit."

We talked. It was easy. It was light. She wasn't an arrogant rich kid. She was just a girl who hated stuffy parties.

"How is Viktor?" I asked, testing the waters.

Her smile faltered. "Fine. He is at a club with his friends."

I said goodbye and went back inside. I found the team huddled in a corner. They looked frantic.

"Where were you?" Naomi hissed. "We thought you got caught."

I just smiled sheepishly. Wang looked toward the door. He saw Melina walking in.

"I think I know where he was," Wang said.

The team turned. They saw Melina.

"Why is she here?" Naomi asked, her voice sharp.

"Her parents are whales," Alicia said. "Platinum cardholders."

"Okay," Naomi said, her eyes narrowing. "Who is targeting her?"

"No one," I said.

My voice was hard. Harder than I intended.

They all looked at me.

"No one touches Melina," I said. "She is off-limits. She is not a target."

The silence stretched. It was tense.

"Relax, Romeo," Naomi said, forcing a laugh. "Just a thought."

"Come on," Alicia interrupted, checking her phone. "We need to go. Before Liam finds me."

As we walked out, Naomi and I locked eyes. There was a challenge there. A warning.

CHAPTER TEN

I barely went to my dorm anymore. Eric had probably coded three new apps and talked to his reflection a thousand times in my absence, but I didn't care. Dmitri's mansion was my new reality. It was where the air conditioning smelled of lavender and ambition.

The team was a strange family. We were bound by secrets and the shared hunger for more. I started to notice things in the quiet moments. Naomi had a crush on me. It wasn't subtle. She would catch my eye across the room and hold the gaze just a second too long.

And whenever Melina's name came up, usually because Harry was making a joke about my "ice princess," Naomi's face would darken like a storm cloud over Lagos.

But Wang... Wang was the enigma. He was the quiet power behind the throne. Dmitri had the charisma, but Wang had the keys.

He knew hackers in Ukraine who could crack a database just for the thrill of it. He had a network of waiters across Los Angeles on his payroll, a silent army of skimmers waiting for the right swipe.

Wang knew drug dealers. He knew money launderers. He knew people who could make problems disappear. It was this network that would eventually save his skin and doom the rest of us.

When the FBI finally came knocking, they didn't want Wang for credit card fraud. They wanted his Rolodex. He walked free because he gave them fifty names. Mine was just one of them. But that was the future. In the present, I was preparing for my date with destiny, also known as Mia Hudson.

We arranged to meet the week after the ball. Her husband, the ancient Jonathan Hudson, was in Tokyo or Dubai or somewhere expensive, closing a deal. Mia was bored. She sent me nudes every night—photos taken in gold-leaf mirrors, her body perfect and lonely. She captioned them with things like *Waiting for you* and *All yours*.

I chose the location carefully. Yang Chow in Downtown LA. It wasn't just for the Slippery Shrimp. It was because of Lee.

Lee was one of Wang's soldiers. He was a waiter there. I had sent him my picture the night before. I told him to make sure he took our table.

On the night of the date, Harry drove me. We took the Bugatti. It roared down the freeway like a panther let loose. I sat in the passenger seat, snapping photos for Instagram.

#LuxuryLife #BugattiBoys #LA.

My follower count was exploding. People back in Nigeria, kids I went to junior school with, strangers who just wanted to touch the hem of wealth.

They all watched my stories on Instagram. They didn't see a criminal. They saw a king. The Nigerian Prince was born.

I arrived at Yang Chow early, at 7:00 PM. My date was at 7:30. I needed to prep the battlefield.

I found Lee. He was small and efficient, moving through the restaurant like water. I caught his eye. He nodded. He studied my face, then my clothes.

Good. I didn't want any mistakes. There were some people who assumed "all Black people look alike."

I sat at a table near the back, drinking water, trying to slow my heart rate.

"Hi," a voice said.

I jumped. I spun around, expecting Mia. It wasn't Mia. It was Melina.

She was wearing a red gown that probably cost more than my father's life savings. Her hair was down, cascading over her shoulders. She looked breathtaking.

My face lit up instinctively. "Melina."

Then I saw him. Viktor.

He was standing behind her, looking like a bulldog in a designer suit. He sneered when he saw me.

"What are you doing here, scholarship student?" Viktor asked. "Checking if they accept food stamps?"

Melina elbowed him in the ribs. "Be nice, Viktor. How are you, Josh?"

"I'm good," I muttered. My joy evaporated.

Then, the door opened. Mia walked in. If Melina was a classic painting, Mia was a pop song. She was bright, loud, and impossible to ignore.

She was wearing a short white dress that showed off legs for days. She scanned the room, saw me, and beamed.

"Josh!" she called out.

Melina froze. She looked at Mia, then back at me. I saw something flicker in her gray eyes. Surprise? Confusion?

Jealousy.

"Are you here alone?" Melina started, "or did you come with a..."

She trailed off as Mia reached my table.

Viktor let out a low whistle. "Damn."

I stood up. I ignored Viktor. I ignored Melina. I kissed Mia on the cheek. She smelled of vanilla and expensive perfume.

"Sorry I'm late," Mia said breathlessly. She didn't even look at the other two.

"Not a problem," I said, pulling out her chair.

I sat down. My heart was racing.

Lee appeared instantly. "Good evening. What can I get for you?"

"I heard the Kung Pao Chicken is legendary," I said, reciting the script.

"It is our specialty, sir."

"I'll have that. And a glass of non-alcoholic wine."

Lee turned to Mia. "And for the lady?"

Mia looked at me like I was the only person in the universe. "I'll have whatever he's having."

Lee nodded and vanished.

I glanced across the room. Melina was sitting with her back to the wall. She wasn't looking at Viktor. She was looking at us. Her eyes were narrowed.

Every time Mia laughed, which was often, because I was turning on the charm, Melina's scowl deepened.

Why did she care? She was the billionaire heiress with the Russian boyfriend. I was just the scholarship kid. But in that moment, seeing her jealousy, I felt a twisted sense of power.

"I got something for you," Mia said suddenly.

She reached into her Birkin bag. She pulled out a small, velvet-wrapped box.

"A thank you," she said shyly. "For making me feel alive again."

I opened the box.

I stopped breathing.

Inside sat a watch. Not just a watch. An Audemars Piguet Royal Oak Concept Flying Tourbillon GMT. The metal gleamed under the restaurant lights.

"Oh my God," I whispered. "Mia... this is..."

She shrugged. "It's just a small gift."

Small gift. This watch was worth one hundred and ninety thousand dollars. I stared at it. I could sell this watch tomorrow. I could take the money, wire fifty-two thousand to my mother, save my father, and still have over a hundred grand left.

I wouldn't have to steal her credit card info. I wouldn't have to commit a felony tonight.

I could be a hero. I could be clean.

But as I held the heavy, cold metal in my hand, something dark whispered in my ear. **Why choose? Why not have both? Why not save your father AND be rich?**

Greed is a patient teacher. It teaches you that enough is never enough.

Eight months later, looking at my collection of thirty-one luxury watches, this Audemars Piguet would be the cheapest one I owned. But tonight? Tonight, it felt like I was holding a star.

Mia beamed as I strapped it on. "It looks good on you."

"Thank you," I said. I took her hand. "You are too generous."

Across the room, Melina watched us hold hands. She looked like she wanted to break something.

Lee brought the food. It was delicious, but I barely tasted it. Mia talked. She talked about her life, and it was a tragedy wrapped in silk.

"I never knew love," she said, picking at her chicken. "My parents... they saw me as a lottery ticket. From the time I was twelve, they told me my job was to marry rich. They spent their rent money on my clothes, my makeup. They were investing in an asset."

She told me about meeting Jonathan. It wasn't an accident. Her father worked on Jonathan's private island. He made Mia walk around the estate in a bikini when Jonathan was visiting.

"They used me as bait," she said, her voice trembling. "And he bit. He didn't care that I was a child compared to him. He has granddaughters older than me. And my parents? They were thrilled. They didn't care about my happiness. They cared about the check."

She looked up at me, her blue eyes wet. "I felt like a pawn my whole life. Until that night at the ball. Until you. You look at me, Josh. You actually see me."

I squeezed her hand. I made my face look sympathetic. "I see you, Mia. You are amazing."

Inside, I felt a flicker of guilt. But I squashed it. I wasn't different from her parents. I wasn't different from Jonathan. I was using her too. She was just a credit limit to me. A five-million-dollar credit limit.

Lee returned. The moment had arrived. He held a black leather folder. He winked at me, a tiny flutter of an eyelid.

"Sir, the bill is $193.17."

I patted my jacket pockets. Left. Right. Inner pocket.

I froze. I let my face fall into a mask of panic.

"Damn!" I said loud enough for Mia to hear. "I left my wallet in my other jacket. The one I wore to class."

I looked at Lee. "Do you take Apple Pay? Or Venmo?"

Lee shook his head sadly. "No, sir. Physical cards only."

"Oh, this is embarrassing," I muttered, looking down.

"Don't worry," Mia said instantly. "I got you."

She reached for her purse and pulled out the platinum StarCred card. It didn't just glint; it hit the table with the heavy, distinctive thud of solid metal.

JONATHAN HUDSON. She handed it to Lee.

Lee took the card, his thumb brushing the embossed lettering. He pulled a wireless handheld terminal from his apron, inserted the card, and waited. He frowned, tapping the side of the device. He pulled the card out, blew into the chip slot and inserted it again.

"My apologies," Lee said, his voice dropping to a confidential, apologetic register. "This table is a dead zone for the Wi-Fi. The handhelds never connect back here. Do you mind if I run this at the main terminal up front?"

"No problem," Mia said, not even looking at him.

Lee nodded and walked away with the card.

"That necklace," I said quickly, locking eyes with her. "The setting is invisible. It looks like the stones are floating. Is it custom?"

She turned to me, smiling, touching the diamonds instinctively. "Oh, yes. Jonathan had it commissioned in Antwerp."

While she talked, I visualized Lee's choreography. It was a dance we had perfected.

He would be at the server station now, a blind spot shielded by the high mahogany counter and the espresso machine. He had twenty seconds.

First, the capture. He would slide his phone out, already open to the camera app. Snap the front of the card. He needed the full sixteen digits and the name clearly legible.

Flip. Snap the back of the card. This was the money shot, the three-digit CVV2 security code.

That code is never stored on the magnetic stripe; without the photo, we couldn't use the card for online shopping. Next, the skim. He would palm the small, square device hidden in his apron pocket, a generic magnetic strip reader, no bigger than a matchbox.

With one fluid motion, he'd run the card through the slot. Swipe. The LEDs would blink green. He now had the Track 1 and Track 2 data. Later, we'd use the photos to load the card onto a burner phone for Apple Pay.

You can't use Apple Pay for a Ferrari, but you can tap for a twenty-thousand-dollar watch if you act like you own the place.

Lee returned to the table exactly ninety seconds later. The card was resting on top of a printed merchant copy, creating a barrier between her hand and the metal.

"All set, ma'am. Sorry about the delay." He placed it down.

Mia scribbled her name.

She didn't check the total. She didn't check for a double charge. She just signed, oblivious to the fact that her digital life had just been copied.

Lee took the leather folder. "Thank you, ma'am. Hope to see you again."

He handed her the card. It was still warm from his hand. As he turned to leave, he gave me a look that lasted a fraction of a second. We have it all. The heist was over. We had won.

We left the restaurant. Melina was still sitting there, watching us leave. I didn't look back.

We couldn't go to her house; Jonathan's security would log me. We couldn't go to Dmitri's; the team was there. So, I drove us to the Beverly Wilshire Hotel.

I paid for the room with cash I had miraculously "found" in my pocket.

As soon as we entered the room, I placed my tongue on the lips between Mia's legs and sent her to heaven. I alternated between my tongue and fingers. After a while, I told her to sit on my face.

We had sex all night. It was fierce and exhausting. Mia screamed my name. She clung to me like a drowning woman clinging to a raft.

As she fell asleep on my chest, I looked at the Audemars Piguet on my wrist. It ticked softly in the darkness.

CHAPTER ELEVEN

Two days later, Wang Wei slid a matte black smartphone across the mahogany table. It didn't make a sound. It just stopped, dead center, in front of me.

I picked it up. It was a rooted Android, modified to look and feel exactly like a high-end iPhone.

"Turn it on," Wang said.

I pressed the side button. The screen flared. No apps, no bloatware, no games. Just the native Wallet app.

I tapped the icon. A digital render of a Platinum StarCred card appeared. JONATHAN HUDSON.

"How?" I whispered, my thumb hovering over the screen. "You need a verification code to add a card to a digital wallet. The second you tried this, the bank sent a text to Hudson's iPhone."

Wang took a sip from his mug, looking bored. "The text did go to his phone. But it also went to the bank's SMS gateway logs."

"The logs?"

"Remember Alicia has her stepfather's RSA token and admin credentials saved on her laptop," Wang said simply. "She didn't need to be in Hudson's house to see the code. She just logged into the bank's administrative portal from her bedroom."

He set the mug down with a soft click.

"She pulled up the outgoing message logs for Hudson's account number. She saw the six-digit code on the server screen before Jonathan even picked up his phone. Jonathan might not even have time to check his text messages."

"Even if he saw it, he might assume it was a technical glitch."

I stared at the device. It felt heavier now. It wasn't just theft; it was total exposure.

"So, she sees everything?"

"She sees what the bank sees," Wang said, his voice dropping into that clinical, lecture-hall rhythm. "We don't need to hack the victim's phone if we own the bank's database. It is the ultimate backdoor. As far as the system is concerned, the code was verified legitimately."

He pointed a slender finger at the screen.

"But the code is only half the battle. The hard part is the fingerprint. Banks look at the hardware ID. If a new phone suddenly appears in a new city, they block it."

"So, this phone…"

"This phone is lying," Wang said calmly. "We rooted the operating system. We spoofed the IMEI and the device ID to match Jonathan's old iPad Air, a device he stopped using six months ago but never removed from his authorized list. We are tunneling the connection through a residential proxy in Calabasas."

He leaned back, a small, cold smile touching his lips.

"The code came from the bank's own brain. The IP address matches his neighborhood. The device ID matches his history. The bank isn't asleep, Josh. We just fed it a dream."

I ran my thumb over the screen. It felt like holding a grenade with the pin pulled.

Dmitri was right. Wang was a god! An evil genius.

"But the limit?" I asked. "Five hundred thousand is a massive spike. Trust or no trust."

"She used her stepfather's credentials to access the 'Private Wealth' management portal," Wang said. "She didn't just set a travel notice; she entered a 'High-Value Pre-Authorization' note on the account. As far as the fraud team is concerned, Jonathan Hudson called his personal banker this morning and said, 'I'm going shopping, don't embarrass me.'"

He leaned forward, his eyes locking onto mine. "But even Alicia cannot disable the Velocity Checks."

"Velocity?"

"Speed of spending. The bank's AI assumes a human being needs time to sign a receipt, bag an item, and walk to the next store. If you tap three times in ten seconds, you trigger a 'Bot Attack' alarm. You must be slow. Chat with the cashier. Ask about the weather. Ask for drinks. Let the system breathe between taps. If you rush, you lose."

I took a deep breath. Who said fraud was easy? "Damn."

"You should get prepared to hit the stores now. The sooner the better," Wang said. "Remember Big Brother is always watching, so you need to be confident. Act like a boss."

He told me about a guy in London, a Ghanaian cleaner who bought eight televisions with a cloned card. He looked nervous.

He stuffed them into his car too fast. The store called the cops. They tracked him down. They found the cards. Game over.

"We don't make mistakes like that," Wang said. "We prepare."

Preparation meant Kate Hamilton. Kate was our secret weapon. She was a makeup artist who worked on Hollywood sets. For the right price, she turned college students into strangers. She could make Trump look like Bob Marley.

She also helped with disguises whenever any of us wanted to use a card to take a major hit.

CCTVs are everywhere, checking not just your face, but also performing a gait analysis by recording the way you walk. If you wear a mask to rob a bank, you can still get arrested based on your walking steps. I kid you not.

I sat in her chair for five hours.

She didn't use heavy prosthetics because those peel under the California sun. Instead, she used 'CV Dazzle' techniques, geometric patterns of temporary ink on my cheekbones and nose. To a human, it looked like avant-garde tribal art. To a facial recognition camera, it broke the mathematical symmetry required to identify a face.

She darkened my skin tone two shades. She gave me non-prescription glasses with thick, reflective frames to scatter IR scanners. She also wove long dreadlocks into my hair.

When she spun the chair around, Josh Balogun was gone. Staring back at me was a stranger. High roller. A music producer or a crypto kid.

"Put a pebble in your right shoe," Kate said.

"Why?"

"Gait analysis. Modern surveillance identifies you by your walk. The pebble forces you to limp slightly. It corrupts the data."

I put on a flat-brimmed cap and non-polarized sunglasses.

"It is showtime," I whispered.

I took a cab to Rodeo Drive. The street was a canyon of wealth. Palm trees swayed high above the clean sidewalks. Tourists took selfies in front of Ferraris. I walked into Christian Louboutin.

I wasn't there just for the red bottoms. Not at all. This was about Geo-Validation.

I needed to ping the local cell towers and make a purchase to cement the "Travel Notice" Wang had set.

"Can I help you, sir?" a sales assistant asked.

"Yes," I said, pitching my voice lower than usual. "I need gifts. My wife is... displeased. I need something to say how sorry I am."

The sales assistant smiled. "Lucky lady. We have just what you need."

I pointed to the shelf. "The Louis Orlato High Tops. The suede ones."

"Excellent choice."

"And the Paloma bag," I said. "The alligator-embossed leather. Black."

"And the So Kates." I pointed to the glittering heels on the pedestal. "The crystal ones."

She rang them up. The High Tops were $1,200. The bag was $2,950. The heels were $3,000.

"Your total is $7,840, including tax," she said.

My heart hammered against my ribs. *Don't look nervous*, I told myself. *Act like you are rich and this is pocket change.*

Sweet Jesus, help me not to get caught. Going to prison wasn't on my bucket list.

I pulled out the phone. My thumb hovered over the scanner.

"Apple Pay," I said.

I held the phone to the NFC reader.

Beep.

The phone didn't send Jonathan's credit card number. It sent a token, a ghost code.

The terminal swirled. Authorizing...

APPROVED.

I walked out with three massive red bags. The bank's AI now saw a trusted device, in the correct city, making a typical luxury purchase. The trap was set.

Next stop: The Timepiece Vault.

I walked in. The staff here wore suits sharper than mine. This was a gray market dealer, unauthorized, expensive, and discreet.

"Patek Philippe," I said. "I'm not browsing. I'm buying."

I pointed to a Patek Philippe Perpetual Calendar Split-Seconds Chronograph. Ref 5370P.

"Three hundred and eleven thousand," the salesman said, testing me.

"Wrap it up." I paused. "And the World Timer. And the Rolex Pearlmaster. And the GMT Master II."

The total was $579,000.

"I'll use the digital wallet," I said.

The salesman hesitated. He looked at the phone, then at me.

"Sir, for this amount, we require a wire transfer. The merchant fees on a credit card are nearly three percent, and the terminal limit..."

I lowered my sunglasses. I stared at him, channeling every ounce of arrogance I had seen in rich people in movies. They always acted like your presence as a pauper annoyed them, and they were bigger than everyone and everything.

"Do I look like I have time to wait three days for a wire to clear?" I snapped. "I fly to Zurich in four hours. Do you want the commission, or should I go to the guy across the street who knows how to run a debit card?"

The greed won. It always won. He did the math in his head. Losing 3% was better than losing a half-million-dollar sale.

"We can do it," he said quickly. "But the POS terminal has a hard limit of $200,000. I have to run it in batches."

"Fine," I said. "Take your time."

He set up the first charge. $195,000.

I tapped the phone. Lord, please let this work.

Beep.

The authorization took four seconds. The bank's algorithm was weighing variables: Location matched. Device ID matched. Spending pattern matched travel notice.

APPROVED.

"Next one," the salesman said. $195,000.

I forced myself to yawn. I needed to avoid velocity triggers. "Do you have an espresso while I wait?"

"Of course." He signaled a junior associate.

Distraction. Normalcy. I pretended to be responding to an email.

"Hold on. Work," I whispered to the sales assistant.

He nodded his head in understanding and gave me some space. I waited for three minutes before telling him to approach with the terminal.

I tapped again.

Beep.

APPROVED.

"Last one," he said. $189,000.

My hand wanted to shake. This was the danger zone. The Velocity Check could mess things up. Two large charges were a coincidence; three was a pattern.

I waited until the associate set the espresso down. I took a sip and shook my head. I needed to buy more time to enable the system to breathe.

"Can I have some champagne instead?"

"Sure," the SA said. After all, I had just spent more than $380,000 and he could see my Christian Louboutin shopping bags. If I had asked him for his kidney at that point, he would've given it to me.

I took a sip of the champagne and asked for tea instead, wasting ten minutes in the process. I asked for the terminal to make the final payment.

I tapped.

Beep.

The terminal screen spun. Processing... Processing...

It was taking longer. The AI was blinking. Sweet Jesus! I began to eye the exit.

APPROVED.

I exhaled, my lungs burning.

I walked out of the store carrying half a million dollars of watches. I went to Beverly Hills Co and bought a bunch of Hublot watches for around $90,000.

I hailed a cab. "Downtown. Fashion District."

Amir's store was a fortress in an alleyway. I knocked. The camera buzzed. The door clicked. Amir was a Hawala broker, part banker, part fence.

I dumped the bags on his desk.

Amir whistled. He picked up the Split-Seconds Patek. He didn't look at the watch; he looked at the Warranty Certificate.

"Dated today," he muttered. "Stamped by the dealer. Box and papers complete."

"Full set," I said. "Unworn."

"This is good," Amir said. "Without the papers, it is just stolen metal. With the papers, it is a commodity."

He tapped a calculator. "I will take it all. Four hundred thousand. Cash.

"Four hundred?" I snapped. "The watches and the stuff from Louboutin are almost $700,000."

"On the internet, yes," Amir said calmly.

"But you are not on the internet. You are in a back room in Los Angeles. I have to wash this inventory. I have to hold it for six months in case the serial numbers are flagged on the Interpol database. That is my risk cost."

I knew he was right. If the serials were reported stolen tomorrow, he couldn't sell them in the US. He'd have to smuggle them to Dubai or Moscow.

But I pushed back. "Five hundred. The Rolexes and Hublots are liquid cash. You can sell those tomorrow."

Amir paused. He looked at the Rolex GMT Master II. "Fine. Four-fifty."

"No! Five hundred or I walk out."

"Damn, even Wang doesn't haggle like this."

"I am not Wang."

If Yoruba people had anything in common apart from our love for eating hot pepper and attending parties, it was our God-given ability to haggle prices.

"Fine," he said in a defeated tone.

He walked to the safe. He didn't pull out loose bills. He pulled out vacuum-sealed bricks of hundred-dollar bills. This was drug money he was laundering through watches. I was just part of the cycle.

He tossed the bricks into my backpack. I walked out of the store. The phone in my pocket felt radioactive. I pulled it out, wiped the screen on my shirt, and dropped it into a storm drain.

I was half a million dollars richer. And Josh Balogun was gone.

Tears welled up in my eyes. I said, *"Ko ni da fun osi."* A Yoruba phrase that roughly translates into *it will not be well with poverty.* Its translation does not make sense in English. That was the day I said goodbye to poverty. It was the day I stopped being poor.

I needed to hide my money first, pack all my belongings, and permanently move into Dmitri's apartment. I could not keep $500,000 cash in my dorm because my roommate, Eric, might stumble upon the money and ask how I got it.

I did not take my money to the bank because Dmitri had earlier warned me not to deposit large sums into my bank account because it would attract suspicion.

It would raise a red flag if someone who had less than $800 in their account suddenly deposited $500,000 into their account. Dmitri advised me to stick to a cash-only policy.

Banks automatically alert the US government whenever a person makes a transaction of over $10,000. That is one of the reasons many drug dealers and credit card scammers prefer to launder their money using offshore accounts or hide the cash in locations known to them only.

Eric was not in the room when I arrived. His absence made it easier for me to arrange my money in my safety drawer carefully. I could not believe it. I started the day poor and was going to bed with $500,000 cash next to me.

I called Jada after I locked my safety drawer. "Hi, love."

She noticed my joyful tone. "You've not been this happy while talking to me lately. What changed?"

"I finally got a loan to help me pay for my dad's treatment," I lied. I could not tell her that I made money from credit card fraud. She might not rat me out to the FBI, but she would never look at me the same way.

"Wow! That is good to know. Remember I told you that everything would be okay."

"Yes. Thank you, Jada. You sold your car and jewelry because of me. I will forever be indebted to you."

"Well, you can buy me a Lamborghini when we're married," she said jokingly.

She did not know that I could afford to buy a Lamborghini at that moment. I was not convinced about the marriage part. Before I saw Melina, I was convinced I would marry Jada, a melanin queen, my first love. However, at that point, I was not sure anymore.

I loved Jada but could not deny the fact that I was attracted to Melina. And dating Melina would boost my social status on campus.

I called my mom after my conversation with Jada and told her that I had been able to get the money for dad's kidney transplant.

Her joy knew no bounds. She started singing and praising God. I was sure that God was probably laughing sarcastically at us. He would never endorse any form of fraud.

"Thank you, my son. I have buried two children. Watching my husband die would have made me lose my mind," she said with tears.

"We will never be poor again, *iya mi*," I vowed. "We will start living life comfortably instead of struggling to survive."

I did not lie to my mom when I said those words. Even now that I am in prison, my sister has enough money to live affluently for the rest of her life. I always ensured that I sent a certain percentage of my ill-gotten wealth to Abisola.

In Nigeria, $3 could get you a haircut, a small loaf of bread, and a 33cl bottle of Pepsi. Now imagine what you could do with over $10 million in Nigeria.

Do I have any regrets? No! I suffer from overwhelming guilt every day because of my past sins, but I have no regrets. If I had not done what I did, my father would have died due to the lack of medical attention.

If I did not do the things I did, my family would still live in abject poverty. I feel guilty but do not regret my actions. If spending a couple of years in jail is the price to pay for making my family enjoy a lifetime of wealth, then I am ready.

I have been poor and rich, and I will repeatedly say that there is nothing as good as being rich.

When you are rich, you will have access to good healthcare, you will be able to enroll your kids at the best schools, and your life will be relatively easy.

Being poor is terrible. No money for hospital bills.

You will bite your fingers as you watch your loved ones die because you cannot afford their medical bills.

No money to buy healthy food. No money to keep your family happy. Being poor can make a person die of depression and hunger.

CHAPTER TWELVE

After the phone call with my mom, the adrenaline faded, replaced by a cold, sharp clarity. I had the money. I had fifty-two thousand dollars for my father and almost four hundred and fifty thousand dollars for myself.

I couldn't stay in the dorm anymore. Eric was too observant. If I started buying things, if I started acting different, he would notice. He would ask questions. And Eric was a good guy. Good guys have consciences. Good guys call the police.

So, I packed my life into two suitcases and moved into Dmitri's mansion. Permanently.

It felt like shedding a skin. I left Josh the scholarship student behind. I became the Nigerian Prince.

My first stop was the Ferrari dealership on Wilshire Boulevard. I walked in wearing my thrift store clothes, carrying a backpack stuffed with cash.

The salesman looked at me like I was lost. He started to guide me toward the exit. Imagine a seventeen-year-old Black boy casually trying to buy a Ferrari.

"Is your dad coming over?" he asked, naturally assuming I came with an adult to buy the car. I mean, I did not look like a rich kid yet. Only the Audemars Piguet gift I got from Mia made me look rich. Even then, the salesman was too busy staring at my black skin and did not notice my left wrist, which had a $190,000 wristwatch.

I ignored his question. "I want the GTC4Lusso," I said, pointing to a sleek, gunmetal gray beast on the showroom floor.

"That is a very expensive car, son," the salesman said condescendingly, barely looking up from his tablet. "Maybe you should try the used lot down the street. They have some nice—"

I unzipped the backpack. I showed him the green bricks.

His attitude changed faster than a chameleon on a disco floor. Suddenly, I was "sir." Suddenly, I was his best friend. He reached for the bag, his eyes wide.

"I'll get the paperwork started," he stammered.

"No," I said, zipping the bag back up.

Wang's voice echoed in my head: *Cash buys groceries. Corporations buy cars.* If I handed over this cash personally, the IRS would be at my dorm room by morning.

"My business manager is on his way," I lied smoothly. "He handles the acquisition. I just choose the toy."

"Wow! You're living a good life," he said, swallowing my lies.

I pulled out my phone and texted Dmitri.

Forty minutes later, while waiting at the salesman's office with a bottle of champagne and some cookies, a man in a sharp gray suit walked in.

I didn't know his name, but he nodded at me like he worked for me. He went into the finance office, shook the salesman's hand, and slapped a folder of documents on the desk.

The car wasn't registered to Josh Balogun. It was purchased by a shell corporation in Delaware. The man in the gray suit took the bag of cash, and I took the keys.

Clean. Untraceable. Mine.

I drove off the lot, the engine purring like a lion in my lap. I felt powerful. I felt unstoppable.

Next was the Christian Louboutin store. I bought ten pairs of sneakers—red bottoms. The kind rappers wrote songs about. I went to Giuseppe Zanotti too. They make the best shoes, so I bought twenty pairs—all stud embellished.

Then Armani. Valentino. Dior. Gucci. Burberry. Dolce & Gabbana. Karl Lagerfeld. Dsquared2.

I moved through the stores like a locust, consuming everything in my path.

I didn't look at price tags. I just pointed. "I want that. And that. And two of those."

I made sure I didn't create profiles at the stores even when the sales assistants wanted me to do so. By creating a profile, the IRS could see my spending history if they dug deeply enough. So, I just spent money without creating any profile.

By the time I returned to the mansion, I had spent more than $300,000—for a new Ferrari and new wardrobe—in one afternoon. I had to hire six Ubers just to carry the shopping bags.

When I got home, I found Wang in the living room, working on his laptop. It was time for the most important transaction.

I couldn't use Western Union because the limit was too low, and the questions would be too loud. They would never allow me to easily send over $50,000 to Nigeria. I gave the $52,000 cash to Wang. He didn't ask questions. He just tapped a few keys, routing the funds through a shell construction firm in Lagos.

"Done," he said.

The hospital received a direct wire transfer twenty minutes later.

I imagined my mother's face when the administrator told her the bill was paid. I imagined my father waking up after surgery, alive, breathing.

That night, I sat in my new room at the mansion. It overlooked the pool. I looked at my reflection in the mirror. I was wearing a four-thousand-dollar robe.

"You made it," I whispered. "You defeated poverty, Josh. You rose above it."

I sipped some champagne while staring at my reflection in the pool. I was a true Nigerian Prince.

Monday morning.

I didn't take the campus shuttle. I didn't walk. I didn't join Harry, Wang, or Dmitri in their cars.

I drove the Ferrari instead. My Ferrari. I pulled into the student parking garage. The engine roared, echoing off the concrete walls. Heads turned.

Conversations stopped.

I parked next to Mark's Lamborghini. I opened the door and stepped out.

I was wearing a Valentino suit. On my wrist was the Audemars Piguet from Mia. On my feet were the red-bottom Louboutin shoes. My gold-framed sunglasses? None other than Bottega Veneta.

Silence. The students who usually looked through me were now staring at me. Their mouths were open.

"Damn!" someone shouted. "Is that the new guy?"

Kyle, the son of a tech billionaire, walked over. He had never spoken to me before. He usually looked at me like I was a stain on the carpet.

"Nice ride, man," Kyle said, running a hand over the Ferrari's hood. "GTC4Lusso? V12?"

"Thanks," I said casually, locking the car with a beep. "Yeah. It handles well."

I walked toward the elevator. The crowd parted like the Red Sea.

"Did you see the watch?" I heard a girl whisper. "That is a Tourbillon. That is almost two hundred grand."

"He must be a Nigerian prince," a guy muttered.

"I heard his dad is a politician. They have oil money," another guy said.

"He was just pretending to be poor," another girl said. "It was a test. To see who was real."

"I wish I had been nice to him," her friend sighed.

I smiled. It was intoxicating. It was better than any drug. I had gone from zero to hero in a weekend.

I walked into the lecture hall, feeling confident. Very confident.

David Lewinson was sitting in the back row, saving a seat for me. He looked up, saw the suit, saw the watch, and his face went slack.

I didn't look at him. I couldn't.

"Hey, buddy!"

I turned. Mark was waving at me from the front row. The Elite row.

"Hi," I said, feeling a flutter of nerves.

"Come sit with us," Mark said, patting the empty chair next to him. "We need to talk about that car."

My jaw dropped. The Elites were inviting me in. The gates of heaven had opened. They accepted me. I got the validation I had been craving. With the Elites as my friends, I could climb the social ladder and create a long-lasting legacy for my kids. I could be the man my father never became.

"Sure," I said.

I walked past the middle row, past the back row, and sat down in the front.

Dmitri gave me a subtle nod. Melina smiled at me. It was a genuine, warm smile. Viktor looked like he had swallowed a lemon.

Dr. Kennedy walked in. He did a double-take when he saw me sitting next to Mark. He opened his mouth, closed it, and started the lecture.

Behind me, the whispers were loud.

"We found his dad," a girl named Chloe whispered to her friend James.

I froze. My blood ran cold. They found him? They found the clerk in Ado-Ekiti who earned less than $50 monthly and drove a Corolla which was older than all the undergraduate students on campus?

"Here," Chloe said, leaning forward and tapping my shoulder. She handed me her tablet.

I looked at the screen.

It was an article about a Nigerian Senator named Dare Balogun. Senator Balogun accused of embezzlement. Senator Balogun buys mansion in London.

"Don't deny it," Chloe smirked. "Same last name. Same face. Why did you hide it?" Of course, she thought all Black people looked alike.

I stared at the screen. Senator Balogun. A corrupt politician.

In Nigeria, names tell a story. Balogun means 'Warlord.' It is a common name. There are thousands of Baloguns. But to these Americans, one Balogun was the same as another.

"You caught me," I lied. I handed the tablet back. "My father is the Senator."

"I knew it!" James exclaimed. "You wanted to be treated normally, right? Like Eddie Murphy in *Coming to America*?"

"Exactly," I said. Stupid kid.

Suddenly, I was the most popular guy in the room. Girls were asking about Nigerian weddings. Guys were asking about oil stocks. I was spinning a web of lies so thick I could barely see out of it.

After class, I went to the restroom.

The door banged open. David marched in. He looked furious.

"What is going on?" David demanded. "Last week your dad was dying. You needed money. Today you are driving a Ferrari. How, Josh?"

I washed my hands, avoiding his eyes in the mirror. "My dad is fine. The money came through."

"Don't give me that Senator crap," David snapped. "We both know your dad is poor. What did you do? Did you rob a bank? Are you dealing drugs?"

"The watch was a gift," I said defensively. "And I am not a drug dealer."

David shook his head. "Josh, listen to me. This isn't you. You are going to crash. You are going to burn."

"You are just jealous," I spat. "You are jealous because I'm not a loser anymore. You are jealous because they like me."

"I am worried about you!" David yelled.

"Stay away from me," I said.

I pulled out my Prada wallet. I counted out $2,000. I threw the bills at his chest.

"Here. That is the twelve hundred you gave me. Plus interest. We are even. We are strangers."

I walked out. I left my only real friend standing in a pile of money on a bathroom floor.

That evening, I went back to the mansion.

Naomi was alone in the living room. She was watching TV. The tension was thick. Ever since she had suggested robbing Melina, things had been weird between us.

"Can we bury the hatchet?" she asked without looking up. "It was a joke, Josh."

She had become my number one enemy after telling the crew to target Melina.

I sat on the couch. "Fine. Buried."

I went to my room. I sat on the bed and looked at the family portrait on my nightstand.

My parents looked back at me, smiling, proud. They didn't know their son was a criminal. They didn't know their medical bills were paid with stolen money.

"I am sorry," I whispered to the photo. "I will quit soon. Once I have enough."

It was a lie. I knew it was a lie. You don't quit when you are winning.

My phone buzzed.

I had been added to the BBC - Billionaire Boys' Club group chat.

It was the inner circle. Mark, Kyle, Viktor, and a few others.

Kyle: *Weekly Challenge time, boys.*

Kyle: *The Burning Challenge. Record yourself burning money. Winner gets 100 points. Go.*

A video popped up. Kyle burning a hundred-dollar bill with a lighter. He laughed as the face of Benjamin Franklin turned to ash.

I stared at the screen. A hundred dollars. That was more than my father's two months' salary.

Then Viktor posted.

A video of him throwing a bundle of cash into a fireplace. $10,000.

Viktor: *Top that, peasants.*

The chat exploded with praise. *King Viktor! Legend!*

I felt a surge of rage. He had Melina. He had the status. He wasn't going to have this.

I walked to my safe. I unlocked it. I took out two bundles. $20,000.

I went to the patio. I put the money in a metal fire pit. I poured lighter fluid on it.

I hit record on my phone.

I dropped the match. The flames roared. $20,000 turned into black smoke in seconds.

I posted the video.

Greg: *Holy shit! Josh just burned $20k!*

Kyle: *Senator money!*

Then Viktor posted again. $50,000.

I saw red. I went back to the safe. I took out ten bundles. $100,000.

It was madness. It was insanity. It was money that could have built a school in my village. A school? More like ten or more schools in Ado-Ekiti. It was money that could have saved some poor Nigerians unable to pay their medical bills.

I took it outside. I piled it up. I lit it. I watched it burn. The smell was acrid. I posted the video.

Josh: *Checkmate! Bow to the Nigerian Prince.*

The group went silent. Then the notifications blew up.

Kyle: *ONE HUNDRED K!*

Mark: *We have a new King! All hail King Josh!*

Viktor didn't post again.

I stood there, watching the last embers of a fortune turn to gray ash. I had won the respect of a group of boys I secretly hated.

I looked at the ash on my hands.

"*Oponu*," I whispered to myself. I was a bloody fool.

I had burned a fortune to impress people who would never truly accept me. But as I walked back inside the thirteen-million-dollar mansion, I told myself it didn't matter.

I could always make more.

CHAPTER THIRTEEN

Kyle posted the Burning Challenge on Instagram, and just like that, I went from a campus curiosity to a campus deity. The "BBC" page wasn't hidden behind encryption like our WhatsApp chat. It was public. And the public loved a spectacle.

My follower count exploded overnight. Thousands of strangers liked the video of me tossing bundles of cash into the fire pit. Comments rolled in like a tidal wave. *King Josh. Legend. Nigerian Prince Energy.*

Soon, freshmen started dressing like me, trying to mimic the swagger I had bought with stolen money. They adopted the uniform: expensive long black coats from Brunello Cucinelli, Karl Lagerfeld, or Valentino.

I refused to touch Loro Piana. It was too plain. That quiet luxury stuff is for kids born into old money, people who don't feel the need to wear the receipts of their struggle on their chest. Not those who watched poverty kill their siblings and wanted to show the world that they had finally defeated poverty.

I wanted loud outfits. I wanted the hardware. Spiky Christian Louboutin sneakers or stud-embellished Giuseppe Zanotti loafers. Gold-framed Bottega Veneta sunglasses. An Audemars Piguet or Hublot on the wrist and a black briefcase in hand. That was how I dressed, and suddenly, that was how my "fans" dressed, too.

It was the life I had dreamed of since I was a boy pushing his father's broken Toyota daily, but it made me broke. Not the "classy broke" but broke as in "constantly-watching-your-gas-level type of broke."

The math was brutal. I had made $500,000 from the Jonathan Hudson card. A fortune. But I had spent over $300,000 on the Ferrari and the clothes. I had sent fifty-two thousand to Lagos to save my father. And then, in a fit of ego, I had burned one hundred and twenty thousand dollars just to beat Viktor in a stupid challenge.

That left me with around $28,000.

And $28,000 in my new world? That was pocket change. It evaporated in four days. A bottle of Ace of Spades at the club was $500. A dinner with the Elites was $1,000. Tipping the valets, buying the drugs, keeping up the charade, every single thing bled me dry.

I was driving a quarter-million-dollar car, but I was checking the price of gas before I filled up. I was a king with an empty treasury.

Then, salvation arrived. Or damnation, depending on how you look at it.

It started in *Principles of Management*. Professor Muller, who had surprisingly kept her job despite the sex tape scandal, divided us into pairs for a semester-long project.

"You will analyze the lifecycle of a startup," she droned. "Transforming a disruption into an institution."

She read off the list.

"Joshua Balogun," she said, looking over her glasses at me. "You are paired with Edward Morrison."

My heart jumped. Edward Morrison. The billionaire boy king. The guy who bragged about falsifying financial reports.

Edward turned in his seat and gave me a lazy salute. "Looks like it is you and me, Nigerian Prince."

After class, we exchanged numbers. "I will email you some files," Edward said. "We can coordinate the project online. I'm flying to St. Barths for the weekend. It's Samantha's birthday."

"Cool," I said. "Send it over."

That night, at dinner in the mansion, the mood was electric. Harry was bouncing in his seat.

Dmitri was grinning like a shark. Wang was actually looking up from his plate.

"You guys look excited," I said, cutting into a steak that cost more than my weekly stipend used to be.

"We have a plan," Dmitri said. "A big one. Fifteen million dollars."

I dropped my fork. It clattered against the china.

"*Oluwa o!*" I screamed. Oh God!

"Fifteen million?" I whispered. "Are you serious?"

"Dead serious," Dmitri said.

I did the mental math instantly. Six partners. Fifteen million. That was over $2.5 million each.

$2.5 million. Imagine taking that type of money to Nigeria and living there permanently. I would be worshipped like a god.

Over 3.5 billion naira. That was retirement money. That was never-worry-about-anything-ever-again money.

"That is too much," I said, my voice shaking. "The credit card companies will notice. They will freeze it in seconds."

Dmitri snorted. "Who said anything about credit cards? This is the big leagues, Josh. This is BEC."

"BEC?"

"Business Email Compromise," Wang said quietly.

"We pretend to be the CEO," Dmitri explained. "We send an email to the CFO. We order a payment. It looks real. It feels real. And they wire the money straight to us."

"Isn't that risky?" I asked.

Harry laughed. He leaned back, picking his teeth. "Isn't being poor risky? Isn't driving a Toyota Corolla risky?"

I took a deep breath. $2.5 million.

I made a vow right then. If we pulled this off, I was done. I would take my $2.5 million, move my parents from Ado-Ekiti to a mansion in Lagos, and never touch a computer again.

I would be a philanthropist. I would be clean. It was a lie, of course. The second lie I told myself. The first was that I was doing this just for my father.

Greed is like saltwater. The more you drink, the thirstier you get. Jeff Bezos doesn't stop. Elon Musk doesn't stop. They have enough money to buy countries, but they still wake up and want more. Why would I be any different?

"So," I said. "What is the plan? Who is the target?"

Dmitri leaned forward. "Your partner. Edward Morrison."

I froze. "Edward? Are you crazy? If we get caught, I get kicked out of college. I go to jail."

"We won't get caught," Dmitri said. "What do you know about Morrison Fits?"

I nodded. Everyone knew Morrison Fits. They were the holy grail of wristwatches.

Mark had shown off his Morrison Fits watch on the BBC chat. It was a hunk of gold and VVS diamonds that cost $580,000. They only made fifty a year. You had to be invited to buy one.

Wang opened his laptop. He spun it around so I could see the screen. An image of an older white man appeared.

"Lukas Schmidt," Wang said. "He supplies the gold and diamonds for Morrison Fits. He has been doing it for ten years. Every quarter, Morrison Fits wires him huge sums for materials."

Wang clicked to the next slide. A middle-aged Black man. He looked serious, wearing a sharp suit and glasses. "This is Denzel Warner," Wang said. "Newly appointed CFO of Morrison Fits. He got the job three months ago. It was a scandal."

"Why?"

"He is an ex-convict," Wang said.

"Served a year for financial misconduct in the nineties. Edward's father hired him to give him a second chance. The media hated it. The shareholders hated it. A Black ex-convict in charge of their finances doesn't sit well with them. He is under a microscope."

"What does Denzel have to do with us?" I asked.

"He'll be the fall guy," Wang said, his fingers dancing over the keys.

I felt a pit in my stomach. Denzel Warner. A Black man trying to rebuild his life. A man who had fought his way back from prison to the C-suite. And we were going to frame him. We were going to destroy him.

I thought about the racism I had seen at Kingsley. This would just confirm every bias they held. *See? You can't trust ex-convicts, particularly the Black ones. They are criminals.* Those stupid rich kids would have a field day intensifying their stereotypical view of life.

"That is cold," I whispered.

"It is $15 million," Harry said. "Cold pays the bills."

"What is my role?" I asked, looking at Wang.

Wang stared at me. "You are the trojan horse. Edward uses his personal MacBook for 'creative work' because he hates the security restrictions on his company laptop. That is his fatal error."

He slid a USB drive across the table.

"You are going to send him a file. 'Project_Notes.docx'. But it isn't a document. It carries a payload, a Zero-Day exploit I bought on the dark web this morning. It cost $80,000."

"$80,000?" I choked. "For a virus?"

"For an unpatched vulnerability in the OS kernel," Wang corrected. "Standard antivirus won't see it. Corporate EDR won't see it. Once he opens it on his unsecured personal network, I own the machine. I can see his screen. I can log his keystrokes. I get his passwords."

"And then?"

"Then I pivot," Wang said. "From Edward's personal email, I send the invoice to Denzel. Denzel sees it coming from the boss's private address. He panics. He pays. We win."

The plan was set.

"You are a dangerous man, Wang," I said, shaking my head.

He shrugged. "That is why you never download attachments. Unless you trust the source with your life."

"Are you in?" Dmitri asked.

I looked around the table. Dmitri, Harry, Alicia, Naomi. They were all looking at me. They were waiting.

I thought about my empty bank account. I thought about the Ferrari that needed gas. I thought about the respect I saw in Mark's eyes when I sat in the front row.

I looked at Denzel Warner's face on the screen one last time. Sorry, brother, I thought. It is you or me.

"I am in," I said.

"Good," Dmitri grinned. "Let's teach these rich assholes a lesson."

CHAPTER FOURTEEN

The project gave Edward and me a reason to meet. Every evening at 6:00 PM, we sat in the library or at a café, huddled over laptops.

Edward was different from the other Elites. He was curious. He asked questions.

"Tell me about Nigeria," he said one evening, sipping an espresso. "I went to Mali on a school trip. Le Rosey organizes these excursions. I loved it. The people were so... warm."

"It is warm," I said. "But it is hard, Edward."

I told him about the poverty. I told him about the forty-eight-dollar monthly wage. I left out the part about my father being one of those people. To him, I was still the Senator's son, observing the poor from a distance.

"Forty-eight dollars?" Edward choked on his coffee. "A month? That is... inhuman. That is less than the tip I leave behind in restaurants. How do they live?"

I couldn't tell him that my father once took care of himself, my mother, and four kids with his $48 monthly salary. The thought of that hardened my resolve. No, I couldn't be like my father. Sick in old age and unable to pay medical bills because he never wanted to get his hands a little dirty. I would be the predator, not prey.

"They barely do," I said. "That is why there is crime. That is why there is fraud. When you are starving, morality is a luxury you can't afford."

"What about aid?" he asked. "The UN? The charities? I've been to several charity balls where we raise millions of dollars in charity for African kids."

"Eaten by politicians in Abuja," I said bitterly. "Old men with big bellies who swallow the country whole. Sometimes the NGOs embezzle the funds too."

Edward looked genuinely angry. "That is terrible. And the schools?"

"Disaster," I said. "ASUU strikes. ASUU is the union of lecturers in Nigeria. Sometimes, universities close for eight months at a time because lecturers aren't paid. A four-year degree takes six years. That is why we leave. That is why we travel abroad, not seeing our parents or friends for decades just because we're seeking greener pastures."

Edward nodded slowly. "I had no idea. I am going to talk to my father. We should set up a scholarship. Specifically for Nigerian students."

I looked at him. He was sincere. He was a good guy. He was trying to help.

And I was about to rob him blind.

The guilt clawed at my throat. *Omo ale ni mi.* I am a bastard.

But I pushed it down.

"Okay," I said, opening my laptop. "Let's look at this report."

I found the file Wang had planted on my desktop. Financial_Decision_Making_Report_v2.docx. It looked innocent. Just a Word document.

"I finished the section on market entry," I said. "I'm sending it to you now. Can you review it?"

"Sure," Edward said.

I attached the file. I hit send.

"Sent."

Edward's phone buzzed. He checked his email. "Got it."

He opened his MacBook. He downloaded the file.

"Weird," he muttered. "It's not opening. Says file corrupted."

My heart stopped.

"Oh," I said casually. "Maybe try again? Or I can resend it as a PDF later."

"Yeah, resend it later," he said.

But the damage was done. The file had executed. Wang was in.

Edward's phone rang. He stepped away to take it.

While he was gone, I texted Wang. *Package delivered.*

Wang replied with a single skull emoji.

Ten minutes later, Edward came back. "Sorry. Business. So, where were we?"

He had no idea that in those ten minutes, Wang had logged his keystrokes. Wang had his password: *IloveMali6@*.

It was almost too easy.

CHAPTER FIFTEEN

The days following the planning session were a study in duality. During the day, I was the charming Nigerian Prince, driving my Ferrari to campus, chilling with the Elites, and pretending to be fascinated by Edward Morrison's life story.

At night, I was either licking the lips between Naomi's legs or watching Wang dissect Edward's digital life.

We didn't just guess Edward's habits; we owned his operating system. The Zero-Day exploit Wang had planted via the "corrupted" Word document gave us a front-row seat to his personal MacBook.

We saw his keystrokes. We saw his passwords. We saw his frustration with Lukas Schmidt, the current diamond supplier for Morrison Fits.

"Schmidt is robbing us," Edward complained to me one evening at a café in Santa Monica. "He thinks because he has the VVS connection, he can charge whatever he wants. But Petra... Petra is hungry."

I nodded sympathetically, sipping my latte. "Competition is good for business, right?"

"Exactly," Edward said. "I am pushing for a switch. My father is hesitant. He likes loyalty, but the numbers don't lie. If I can close the Petra deal, I save the company ten percent annually."

He didn't know he was handing me the blueprint to his own robbery.

Back at the mansion, Harry was our linguistic chameleon. He studied Edward's emails like they were sacred texts.

Harry was obsessed with two things in life—cocaine and Alicia. But the guy had crazy observational skills. He could detect patterns.

"Look at this," Harry said, pointing to a screen. "When Edward emails Denzel, he always puts a full stop after his signature. Edward. Not Edward or Edward Morrison. Just Edward with a full stop."

"A code?" I asked.

"Authentication," Wang said. "A subtle way to prove it is really him. If we miss that dot, Denzel gets suspicious."

"And look at the capitalization," Harry added. "He never capitalizes 'finance' or 'accounting'.

He treats them like verbs, not departments. And he uses the word 'expedite' a lot. We need to sound like him. Arrogant, impatient, but specific."

We waited for the perfect moment. The diamond industry moves in cycles. Petra Diamonds held tenders, which were sales events where raw diamonds were sold in lots. The next tender was in three days.

We were ready.

Wang had set up the infrastructure. We weren't going to spoof the domain. Not at all. That was for amateurs. Baby scammers.

Since we had access to Edward's personal email—which he often used to bypass corporate filters)—we were going to send the order from the real account.

The day of the tender arrived. We placed a bid. Not a real one, but a digital phantom that inserted itself into the communication stream between Petra and Morrison Fits.

Bid Accepted: $15,000,000 for Lot 44B.

Harry drafted the email. It was a masterpiece of mimicry.

To: Denzel Warner

From: Edward Morrison

Subject: **Fwd: Petra Tender - URGENT Payment**

Denzel, we won the tender. Finally dumping Schmidt. See attached invoice from Petra. Wire the $15M immediately. I want this expedited before the European markets open tomorrow. Don't let compliance slow this down.

Edward.

The full stop was there. The tone was perfect. The attached invoice looked impeccable, right down to the Petra logo and the VAT number. But the IBAN pointed straight to our shell account in the Caymans.

Wang hit send.

We waited. The server room was silent except for the hum of the cooling fans.

Ten minutes later, Denzel replied.

Edward, fantastic news. However, this is a new beneficiary account. Corporate protocol strictly requires verbal confirmation for any transfer over five million. I need to call you.

"He is checking," I whispered. "He's going to call Edward's real phone."

"No, he isn't," Wang said calmly. He opened a program I hadn't seen before. A waveform visualized on the screen.

"What is that?"

"AI Voice Cloning," Wang said. "I harvested five minutes of Edward's audio from his Instagram stories and your recorded conversations. That is all the neural network needs."

Wang typed a sentence into the text box.

Denzel, I am walking into a meeting with my father! Stop wasting my time and send the damn wire! I'm losing signal!

He picked up a burner phone and dialed Denzel's direct line. He held the microphone to the computer speaker.

We heard Denzel pick up. "Edward?"

Wang hit Generate.

Edward's voice, exact in pitch, cadence, and arrogant drawl, blasted through the room.

"Denzel, I am walking into a meeting with my father! Stop wasting my time and send the damn wire! I'm losing signal!"

"I—I. Yes, sir. Understood, sir," Denzel stammered. "Initiating now."

The line went dead.

Five minutes later.

Wire Initiated: $15,000,000.00

The room exploded. Harry snorted an entire coke line on the table. Alicia screamed in joy and popped a bottle of Champagne. Naomi hugged me so hard I couldn't breathe.

"Fifteen million dollars!" Harry shouted. "We are kings!"

Wang didn't celebrate. He was already working on the cleanup.

"Deleting local copies," he said. "Scrubbing the sent folder on Edward's laptop. Scrubbing Denzel's inbox."

"Does that mean the evidence is gone?" I asked.

Wang shook his head, his eyes glued to the code. "No. Morrison Fits is a publicly traded company. It is bound by the Sarbanes-Oxley Act. The company uses immutable email archiving, probably Mimecast. Every email is backed up on a separate server that even I can't touch."

"Then why delete the local copies?"

"To blind Denzel," Wang said. "When he goes to look for the email to prove his innocence, it won't be there. He will panic. He will sound crazy. By the time their IT forensics team pulls the deep archives to prove the email was real, the money will be gone."

"Where is it going?"

"Everywhere," Dmitri said, pointing to a diagram on the whiteboard. "Caymans first. Then a shell company in Hong Kong. Then a construction firm in Dubai. Then Estonia. Finally, a bank in Moscow where we buy Bitcoin. Ten hops. Ten jurisdictions."

"By the time the FBI traces the first hop," Wang said, "we will be ghosts."

But Wang wasn't done. He opened another window.

"What are you doing now?" I asked.

"Creating a narrative," Wang said.

He accessed Denzel's personal bank accounts. We had his passwords from the keylogger.

"Denzel sent five thousand dollars to his mother last week for surgery," Wang noted. "Let's make him look generous."

He wired $400,000 from the stolen funds into Denzel's mother's account. Then another $250,000 to Denzel's brother in Chicago.

"Why?" I asked, horrified.

"To bury him," Dmitri said coldly. "When the money goes missing, who do they look at? The CFO with a criminal record whose family just got $650,000 from an anonymous source. It is an open-and-shut case."

I felt sick. We weren't just stealing; we were framing an innocent man. A Black man like me. I knew how hard it was to reach the top while being Black. Yet, I destroyed another Black man's life. His life and his family to cover our tracks.

"That is evil," I whispered.

"That is insurance," Dmitri corrected.

Suddenly, a loud CRACK echoed through the room.

I jumped. Wang was standing over his laptop—the Alienware he used for the hack. He had just smashed the screen with a heavy glass ashtray. He then stomped on the keyboard until keys flew like shrapnel.

He gathered the pieces and threw them into the fireplace.

"What the hell?" I yelled. "That was brand new! That cost three grand!"

Wang stared at the fire, his face illuminated by the flames.

"Where do deleted files go, Josh?" he asked softly. "When you hit delete, where does the data go?"

"It... goes away?"

"No," Wang said. "It stays on the drive. It is just marked as 'free space'. A good forensic team can recover it in an hour. And the Hardware ID leaves a fingerprint on the network. The only way to truly delete data is fire."

The money moved through the labyrinth. Caymans. Hong Kong. Dubai. Estonia. Moscow.

By the time the Bitcoin hit our wallets, the $15 million had been washed clean. We split it six ways. Two and a half million dollars each.

In Nigeria, that is billions of naira. I was a billionaire in my home currency.

Two months later, the news broke.

I was sitting in the student lounge, watching CNN.

BREAKING NEWS: **CFO of Morrison Fits Arrested in $15 Million Embezzlement Scheme.**

They showed Denzel Warner being led out of his office in handcuffs. He looked bewildered. He looked broken.

"Authorities say Warner diverted company funds to offshore accounts linked to his family members," the reporter said. "This is not his first run-in with the law..."

I turned off the TV. I couldn't watch.

Denzel was the pawn. We were the grandmasters. And the game was rigorous.

In life, you can either be the predator or prey. I refuse to be the prey. I learned from Belfort to always be the wolf.

I am a predator wearing black Karl Lagerfeld coat, gold-framed Bottega Veneta sunglasses, and spiked Giuseppe Zanotti shoes.

My life was good at that moment. I was a millionaire, but I was still sad. The sad part about making money illegally is that you cannot help your family financially as much as you would have loved to do because they will get suspicious and start asking questions about how you suddenly became rich.

I called my mom on her cellphone a few days after receiving my share of the money that we got from Morrison Fits.

She seemed excited to hear my voice. "Why not call me on WhatsApp instead?" she asked. "You know regular phone calls are expensive."

"It's not a problem. Besides, WhatsApp calls are always terrible because of the poor internet connection," I replied.

"That is true. I have good news for you, my son."

"What is it?"

"I got a new job at a nearby school to work as a teacher," she said with excitement in her voice. "They'll be paying me 85,000 naira, my son. I can use the extra money to buy more groceries now that things are super expensive in the country…"

I stopped listening and converted 85,000 naira to dollars on Google. It was just $59. My mother was happy to earn $59 monthly, while I had over $2 million in my blockchain wallet. I wanted to smash my phone against the wall and tell my parents to resign from their jobs.

I wanted to buy a good house for them in Banana Island and a Range Rover Autobiography, but I could not do anything because my parents would start asking about my source of sudden wealth. They would wonder how a scholarship student got so rich.

My mother had no idea that her son was known as *the Nigerian Prince* on Instagram. A big boy who gave away $100 weekly to his most active followers. She did not know how rich I had become.

"Are you there, my son?" my mom asked when she noticed that I had gone quiet.

"Why can't you resign, mummy? My scholarship allowance has been increased to $2,000 monthly. I can send $1,000 to you and daddy every month. You don't have to work anymore."

"No!" my mom yelled. "You should save your money. You will start a family after college. You need to save money to take care of yourself and your family after college. Don't worry about your father and me. We will survive. All that is important is for you to get good grades and get a respectable job after your graduation."

I wanted to yell at my mom. I wanted to tell her that I had become a millionaire and no longer needed to get a job after graduation. I had enough money to "create jobs."

I wished she could know that I owned a Ferrari worth more than a quarter million dollars. I wanted to tell her that I lived in Beverly Hills. I had many things I wanted to say to her.

I exhaled. There was nothing I could do to convince my mom to quit her job. "Okay, ma."

"How are things between you and Jada?"

I rolled my eyes. It was an unexpected question. My mom and Jada loved each other so much. I could not explain to my mom that I had lost interest in Jada and had my eyes on a rich white girl.

"Things are fine between us," I lied.

My mom and I talked for some minutes before I hung up. I was not happy because I could do nothing to help my family financially without attracting suspicion.

I went to bed that night with a heavy heart and a feeling of dejection because I could not live with myself knowing that I was a millionaire while my parents were living in abject poverty.

It was sad that the money I spent on strippers whenever I went to the club was more than my father's yearly salary.

I played Yanni's *Ethnicity* album on my MacBook pro as I struggled to sleep that night. I kept turning on my bed at intervals as I thought about my family.

I had barely slept when a sound like thunder shook the house. I sat up, heart hammering. Was it an earthquake? Then the door flew open.

Naomi burst in. Her eyes were wide with terror. She was wearing an oversized t-shirt, her hair wild.

"FBI!" she screamed. "Josh! FBI! They are at the gate!"

Time stopped.

CHAPTER SIXTEEN

I could not react. My body felt like it had been turned into stone. I was not sure I could even breathe at that moment because the air in the room felt too thick to inhale.

My worst fears had finally walked through the door. I glanced at the golden table in the corner of my room. My laptop was wide open. It was powered on.

The screen glowed in the darkness like a lighthouse guiding a ship to a crash. I had forgotten to turn it off the previous night because I was playing Yanni's Ethnicity album.

I always played the album whenever I had trouble sleeping. Yanni's talented piano skills usually had a way of making me feel calm, but right now, the music sounded like a funeral dirge.

"Shut down your laptop!" Naomi yelled. Her voice cracked with a terror I had never heard before.

I tried to move my arm, but my brain was disconnected from my muscles. I had a full-blown panic attack. My heart hammered against my ribs like a trapped bird.

I imagined myself being dragged to an American jail in the middle of the night. I saw the headlines in Nigeria. *Another Nigerian Prince Caught.*

I thought of how my actions would ruin the reputation of my people. The country already had a terrible public image. I was about to become another statistic.

Another reason for the world to look down on Nigerians.

I would be the face of their shame on every news outlet.

Igbo and Hausa people on *Instablog9ja* would accuse Yoruba people of ruining the country's reputation abroad.

African Americans on *TheShadeRoom* would accuse Nigerians of ruining Black people's reputation in the U.S. *Fuck!*

I thought of my parents.

Mogbe! I am finished.

My mother would collapse. My father would wish the kidney failure had taken him before he lived to see this disgrace. In Yoruba culture, a good name is worth more than gold. *Oruko rere san ju wura ati fadaka lo.* I had just thrown my family name into the mud.

My entire life flashed before me. I saw my childhood in Ado-Ekiti. I saw the broken Toyota Corolla. I saw Jada's face.

While I was lost in my terrified thoughts, the door to my room burst open.

A man in tactical gear charged in. He was huge. He looked like a mountain made of Kevlar and rage. He tackled me to the floor.

My face hit the expensive carpet. The air left my lungs in a painful whoosh. He held me tightly, his knee pressing into my spine, making it difficult for me to breathe.

I turned my head to the side, gasping. I saw Naomi. She was pinned on the floor by another agent. Her hair was over her face, and she was screaming.

"His laptop is unlocked!" the agent who pinned me yelled.

Two other agents arrived immediately. They grabbed my laptop. They pulled the USB drive. They bagged it.

"Secure the perimeter!" someone shouted.

The agent on my back grabbed my wrists. He snapped a pair of cold steel handcuffs onto them. The metal bit into my skin.

"Get up!" he barked.

He dragged me to my feet. My legs were like jelly. He shoved me toward the door. I stumbled into the hallway. They were dragging Naomi too.

"You have the right to remain silent," one of the FBI agents recited.

His voice was deep and robotic. "Whatever you say can and will be used against you in a court of law."

I began sobbing. I could not stop it. The tears flowed hot and fast. My life was over. I was twenty years old, and my life was over. I would never see Ado-Ekiti again. I would never see the warm and cold springs flowing next to each other in Ikogosi-Ekiti. I would never eat my mother's jollof rice again. I would die in a cage.

We reached the living room.

Dmitri, Wang, and Harry were already there. They were on their knees. Their hands were cuffed behind their backs. Their faces were blank. Alicia was crying silently.

The agent pushed me down next to Dmitri. I bowed my head. I prayed to God. *Olorun, please. I am sorry.* I will never do it again. Just save me.

Then, a sound cut through the silence. It was not a siren. It was not a gunshot.

It was laughter.

One of the FBI agents was laughing.

What the actual fuck!

I looked up, confused. The agent who had tackled me was clutching his stomach. His shoulders were shaking.

Then Dmitri started laughing.

I blinked. Was I going crazy? Was this the madness that comes before prison?

I looked around. Harry was grinning. Wang was shaking his head with a small smile. Even Alicia stopped crying and started giggling.

"Where did you get this kid?" the agent asked, pulling off his tactical mask. He was just a regular guy underneath. He pointed at my jeans. "I think he has wet his pants."

I looked down. There was a dark stain on the crotch of my jeans.

Dmitri rolled on the floor laughing. He could not breathe. "Oh my God! Josh! Look at you!"

The "officers" unlocked our handcuffs. They took off their helmets. They were smiling at me like we were old friends.

I remained stupefied. My brain could not process the shift. I did not know much about FBI agents, but I was sure that they were not the type to crack jokes in the middle of a raid.

"What is going on?" I whispered. My voice was hoarse. "Why are they unlocking us?"

"It is a drill," Wang explained. He stood up and dusted off his knees. His face was serious again. "These people are actors. We organize drills like this occasionally. We need to evaluate how we would react if the real FBI visited us."

He looked at me with cold eyes.

"You failed, Josh. You made a huge mistake. You hesitated. You left your laptop open. You didn't activate the kill switch."

I stared at him. I still did not believe it. My heart was still racing at a thousand miles per hour.

"But... they have guns," I stammered. "They have uniforms."

"Costumes," Harry said. "Props. Hollywood magic." I could see some white stains on his nose. Cocaine as usual. The boy was always high.

The men smiled broadly at me. One of them patted me on the back. "Sorry about the tackle, kid. You have to sell it, right?"

I sighed. The air rushed back into my lungs. I sat on the bare floor, feeling the strength drain out of me.

I had already pictured myself wearing an orange jumpsuit for twenty years. I had already said goodbye to my future.

"Fuck you all!" I screamed. "I almost had a heart attack! Do you know what you just did to me?"

The actors left afterward, taking their fake guns and their real cash payment. They were still talking about how the new guy wet his pants.

"You should have seen your face," Harry said amidst tears of laughter.

"You were crying like a baby. Please sir, I want my mommy."

"I thought I would be spending the next few years in a federal prison," I snapped. "It is not funny."

Dmitri stepped closer to me. He was not laughing.

"You should not engage in crime if you are not ready to spend time in prison," Dmitri said tonelessly. "Don't do the crime if you can't do the time. Panic gets you caught. Panic gets us all caught."

"Fuck you," I said again.

"We do this for a reason," Dmitri explained. "Random drills. We need to be ready. Everyone was coordinated tonight except you. You froze."

I stood up. My legs were shaking. I felt humiliated. I felt small.

I looked at them. My partners. My friends. They were monsters. They played with fear like it was a toy.

"At this point, I am not even sure I want to engage in fraud anymore," I said quietly. "I am not ashamed to say that I am scared of prison. Being a Black man in America is hard enough. But being a Black male ex-convict? That is a death sentence."

I stormed off to my room. I slammed the door. I locked it. I leaned against the wood and slid down to the floor.

I closed my eyes. Thank you, God. Thank you. I should have seen it as a sign. A warning from the heavens. The universe had given me a glimpse of my future. It had shown me the end of the road.

After that drill, I should have packed my bags. I should have taken my remaining cash and run. I should have gone back to being Josh the scholarship student.

But I didn't. I was in love with the Nigerian Prince persona. If you've ever been poor, then suddenly got rich, trust me, you will do whatever you must do to avoid returning to poverty.

CHAPTER SEVENTEEN

My phone rang the next morning like a drill boring into my skull. I groaned, rolling over on sheets that probably cost more than my mother's salary.

My eyes felt like they were packed with sand. The fake raid the night before had left me with a hangover of adrenaline and fear.

I swiped the screen.

"Hello," I rasped.

"*Don't tell me you still sleepin' when it's 'bout eleven in da mornin'.*"

Jada's voice was loud and sharp, cutting through the silence of the mansion.

"I could barely sleep," I muttered. "Had things to do." Like almost peeing my pants because my friends are psychopaths.

There was a pause on the line. A heavy, loaded silence.

"Is something wrong?" I asked, sitting up.

"*April 19 is just a couple days 'way,*" she said. Her tone was flat. Dangerous.

I blinked. My brain was a blank slate. "Okay? What is happening on April 19?"

"It's our anniversary, you asshole," she snapped. "Three years. Three damn years."

I winced. Shame washed over me, hot and prickly. How could I forget?

Jada was my anchor. She was the one who sold her car for me. She was the girl who liked me on the airplane from Lagos. She was the one who loved me when I was nobody.

But lately, "nobody" felt like a stranger. "Josh the Nigerian Prince" didn't have room in his head for anniversaries. He had room for Ferraris, for wire transfers, for Melina.

"Jada, I'm sorry," I stammered. "I stayed up all night working on a group project. My brain is fried. You know I would never forget us."

"*You ain't ever forgot before,*" she said, her voice softening just a fraction, but still laced with hurt. "*We never been apart on our anniversary.* I feel... I feel like I don't know you no more, Josh. This long distance? It's killing us. We need to link up."

The fog in my head cleared instantly. She was right. We needed this. I needed to remember who I was before the money, before the lies.

"Why don't you come to LA?" I asked.

"Nah," she sighed. "Remember last time? Your dorm room? We couldn't even kiss without Eric typing in the corner. It was awkward as hell."

I smiled. "Things have changed, Jada. I don't live in the dorm anymore. I live somewhere else now. Private room. Soundproof."

"For real?"

"For real. Don't worry about anything. I have it planned."

"*A'ight then,*" she said, sounding hopeful. "*I'm boutta roll over to Greyhound, see if I can cop a cheap ticket.*"

Greyhound. Fifty-nine hours on a bus. Smelling strangers' sweat, eating vending machine food, cramping in a seat designed for torture.

I looked around my room. The silk curtains. The view of the hills.

"No," I said firmly. "No bus. I'll handle the ticket. Check your email in five minutes."

"Thanks, baby. I love you."

"I love you too," I said. "And get ready. You won't be sleeping much."

"Yes, daddy," she purred. "I'm wet already."

I hung up. I went straight to PrivateFly.

I didn't even look at commercial flights. Delta First Class was for peasants.

The Nigerian Prince would rather chew a rock than allow his loved ones to fly a commercial first-class flight. I found a Learjet 75 available out of Detroit. $28,400.

Click. Booked.

I sent the confirmation.

Five minutes later, my phone blew up.

"JOSH!" she screamed. "A private jet? A whole-ass private jet? How did you get the money, *bruh?*"

I rolled my eyes. I was getting good at lying. It came as naturally as breathing now.

"A friend," I said smoothly. "He heard me on the phone. He couldn't stand the idea of my girl on a bus for three days. He offered his family's plane account."

"*But you said you ain't got no friends except David and that nerd Eric,*" she said suspiciously.

"Things change," I said.

"People realized I'm smart. They want to be around me. Also, I've been helping him with his assignments, so he feels indebted to me."

"Damn," she breathed. "I'm gonna take a thousand pictures. *I'm gonna be bougie as hell.*"

A week later, I pulled up to the private terminal at Van Nuys in the Ferrari.

Jada walked out of the sliding doors. She looked beautiful, in a simple way. She was wearing leggings and a hoodie, her hair in braids. But when she saw me, her steps faltered.

She stopped. She looked me up and down.

I was wearing a $7,500 Saint Laurent jacket. Amiri pants with the rips perfectly engineered. Giuseppe Zanotti on my feet. And an iced out Patek Philippe on my wrist.

"Josh?" she asked, like she wasn't sure. "Is that really you?"

I smiled and hugged her tight. "It's me, Jada. It's so good to see you."

She hugged me back, but she was stiff. *"You ain't the same.* You look different. You smell like money. *You talk like them white boys now."*

It was true. My accent had shifted. The Detroit edge was gone, smoothed over by hours of mimicking Edward and Dmitri.

I spoke the language of wealth now. I led her to the Ferrari.

"Who owns this?" she asked, eyeing the prancing horse emblem.

"My friend," I lied again. "You'll meet him."

We drove in silence. The air was thick with unspoken questions. I wanted it to be romantic, like a movie reunion. Instead, it felt like an interrogation.

"It's still me," I said, reaching for her hand.

She pulled away slightly. "Really? Last time I saw you, *you was crying about your pops being sick. Now you got a PJ and a Ferrari? Who you tryna play, bruh? I might be Black, but I ain't stupid."*

"I told you, rich friends," I said, gripping the steering wheel tighter.

We pulled into the neighborhood. Jada gasped at the mansions.

"Damn," she whispered.

I parked in the garage next to Harry's Bugatti. Jada stared at the lineup of cars.

"Does your friend own all these?"

"He lives with a couple of other students."

"What does he do?" she asked, her eyes narrowing.

I needed to shut this down. I needed to flip the script. Psychological manipulation.

"His father is a Russian billionaire," I snapped. "Why are you so suspicious? I bring you to a palace, I fly you private, and all you do is complain and ask questions. Can't you just be happy?"

Guilt flashed across her face. "I'm sorry, Josh. I didn't mean to..."

"This isn't how I pictured it," I said, playing the wounded victim. "I thought you'd be excited."

"I am," she said, her voice trembling. "I'm sorry."

I softened. "There is one way you can make it up to me."

I looked at my lap. Jada understood. She unzipped my pants. She went down on me right there in the Ferrari, surrounded by millions of dollars of horsepower.

Her tongue sent me to heaven. Hands on the Ferrari steering wheel, my rod in her tight mouth, my head in a haze. Deadly combination. It felt good.

The next night was our anniversary.

I took her to Nobu Malibu. It was the place to be seen. The ocean crashed against the rocks below, the patio lit by soft lanterns.

We walked in, and my stomach dropped. Sitting at a prime table near the railing were Mark, Viktor, and Melina.

Melina looked like a goddess. She was wearing a white Chanel dress that glowed against her skin. Beside her was Viktor, looking smug. And Mark was with a girl who looked like a supermodel.

Jada was wearing a dress from Zara. It was cute, but next to Melina's couture, it looked like a rag.

"Josh!" Mark called out, waving. "Hey man!"

I froze. I wanted to turn around and run.

"*These yo' homies?*" Jada asked loudly.

I cringed. "Yeah."

"Come join us!" Mark insisted.

We walked over. They pulled up chairs.

"This is Jada," I said, my voice tight.

Melina looked at Jada. Her gaze was cool, analytical. She scanned the Zara dress, the simple gold-plated jewelry. Not even actual 24k gold. Then she looked at me. Her eyebrow raised slightly.

Mark introduced everyone. The model was Zoe, from Paris. Of course. He came across her OnlyFans account. Jerked off to her a couple of times and wanted her in flesh. So, he sent his father's private jet to fly her from Paris to LA.

We ordered. Seven courses. Jada looked at the menu like it was written in alien hieroglyphs.

"What college do you go to, Jada?" Mark asked politely, trying to break the awkward silence.

Melina's eyes were on Jada. My eyes were on Melina. Viktor's eyes were on me.

Jada took a sip of wine. She held the glass by the bowl, her hand wrapping around it like a mug. I saw Melina notice. I saw Viktor smirk.

"*I don't study at no college,*" Jada said. "My cousin went to college, now he works at a bar. *Ain't no use wasting time on that and racking up student loans.*"

I closed my eyes. Please stop.

"So, you don't study at all?" Melina asked. Her voice was polite, but the judgment was dripping off every syllable.

"*Nah, sis,*" Jada said. She drained her glass and waved at the waiter. "*Yo! Can I get a refill? This shit good.*"

I wanted to die. I wanted the floor to open up and swallow me whole.

Here I was, trying to be the sophisticated Nigerian Prince, the peer of billionaires, and Jada was shattering the illusion with every word.

She was loud. She was unpolished. **She was everything I used to be, and everything I was trying to hide**.

"How did you two meet?" Viktor asked, a cruel glint in his eye. He was enjoying this. He was loving watching the scholarship boy squirm.

Jada burped. Softly, but audibly.

"We met—" she started.

"Tinder," I blurted out. "It's a blind date."

Silence slammed into the table.

Jada froze. Her mouth hung open. Her eyes filled with instant, shocking tears.

"That figures," Viktor muttered, chuckling.

Jada stood up. Her chair scraped loudly against the patio stones.

"I lost my appetite," she whispered.

She turned and ran. She ran past the host stand, past the valet, out into the night.

I sat there. My heart was pounding. I felt sick. I had just denied the girl I loved. I had erased three years of history because I was ashamed.

The girl who sold her car and jewelry to help me foot my father's hospital bills. The girl who knew and loved the real Josh Balogun.

"Aren't you gonna go after her?" Mark asked, raising an eyebrow.

I looked at Melina. She was watching me intently. If I ran after Jada, I admitted I lied. If I stayed, I was a monster.

"She isn't my girl," I said, my voice cold and dead. "Just a Tinder date. Won't see her again. Good riddance."

Melina smiled. A small, satisfied smile.

We finished dinner. I ate the wagyu beef. It tasted like ash. I drank the sake. My phone buzzed in my pocket. Jada. Again and again. I ignored it.

An hour later, we walked out. Viktor led Melina to his Porsche. He opened the door for her. She looked back at me one last time before getting in.

I walked to the Ferrari. Jada was standing there, leaning against the fender. Her face was streaked with mascara.

I walked up to her. "Jada, listen…"

"Tinder date?" she choked out. "Blind date? Josh, it's our anniversary. Three years."

"I panicked," I said. "You were acting weird. You were embarrassing me."

"Embarrassing you?" she screamed. "Because I speak like I'm from Detroit? Because I don't hold a glass with my pinky out?"

"Yes!" I shouted back. "Yes! Look at them, Jada! Look at Melina! She holds herself with class. You were eating like you were starving. You were drinking like a fish. You don't fit in here!"

"I don't fit in because I'm real!" she yelled. "And you know why I was drinking? Because you couldn't keep your eyes off her! That white girl! You were staring at her like you wanted to eat her! On our anniversary! You told me you would never leave me. Not for a white girl."

I stopped. I hadn't realized I was doing it. But she was right.

"You aren't the man I loved," Jada said, her voice dropping to a whisper. "I don't know who this is. This... Nigerian Prince. You are a stranger. A stranger with a nice car and a fake soul. You don't even know who you are anymore, Josh."

I got angry. "I am the man my father never became. A man who doesn't have to worry about paying bills every night. A man who would not be too poor to take his sick children to the hospital."

"I can't be with you anymore, Josh."

"Are you breaking up with me?" I asked.

The crickets chirped in the bushes.

She laughed, a dry, broken sound.

"No. I'm doing you a favor. It's obvious you love the white girl. Go be with her. Go be with your ice princess. She knows how to hold a wine glass. She knows how to eat with a fork and a damned knife properly. Maybe she won't notice that your hand is empty when you try to hold hers."

She leaned in and kissed my cheek. Her lips were cold.

"You will always have a place in my heart, Josh. But I can't stay in yours. It's too crowded with lies."

She walked away. She called an Uber and left.

The next day, she took a bus back to Detroit. She blocked my number. She deleted our photos on her Instagram.

I sat in my room at the mansion, surrounded by my luxury. I was single. I was free. I could pursue Melina now.

But as I looked at the empty space beside me in the king-sized bed, I felt an ache in my chest that no amount of money could fix.

CHAPTER EIGHTEEN

Jada left, and with her, the last shred of my old life disappeared. The mansion was quiet, but my head was loud. Guilt is a strange companion. It doesn't scream; it whispers. It waits until you are alone, then it sits on your chest and reminds you of everything you have lost.

I wasn't a big drinker. Just a little champagne and espresso martini here and there. In Nigeria, my father drank palm wine on special occasions, but I never liked the taste of alcohol. But that week, the silence was too heavy. So, I started going to bars.

I hit the spots the Elites frequented—*The Nice Guy, Delilah, Warwick*. I sat in dark corners, nursing bottles of expensive whiskey that tasted like gasoline. I had money in my pocket, a Ferrari in the valet lot, and a Rolex on my wrist. But I had no one.

David was gone. Jada was gone. My parents thought I was a saint. My new friends, Mark, Kyle, and Viktor—more like a frenemy—only liked the "Senator's Son." The Nigerian Prince. They didn't know Josh. They knew a character I was playing.

One night, at the bar of the Beverly Hills Hotel, I met Marie.

She was a redhead with green eyes that looked like they had seen everything and judged nothing. She was wearing a dress that clung to her like a secret. She wasn't just a girl at a bar. She was a professional. An escort.

I was drunk. The kind of drunk where the room spins and your tongue feels too big for your mouth. I don't remember much of our conversation. I just remember waking up the next morning in a hotel suite I didn't recognize.

Marie was sitting naked in a chair by the window, smoking a cigarette. She looked at me and smiled.

"Good morning, Prince," she said.

That was how it started. Marie became my escape.

She wasn't cheap. $2,000 a night. But she listened. That was the real service. Sex was just the handshake. The real transaction was confession.

I told her everything—well, my family background, definitely not my life as a fraudster. I told her about Ado-Ekiti. I told her about the scholarship. I told her about Jada. I cried in her arms, tears soaking into her Versace robe, and she just stroked my hair and told me it was okay.

"You are lonely, Josh," she said one night, blowing smoke rings at the ceiling. "Money makes you lonely."

"It pays the bills," I muttered.

One morning, lying next to her, I checked my phone. I opened my crypto wallet. My stomach dropped. Bitcoin had crashed. I had lost $56,000 while I slept. $56,000. Gone. Vaporized.

"What is wrong?" Marie asked, trailing a finger down my chest.

"I lost money," I said, staring at the screen. "A lot of money."

"How?"

"Bitcoin dropped."

"Oh," she said. She didn't understand.

To her, money was cash on the dresser. Money was tangible.

I realized then that crypto was a trap. It was volatile. It was gambling. I needed something solid. I needed banks. I needed laundering.

I left the hotel two hours later. I never took Marie to the mansion. That was a line I wouldn't cross. The mansion was for business.

I went to Dmitri. We sat by the pool, the water glittering in the California sun.

"I need to wash the money," I said. "I can't keep it in crypto. It is too risky."

Dmitri nodded. He took a sip of his matcha. "You need a lawyer. A specific kind of lawyer."

"Who?"

"Julian Schneider," Dmitri said. "He is Swiss. He is expensive. But he is a magician."

We didn't fly direct. Direct flights leave trails. The IRS watches flights to Switzerland like hawks. They know that Zurich is the piggy bank for American secrets.

So, we got creative. We flew to Cologne, Germany first.

I was nervous. I had heard stories about Germany. Stories about cold stares and racism. But Cologne surprised me. The people were reserved, yes, but polite. They gave directions. They smiled when I butchered their language. I saw Black people, Asians, Arabs. It was quite diverse.

From Cologne, we took a train to Paris. No passport checks. The Schengen Zone was a criminal's best friend. We were ghosts moving through borders that didn't exist.

Paris to Milan. Milan to Zurich. By the time we arrived in Switzerland, our digital footprint was a mess of zig-zags that led nowhere.

Julian Schneider's office was not in a glass tower. It was a fortress in the hills outside Zurich. Four checkpoints. Armed guards with earpieces.

We walked in.

I blinked. The reception area looked like a high-end strip club. Velvet furniture. Dim lighting. And the staff...

Every single employee was a Black woman. Stunning. Tall. Wearing skirts so short they were barely legal. I swear, I had seen handkerchiefs longer than some of those skirts.

"Julian has a... type," Dmitri whispered.

We walked past four checkpoints to the inner sanctum. The door opened.

Julian Schneider was sitting behind a massive desk made of black glass. He was a white man in his fifties, tan and fit.

He was also half-naked.

His shirt was on the floor. His pants were unbuttoned. Two women who were gorgeous, Black, and completely nude were sitting on his lap, giggling.

A pile of white powder sat on the desk like a paperweight.

"Is this a bad time?" Dmitri asked, not blinking an eye.

Julian snorted a line of coke. He threw his head back and sneezed.

"No, my friend!" he roared. "Never too busy for you!"

He slapped the women on their behinds. "Ladies, party is over. Business time."

They stood up, unbothered, and sauntered out. Julian watched them go with a look of pure worship.

"God took his time with Black women," he sighed, buttoning his pants. He didn't even try to hide his erection.

He looked at me. His eyes were sharp, intelligent, and completely soulless.

"So," he said. "The Nigerian Prince. I have heard about you."

I smiled. "Good things, I hope."

"Profitable things," Julian corrected.

Dmitri explained the situation. I had $2 million to wash. I wanted to keep some in crypto, but I needed a chunk of it legitimate. Clean. Spendable.

"My fee is twenty-five percent," Julian said.

I did the math. $500,000.

"No," I said instantly. "Ten percent."

Julian laughed. A loud, barking sound. "Dmitri, tell your friend I don't haggle. This is Switzerland, not a bazaar."

"I am sorry, Julian," Dmitri said smoothly. "But he is new. He is learning."

"Twenty percent," Julian countered. "Final offer."

"Fifteen," I said. "Or we walk."

Julian stared at me. The room went quiet. I held his gaze. I had negotiated with Amir for watches. I could negotiate with a coke-head lawyer.

"Fifteen," Julian muttered. "Fine. But only because Dmitri is family."

He pressed a button on his desk. A screen descended from the ceiling.

"We cannot just invest," Julian explained. "The IRS asks questions. 'Where did Josh get a million dollars?' We need a source."

He typed on his keyboard.

"Gambling," Julian said. "You are a lucky man, Josh. You went to a casino in downtown LA. You played high-stakes poker. You won big."

"I don't play poker," I said.

"You do now," Julian grinned. "I know a manager. He owes me. He will create the records. Receipts. Cash-out slips. Tax forms. It will be bulletproof."

"And then?"

"Then we invest," Julian said. "Shell companies. Boring businesses. A nail salon. A taxi service. A spa."

"Why those?"

"Because they are cash businesses," Julian said. "Hard to track inventory. Who knows how many nails you painted today? Five? Fifty? We cook the books. On paper, your salon is the busiest place in LA. In reality? Maybe five customers a week."

"And the money?"

"The money comes back to you as 'profit'," Julian said. "Taxed. Clean. Legal."

It was brilliant. It was simple.

We set it up.

Within three weeks, I was the proud owner of a nail salon called *Polished Princess*, a taxi fleet with two cars, and a spa called *Royal Serenity*.

Julian handled the details. No CCTV cameras. We paid actors to walk into the salon and sit for hours, just in case the FBI was watching from a van down the street.

It worked. The IRS never looked twice. I paid my taxes on my "gambling winnings" and my "business profits," and I slept like a baby.

One night, I looked out the window into the dark sky outside.

My life was a movie. I was the poor boy from Ado-Ekiti who beat the system. I had millions in the bank. I had a Ferrari. I had a lawyer who snorted coke off models.

Just like Jordan Belfort, I used my intelligence to rise above poverty.

I thought about my parents. My father earned forty-eight dollars a month. forty-eight dollars! I spent more than that on my Balmain socks.

I wanted to tell them. I wanted to scream it. I am rich! We made it! But I couldn't. Silence was the price of safety.

I settled into my new routine. I was a businessman now. A "legitimate" one.

But the emptiness was still there. Jada was gone. David hated me. Marie was a paid friend.

Dmitri was always there for me. However, we were so different. I wanted to be rich while Dmitri wished to be wealthy. I just wanted to have money to live a good life, while Dmitri wanted to have sustainable wealth that could be passed down to his children.

To me, wearing limited-edition wristwatches was proof that I was rich, but to Dmitri, owning companies and investing in real estate were all he wanted.

CHAPTER NINETEEN

Two weeks before Christmas, my inbox chimed.

From: Office of the Dean of Student Affairs

Subject: Urgent Meeting - Academic Standing

I stared at the screen. The Dean of Student Affairs was a woman named Dr. Evelyn Vance.

She was known for two things: her impeccably tailored suits and her ruthless efficiency. She didn't invite students for tea. She invited them for executions.

I went the next day. Her secretary, a severe woman with gray hair, made me wait for twenty minutes. It was a power move.

I sat there, drumming my fingers on my knee, checking the time on my custom-made Vacheron Constantin wristwatch.

Finally, the door opened.

"The Dean will see you now."

I walked in. Dr. Vance was sitting behind a desk that looked like it was carved from a single piece of oak. She didn't look up immediately. She let me stand there, soaking in the silence.

"Good morning, Mr. Bal... Bal..." She stumbled over my name.

"Josh," I said sharply. "You can call me Josh."

I was sick of people butchering my name. Balogun meant Warlord. It demanded respect. But here, it was just a collection of syllables they couldn't be bothered to learn.

"Right," she said, adjusting her glasses. She looked up. Her eyes widened.

I was wearing a long Saint Laurent wool coat that cost $5,500. Louis Vuitton pants. My loafers were Christian Louboutin. My wristwatch was custom-made by Vacheron Constantin. And around my neck hung a diamond chain from Eliantte worth $85,000.

She stared. She looked at the file on her desk: Joshua Balogun, Financial Aid Recipient. Then she looked back at me. The math didn't add up.

"I called you here concerning your grades, Josh," she said, forcing her eyes away from the diamonds.

She slid a transcript across the desk. It was a sea of red ink. D's. F's. Incompletes.

I looked at it without emotion. It wasn't surprising. I had spent the semester in Paris, Cologne, Zurich, and the back rooms of exclusive nightclubs. I had spent my time laundering money, not studying macroeconomics.

Why would I care about a lecture on wealth accumulation when I was accumulating more wealth in a week than my professor made in a decade?

"I am sorry," I said, putting on my best contrite face.

"As a scholarship student," she said sternly, "your GPA must be 3.5 or above. You are currently at a 2.1. If this continues, we will revoke your scholarship."

I almost laughed. I could pay the tuition ten times over with the cash in my safe. I didn't need their charity anymore.

But I needed the cover. If I lost the scholarship, questions would be asked. How is he paying? Where is the money coming from?

I needed to play the game.

"Things here are different," I said, making my voice small. "The practical approach... it is hard for me. In Nigeria, we learn theory. And the environment... it is overwhelming."

Dr. Vance softened slightly. "It is an adjustment, I understand."

"And attendance," she noted, tapping the paper. "You have missed sixty percent of your classes."

Time for the ace in the hole.

I looked down at my expensive sneakers. "It is hard being poor and Black here, Dean Vance," I whispered. "The students... they look down on me. I get comments. I get stares. I skipped class because I was tired of being treated like I didn't belong."

It was a lie, of course. The students loved me now. I was the Nigerian Prince. But Dr. Vance didn't know that. She saw a vulnerable scholarship boy.

She shifted uncomfortably. White guilt was a powerful currency in academia.

"I am so sorry to hear that," she said. "We have zero tolerance for bullying."

"I know," I said. "I just... I felt alone."

"You can see a counselor," she offered. "We don't want... well, you know about the suicides. We want you to succeed, Josh."

"I will do better," I promised. "No more skipping."

She nodded. She even offered me coffee. We chatted for ten minutes about "cultural integration." I walked out of her office with my scholarship intact and a free latte.

I checked my watch. *Financial Decision-Making* was starting in ten minutes.

I walked into the lecture hall. I didn't head for the back row. I walked straight to the front.

Greg, the son of a hedge fund manager, waved at me. "Josh! Over here!"

I sat down next to him. "Hey, man."

"Tonight," Greg whispered. "Club Warwick. BBC meeting. Be there."

"I'm in," I said.

I sat through the lecture, taking notes on a notepad that cost fifty dollars. I was bored out of my mind, but I had made a promise to the Dean. And more importantly, I needed to keep my cover.

That night at Warwick, the bass was thumping so hard I could feel it in my teeth. We had the best table. Bottles of Ace of Spades with sparklers were arriving every ten minutes.

"Christmas break!" Mark shouted over the music. "What is the plan?"

"Paris," Viktor suggested. "I know a place."

"Paris it is," Mark agreed. "No parents. No rules."

Viktor pulled out his phone. Right there in the club, he booked a penthouse rental. Five bedrooms. Avenue Montaigne. $16,000 a week.

"Two weeks," Viktor said, hitting confirm. "Done."

"I got food and drinks," Greg volunteered. "Let's dent my dad's card."

I looked around the circle. Everyone was contributing. I couldn't be the freeloader. I was the Nigerian Prince. I had a reputation to uphold.

"I got the flight," I said loudly.

The table went quiet.

"For ten people?" Mark asked. "That is a big plane, Josh."

"Ultra Long Range," I said, pulling out my phone. "Gulfstream G650. Non-stop LA to Paris."

I logged into PrivateFly. I found the jet. $252,790. I hit *Pay*.

I showed the screen to Mark.

"Holy shit!" Mark yelled. He grabbed my shoulder. "King Josh! That is a quarter million dollars!"

The group erupted. They toasted me. They posted it on Instagram. *Nigerian Prince drops 250k on the PJ. Legends only.*

I smiled and drank my champagne.

$250,000. That was roughly three years of income for the average American household. That was more than my father would ever earn in his lifetime, and I had spent it in ten seconds to impress a group of boys I didn't even like.

I felt a flash of vertigo. I remembered the hunger. I remembered my siblings dying because we couldn't afford to pay their medical bills.

Now I was burning money like it was paper.

Two days before the trip, I needed cash. Not digital numbers. Cold, hard cash. I contacted Mr. X.

Mr. X was Wang's contact. A ghost in the machine. Mr. X turned crypto into paper without questions.

I sent a message on the encrypted app. *Need 100k. Detroit pickup.*

Transfer received, Mr. X replied. *Location sent.*

I flew to Detroit the next morning. Not on a private jet this time, but first class. I landed and rented a car. The location was a cemetery on the outskirts of the city. St. Mary's.

I walked through the rows of headstones. It was gray and cold. I found the grave. Mary Simpson. Beloved Daughter. 1998-2014.

I knelt down. I felt under the loose sod behind the headstone. My fingers brushed a heavy, waterproof bag. I pulled it out.

$100,000.

I checked the contents. Crisp, new bills. I walked back to the car. I drove to the old neighborhood.

The houses were smaller than I remembered. The paint was peeling. The porches sagged. I pulled up to Jada's house.

It looked the same. The same cracked driveway. The same wind chimes on the porch. I took a pen and a piece of paper from the glovebox.

Use this money to start a business, Jada. Thank you for everything. -J

I put the note in the bag. I got out. I walked up to the door. My heart was pounding. I didn't want to see her. I couldn't handle the look in her eyes again.

I put the bag on the mat. I rang the doorbell. I ran back to the car. I slumped down in the seat, watching the mirror.

Thirty seconds later, the door opened. It was Jada's little brother, Malik. He looked bored. He looked down and froze.

He bent down and opened the bag. His eyes popped. He screamed something into the house.

A moment later, Jada's mom came out. Then Jada. She was wearing sweatpants and a t-shirt. She looked tired. Malik showed them the money. Her mom started screaming, dancing, praising Jesus.

Jada didn't dance. She reached into the bag. She pulled out the note. She read it. She looked up. She looked at the street.

Our eyes met in the rearview mirror.

I zoomed off.

CHAPTER TWENTY

Our trip to Paris changed. Viktor, being Viktor, insisted on chartering a second jet for his entourage of sycophants, and hangers-on. I didn't mind.

I had a feeling that he did it because he felt hurt that I booked the group's private and wanted to prove that he could do it too. It didn't matter to me. It simply meant less of his voice in my ear for twelve hours.

We touched down at Le Bourget. The sky was a pale, watery gray. Four Rolls-Royce Wraiths were waiting on the tarmac, their engines idling silently. We were whisked away to the penthouse Viktor booked.

Paris was exactly as they say it is. It is a city designed for romance, for excess, for dreams. But for the first two days, it was just a backdrop for Viktor's debauchery.

On the second night, we were in the living room, playing poker, drinking vintage wine that Greg had ordered on his father's tab.

"Let's hit Pigalle," Greg said, tossing a chip onto the pile.

Dmitri frowned. "Pigalle?"

"Red light district," Greg grinned. "The Moulin Rouge. But better. The girls there... they do things that are illegal in our country."

Viktor stood up immediately, knocking his chair over. "What are we waiting for?"

The room went quiet. Everyone looked at Melina. She was sitting on the sofa, sipping champagne. Her face was perfectly composed, but her knuckles were white around the glass.

Cheating was one thing. Everyone knew Viktor cheated. But announcing it in front of her? That was cruelty.

Melina smiled. It was a tight, brittle smile. "Go have fun, boys."

"See?" Viktor crowed, grabbing his jacket. "She gets it. Come on. Melina can stay here and gossip with the girls."

"I think I'll pass," I said.

Viktor stopped. He looked at me with disdain. "Suit yourself, virgin boy. More for us."

They left. The door slammed shut, leaving a ringing silence in its wake.

The other girls awkwardly excused themselves to go shopping or sleeping. Soon, it was just me and Melina.

I stood up. "I'm going to my room."

"Wait," she said.

I stopped.

She put her glass down. "Why did you stay?"

"Because I don't pay for sex," I lied. Not technically a lie because I paid Marie $2,000 per night to listen to me rant about my lonely life. The sex was always a bonus. "And because I don't like watching him hurt you."

She flinched. "He doesn't hurt me."

"He humiliates you," I said. "In Yoruba, we say *eni to ba lori o kin ni fila*. The person with the head doesn't have the cap. It means valuable things often belong to people who don't appreciate them. Viktor has you, and he treats you like an accessory."

She looked away. "It is complicated."

"It doesn't look complicated," I said. "It looks painful."

I walked out. I went to my room and poured a glass of Hennessy. I stood by the window, looking at the lights of the city.

Ten minutes later, there was a knock on my door. It was Melina.

"Can I come in?"

"Sure."

She walked in. She sat on the edge of the bed. She looked small.

"Why are you with him?" I asked, cutting straight to the bone.

"You have money. You have beauty. Why stay with a bastard who cheats on you in public?"

Her eyes filled with tears. "He loves me. In his own way."

"Bullshit," I said. "That isn't love. That is ownership."

"We are engaged," she whispered.

I froze. "Engaged?"

She held up her hand. I had always noticed the ring, a massive diamond, but I assumed it was just fashion. "Since we were seven," she said. "It was an arrangement. My father's winery was going bankrupt. Viktor's father bailed him out. The price was a merger. Me and Viktor. Our child will inherit the company."

I stared at her. "You are being sold? Like a piece of land?"

"It saved the company," she said defensively. "The winery is worth a billion dollars now. If I leave him, the contract voids. My father loses everything."

I threw my glass against the wall. It shattered. Melina screamed.

"Your father's winery?" I shouted. "Your mother has a fashion empire worth half a billion! You wouldn't starve! There are families in Africa living on less than $50 a month, and you are throwing your life away for a vineyard?"

"He worked hard for it," she said weakly.

"Your happiness is worth more than grapes!" I yelled.

She looked down at her hands. "It is different here, Josh. In our world, duty comes first. We marry for alliances. Love is... secondary."

"That is stupid," I said. "You deserve better."

She looked up at me. Her eyes were searching mine. "And you?" she asked. "Are you engaged?"

"No," I said.

"Then show me," she whispered.

"Show me what it is supposed to be like."

She stood up. She walked over to me. She kissed me. It wasn't tentative. It was desperate. I froze, but not too long.

I made love to Melina. I took my time to please her. I worshipped her love spot with my tongue. I made her scream multiple times.

I told her to sit on my face and made her gush out her love juices five times before I entered her from behind. She gasped. She moaned. She cried. She screamed. She spoke in tongues.

Afterward, she lay in my arms, tracing the line of my jaw. "*Merci*," she whispered.

"For what?"

"For seeing me."

The next day, we became conspirators.

"I am going shopping," Melina told Viktor over breakfast. He was hungover, wearing sunglasses indoors.

"Take my card," he grunted, waving a hand.

"I am going for a walk," I told Dmitri. "Clear my head."

Melina and I met at the Champ de Mars. We walked to the Eiffel Tower. We took pictures like tourists. In one photo, taken by a random stranger, we weren't looking at the camera. We were looking at each other. The hunger in our eyes was unmistakable.

We walked along the Seine. We found a street artist, a Black woman with a Togolese flag on her wrist.

"*Un portrait, s'il vous plaît*," I said.

She pointed to a single chair. "Sit."

I sat down. I pulled Melina onto my lap.

"*Regarde ton amant avec amour*," the woman said. Look at your lover with love.

I looked at Melina. I saw the trap she was in. I saw the fear. But I also saw the spark of rebellion.

The artist sketched quickly. When she handed us the paper, I gasped. She had captured it perfectly. She caught the way Melina leaned into me, seeking safety. The way I held her, possessive and protective.

"*She love you,*" the artist whispered to me as I paid her.

"I love her too," I said.

We walked to Cartier. Melina bought a bracelet for $13,000. I offered to pay.

"No," she said firmly. "I buy my own things."

I admired that.

Viktor sensed the change when we flew back to LA. He saw the way Melina didn't laugh at his cruel jokes anymore. He saw the way she looked out the window of the jet, a small, secret smile playing on her lips.

He knew he was losing her. But he didn't know he had already lost her to the Nigerian Prince sitting three seats away.

The trip cost me a fortune. But as I watched Melina sleeping on the flight home, I knew it was the best investment I had ever made.

For the first time since Jada and I broke up, my mind was at ease.

CHAPTER TWENTY-ONE

I placed the charcoal drawing of Melina and me in a gold frame. I hung it on the wall right next to my bed. It was the first thing I saw when I woke up and the last thing I saw before I closed my eyes.

I also changed my phone wallpaper to the picture we took in front of the Eiffel Tower. In that photo, the iron lattice of the tower rose behind us like a ladder to the heavens, but we were not looking at the architecture. We were looking at each other. The hunger in our eyes was unmistakable.

In Yoruba culture, we believe deeply in *ayanmo*. It means destiny. We say Ayanmo ko gbo ogun. Destiny cannot be changed by medicine or charms. Looking at that picture, I felt that Melina was my *ayanmo*. She was the destination my soul had been walking toward my entire life.

Two weeks after we returned from Paris, the quiet routine of our lives was shattered. Dmitri summoned us.

We gathered in the living room of the mansion. The air conditioner was humming its low, expensive tune. The leather couches were cool against my skin. It was our war room.

"I have a plan," Dmitri said. He was standing by the window, looking out at the swimming pool. He turned to face us. "It can fetch us a lot of cash before the end of this month. Are you guys in?"

I shifted uneasily in my seat. I still had millions stashed away, and Julian was still in the slow, careful process of laundering the money from the Morrison Fits job through my nail salons.

We had also made some bucks from other stunts we pulled. I had more money than I could spend. But greed is like drinking saltwater. The more you drink, the thirstier you get.

"I'm in," I said.

The others nodded. Harry was cleaning his fingernails with a switchblade.

Naomi was scrolling on her phone. But they all said yes. No one ever gets tired of making money.

Dmitri walked to the large television screen on the wall. He tapped his tablet, and an image appeared.

It was a middle-aged Arab man. He had a thick mustache and eyes that looked like they could calculate compound interest in a split second.

"This is Faizal Badawi," Dmitri announced.

"He is the CEO of Apex Green Energy. A top energy company here in America. If this deal goes well, we are looking at ten million dollars."

Wang whistled sharply. "Wow."

"As you all know," Dmitri said, a small smirk playing on his lips, "I am quite famous as a successful hotelier. I own several hotels across Europe. On paper, at least."

Harry rolled his eyes. "We know you are successful, Dmitri. We live in your thirteen-million-dollar house. How is this related to the task at hand?"

Dmitri ignored him. He was used to Harry's impatience.

"I reached out to Faizal," Dmitri continued.

"I told him about my plans to expand my hotel business to Africa. I told him I want to build the first fully green, self-sustaining luxury resort in Lagos. I told him I admire his company's work in renewable energy."

"And he bought it?" Alicia asked.

"Hook, line, and sinker," Dmitri said. "After weeks of emails and calls, Faizal agreed. He is flying to Los Angeles this weekend to meet me. He wants to discuss the project in person."

I frowned. This didn't make sense. Our entire operation was built on anonymity.

"I don't understand," I said. "How will we get money from him if he knows your identity? If the money disappears, the police will come straight to your front door."

Dmitri shook his head. "I am not planning to scam him during the meeting. The meeting is just the bait. The meeting sets the stage."

He paused for dramatic effect. "We are going to pull an *Evil Maid attack.*"

The room went silent.

I shook my head. "What does Evil Maid mean? Are we going to dress Naomi up in a French maid outfit?"

Naomi threw a cushion at me. "Dream on, Josh."

Wang spun his laptop around on the coffee table. His face was lit by the blue glow of the screen. "It means we gain physical access to his device while he is away from it," Wang said. His voice was calm, clinical.

"Or better yet, we trick him into plugging into our hardware. Specifically, using a Human Interface Device attack. The media calls it *advanced Juice Jacking.*"

"Juice jacking?" I asked. "I thought that was a myth. Like putting razors in Halloween candy. Doesn't the iPhone block USB data connections by default now?"

"Old school juice jacking is dead," Wang corrected. "You can't just modify a public USB port at the airport to steal data anymore. Modern phones and laptops go into 'Charge Only' mode unless you unlock them and tap 'Trust This Computer.' The security protocols are too strong."

He leaned forward. His eyes were shining with the excitement of a predator. "But there is one thing computers still trust blindly," Wang said.

"What?" I asked.

"Keyboards," Wang grinned.

He reached into his bag. He pulled out a device.

It was a USB-C docking station. It looked sleek and expensive. It was the kind of Belkin dock you find on the desk of every five-star hotel room in the world. It had ports for HDMI, USB, and ethernet.

"This looks like a standard Belkin dock," Wang said, tossing it gently in his hand. "But inside, I have soldered a wicked little microcontroller. An O.MG chip. To the computer, this isn't just a charger or an HDMI adapter. It identifies itself as a keyboard."

"I don't get it," I said.

"Computers trust keyboards," Dmitri explained. "They have to. If you plug in a mouse or a keyboard, the computer accepts the input without asking for permission. It assumes a human is attached to the other end."

Wang tossed the dock to me. I caught it. It felt heavy. Solid.

"Plug your phone into that," Wang ordered. "Let's pretend you are Faizal. You are in your hotel room. You need to charge your phone. Or maybe you want to connect your laptop to the hotel TV to practice your PowerPoint presentation."

I rolled my eyes. "Okay. Dazzle me."

I took the lightning cable from the table and plugged my iPhone into the dock. For a second, nothing happened. The battery icon turned green to show it was charging.

Then, my screen flickered. It happened so fast I almost missed it.

A browser window opened automatically. It navigated to a URL I didn't type. It downloaded a file. Then the window closed. It took less than two seconds.

"What the hell?" I whispered, staring at my phone.

"The dock just injected keystrokes at superhuman speed," Wang said, looking pleased with himself. "It typed in a command script faster than any human fingers could move. If that was a laptop, it would have opened the terminal, disabled Windows Defender, and downloaded my Remote Access Trojan before Faizal even realized his battery was charging."

"And once the RAT is installed?" I asked, feeling a cold chill run down my spine.

"Then I own the device," Wang said. "I don't need the dock anymore. The malware establishes a reverse shell back to my server. I can see his emails. I can download his files. I can turn on his webcam. I can log every password he types."

I unplugged my phone hurriedly. It felt like holding a grenade. "Is it off now? Did you hack me?"

Wang laughed. It was a dry, rusty sound. "The injection is done, Josh. The malware is already running in the background. Even if you fly to Australia, as long as that phone has an internet connection, I am inside."

Dmitri walked over and took the dock from my hand. He held it up like a trophy.

"This is the plan," Dmitri said. "I booked the hotel suite where Faizal Badawi will stay. The Ritz-Carlton. Since the room is in my name, I have the keycards."

He placed the dock on the table.

"We go in before he arrives," Dmitri continued.

"We swap out the hotel's standard docking station and HDMI cables with Wang's modified hardware. Faizal is a businessman. He will need to charge his laptop. He will need to connect to the TV to practice his presentation. The moment he plugs in, the chip executes the payload."

"Fuck," Alicia breathed. She looked at Dmitri with a mixture of fear and adoration. "You are such an evil genius, Dmitri."

We spent the next hour assigning roles. It was like planning a military operation.

Alicia would accompany Dmitri to pick Faizal up at the airport. She was the distraction. Her job was to be charming, beautiful, and engaging, keeping Faizal's eyes off his phone until he was safely in the trap.

Harry's role was surveillance. Once Wang established the connection, Harry would monitor the inbox.

He would sit for hours, watching the emails flow, waiting for the perfect moment to inject a fraudulent invoice.

Naomi and Wang would handle the exfiltration. They would download the proprietary data and record the passwords.

And then there was me.

"Josh," Dmitri said, turning to me. "We need a bucket."

"A bucket?"

"A place to catch the rain," Dmitri said. "We are going to divert a ten-million-dollar payment. We need a bank account. And it needs to be bulletproof."

My talent wasn't coding. I couldn't write a script to save my life. I wasn't like Wang.

My talent was money laundering. I was the god of the wash. I understood the flow of money. I understood how to make dirty cash look clean. I knew how to layer transactions so deep that even the IRS got a headache trying to follow them.

"I need an account," Dmitri said.

"But not just any account. It has to be in Faizal Badawi's name."

I raised an eyebrow. "You want me to open an account in the victim's name? Without the victim being there?"

"Exactly," Dmitri said. "If the finance department at Apex Green Energy sees a request to change the receiving account, they will check the name. If the account name matches the vendor or the CEO, they push the button. If it is some random shell company, they pause."

Creating a bank account where illegal money would be deposited was hard enough. Creating the account in the victim's name was almost impossible.

It required passing Know Your Customer protocols. It required passports. It required utility bills.

But I was a Yoruba man. In my culture, we have a saying. *Ona kan o w'oja*. There is not only one road to the market. If the main road is blocked, you find a bush path.

If I could defeat my family's generational poverty, there was no giant too tall for me to defeat. "I can do it," I said.

One of the main reasons BEC scammers get caught is the bank account. They use a mule account. Or they use a hacked account that gets flagged. To escape scot-free after a successful BEC fraud, you need a ghost account. An account that exists only to catch the money and then vanish.

The perfect place to set up such a bank account was in the Cayman Islands. And I knew the right person to contact.

I pulled out my burner phone. I scrolled through the contacts until I found the number. Julian Schneider.

Julian was our Swiss lawyer. The man who sniffed cocaine off models' backs in his office. He was expensive. He was dangerous. But he knew people who were willing to bend the law until it snapped.

CHAPTER TWENTY-TWO

The meeting took place on a Saturday afternoon. The sky over Los Angeles was a blinding, smoggy blue. Dmitri and Alicia drove the Rolls-Royce to LAX, playing the part of the perfect, wealthy couple.

Faizal Badawi landed in Emirates First Class. He looked every inch the CEO. The man was impeccably groomed, wearing a suit that cost more than a Honda Civic. Dmitri shook his hand; Alicia smiled her thousand-watt smile, and they drove him to the Ritz-Carlton.

We were already in position.

An hour earlier, Wang and I had slipped into the suite dressed as maintenance staff. Wang swapped the standard Belkin dock on the mahogany desk with his modified version. It looked identical. Same brushed aluminum finish. Same black cables. But inside, the O.MG Elite implant was waiting like a spider in a web.

We watched the feed from the server room back at the mansion. It was like watching a movie, but the stakes were ten million dollars.

Faizal walked into the suite. He tossed his jacket on the bed. "Nice view," he muttered, glancing at the window. He walked to the desk. He pulled his laptop out of his bag.

"Do it," Harry whispered, staring at the screen. "Plug it in."

Faizal hesitated. He checked his phone. Then, he plugged the USB-C cable into his laptop.

Click. The trap sprang.

On the screen, nothing happened. But in the background, the implant was screaming.

It identified itself as a keyboard. It injected a keystroke payload at lightning speed, around three hundred words per minute. It bypassed the "Trust This Computer" prompt because computers trust keyboards implicitly.

In less than two seconds, it opened a hidden terminal, disabled Windows Defender, and downloaded Wang's Remote Access Trojan.

"We are in," Wang said, leaning back in his chair. "I own his machine."

We watched as Faizal typed an email to his assistant. Wang's keylogger captured every stroke. We got his passwords for his bank, his cloud storage, his corporate VPN. We got everything.

Harry spent the next few hours studying Faizal's emails. He built a linguistic profile.

"He is concise," Harry noted. "He doesn't use pleasantries. He signs off with 'Regards, FB.' Not Faizal. Just FB."

While they handled the tech, I had to handle the money.

This was the choke point. Most BEC scams fail because the receiving bank account looks suspicious. A CEO sending ten million to "Shell Corp LLC" in Cyprus raises flags. But a CEO sending money to himself? That is just asset management.

Julian Schneider set me up with Robert Bodden at Alexandria Bancorp in the Cayman Islands.

Robert was a professional. He didn't ask why a Nigerian student in LA wanted to open an account for a Saudi energy CEO. He just asked for his cut.

"Ten percent," Robert said over an encrypted line.

"And I need documents. Passport. Utility bill. Proof of funds," he added.

"Done," I said.

I went to work. Faizal kept high-resolution scans of his documents in a folder labeled *Personal*. It was shockingly easy. I downloaded his Saudi passport and his driver's license.

But Robert needed more.

"He needs a liveness check," I told Wang. "A video selfie. Faizal holding his passport and blinking."

Wang didn't even look up from his screen. "We have hours of Zoom footage. I can deepfake it."

Wang pulled up a rendering tool. He mapped Faizal's face onto mine. I sat in front of the webcam, holding a blank piece of paper. On the screen, it looked exactly like Faizal Badawi holding his passport. I blinked. The avatar blinked. I turned my head. The avatar turned.

We passed the check in thirty seconds.

For proof of funds, I used Faizal's own bank statements—$24 million in Chase, $10 million in Wells Fargo.

For the utility bill, I used his Verizon invoice. But the physical address was tricky. You can't just make up an address for a bank account. They check databases. I didn't buy an apartment. It would leave a paper trail. I created a ghost.

I photoshopped a lease agreement for a penthouse in Tribeca. I forged a Con Edison electric bill. Then I routed the mail from that address to a virtual office service that scanned incoming letters and emailed them to me.

To the bank, Faizal had a luxury apartment in New York. To the world, the apartment didn't exist.

Two days later, the account was open. We were ready.

The strike happened when Dmitri and Faizal flew to Africa to inspect potential hotel sites. They were in the air, somewhere over the Atlantic, unreachable.

Just in case Faizal bought Wi-Fi on the plane, Harry set up an **Inbox Rule** on his email server. Any email containing the words "CFO," "Wire," or "Transfer" was automatically moved to a hidden folder. The notifications would never hit his phone.

Harry logged into Faizal's Outlook using the stolen session cookies. He didn't even need the password.

He drafted the email.

To: **CFO** From: **Faizal Badawi** Subject: **Acquisition Opportunity - Confidential**

Hamid,

I am currently en route to Lagos. An opportunity has come up to acquire a boutique hotel chain quietly. I need you to wire $10M to my private holding account in Cayman immediately to secure the deal. We will formalize the paperwork upon my return.

Details attached.

Regards, FB

It was perfect. Faizal often moved money around for deals. His CFO was used to it. And the money was going to an account in Faizal's own name. Why would he suspect fraud?

Harry hit send. We waited.

Three hours later, the notification pinged on my phone.

Incoming Wire: $10,000,000.00.

"Boom," I whispered.

We didn't celebrate immediately. We had to clean the money.

Robert took his million. He moved the remaining nine million through a labyrinth of shell accounts in Panama, Belize, and Seychelles. Finally, it hit Mr. X.

Mr. X took twenty percent. He converted the rest into Bitcoin using an OTC trading desk to avoid crashing the price.

Then Wang split it up.

My phone buzzed again.

Wallet Updated: + 65 BTC.

$1.2 million.

We partied hard that night. Harry was on a bender, mixing Xanax and cocaine until his eyes rolled back in his head. Alicia watched him with a mixture of love and terror.

Naomi and Wang smoked a joint on the balcony, looking out at the city we were slowly conquering.

I called Marie. She came over to the hotel, never the mansion, and we spent the night lost in expensive sheets and physical distraction.

Lying there, staring at the ceiling, I made a decision. I was done with school.

Why bother? Why study for four years to get a job paying twenty dollars an hour when I could make a million in a week?

Education was for people who played by the rules. I had found a cheat code.

Money is a strange drug. It solves every problem you have, only to create new ones you never imagined. It is freedom, but it is also a cage.

I thought about Bill Gates. In his sixties, worth billions. Still working. Still chasing. Why? Because the hunger never stops.

I looked at my bank account balance. I looked at the Ferrari key on the nightstand. Then I gave poverty my middle finger.

CHAPTER TWENTY-THREE

I was not just rich anymore. I was wealthy. I had $1.2 million from the Faizal Badawi job, plus the leftovers from my previous scams. But money, like water, evaporates when you leave it out in the sun.

The problem with having money is that you run out of things to want. When I was poor, I wanted everything. New shoes. A full fridge. A car that started. Now, I had a closet full of Christian Louboutin and Giuseppe Zanotti shoes, a pantry stocked by a personal shopper, and a Ferrari. The hunger was gone, replaced by a dull, persistent boredom.

Everyone on campus knew me now. The Nigerian Prince.

"Josh! Over here!"

"Come sit with us, Josh!"

I walked through the quad like a celebrity. People who wouldn't have spat on me before were now desperate for my attention. It was intoxicating, and it was hollow.

My relationship with Melina deepened. We weren't "official" because Viktor's ring was still on her finger, but we were everything else. We went on dates to Nobu and Spago. She came over to the mansion, much to Naomi's irritation.

Naomi would sit by the pool, watching us with narrow eyes, smoking cigarettes like she was trying to burn a hole in the air. Whenever Melina wasn't around, I would sleep with Naomi. She always wanted more. She wanted us to be exclusive and official even though she knew I loved Melina.

But while my life was ascending, Harry's was crashing. Harry's addiction spiraled. Before, he got high to celebrate. Now, he got high to survive. He started his day with crushed OxyContin to numb the pain, then snorted cocaine to wake up. A "rich kid speedball."

He looked terrible. His skin was gray and papery.

His eyes were sunk deep into his skull. He was twenty-one, but he looked forty. Alicia cried every time she looked at him. She paid for rehab clinics in Malibu, in Switzerland, in Arizona. Harry would go, stay for three days, and walk out. He didn't want to be saved.

"Why?" I asked Dmitri one night as we watched Harry nodding off at the dinner table. "He has everything. Money. Alicia. Why kill himself?"

"His mother," Dmitri said quietly. "She died when he was sixteen. Overdose. He found her. Drugs are the only way he can stop seeing her face."

Dmitri was thriving. He was on the cover of Forbes, the "Russian Hotel King." He was building a resort in the Caribbean with laundered money. Naomi launched a lingerie line. Wang... Wang was a ghost. He made phone calls in Mandarin at 3 AM. He was moving money in ways even I didn't understand.

And Alicia? She bought an island in Greece. She bought restaurants. She was building an empire to distract herself from the fact that the love of her life was dying in front of her eyes.

Me? I was an idiot. I didn't invest. I spent. I bought Richard Mille watches. I made Eliantte's store my second home. New iced-out jewelries every week. VVS only.

I bought limited edition sneakers. I threw parties. I was chasing likes on Instagram. My follower count hit 300,000.

But money changes you. It strips away your empathy. I stopped going to church. I stopped thinking about Denzel Warner sitting in a jail cell. I stopped caring about the scholarship kids in the back row.

I saw David Lewinson one day in the library. He looked tired. He looked poor.

"Josh," he said, tentative.

I looked through him like he was glass. I kept walking. He was invisible to me the way I was invisible to the Elites in the past.

I slept with expensive escorts. OnlyFans models. I tried designer drugs at parties in the Hills. I did everything I could to fit into a world that would never truly accept me.

One night, at a BBC party in a mansion in Bel Air, Martin Berg, son of a German industrialist, was showing a porn video on the big screen.

"She is hot," Alec laughed. "I would pay fifty grand just to touch her."

I didn't say anything. The next day, I called Julian Schneider.

"Find her," I said. "The actress."

Julian found her. She wanted $100,000. I paid it. I filmed us having sex. I sent the video to the BBC group chat.

Legend, they typed. *King*.

I look back now, and I hate that boy. There are children starving in Ekiti State. There are kids like my brother dying of tuberculosis.

And I spent $50,000 on a sex tape to impress a bunch of trust fund babies.

My arrogance peaked at a club called *Blue and Black*. I was at the gym when the text came through. VIP party. Blue and Black. Now.

I didn't go home to change. I went straight there in my gym clothes. Nike sneakers, Puma sweatpants. I took an Uber.

I walked up to the velvet rope. Two bouncers blocked my path. They looked me up and down with sneers.

"Sorry, sir," the shorter one said. "Private event."

"I know," I said, wiping sweat from my forehead. "My friends are inside. It's our party. "

"People like you aren't allowed in here," he said firmly.

People like me. *Black. Sweaty. Not arriving in a G-Wagon.*

I nodded slowly. I pulled out my phone.

"Julian," I said when he answered.

"Yeah?" Julian sounded groggy. It was late in Zurich.

"I need you to buy a club," I said. "Blue and Black. Beverly Hills."

"What?" Julian asked. "Now?"

"Now," I said. "Find the owner. Buy it. In my name."

"I am on it," Julian said. He didn't argue. He knew when I was in a mood.

I stood there, staring at the bouncers. They smirked at each other. They thought I was crazy.

Ten minutes later, Julian called back. "Owner is an NBA player," Julian said. "He says it's not for sale. But everyone has a price. It is valued at $2 million. Offer three, he signs."

"Offer $3 million," I said loud enough for the bouncers to hear. "I want immediate operational control. Tonight."

"Three million?" Julian gasped. "Josh, that is a bad investment..."

"Do it," I snapped.

Twenty minutes later, a middle-aged white man came running out of the club. He looked panicked. He looked around the entrance.

He walked right past me. He went to a white kid in a suit. "Excuse me, sir," he said. "Are you Mr. Josh Bal...?"

"No," the kid said.

The manager looked confused. He turned. He saw me. The Black kid in sweatpants.

"Excuse me?" I said.

He walked over, skeptical. "Can I help you?"

I showed him my ID. Joshua Balogun.

His face went white. "I... I am so sorry, sir. I didn't know." He bowed. Actually bowed.

"Is this guy bothering you?" the short bouncer asked, stepping forward. He balled his fists.

"Shut up!" the manager hissed. "This is the new owner. He owns the club."

The bouncers froze. Their jaws dropped.

"We are sorry, sir," they stammered.

"It is okay," I smiled. "What are your names?"

"Lucien," the short one said.

"Martin," the other said.

"Nice to meet you," I said. "You are both fired."

"What?" the manager gasped. "Sir, we can't just…"

I stared at him. "Do you want to be fired too?"

"No, sir."

"Then get them out of my sight."

I walked into the club. I owned it. I made Marie the manager a week later. We used it to wash cash. It was the ultimate power move.

But power is fragile.

February 14th. Valentine's Day. Melina and I flew to London. Viktor thought she was shopping in Milan. He was an idiot.

We stayed at *The Connaught*. We ate at *The Araki*. We walked through Hyde Park in the rain.

That night, in the back of an Uber, we couldn't keep our hands off each other. We stumbled into the hotel room, stripping off clothes, drunk on expensive wine and each other.

My phone rang. I ignored it. It rang again. And again.

"Answer it," Melina whispered, kissing my neck.

I grabbed the phone. "What?" I barked. Who the hell was ruining my orgasm?

"Harry is dead," Dmitri said.

The world stopped.

"What?" I whispered.

My lust evaporated, replaced by a cold, hollow pit in my stomach.

"Overdose," Dmitri said. His voice was flat, empty. "Wang found him. It was too late."

I dropped the phone. It shattered on the floor.

Melina sat up. "Josh? What is it?"

"Harry," I said. "He is dead."

She covered her mouth. "No."

We held each other that night, but we didn't sleep. Harry was twenty-one. He was rich. He had everything. And he died alone in a bathroom with a needle in his arm.

We flew back for the funeral. It was a grim affair. The BBC boys were there, looking uncomfortable in black suits. Alicia was a wreck. She looked like a ghost.

Then, Harry's father arrived. He was a tall man with a military bearing, stone-faced.

Alicia saw him. She screamed. She flew at him, claws out. She scratched his face. She pummeled his chest.

"You killed him!" she shrieked. "You killed him! Where were you?"

Dmitri grabbed her, pulling her back.

"He needed you!" she yelled, sobbing. "He lost his mother! He needed a father! You cut him off! You let him die!"

Harry's father stood there, bleeding from a scratch on his cheek. He didn't fight back. He walked to the casket. He looked at the photo of Harry smiling.

"My beautiful boy," he whispered. "I am sorry."

I watched him. I felt a deep, aching sadness.

I walked up to him. "I am sorry for your loss, sir." I sympathized with him because I knew how it felt to lose a relative. We lost a friend, but the poor man lost his only son. His pain was unimaginable.

I had lost four young people I cared about. First, I lost two of my siblings. Then Tunde-Sean died from a gunshot wound during a shootout, and Harry died of a drug overdose. I wondered who was next.

CHAPTER TWENTY-FOUR

The next few weeks at the mansion were quiet, but it was the kind of quiet you feel before a tornado touches down. The air was heavy.

Alicia was gone. After Harry's funeral, she tried to swallow a bottle of sleeping pills. Her stepfather, Liam, found her and shipped her off to a psychiatric facility in Switzerland. Without her, the house felt empty.

Wang was disappearing too, but in a different way. He spent his days in a haze of marijuana smoke, staring at the wall. He and Harry had a bond none of us understood. Now that Harry was gone, Wang seemed untethered.

Naomi cried herself to sleep. I could hear her through the thin walls. And me? I relied on Marie. I paid her to hold me while I shook with anxiety.

Only Dmitri seemed unaffected. "We need one last hit," Dmitri announced one evening. "A retirement fund."

"We have millions," I said, exhausted. "Isn't it enough?"

"It is never enough," Dmitri said.

This next target turned out to be our last. It wasn't a clever hack or a corporate takedown. **It was a sin.**

Dmitri summoned us to the living room. Sitting there was a man I had never seen before. He was older, Black, wearing a suit that had seen better days.

"This is Mr. Kofi," Dmitri said. "A contact from Accra."

Mr. Kofi stood up. "Hello," he said. His accent was thick, unmistakably Ghanaian.

I narrowed my eyes. "Who is this? The rule is no outsiders."

I balled my hands into fists. One of the essential rules of our team was that we did not bring strangers into our inner cycle. We tried to keep our business among ourselves for safety purposes and to make more profits.

The problem with organized crime is that you must ensure that everyone is trustworthy.

A single snitch can lead to the downfall of an entire syndicate.

Another problem is also the issue of sharing profits. Organized crime syndicates often share their proceeds with everyone involved, depending on the role they play.

Our syndicate consisted of six people before Harry's death, and we split our profits evenly. Besides, the man looked like he was old enough to be our grandfather.

"Relax," Dmitri said in a casual tone. "This man is here to discuss an important transaction that will fetch us more money. Besides, you are both Africans. You should be nice to each other."

"Well, Nigerians and Ghanaians do not exactly like each other," I replied.

I was not lying when I told Dmitri that Nigerians and Ghanaians did not like each other.

In the mid-20th century, many illegal Ghanaian immigrants were living in Nigeria until the president of Nigeria in 1983, Shehu Shagari, ordered for mandatory deportation of Ghanaians in Nigeria.

Ever since then, there has been a slight tension between Ghanaians and Nigerians. One of the most popular phrases in Nigeria is *Ghana Must Go*.

Mr. Kofi rolled his eyes, as if my existence bored him. "The target is the TP Energy Foundation."

I knew the name. Taylor Peterson was a tycoon, a child of immigrants who made it big in energy. His foundation donated millions to Africa every year.

"This year," Kofi said, "they are releasing a Capital Development Grant. Ten million dollars. It is a single bulk transfer intended to build a hospital in Liberia."

"And?" I asked.

"My NGO applied," Kofi said smoothly.

"We were rejected. But I know the schedule. The transfer happens next Friday. I want you to divert that payment to me."

Wang looked up from his joint. "You want us to steal a hospital? From sick kids?"

"I want to redirect funds," Kofi corrected. "I take thirty percent. You take seventy."

"I am out," Wang said instantly.

Dmitri turned to him. "What?"

"Defrauding tax-evading billionaires is one thing," Wang said, standing up. "Stealing from a charity? That money is for medicine. For infrastructure. If we steal it, people actually die. Children. I am not doing it."

"Come on, Wang," Dmitri sneered. "Did Harry's death make you soft?"

"Harry's death was a warning from God!" Wang snapped. "We have enough money. Why cross this line?"

"Because it is ten million dollars," Dmitri said coldly. "If you don't want your share, fine. Go to your room and smoke. Josh, Naomi, and I will do this."

Wang shook his head. "If we succeed, what will we do with the money? We will probably buy expensive wristwatches or buy new cars while those poor kids slowly starve to death. God might kill us like Harry! This is a big sin."

"Your friend's death was not a warning from God. Harry only died because he was a fucking junkie. It has nothing to do with God."

Wang glared at us with pure disgust. He stormed off, slamming his door.

We turned back to the plan.

"The Foundation's database is a fortress," Dmitri said. "We can't brute force it. We need an inside man."

"Who?"

Dmitri pulled up a photo. "Annalise Peterson. Taylor's sister. The CFO. She approves the wire batches every Friday."

"She won't help us," I said.

"She doesn't have to know," Dmitri smiled. "We need someone to establish a sort of relationship with Annalise and find a way to install a hardware keylogger on her office computer," Dmitri said.

Everyone turned to me in unison with smiles on their faces.

"Why is everyone staring at me?" I asked, feeling uncomfortable. "It's creepy."

"I think you should do this," Naomi said.

"Why should I?"

Dmitri rolled his eyes. "Because you have a way with women. I mean, you're dating Melina and ten other girls. You're a true *Yoruba demon*. Even Casanova will be jealous of you."

"For your information, I don't have a girlfriend."

I had several hookers on my speed dial and had Marie and Melina whenever I needed someone to bare my soul to.

However, I was not in a defined relationship with any of them. Marie saw me as an exclusive client while Melina was still engaged to Viktor.

"We just need her credentials. Josh, you are up."

My role was Social Engineering. I needed to get close enough to Annalise to install a hardware keylogger.

I stalked her digital life. Instagram told me she ate lunch at The Maybourne every day at 2:00 PM.

I started showing up. After three days, I bumped into her. A spilled coffee. A charming apology. A conversation about my studies at Kingsley.

She bought it. She was lonely, overworked, and charmed by the polite Nigerian student.

A week later, she invited me to tour the Foundation's offices. The office was bustling. Photos of smiling African children lined the walls. Children with polio. Children with malnutrition.

I felt a pit in my stomach. Wang was right. This was evil. But the greed... the greed was louder than the guilt.

"Can I get you some water?" Annalise asked when we reached her office.

"Please," I said.

The moment she stepped out, I moved.

I didn't use a software virus. Too risky. I reached behind her desktop tower. I unplugged the USB keyboard and inserted a hardware keylogger, a tiny device the size of a thumb drive. It sat between the keyboard cable and the computer.

It recorded every keystroke to an internal memory chip. It was invisible to antivirus software because it operated on the physical layer.

I reconnected the keyboard. I sat back down. Annalise returned with the water. I drank it. I smiled. I left.

Two days later, I returned to "drop off a thank-you note." I distracted the receptionist, slipped into the empty office while Annalise was in a meeting, and retrieved the device.

We took it back to the mansion. Wang refused to help, so Dmitri decrypted the logs.

There it was. Her username. Her password. And the 2FA bypass code she had foolishly typed into a sticky note app on her desktop.

Friday came. The batch transfer day.

We waited until 1:00 AM. Dmitri logged into the Foundation's payment portal using Annalise's credentials via a residential proxy to mask our location.

We found the scheduled transaction: $10,000,000.00 to Liberia Health Initiative.

"Here is the smart part," Dmitri said. "We don't change the beneficiary's name. If we change the name, the bank's mismatch filter might catch it. We only change the Routing and Account Number."

He pasted in the details of the Cayman Islands account I had set up for the Faizal job.

He hit Save.

At 9:00 AM the next morning, the automated clearing house system ran the batch. It saw the approval from the CFO. It processed the wire.

By noon, ten million dollars was sitting in our Cayman account. We moved fast. We funneled it through a shell company in Hong Kong, bought fake machinery invoices to wash it, and finally converted it into Monero and Bitcoin.

Mr. Kofi got his thirty percent. I got my share, over two million dollars. I bought a Rolls-Royce Wraith to match Dmitri's. I bought a rose gold Rolex for Melina.

I was worse than the devil. We noticed Wang becoming more reclusive, but we ignored him. It proved to be our fatal mistake.

I should have noticed the black sedan parked down the street for three days. I ignored it. I thought the Hills were safe.

It happened on a Tuesday night.

Dmitri and I were in the living room, talking about our crypto balances. Mr. Kofi was asleep on the sofa, snoring softly. Naomi was in the shower.

BOOM.

The front door exploded inward. Glass shattered. Wood splintered.

"FBI! OPEN UP!"

"Wang! The Kill Switch!" Dmitri screamed.

Wang had a script set up on his main server. A Cryptographic Erasure command. It wouldn't explode the laptops, that is a movie myth. But it would **overwrite the LUKS encryption headers on every hard driv**e in the house. Without those headers, the data on the drives would become random, unreadable static. Even the NSA couldn't decrypt it.

Wang stood by the server rack in the corner. His hand hovered over the Enter key.

Dmitri ran toward him. "Hit it! Hit the button!"

Wang looked at Dmitri. Then he looked at the door where the agents were pouring in with assault rifles and tactical shields.

He looked at me. His eyes were sad.

He stepped away from the keyboard.

"No," Wang whispered.

"You traitor!" Dmitri lunged at him, tackling him to the floor.

It was too late.

"HANDS! LET ME SEE YOUR HANDS!"

Agents swarmed the room. They pulled Dmitri off Wang.

They pinned me to the carpet. The air smelled of cordite and sweat.

An agent in a windbreaker walked over to the computers. He didn't plug in a flash drive, that would ruin the chain of custody.

He pulled a Mouse Jiggler from his pocket, a small USB device that simulates mouse movement. He plugged it into Dmitri's open laptop to keep the screen from going to sleep and locking us out.

Then he shouted, "Tech team! Bag and tag!"

Specialists ran in carrying silver Faraday bags which were lined with metallic mesh that block all radio signals. They disconnected the power cords, slammed the laptops shut, and immediately sealed them inside the bags to block any remote-wipe signals from the cloud.

"Evidence secured," the agent said.

I looked at Mr. Kofi, who was crying on the floor. I looked at Dmitri, who was bleeding from the nose.

And I looked at Wang. He was sitting calmly against the wall, watching us. He hadn't run. He had stayed to make sure we got caught.

My life was over.

Part 2

The Wages of Sin

CHAPTER TWENTY-FIVE

The next few days were a blur of fluorescent lights, cold interrogation rooms, and the scratching of pens on plea agreements. Wang had given them everything. The logs. The emails. The crypto wallets. It was over before it started.

Because Wang had flipped, implicating not just us but Mr. X, Julian Schneider, and a network of fifty other money launderers, the US Attorney was feeling generous. Or maybe it was just because we were kids.

"You are lucky," my lawyer, a sharp-faced man named Mr. Klein, told me. "The guidelines for a fifty-million-dollar fraud usually start at fifteen years. But because you were a minor when the conspiracy began, and because Wang handed them the Cartel connection on a silver platter, they are offering a deal."

I took it. I gave up everything. The Ferrari. The watches. The millions in the Cayman account. Even the crypto wallet.

I was sentenced to eighteen months. Dmitri got five years, which was a miracle sentence, considering he was the mastermind, but he had given up the names of his Russian contacts. Naomi and Alicia got one year each.

During the sentencing, I looked back at the gallery. Aunt Moji was there. She wasn't crying. She just looked... tired. She looked at me like I was a stranger who had stolen the face of the nephew she loved.

I was sent to Taft Correctional Institution. It was a low-security facility, a "Club Fed" for white-collar criminals. It was ironic.

I had idolized Jordan Belfort, the Wolf of Wall Street. Now I was following in his footsteps, right down to the prison cell.

Dmitri was sent to a different facility. The Bureau of Prisons separates co-defendants to prevent collusion. I didn't see him again. I only heard rumors. Life inside was monotonous. It wasn't the violence of a maximum-security prison.

There were no shanks in the shower. But there was a quiet, suffocating despair.

I made a friend. Alejandro Rodiles. He was a former lawyer who had laundered money for the Sinaloa Cartel. He was old enough to be my father, with gray hair and sad eyes.

"Money is just water," Alejandro told me one day as we walked the track. "It flows where gravity takes it. We were just the plumbers."

Six months into my sentence, Mr. Klein came to visit. He looked pale.

"Wang is dead," he said.

I froze. "Dead? He is in Witness Protection. He is safe."

Klein shook his head. "It is unprecedented, Josh. The Marshals never lose a witness. But Wang... he must have broken protocol. Maybe he made a call. Maybe he logged into an old account."

"How?" I whispered.

"It was a message," Klein said, his voice dropping. "They found him in a safe house in Arizona. Dismembered. His head... it was on the kitchen table next to his mother's. His penis was stuffed inside his mouth. It was a Cartel hit. Professional. Brutal."

I felt sick. Wang, the genius. Wang, who loved his family so much he became a criminal to save them. He had saved himself by selling us out, only to be butchered like an animal.

"And Dmitri?" I asked.

"He heard," Klein said. "He attacked a guard in the cafeteria. Beat him half to death. They threw him in the SHU. He is probably heading to a Supermax now."

I went back to my cell. I lay on the bunk and stared at the concrete ceiling. Harry was dead. Wang was dead. Dmitri was buried in solitary.

We had flown too close to the sun, and now we were burning.

A week later, Klein returned. He slid a card across the table. It was a wedding invitation. Cream cardstock. Gold lettering. The Marriage of Melina Dervishi and Viktor Petrov.

"No," I whispered.

"She is moving on," Klein said gently. "It is what people do."

I ripped the card in half. Then I ripped it again. I wanted to scream. I wanted to break the glass partition.

But the worst was yet to come. Aunt Moji visited a month later. She sat down, and for the first time, I saw tears in her eyes. I thought she was sad to see me in prison, but I was wrong.

"Your parents," she choked out.

"What?" I asked. "Are they okay?"

"They are dead, Josh."

The world stopped spinning. The air left the room.

"How?"

"Your father... his hypertension came back. The stress of your arrest killed him. He died three days ago."

She took a breath. "And your mother... she found him. She couldn't take it. She took pills. Swallowed a bunch of them. She is gone."

I didn't scream. I didn't cry. I just fell. I fell into a darkness so deep I thought I would never hit the bottom.

I woke up in the prison infirmary, handcuffed to the bed. My parents were dead. I had killed them. Not with a gun, but with my greed. I had tried to save them with stolen money, and instead, I had bought their coffins.

I thought about the Bible verses my mother used to read to me. **For the wages of sin is death**. I had been paid in full.

I changed after that. I stopped talking. I spent my days in the library, reading everything I could find. Philosophy. Economics. History. I was looking for the answer to a question I couldn't even formulate.

I started praying again. Not for money. Not for freedom. For forgiveness.

Jada visited me near the end of my sentence. She came with Klein. She looked different. Older. Stronger.

"I am sorry about your parents," she said softly.

I couldn't look at her. "It is my fault."

"How is Abisola?" I asked.

"She is with one of your uncles," Jada said. "I send her money. From the salon."

"The salon?"

"Yeah," she smiled a sad smile. "I used the money you left. I opened a shop. It is doing well."

I felt a tear slide down my cheek. At least one good thing had come from my crimes. "And you?" I asked. "Are you happy?"

"I am," she said. "I am seeing someone. Devante. He treats me right."

It hurt. It hurt like a physical blow. But I nodded. "I am glad."

"Don't give up, Josh," she said as she left. "You are still the smartest boy I know."

Eighteen months. It sounds like a long time, but it goes fast when every day is exactly the same.

The day I was released, the sky was gray. I walked out of the gate with a plastic bag containing my clothes and forty dollars.

I didn't want to celebrate. I didn't want a steak dinner. I just wanted to disappear. I took a Greyhound bus to Detroit. I went straight to Aunt Moji's house. It looked smaller. Or maybe I had just seen too many palaces.

My cousin opened the door. He had grown. He looked at me with suspicion. Aunt Moji let me in. She didn't hug me.

She gave me a bed in the basement.

"You can stay," she said. "Until you get on your feet."

I spent my days walking. I walked through the neighborhoods of Detroit. I sat at bus stops, watching people go to work. Watching them struggle.

They were poor. But they were free.

I had been a millionaire. I had driven a Ferrari. I had worn a watch worth more than this entire block.

But as I sat there in the cold wind, shivering in my thin jacket, I realized something. I was alone. Poor and miserable. I had nothing left. No one left either.

CHAPTER TWENTY-SIX

I wanted my release to be a fairy tale. I wanted to step out of those gates and have the world apologize. But the world doesn't apologize. It just keeps spinning.

The reality was a parole officer named Mr. Henderson who smelled like stale coffee and disappointment. It was weekly drug tests. It was a curfew. And it was living in Aunt Moji's basement.

Aunt Moji had changed. The woman who once bragged about my SAT scores now looked at me like I was a ticking bomb.

"Where were you?" she would demand if I came home five minutes late. "Are you scamming again? Are you bringing the police to my door?"

"I was at the library, Auntie," I would say, tired to my bones.

"Lies," she would hiss. "Just like your father. Full of lies."

That stung. My father never lied. He was honest. A poor but honest man.

I needed a job. Desperately. But try getting hired in corporate America with a federal fraud conviction.

The moment they ran a background check, the door slammed shut. Banks were out. Tech companies were out. Anything involving money or data was forbidden by law.

So, I went to Amazon. Amazon didn't care about my past. They just cared if I could lift a box. They have a "Second Chance" program, which is corporate speak for "We need bodies."

I worked the night shift in a warehouse in Romulus. Ten hours of standing on concrete. Ten hours of pick, pack, scan. My back screamed. My feet bled.

I was a genius who could code in Python and launder millions through the Cayman Islands, and now my entire existence was reduced to moving cardboard from Point A to Point B.

I enrolled in a community college. It was part of my parole agreement. *Maintain employment and education.*

I took classes during the day. It was exhausting. I slept four hours a night. I lost weight. My eyes were permanently bloodshot.

The worst part was the TV in the breakroom. Every time I looked up, I saw them. My old life.

Forbes 30 Under 30: Edward Morrison.

There he was, smiling on the screen. The boy whose email I hacked. The boy whose company I robbed. He was being hailed as a visionary.

And Melina. She was in Vogue. The new face of Dervishi. She looked beautiful. She looked happy. She was wearing the ring Viktor gave her.

I would stand there, holding my lukewarm coffee, watching the people I used to rule with. They were ascending. I was scanning barcodes for fifteen dollars an hour.

It took me a year to get my certificate in Business Administration. A year of hell. I graduated at the top of my class. It wasn't hard. My competition was bored teenagers and tired single moms.

But still, it was an achievement. I went home that night, holding the piece of paper. I wanted to celebrate.

"Auntie," I said, walking into the kitchen. "I got my certificate."

Aunt Moji was washing dishes. She didn't turn around. "That is nice," she grunted.

That was it. No hug. No "well done." Just a grunt.

I went to my room, the basement. I sat on the cot and cried.

I missed my mother. She would have danced. She would have sung.

I wiped my face. I opened my laptop. I just wanted to check Facebook. To see if Jada was okay.

Suddenly, the door flew open. Aunt Moji stood there.

Her eyes were wild. "What are you doing?" she screamed. "Why is the door locked? Are you hacking? Are you scamming people again?"

"I am checking Facebook!" I yelled, slamming the laptop shut. "Stop it! I am trying, Auntie! I am working! I am studying! Why can't you see that?"

She walked over and slapped me. *Thwack.*

"Do not raise your voice at me in my house!" she shouted. "I am protecting this family! I don't want Devante to end up in prison like you!"

Something inside me snapped.

"At least, I am alive, which is more than I can say for Tunde-Sean. I'm sure Devante would rather go to prison than die like a gangbanger." I said, my voice cold.

She slapped me again. Harder. My lip split.

"Get out," she whispered. "Get out of my house. Now."

She threw me out.

I stood on the sidewalk with a duffel bag. It was 2 AM in Detroit. The air was freezing. I started walking. I didn't know where to go. I was three blocks away when I felt the cold steel of a knife against my throat.

"Run it," a voice growled in my ear.

I didn't fight. I dropped the bag.

"Wallet," the mugger demanded.

I handed it over. My Amazon ID. My library card. Forty dollars.

"Shoes," he said.

I looked down at my Nikes. They were the only decent thing I owned. Damn, I missed my Louboutin sneakers and Giuseppe Zanotti shoes.

"Please," I whispered.

He pressed the knife harder. A drop of blood trickled down my neck. I took them off. He took my jacket too.

I stood there in the snow, barefoot, shivering, watching him run away with everything I had left.

I looked up at the sky. It was black and empty.

"Is this it?" I screamed at the sky. "Is this the plan? I paid my debt! I served my time! Why are you still punishing me?"

I collapsed on the sidewalk. I curled into a ball. I wanted to die. A homeless man pushed a shopping cart past me. He stopped. He threw a dirty blanket over me.

"Rough night, kid," he muttered.

I slept under that blanket, on the concrete, praying I wouldn't wake up. But I did wake up. Survival is a stubborn instinct. I found a room. It was a rat-hole in a bad neighborhood. The landlord didn't ask for a background check; he just asked for cash upfront.

My neighbors were dealers. I heard them through the thin walls. Counting money. Cleaning guns. Bragging about bodies. I needed more money. Amazon wasn't cutting it. My sister, Abisola, had gotten into university in Nigeria. She needed tuition. I was her only hope.

I moved to LA. I thought a change of scenery would help. I thought the sun would burn away the bad luck.

I rented a studio apartment in East LA. My neighbors were two Mexican guys, Carlos and Fernando. They looked scary. Tattoos up to their necks. They watched me with suspicion every time I left the house.

I got a job managing a nightclub. It was a step up. No more lifting boxes. I was good at it. I knew how to run a club. I had owned one, once.

But a month later, $2,500 went missing from the safe. I didn't take it. I swear. But who does the owner blame? The Black ex-con with a fraud conviction.

"Get out," the owner said. "And be glad I don't call the cops."

Fired again.

I applied everywhere. No one called back. Having a criminal record is a scarlet letter.

Finally, I hit rock bottom. Burger King.

"Can you mop?" the manager asked.

"Yes," I said.

So, I became a cleaner. The Nigerian Prince, the god of money laundering, the boy who drove a Ferrari, was now cleaning toilets and wiping ketchup off tables.

It was humiliating. But the worst part was the recognition. Kids would come in. High schoolers. They would stare at me. Then they would pull out their phones.

Click.

Later that night, I would see it on Instagram.

POV: When your idol cleans your table. #NigerianPrince #FallenOff

The comments were brutal. *He is a loser. Karma. Fake it till you break it.*

One Tuesday afternoon, the bell on the door chimed. I was wiping a table near the window. I looked up.

I froze.

It was David Lewinson. He was wearing a Zegna cashmere suit. Beside him was a woman. Chloe. Our classmate from Kingsley. She was pregnant.

I ducked my head. I tried to run to the back.

"Hey! You missed a spot!" my manager yelled. "Josh! Get back here!"

David turned. He saw me. His eyes went wide. "Josh?"

I stopped. There was no escape. I turned around. I forced a smile. "Hi, David. Hi, Chloe."

David walked over. He looked shocked. "Josh... it is really you."

He looked at my uniform. The grease stains. The name tag.

"You work here?"

"Hard to get a job with a record," I said, shrugging. "Gotta pay the bills."

I looked at Chloe's stomach. "Congratulations."

David smiled, touching her belly. "Yeah. A girl. We are excited."

"That is great," I said. "Really."

"What are you up to?" I asked, trying to change the subject.

"I have a tech startup," David said. "San Francisco. Chloe is an accountant at Apple."

A tech startup. An accountant at Apple. They were living my dream. They were living the life I threw away.

I felt a surge of rage so hot it blinded me. I threw the tray on the floor. Clatter. Fries and soda went everywhere.

I ran. I ran out the back door. I ran until my lungs burned. I couldn't do it anymore.

I couldn't be the cautionary tale. I went home and pounded on my neighbor's door.

Carlos opened it. He had a gun in his hand. "What do you want, pendejo?"

"Fentanyl," I gasped. "I need Fentanyl. I have money." I pulled out my wallet. I offered him everything I had.

Carlos grabbed me by the collar. He slammed me against the wall. "You a cop?" he hissed. "You trying to set me up?"

"No," I sobbed. "I just want to forget. I just want it to stop. Please."

Fernando walked up behind him. "Let him go, Carlos. Look at him. He is broken."

Carlos let me go. He handed me a blunt instead.

"Sit," Fernando said.

We sat on their stoop. I smoked. The weed dulled the edge of the pain.

"You ain't a junkie," Fernando said. "I can tell. You got smart eyes. Why you living in this dump?"

"Prison," I said. "Fraud. Eighteen months."

"Fraud?" Carlos laughed. "You? You look like a choir boy."

"I laundered more than $50 million," I said. "BEC scams. Credit cards. Synthetic identities."

The laughter stopped. Carlos and Fernando exchanged a look.

"Laundering?" Carlos asked. "You know how to wash?"

"I know how to make money disappear," I said. "I know how to layer. I know how to set up shell companies that the IRS can't touch."

"And you got caught? Maybe you ain't so smart."

"My partner ratted," I said.

"Where is he now?"

"Dead," I said. "Cartel hit. Dismembered."

Carlos nodded appreciatively. "Good. Rats get what they deserve. Snitches get stitches."

He leaned in close. "Listen, *ese*," Carlos said. "The Professor needs someone like you. Someone smart. Someone who can move money without touching it."

"The Professor?"

"Our boss," Fernando said. "Our cartel has a liquidity problem. Too much cash. Needs to be digital."

I stared at the blunt in my hand. Here it was. The crossroads. I could go back to Burger King. I could clean toilets for the rest of my life. I could be poor and righteous.

Or I could be rich again. I thought about David's suit. I thought about Chloe's ring. I thought about the Ferrari.

But then I thought about my father. I thought about my mother. I thought about the promise I made to God in that prison cell.

Your word I have hidden in my heart, that I might not sin against you.

I stood up. I dropped the blunt. "No," I said.

Carlos frowned. "No?"

"I can't," I said. "I am done. I am a changed person."

"Offer stands," Carlos said. "Think about it. Burger King... or being a King."

"Never," I said. "Let's pretend we never had this conversation."

I walked back to my apartment. I locked the door. I sat on my bed. I opened my Bible to Psalm 23.

The Lord is my shepherd; I shall not want.

I read it over and over again until I fell asleep.

PART 3

LEVIATHAN

CHAPTER TWENTY-SEVEN

I told my pastor that I needed a job. Any job. Preferably one where I wouldn't have to look people in the eye.

He introduced me to Mrs. Garcia. She was a small, fierce Filipina woman who had started her cleaning agency with a bucket and a sponge and built it into an empire. She knew about my record. She knew about the fraud. But she was a Christian woman, and she believed in redemption.

She gave me a roster. Fifteen houses a week. The pay was abysmal, barely enough to cover rent and send money to Abisola. But it was honest.

I scrubbed toilets in houses that looked like the ones I used to party in. I polished marble floors that reminded me of Dmitri's mansion. It was humbling. It was depressing. But I kept my head down. I worked hard.

I avoided Carlos and Fernando. I left my apartment at dawn and returned late at night, locking myself in with my Bible. I had no girlfriend, no money for dates, no social life. I was a monk in a hoodie.

For six months, I was good. I was clean. Then, disaster struck. One of my regular clients was a young Black doctor named Amber. She lived in a condo in Santa Monica. I liked cleaning her place; she had good taste in art.

One Tuesday, I finished cleaning and left. Two hours later, my phone rang. Mrs. Garcia.

"Josh," she said, her voice tight. "Did you see any cash at Dr. Amber's house today?"

"No, ma'am," I said.

"She says she left $800 on her dresser. It is gone."

My stomach dropped. "Mrs. Garcia, I didn't take it. I swear."

"She is adamant, Josh. She says you were the only one there."

I tried to explain. I begged. I asked Mrs. Garcia to check my pockets, check my bag. But the shadow of my past was too long. To them, I wasn't Josh the cleaner. I was Josh the fraudster. Once a thief, always a thief.

Amber threatened to call the police. To avoid a scandal, Mrs. Garcia paid her the eight hundred dollars out of her own pocket.

But the cost was my job.

"I can't keep you, Josh," Mrs. Garcia said, handing me my final check. Her eyes were sad. "I trusted you."

"I didn't do it!" I shouted, tears stinging my eyes. But she just closed the door.

That night, I sat in my apartment. I didn't read my Bible. I looked at the ceiling and cursed God.

Why? I am trying! I am doing everything right! Why do you keep punishing me?

I spent the next week applying for jobs. Rejection after rejection. I started drinking again. Then, I bought a small bag of cocaine from Fernando. Just a little. To numb the rage.

A month later, the money ran out. Abisola called, needing tuition. My landlord threatened eviction. I was cornered. I became desperate. And desperation makes you capable of anything.

I walked next door. I knocked on Carlos' door. He opened it, shirtless, revealing a tapestry of prison tattoos.

"I am in," I said.

Carlos grinned. "Took you long enough, *ese*."

"Does the offer still stand?"

"The Professor always needs talent," Carlos said. "But you know the rules. Once you are in, the only way out is in a box."

"I know," I said. "I don't care. I just need to eat."

I walked back to my apartment to pack a bag.

As I reached my door, I saw my pastor standing there. He looked worried.

"Josh!" he called out. "I have been trying to reach you."

I turned away. "Leave me alone, Pastor. God has left the building."

"No, listen!" he said, grabbing my arm. "Mrs. Garcia called me. Amber found the money."

I froze. "What?"

"She found it," the pastor said, breathless. "It fell behind the dresser. She felt terrible. She wants to apologize. Mrs. Garcia wants you back."

The world seemed to tilt. It was thirty minutes too late. If he had come an hour ago... if I hadn't knocked on Carlos' door...

"It is too late," I whispered.

"What do you mean?" the pastor asked. "You have a job again!"

"I have a new job," I said, my voice dead. "Tell Mrs. Garcia thanks. But I am gone."

"God won't give up on you, Josh."

I pulled my arm free and slammed the door. I slid down to the floor and wept. Fate was a cruel comedian.

Two weeks later, a black SUV picked me up. I was blindfolded. We drove for an hour. When the blindfold came off, I was standing in a mansion that rivaled Dmitri's. Marble floors. Gold leaf. Armed guards with assault rifles standing like statues in the corners.

"This is nice," I muttered to Carlos.

"The Professor does well," Carlos smirked.

We walked into the living room. Sitting in a high-backed leather chair was a teenage girl. She couldn't have been older than nineteen. She was stunning. She had long dark hair, sharp features, eyes that burned with intelligence. She looked like a telenovela star.

Jesus Christ. These Latinas. My God! I could spend an entire month writing poems singing their praises. They were simply perfect. Very feminine. Very sensual.

"Is she The Professor's daughter?" I whispered.

Carlos jabbed me in the ribs. "Shut up. That is The Professor."

My jaw dropped. I was expecting a scar-faced narco in his fifties. I mean, after watching El Chapo, Breaking Bad, and Narcos, you can't blame me for expecting The Professor to be a middle-aged man.

"You look surprised," she said. Her voice was smooth, cultured.

"I was... expecting someone else," I admitted.

"My father died two years ago," she said, swirling a glass of wine. "My brothers died in the war. I inherited the throne."

She stood up. She was small, but she commanded the room. "Carlos says you are a wizard with digital finance."

Those tits, my Lord. I could see her nipples poking through her top.

"I know my way around," I said.

"Good. Because I have a problem." She gestured to the corner of the room.

I have a problem too. You're making my third leg rise in its fury, and I don't want your men to castrate me. I don't want my dick to lead me to my death.

Stacked against the wall were pallets. Pallets of cash. Shrink-wrapped bundles of hundred-dollar bills. Millions.

"We have too much paper," she said, disgusted. "Trucks get seized. Cash is heavy. It smells. I need ghosts."

"You want me to launder it?"

"I want you to digitize it," she corrected. "I need to move funds to Sinaloa instantly. No mules. No tunnels."

"I can do it," I said.

"I need to test you first," she said.

She snapped her fingers. A guard brought a black duffel bag and dropped it at my feet.

"Open it."

I unzipped it. It was full of cash.

"$100,000," she said. "Dirty street money."

She slid a piece of paper across the table. It had an account number on it. Banco Azteca, Mexico City.

"I want $80,000 in that account by Friday noon," she said. "Without physically moving the bills across the border."

This was the ultimate test. Placement. The hardest part of laundering. Taking physical cash and getting it into the digital system without triggering the ten-thousand-dollar IRS reporting limit.

"Your cut is ten percent," she said. "Use another ten percent for operational costs. If you fail... my men will find you. And if you run..."

She didn't finish the sentence. She didn't have to.

"I won't run," I said.

Why would I run and never see your beautiful face again? Or those hips and sexy legs. Never!

I picked up the bag. It was heavy. They blindfolded me again and drove me back to my rat-hole apartment.

I stood in the middle of the room, surrounded by peeling paint and the smell of weed from next door. I had $100,000 on my bed.

I had three days to turn paper into digital air. And if I failed, I was dead.

"Let's get to work," I whispered.

There are three things cartel leaders never joked with. The first is vengeance, the second is their drug shipments, and the third is money.

CHAPTER TWENTY-EIGHT

I spent the rest of the night scheming on how to digitize $100,000 cash without triggering a federal investigation. I wished Dmitri could be with me at that moment because the guy always had a plan. But I was the only one left standing.

As a Yoruba guy, I knew that nothing was impossible. My father used to tell me that there was nothing that could stop a determined man.

I looked at the bag of cash. The problem wasn't moving it; the problem was the Bank Secrecy Act.

If I walked into a bank and deposited $100,000, the teller would file a CTR (Currency Transaction Report) immediately. The IRS would be at my door in an hour.

I needed to bypass the banks entirely. I needed to turn this paper into Bitcoin, but even crypto exchanges required ID now.

Then, the idea hit me. Bitcoin ATMs.

Los Angeles was full of them. Liquor stores, gas stations, malls. They allowed you to feed cash in and get Bitcoin out. The catch? They required ID for anything over $900.

But I was a programmer. I could automate the evasion.

I opened my laptop. I didn't have much time. I wrote a Python script to generate 125 unique Bitcoin paper wallets, printable QR codes that function as temporary deposit addresses.

My plan was "Digital Smurfing."

I wouldn't make one big deposit. I would make 125 small deposits of $800 each. $800 is below the ID verification threshold.

By using a different wallet address for every single transaction, the ATM network wouldn't flag me as a single user. It would look like 125 different people buying small amounts of crypto across the city.

I spent the next three days living in my car.

I mapped out every Bitcoin ATM in Los Angeles County. I drove from Compton to Van Nuys, Santa Monica to Pasadena.

It was grueling work. I would walk into a sketchy liquor store, wearing a hoodie and sunglasses.

I'd scan a fresh QR code from my stack of printouts. I'd feed $800 in twenties into the glowing machine.

Whir. Click. Sent.

Then I would take a Lyft five miles to the next machine. For every $800 I fed in, only about $736 worth of Bitcoin hit the wallet. The rest was the fee.

I felt like a ghost haunting the city's financial edges. I was carrying a backpack worth a fortune, looking over my shoulder constantly, terrified of being robbed or stopped by the cops.

By Thursday night, my fingers were black from handling dirty bills. The bag was empty.

I returned to my apartment and opened my laptop. I loaded the private keys for all 125 paper wallets.

There it was on the blockchain. $92,000 in Bitcoin (after the ATM fees). But it wasn't safe yet. The blockchain is a public ledger. If the Feds seized the ATM logs, they could trace the coins to me.

I executed Phase Two: The Wash.

I ran the funds through a CoinJoin mixer, which is a protocol that takes coins from hundreds of users, mixes them together in a digital blender, and spits them out into new wallets. It breaks the transactional link between the sender and the receiver.

It took six hours for the mixer to finish. The mixer took another 1.5%, which was about $1,380.

On Friday morning, I sat in front of my screen. I had the Mexican bank account number The Professor had given me.

I went to a peer-to-peer exchange that allowed crypto-to-fiat payouts in Mexico. I sold the clean Bitcoin.

Transfer Initiated.

I watched the confirmation screen.

Amount Sent: $80,000.00 Destination: Banco Santander, Sinaloa.

I sat back. The math had worked. I had my $10,000 cut, plus a little extra cash.

I closed my laptop and exhaled. I had turned a bag of dirty street money into clean digital funds in a Mexican bank account, all without ever crossing the border or showing my ID.

I sent a secure message to The Professor via the encrypted app she gave me. *Done.*

Her reply came one minute later. *Impressive. Welcome to the family*

The Professor began to grow fond of me, and I no longer needed Carlos to set up a meeting with her. I visited her regularly, and she began to tell me more about the cartel.

I got to know more about the politicians that worked for the cartel and other important cartel members. Mexican cartels relied a lot on anonymity. That was the primary reason many of them always used their nicknames instead of their real names.

The Professor's real name was Camila, but her cartel members all knew her as *The Professor*. Most of them did not even know that she was a teenage girl. Many people assumed she was an old man. Only top members of the cartel knew her real identity.

"You need to think of a nickname. It is really dangerous to use your real name in the world of drug trafficking. The DEA can easily find your real name in their records and trace you. Worse still, rival cartel members might want to kill you," The Professor said.

I tried to think of a nickname but could not think of any. While brainstorming, my phone vibrated gently. It was a notification from a bible app.

After my release from prison, I downloaded an app that sent me random bible verses daily. The notification was from Isaiah 27:1:

"In the day the Lord with his sore and great and strong sword shall punish **LEVIATHAN** *the piercing serpent...."*

I did not continue reading. My eyes were stuck on the word *Leviathan*. I felt a sort of magnetic pull to the name. I did a mental wordplay and arranged the alphabets to form *Nate Haliv*.

"What is it?" The Professor asked.

"I think I've just found a perfect name. I would love to be called Nate Haliv."

The Professor frowned. "What sort of name is that?"

I shrugged. "Just a random name."

I became known as Nate Haliv in the world of narcotics. To all my friends and my pastor, I was Josh Balogun, an ex-convict who worked at a cleaning agency to make ends meet, but in the world of narcotics, I was Nate Haliv, The Professor's most trusted ally and a high-ranking member of the cartel.

I was also the man rocking The Professor's bed at least twice every week with hardcore, raw, primal sex. I always ensured she was thoroughly pleased.

I only revealed my identity to a few members of the cartel. I mostly communicated with them via phone calls, and my voice was always scrambled during the call.

None of the cartel members could have guessed that I was an African guy. They thought I was also Mexican or an intelligent white lawyer skilled at moving money across international borders.

It was not easy being Josh Balogun and Nate Haliv at the same time. Josh Balogun had to work as a cleaner from Monday to Saturday, and he had to go to church every Sunday and Wednesday.

He also had to see his parole officer weekly, while Nate Haliv had to work on the cartel's finances and ensure that every cartel member got paid regularly without any delay.

It was tiring because any slight mistake in the management of the cartel's funds could make them think I was stealing from them.

There is nothing worse than being punished for stealing from a cartel. They will literally make the thief beg for death.

I opened my heart to a church member after a while. After I heard about Melina's marriage, I had been distraught and shut women out of my life.

However, Zendaya, a Black church girl who looked nothing like my exes, caught my attention. It began with an innocent smile. She smiled at me while she was singing among the choristers during one of our church services.

Her smile made me freeze, and I could not look away from her. She was not as beautiful as The Professor or Mia, but something about her was irresistible.

Zendaya thought of me as a poor ex-convict who needed to be saved. She grew fond of me after I told her that I worked as a cleaner because many companies were not eager to hire a Black ex-convict.

Zendaya made dinner for me regularly, and we often hung out, but she never knew I was richer than I appeared. She had no idea that I managed the finances of a top Mexican drug cartel. We enjoyed each other's company a lot, and our love led to my downfall.

I got my first big test as Nate Haliv a couple of weeks after I picked the nickname.

The Professor summoned me to her mansion in the Hollywood Hills. The air was thick with cigar smoke and the scent of expensive leather. She looked serious, her usual playful demeanor replaced by the cold, calculating stare of a cartel boss.

She didn't look like the woman who had just squirted all over my face the previous night. She seemed so…professional.

"I have a liquidity problem," she said, sliding a glass of wine across the table to me. "I need to move $8 million from Los Angeles to a partner in Rome, Italy. I need to pay a 'consulting fee' to a Camorra boss who facilitates our shipments through the Port of Naples."

I took a sip of the wine, trying to hide my nervousness. "$8 million? That's too much to structure through Bitcoin ATMs. The fees would eat us alive, and the volume would trigger blockchain analytics alerts. We can't use the smurfing method for that volume."

"I know," she said sharply. "And I can't ship the cash. $8 million in hundred-dollar bills weighs almost one hundred and eighty pounds. It takes up two large duffel bags. If I put that on a private jet, Customs will seize it before the wheels leave the tarmac. I need you to find a way to move that value across the Atlantic without using the banking system and without a cargo plane full of cash."

I spent the next few days in a state of high anxiety. I was a cyber-criminal, a money launderer, but this was a logistics nightmare. I needed a vessel, something that held immense value but had low physical mass. Something unregulated. Something invisible to the banking radar.

I was brainstorming in my cramped apartment when Zendaya visited. She was my anchor. In a world of cartels, encrypted phones, and dirty money, Zendaya was the only thing that felt real.

She brought a sense of comfort and normalcy that I desperately craved.

"It's so good to see you," I told her, hugging her longer than usual.

Zendaya pulled away and smiled, her eyes lighting up. "I have news. Big news."

"Tell me."

"I'm participating in a showcase," she said, vibrating with excitement. "It's not a gallery. It's an underground art collective. A 'Dark Market' event in the Arts District. They don't advertise. It's for high-net-worth private collectors who want to buy art without the pretension, or the records, of the big galleries."

"That sounds... exclusive," I said.

"It is. I'm so lucky they accepted my piece. I doubt anyone will look at my work, though. The rumor is that a major private seller is offloading a blue-chip piece during the event. **A work by Jean-Michel Basquiat.**"

I froze. The name hit me like a physical blow. Basquiat.

I knew about the art world from my days pretending to be a rich kid at Kingsley University. Jean-Michel Basquiat was the holy grail of modern art. His works were raw, chaotic, and incredibly valuable.

While his massive canvases sold for over a hundred million, his smaller works, oil sticks on paper, sketches, and lesser-known compositions, regularly traded in the single-digit millions.

But more importantly, art was the last great loophole. It was the "Wild West" of finance.

If you buy a house, there is a paper trail. If you buy stocks, the SEC watches. But art? Art is subjective.

You can buy a painting for eight million dollars, roll it up into a tube, carry it on a plane as "personal effects," and sell it in Italy for the same price. No customs declaration for currency. No bank wire. Just a piece of canvas with paint on it.

I looked at Zendaya, my mind racing. "A Basquiat? Are you sure?"

"That's the rumor," she said. "It's a private treaty sale happening in the back room. Cash and crypto only. No questions asked."

I hugged Zendaya tightly, burying my face in her hair so she wouldn't see the predatory gleam in my eyes. "Thank you, Zendaya. You have no idea how proud I am of you."

She thought I was congratulating her. In reality, she had just given me the solution to an eight-million-dollar problem.

I did my research that night. The art market is a common vehicle for Trade-Based Money Laundering (TBML). High-value art can be stored in "Freeports," high-security warehouses in places like Geneva or Singapore, where they change hands tax-free. But for this to work, I needed to physically move the asset to Italy.

I pitched the plan to The Professor the next morning, after she had just finished riding me like a wild cowgirl.

"Art?" she asked skeptically while lighting her cigar. "You want me to trade $8 million cash for a drawing?"

"It's not just a drawing," I explained.

I reached out to my laptop and pulled up the auction history on my laptop. "It's a bearer bond. It's a global currency. A Basquiat holds its value better than the Peso. We buy it here in a private sale using the cash hoard you have in the safe houses. I fly it to Italy. I hand the painting to your Camorra partner. He puts it in a vault or sells it. The value moves across the border without a single dollar crossing a wire. We can even arrange a private sale in Italy and give him the actual cash. It's a win-win situation."

The Professor lit a cigarette, studying the screen. "And the Customs officers?"

"It's a painting," I said. "I declare it as a 'commercial sample' or a reproduction worth a few hundred dollars. Unless they have a Christie's art appraiser on shift at LAX, they won't know it's worth eight million.

"To the X-ray machine, it's just organic material. Canvas and wood. They are more concerned about drugs, bombs, and undeclared cash at airports.

No one cares to investigate paintings. I doubt if most custom officers can even recognize Basquiat's paintings at first glance."

She exhaled a plume of smoke while I spanked her sexy ass. My good Lord. It was soft. Like a loaf of *Agege* bread. "Do it. But Nate... if you lose this painting, or if it turns out to be a fake, you will wish you died in prison."

The event was held two days later in a nondescript industrial warehouse in the Arts District. This wasn't a Sotheby's event with champagne and tuxedos.

This was the gritty underbelly of the art world, the secondary market where tax evaders, cartels, and eccentric billionaires traded assets off the books to avoid capital gains taxes.

Security was tight. I had to show proof of funds, a crypto wallet balance I had prepared, just to get the location.

The dress code was strict: black tie, masks mandatory. It added a layer of anonymity that made everyone comfortable.

I wore a sleek black suit and a full-face mask reminiscent of the Black Panther movie. I carried a backpack, but not for the money. The money, four million in physical cash and four million in stablecoins (USDT), was split.

The cash was waiting in a reinforced van outside, guarded by Carlos and three of The Professor's soldiers. We wouldn't move the physical cash until the deal was sealed.

I entered the main hall. It was dimly lit, with spotlights focused on the easels.

"The undercard auction is beginning," the announcer said. He was a British man with a voice like velvet. "First item: The Black Mona Lisa by local artist Zendaya Palmer."

I watched from the shadows as Zendaya stepped onto the small stage. She looked terrified but radiant. She held up her canvas. It was a stunning reinterpretation of Da Vinci's masterpiece, but the subject was a Black woman with a powerful afro and piercing eyes.

"Opening bid: $1,000," the announcer said.

Silence. The room was full of sharks waiting for the Basquiat. They didn't care about local art.

"Five hundred?" the announcer tried.

I couldn't watch her fail. I raised my paddle.

"$50,000," I said, disguising my voice with a rough growl.

The room went silent. Zendaya gasped, her eyes scanning the crowd, trying to find the source of the voice.

"I have fifty thousand," the announcer said, stunned. "Do I hear fifty-five?"

Silence.

"Sold! To the gentleman in the Panther mask."

I walked to the side desk, tapped my phone to transfer the Bitcoin equivalent of $50,000 to the house wallet, and collected the painting. I saw Zendaya staring at me, tears in her eyes. She didn't recognize me. To her, I was just a wealthy, eccentric patron. I had just laundered $50,000 of drug money into my girlfriend's pocket, and she thought it was a miracle.

But that was just the appetizer.

"Gentlemen," the announcer said, his voice dropping. "For those interested in the Lot Alpha, please proceed to the secure viewing room."

I walked to the back. Two massive bodyguards checked my credentials again before letting me into a smaller, climate-controlled room.

There were only five of us in there. Me, a Russian oligarch type, a tech billionaire I recognized from the news, and a representative from a Saudi sovereign fund.

And there it was.

Jean-Michel Basquiat's Untitled (Head) (1982).

It wasn't one of the massive murals. It was a smaller work, oil stick and acrylic on paper, roughly 30 by 22 inches. But the power was undeniable. The skull-like visage screamed from the paper in violent strokes of black and red.

Works like this had been hammering at auction for between six and nine million dollars consistently for the last three years.

The seller was a nervous-looking man in a white suit. Obviously, he wasn't the owner; he was a fixer.

"This is a private treaty sale," the fixer said. "Authentication papers are provided by the Basquiat Estate Committee. Provenance is impeccable, previously held in the collection of a Swiss banker. The asking price is eight million dollars. Firm."

This wasn't an auction. It was a race. The first person to prove liquidity got the asset.

"I offer seven," the Russian grunted.

"The price is eight," the fixer repeated. "And I require immediate settlement."

"I can wire the funds within three days," the tech billionaire said. "My bank in Zurich requires compliance checks."

The fixer shook his head. "No wires. No banks. Immediate settlement. Crypto or physical."

The other buyers hesitated. Moving that much crypto instantly was risky due to volatility, and nobody carried that much cash.

Except me. "I'll take it," I said, stepping forward. "Eight million. Settlement tonight."

The room turned to look at me.

"How?" the fixer asked.

"My associates are outside," I said. "We have fifty percent liquidity in secure transport. The other fifty percent is USDT-ERC20. You can count the paper now and verify the hash on the blockchain."

The fixer looked at me, then at the painting. "Show me."

I signaled Carlos via text.

Ten minutes later, the back door of the warehouse opened. Carlos and his men brought in two massive duffel bags.

The fixer's eyes widened. We settled on the split—$4 million in physical cash (which the fixer clearly needed for his own off-the-books debts) and $4 million in Tether transferred peer-to-peer.

It took an hour to verify the bills and the blockchain transaction. The tension in the room was suffocating. If the Russian decided to hijack the deal, it would turn into a shootout. My hand hovered near the gun tucked in my waistband.

I had never killed, but if I had to kill to protect a Mexican drug lord's money, I would gladly do it.

Mexican drug lords don't play with money. They might have $100 million cash, but if anyone steals even $1 from them, they will skin the person alive to make an example out of them.

You can ask people who stole from Pablo Escobar or El Chapo. Oh no! You can't, because they are dead. As dead as my feelings for Melina.

"It's done," the fixer said, checking his ledger. "The Head is yours."

I didn't admire the art. I didn't marvel at the brushstrokes. I watched as the specialized art handlers crated the painting in a heavy-duty, humidity-controlled travel tube.

I walked out of that warehouse carrying eight million dollars in a tube slung over my shoulder.

I returned to my rat-infested apartment at 3:00 AM. I was vibrating with adrenaline.

I carefully placed the tube containing the Basquiat behind my stained sofa, covering it with a dirty blanket. I placed Zendaya's Black Mona Lisa next to it.

Then I shoved the remaining operational cash, about $20,000 I had skimmed for "logistics," under my mattress.

I sat on the floor, staring at the sofa. I was guarding a fortune that could buy this entire neighborhood ten times over.

A sudden knock on the door made me jump out of my skin. My heart hammered against my ribs. Had I been followed? Did the Russian track me? Was this a hit squad coming to reclaim the painting?

I grabbed the Glock 19 Carlos had given me. I racked the slide, checking the chamber. I crept toward the door, my breathing shallow.

"Who is it?" I shouted, aiming the gun at the wood.

"Josh? It's me, Zendaya."

The air left my lungs in a rush. I quickly engaged the safety and hid the gun in the drawer of my bedside table, covering it with socks.

I unlocked the multiple deadbolts and opened the door.

Zendaya stood there, her face flushed, holding a bottle of cheap champagne.

"You look like you've seen a ghost," she said, stepping inside. *Yes, my own ghost.*

"Just... rough night," I stammered. "Bad dreams."

She didn't notice my sweat. She sat down on the sofa, leaning back against the blanket that covered eight million dollars.

"You won't believe what happened," she said, popping the cork. "The Black Panther guy! He bought my painting for fifty thousand dollars! Cash!"

"That's... that's incredible," I said, my voice trembling. "I told you your art was worth it."

"I'm rich, Josh!" she laughed, pulling me down onto the sofa next to her. "I can pay off my student loans. I can get a studio. I can finally breathe."

She kissed me, tasting of cheap wine and joy. I kissed her back, but my eyes were open, staring at the wall.

"I want to take you out," she said, pulling away. "Let's go to KFC. I know it's late, but I'm starving."

I forced a laugh. I can't step out. Not when my life depended on protecting a drug lord's $8 million painting. "I'm not sure I wanna step out."

"Come on," she said, standing up. "My treat. I know money is tight for you."

The poor girl thought I didn't want to go out because I was "broke." If only she knew how much money I had in my crypto wallet.

"Fine," I said, trying not to trigger her suspicions.

We walked to the all-night KFC a few blocks away. The neighborhood was quiet, but I scanned every rooftop, every parked car, looking for cartel hitmen. We sat in a booth, eating greasy chicken under the fluorescent hum of the lights. Zendaya was glowing.

"I'm just so happy," she said, biting into a biscuit. "And I'm happy you're here to share it with me."

"Me too," I said.

Her expression darkened slightly. "I just wish... I wish I knew who the buyer was. I hope he's a good person. Not like... you know."

"Like who?"

"Like my ex," she said, her voice turning bitter. "I never told you the full story, did I?"

"No."

"His name was Marcus. He was charming. Sweet. Went to church. Just like you." She stabbed a fork into her coleslaw. "Turned out he was moving product for the gangs. Pills. Fentanyl."

I stopped chewing. The chicken turned to ash in my mouth.

"He sold a bad batch to my younger brother," she whispered, tears forming in her eyes. "My brother overdosed in his bedroom. Marcus killed him."

"I'm... I'm so sorry, Zendaya."

"I hate them," she said, looking up at me with a ferocity that terrified me. "Drug dealers are the worst set of people on earth. Selling poison to people for money."

Well, I wasn't technically a drug dealer. I was just their launderer. But I wasn't sure Zendaya would be interested in my duties.

She reached across the table and took my hand.

"My dad is a Police Captain," she said. "Did I tell you that?"

I froze. "No. You didn't."

"He runs the major crimes unit," she said proudly. "He taught me that there is no gray area. You are either on the side of the law, or you are against it. Zero tolerance. If I ever found out someone I cared about was involved in that life... I would turn them in myself. In a heartbeat."

Fuck me!

She squeezed my hand.

"That's why I love you, Josh," she said softly. "You have nothing. You scrub toilets. You are an ex-con. But you are honest. You are trying to do it the right way. That makes you better than any rich guy in a fancy car."

I looked into her eyes. They were full of love and absolute moral clarity. I loved her. I truly did. She was the light in my darkness.

But I was currently hiding an eight-million-dollar cartel asset in my apartment. I was Nate Haliv. I was exactly the monster she hated.

"I love you too. I will never lie to you, Zendaya," I lied, my voice cracking.

We finished our meal in silence.

The next morning, the real work began. I had the asset. Now I had to move it. I lied to Zendaya that Aunt Moji was seriously ill, and I had to visit her in Detroit. I shed a few tears to make her believe me. I told her how Aunt Moji had brought me from Nigeria to the U.S. How she was like a mother to me.

She fell for my tricks. She wanted to take some time off work to follow me to be with Aunt Moji, but I screamed a loud no. I told her that I would like to be alone with my aunt. She prayed for my journey and Aunt Moji's health. Poor girl.

I booked a commercial flight to Rome. I didn't use a private jet; private jets were scrutinized for narcotics. Commercial flights were chaos.

I packed the Basquiat into a specialized architect's drafting tube. I stuffed the remaining space with blueprints for a fake construction project in Tuscany. I forged documents showing I was an architectural consultant.

At LAX, I walked up to the TSA checkpoint. My heart was pounding so hard I thought it would trigger the scanners.

"What's in the tube?" the TSA agent asked.

"Blueprints," I said, keeping my voice steady. "I'm presenting a hotel design in Rome."

He ran it through the X-ray. Canvas, paper, plastic. No metal. No explosives. No organic density of cash bricks. The X-ray cannot distinguish between a blueprint worth five dollars and a Basquiat oil stick drawing worth eight million.

"Have a safe flight," he said.

I boarded the plane. I placed eight million dollars in the overhead bin, sandwiched between a duty-free bag and a stranger's coat. The flight was twelve hours of torture. Every time the seatbelt sign chimed, I jumped. I was wide awake throughout the flight. My life depended on the safety of the painting. The last thing I needed was for a random stranger to poach it.

CHAPTER TWENTY-NINE

We landed in Rome in the morning. This was the true test. TSA lets you leave with anything, but Italian Customs (Guardia di Finanza) looks for things coming in. They hunt for undeclared cash, narcotics, and luxury goods to tax.

I walked toward the "Nothing to Declare" lane. My heart hammered against my ribs. If they stopped me, they would find a painting worth eight million dollars.

I had no export license from the US, no import declaration for Italy, and no VAT receipt. It would be seized immediately.

Two officers were standing by the exit, chatting and drinking espresso. They were profiling passengers, looking for nervous drug mules coming from South America or tourists with too many designer shopping bags.

I adjusted my glasses, slung the tube casually over my shoulder like a bored student and walked right past them.

I stepped out into the Roman sun. I had successfully moved eight million dollars across the Atlantic without a single bank wire.

I didn't check into a hotel. I went straight to the meeting point. The Professor had arranged a buyer, a "fence" for high-end art named Ernesto Rossi.

Ernesto was an old-school operator. He didn't have a gallery; he operated out of a heavily fortified villa in the hills outside Rome.

He collected rare art for the Camorra, using dirty cash to buy assets that could be stored in vaults. I met him in his study. The room smelled of old paper and cigars.

"Let me see it," Ernesto said.

I uncapped the tube and carefully unrolled the canvas. Jean-Michel Basquiat's Untitled (Head).

Ernesto put on a pair of jeweler's loupes. He spent twenty minutes inspecting the brushstrokes, the signature, and the provenance papers I had brought.

"It is authentic," he murmured. "Beautiful aggression."

"The price is eight million," I said. "As agreed."

"I have the liquidity," Ernesto said. He pressed a button on his desk.

Two men entered carrying four large, reinforced suitcases.

"Eight million dollars in Euros and USD," Ernesto said. "Mixed denominations. Unmarked."

I didn't count it all, that would take hours, but I spot-checked the bundles. They were real.

"Pleasure doing business," I said.

I left the villa with four heavy suitcases. I had converted the painting back into liquid cash. Now, I had to deliver it to The Professor's partner.

I chartered a private van to drive me south. The destination wasn't Turin; it was Naples, the heart of the Camorra.

We arrived at a massive estate overlooking the Gulf of Naples. The gate was manned by guards carrying submachine guns.

"*Chi sei?*" a guard asked rudely, aiming his weapon at the windshield.

What's with these drug lords and violence?

I raised my hands. "I don't speak Italian. I am here to see Don Alberto. I am from The Professor."

The mention of the name made him pause. He spoke rapidly into his radio. A moment later, the heavy iron gates swung open.

Italian Mafia members are different from the Mexican cartels. The cartels are brutal and militaristic. The Camorra are ancient, tribal, and sadistic. They don't just kill you; they erase your entire lineage.

The van pulled up to the main house.

I was escorted inside by three silent men who checked me for wires. They ignored the suitcases; they knew what was inside.

I was led into a lavish living room with marble floors and gold-leaf ceilings.

An older man, perhaps in his late sixties, sat on a velvet sofa. He held a glass of red wine. This was Don Alberto, a man whose name appeared in Interpol notices but who lived like a king in plain sight.

"You must be Nate Haliv," Alberto said. His English was heavily accented but precise.

"Yes, sir," I said.

His men brought the suitcases in and set them on the floor. One of them, a man named Francesco, unzipped a bag and nodded to Alberto.

"The payment is complete," Alberto said. "Eight million."

"As The Professor promised," I said.

Alberto studied me over the rim of his glass. "Tell me, Nate Haliv. How old are you? 19? 20?

"How did a young boy like you move eight million dollars from Los Angeles to Italy in twenty-four hours? My own men struggle to move half that amount without the *Guardia di Finanza* sniffing around."

I kept my face neutral. "I didn't move money, sir. I moved art. I bought a Basquiat in LA, flew it here as a blueprint, and sold it to a private collector in Rome this morning."

Alberto's eyes widened. Then he laughed. It was a dry, raspy sound.

"Ingenious," he said. "The banking system hunts for numbers. The dogs hunt for powder. But nobody hunts for paint."

"It's a loophole," I said. "Subjective value."

"You are smart, *mio amico*," Alberto said. "My men... they have muscles, they have loyalty. But they lack imagination."

He gestured to the seat opposite him. "Sit."

I sat down, feeling the adrenaline begin to fade, replaced by exhaustion.

"You will stay for dinner," Alberto said. "You cannot fly back tonight. We celebrate."

"Thank you, sir," I said.

I knew better than to refuse an Italian Don. It was either I joined him for dinner, or I became his dinner.

The dinner was an opulent affair. Course after course of seafood, pasta, and wine. The room filled up with Alberto's lieutenants and a bevy of beautiful women.

My third leg stiffened multiple times as I stared at the women. Lord Jesus, these Italian women.

After dinner, Alberto called me to the balcony. We looked out over the lights of Naples.

"You cannot return to America just yet, Nate," he said.

My stomach dropped. I thought of Zendaya. I thought of my cover in church. "Sir, I told my family I would only be gone for a few days."

"They will wait," Alberto said dismissively. "I have a problem. A problem you can solve."

He lit a cigar.

"You delivered eight million to me. But I have another twenty million sitting in a vault in the basement. Cash. From the ports. From the waste management contracts."

He puffed on the cigar.

"The European banks are tightening their grip. The KYC rules, Know Your Customer, are strangling us. I need to hide this money. I need it to disappear from Italy and reappear in a place where the authorities cannot see it."

"You want me to wash it," I said.

"I want you to make it invisible," he corrected. "Can you do this?"

I looked at the city lights, my mind racing through the options. Moving twenty million dollars out of Europe was harder than moving it out of the US. The Eurozone had unified reporting standards (CRS).

"I can do it," I said. "But we can't use art for this volume. We need a structural solution."

"Go on."

"Hong Kong," I said.

Alberto frowned. "Hong Kong? The Chinese monitor everything."

"They monitor political dissidents," I said. "They welcome capital. Hong Kong is a territorial tax system. They don't tax income earned outside the city. But the problem isn't Hong Kong; the problem is getting the money into Hong Kong without triggering a report back to Italy."

"And how do we do that?"

"We need a firewall," I said. "If you open an account as an Italian citizen, the bank will report your balance to the Italian authorities under the Common Reporting Standard (CRS). You need to be someone else."

"I cannot use a fake passport," Alberto said. "The biometrics are too good now."

"Not a fake one," I said. "A real one. A purchased one."

I turned to face him.

"The Commonwealth of Dominica," I said. "It's a small island in the Caribbean. They have a Citizenship by Investment program. For a donation of $100,000, you legally become a citizen. You get a passport. A real one."

"And this helps me how?"

"Dominica does not enforce the same strict reporting standards to EU countries if structured correctly," I explained.

"We buy you a Dominican passport. Then, we use that passport to incorporate a shell company in Hong Kong.

"When the Hong Kong bank asks for the beneficial owner, you show the Dominican ID, not the Italian one."

"So, the bank reports to Dominica?"

"Exactly," I said. "And Dominica... well, their record-keeping is notoriously slow. By the time any regulator connects the dots, the money has moved to a trust in the Cook Islands."

Alberto stared at me, the ash on his cigar growing long.

"You know this for a fact?"

"It's standard procedure for high-net-worth individuals who value privacy," I said. "It's perfectly legal on paper. It relies on the bureaucracy of international treaties."

"Twenty million," Alberto said softly. "You can move it?"

"I need two weeks," I said. "I need to process the citizenship application. We expedite it with a donation. Once the passport is in hand, I fly to Hong Kong. I set up the corporate structure. I open the accounts. Then, we use a 'Trade Misinvoicing' scheme to wire the money from your Italian front companies to the Hong Kong shell, paying for non-existent consulting services."

Alberto smiled. It was the smile of a predator who had just found a new way to hunt.

"I don't understand 'trade misinvoicing' or any of those things. I only know how to shoot my gun. But Camila was right," he said. "You are a wizard."

He crushed the cigar out on the railing.

I nodded, maintaining my composure. "I will get it done."

Alberto leaned toward me. "You like Italian women, Nate?"

"They are very beautiful," I said politely. Hell, beautiful was an understatement. They were goddesses, just like my Latinas.

He laughed and snapped his fingers. "Francesco! Bring the girls."

Four stunning women walked in. They were dressed in evening gowns that left little to the imagination.

"For you," Alberto said, gesturing to me. "To help you relax after your flight."

I swallowed hard. I was a twenty-year-old kid from Nigeria, sitting in a Mafia palace, being offered a harem. It was every rapper's fantasy. I had never had a threesome, not to mention having sex with four women at once.

That night was a night like no other. The Italian girls did things no girl had ever done to me. I found myself screaming in ecstasy and swearing in languages I never knew I could speak.

CHAPTER THIRTY

I returned to America two days later, leaving the vineyards of Naples behind. Don Alberto didn't want me to go. He had enjoyed our conversations about the inefficiencies of cash.

He called me a prodigy, a gift from God sent to organize the Camorra's finances. I didn't tell him God had stopped taking my calls a long time ago.

I didn't bring my $800,000 fee back in cash. Walking through LAX with a suitcase full of Euros/USD was asking for a seizure.

Civil asset forfeiture laws meant the TSA could take it just because they didn't like my face.

Instead, I instructed Alberto's financier to pay me in USDT, Tether. A stablecoin pegged to the dollar. We settled the transaction peer-to-peer on the TRON network before I even boarded the plane. Low fees, instant settlement, and completely invisible to the banking system.

When I landed in LA, I didn't rush to the dealership. The Ferrari days were over. The new Nate Haliv didn't flash cash. He buried it.

I couldn't invest in startups or stocks. *Know Your Customer* laws meant I couldn't write a check without exposing my identity. So, I turned to DeFi, Decentralized Finance.

I moved my $800,000 into liquidity pools on the Ethereum network. I staked my stablecoins in Aave, earning a quiet four percent annual yield. It wasn't flashy, but it was safe. It was outside the system.

I stored the private keys on a Ledger Nano X, sealed it in a watertight bag, and buried it in the soil of a potted ficus plant on my balcony.

I was rich, but I was still living like a pauper in a rat-infested apartment.

Zendaya was overjoyed to see me. She threw her arms around my neck, smelling of cocoa butter and innocence.

With The Professor, my dick was always hard. Same with the women in Italy. But with Zendaya, my heart was always tender. God knows I loved and still love that beautiful Black girl.

"How was Detroit?" she asked.

"Cold," I lied. "Aunt Moji sends her love."

She didn't know I had just spent the weekend laundering millions for the Italian mafia. She didn't know I had thrown the painting tube into a dumpster three blocks away before coming over. To her, I was just Josh, the hardworking cleaner who loved his family.

But I couldn't get comfortable. Alberto's mission was ticking in my head like a bomb.

Get the Dominican passport. Go to Hong Kong.

It sounded simple. It wasn't.

To get a Dominican passport by investment, you need to pass a due diligence check. They run your biometrics against Interpol and the FBI. If I applied as Josh Balogun, my felony conviction would light up the screen like a Christmas tree. REJECTED.

I needed a new skin. I needed a **Synthetic Identity**. A real person who didn't exist.

I couldn't create it in America. The systems were too integrated. Social Security, credit bureaus, and DMV all talked to each other.

I needed to go back to the source. My roots. I had to go to Nigeria.

But I couldn't just fly to Lagos. If I flew direct, the manifest would record "Josh Balogun" entering the country. If the Feds ever investigated my new identity, they would see that Josh Balogun was in Nigeria on the exact day "Nate Haliv" was born. It would be a red flag.

I needed an air gap. I needed to disappear from one ledger before appearing in another.

I sat Zendaya down on the floor of my apartment.

We were eating takeout Chinese food, Kung Pao chicken. I remembered my date with Mia.

"I have to go away again," I said quietly.

She paused the TV. Her fork stopped halfway to her mouth. "What? You just got back."

"I know," I said. "But... remember that businessman? The one I cleaned for?"

"The one with the cocoa?"

"Yeah," I lied. "He offered me a contract. A big one. He wants to cut out the middlemen. He wants to buy directly from the farmers in West Africa. He needs someone on the ground. Someone who understands the culture."

"Where?"

"The Benin Republic," I said.

Zendaya frowned. "Benin? Josh, they speak French there. You don't speak French."

"I know," I said smoothly. "But the farms are near the border. They speak Yoruba too. He needs a translator. A negotiator. He trusts me."

"How long?" she asked. Her voice was small.

I took a deep breath. "Three months."

"Three months?" She stood up, pacing the small room. "Josh, that is a quarter of a year! We just started this. You can't just leave."

"The pay is twenty thousand dollars," I said.

She stopped.

"Twenty thousand," I repeated. "Zendaya, that changes everything. It pays off my debts. It gets me a car. It gets us a real apartment. No more rats. No more gunshots next door. I am doing this so I can stop cleaning toilets. I am doing this for us."

She looked at me. Her eyes searched mine for deception.

256

I held her gaze, using every ounce of manipulation I had learned from Dmitri. I channeled the Nigerian Prince.

"I promise," I said, taking her hands. "I will FaceTime you every day. The time will fly."

She softened. She sat back down and leaned her head on my shoulder.

"I am going to miss you," she whispered.

"I will miss you too," I said.

We kissed. Then she lay on the couch, slowly took off her clothes and spread her legs wide. An open invitation.

I walked to the fridge, grabbed a bowl of ice cream and scooped a copious amount on her love spot. Then I licked it clean with my tongue.

I spent the next week tying up loose ends. I paid my rent three months in advance with cash. I bought a burner laptop, a cheap Dell from a pawn shop.

When I boarded the plane at LAX, I didn't look back. I was leaving Josh Balogun behind.

I flew Air France via Paris to Cotonou, Benin Republic.

To the US authorities, to the airline database, Josh Balogun landed in Benin. That was the official story.

I spent one night in a cheap hotel in Cotonou to establish a digital footprint. I logged into my email. I bought a bottle of water with my debit card. Ping. Location confirmed.

Then, I went dark.

I took a bush taxi, a battered Peugeot 504 station wagon that smelled of gasoline and dust, to the Seme Border.

The Seme Border is chaos incarnate. It is a hive of smugglers, traders, hawkers, and corrupt officials.

The air is thick with the smell of exhaust and roasting corn. It was the perfect place to disappear.

The taxi dropped me on the Benin side. I walked across the dusty stretch of No Man's Land toward the Nigerian Immigration Service post. This was the choke point. I needed to enter Nigeria, but I couldn't have a stamp in my passport. A stamp was a record. A stamp proved I was there.

I watched the officers. They were sweating in their uniforms, yelling at a woman smuggling bales of second-hand clothes. I spotted an older officer. He had tribal marks on his cheeks. Definitely a Yoruba man. He looked tired. He looked like he had bills to pay.

I approached him. I switched to Yoruba.

"*E kaale*, sir," I said, bowing slightly. Good evening, sir.

He looked me up and down. He saw my American clothes. He saw my fresh haircut. He saw an ATM.

"*Ki lo n sele?*" he asked. What is happening?

"Oga, I have a big problem," I said, leaning in, lowering my voice. "I am coming from Cotonou. I went to visit my uncle. But... I misplaced my passport in the taxi. I think it fell out of my bag."

He frowned. "No passport? You cannot enter. Go back to the embassy."

"Sir, please," I pleaded. "I am a son of the soil. I am from Ado-Ekiti. I went to Cotonou because we had a group project in school. If I go back to Cotonou, I will be stranded. I just want to go home to Lagos."

The mention of Ado-Ekiti softened him. It established kinship. I wasn't a stranger; I was a brother who had lost his way.

"*Ekiti kete*," he muttered. "But this is irregular. The Comptroller is watching."

"I know, sir," I said.

I reached into my pocket. I pulled out a folded $100 bill.

In naira, this was a fortune. It was his kid's school fees for an academic term. It was rent.

I shook his hand, pressing the bill into his palm. The universal handshake.

"I just need to pass," I whispered. "Just a brother going home."

He felt the crisp paper. His eyes darted left and right. The chaos of the border was our cover. Hundreds of people were pushing past with sacks of rice and jerrycans of fuel.

He shoved the bill into his pocket.

"Pass," he grunted, pointing to a pedestrian gate that bypassed the biometric scanners. "Go quickly. Don't look back."

"*E se*, sir," I said.

I walked through the rusted metal gate. I stepped onto Nigerian soil. There was no stamp. No scan. No record. To the world, Josh Balogun was sleeping in a hotel in Benin. But in reality, I was in Lagos. And I was a ghost.

The road from Badagry to Victoria Island was filled with blaring horns, shouting bus conductors, and the thick, choking scent of diesel fumes mixed with the salty Atlantic air.

Lagos does not welcome you with open arms. It welcomes you with a slap to the face and dares you to slap back.

I arrived at Eko Hotels & Suites looking like a refugee from a war I had started myself. My clothes were dusty from the road, and my backpack felt heavy.

I walked through the sliding glass doors, and the noise of the city vanished, replaced by the hushed, expensive hum of central air conditioning and the soft clinking of silverware from the lobby restaurant.

I approached the reception desk. The marble floor reflected the chandeliers above, making me feel like I was walking on water.

"Checking in," I said, keeping my voice low. "The name is Chibuzor Okafor."

The receptionist was a young woman with impeccable makeup and braids that were twisted into a crown on her head. She typed something into her computer and then looked up. Her eyes lingered on my face a second too long.

"Passport, please," she said.

My heart did a slow, heavy thud against my ribs. I did not have the fake passport yet. I only had Josh Balogun's passport, and that document was a one-way ticket to a federal prison cell.

I reached into my pocket. I didn't pull out a document. I pulled out a crisp, new $100 bill. In Lagos, Benjamin Franklin speaks louder than any government official.

I slid the bill across the cold marble, tucking it discreetly under my credit card.

"I am in the middle of renewing it," I lied. My voice was smooth, practiced. It was the voice of the Nigerian Prince. "Can we waive the scan for tonight? I just need to sleep."

She hesitated. Her eyes flicked down to the money, then back to my face.

She looked around the lobby to ensure her manager wasn't watching. Her hand moved like a cobra, snatching the bill and making it disappear into her pocket.

"Of course, sir," she said. Her smile was professional, but her eyes were still searching mine. "We can make an exception."

She started typing again, but she kept glancing up. It was making my skin crawl.

"Have we met before?" I asked, clearing my throat. I tried to sound casual, but my palms were sweating.

She stopped typing. She tilted her head. "No. But... you look exactly like that guy on Instagram. *The Nigerian Prince.* I used to follow him."

My blood ran cold. It felt like someone had poured ice water down my spine.

I had deleted the account. I had scrubbed the internet. But the internet is a graveyard that never truly closes. 400,000 followers. My face was a digital artifact, burned into the retinas of strangers across the globe.

"I get that a lot," I said, forcing a laugh that sounded like dry leaves crunching. "I wish I had his money."

She laughed too, but the suspicion didn't leave her eyes entirely. She placed a keycard on the marble.

"Room 504. Enjoy your stay, Mr. Chibuzor."

I looked at her. Really studied her. She was older than me. She was in her mid or late twenties.

But the Nigerian Prince doesn't discriminate. He needs someone to massage the royal rod, and this lady looks like she can perform exorcism and miracles with her tongue.

"What's your name?"

"Nneka," she replied.

"Can I have your number, Nneka?" I asked.

She stiffened slightly, her professional mask slipping back into place. She glanced toward the supervisor standing near the concierge desk, then up at the dark dome of the CCTV camera mounted above us.

"I can't do that, sir," she said, her voice dropping to a hush. "It's against company policy. If my manager sees me fraternizing with guests, I could get fired."

I leaned in closer, resting my elbows on the cool marble counter. I lowered my voice to match hers, flashing the charm that had convinced Mrs. Garcia to hire a felon and Zendaya to date a cleaner.

"I'm not asking you to break the rules," I lied smoothly. "I'm just asking for a tour guide. I've been away a long time. I need someone who knows the city. Someone I can trust." I paused, letting my eyes drift over her face. "Besides, it would be a crime to visit Lagos and not spend time with its most beautiful citizen."

She bit her lip, fighting a smile. She looked at me, weighing the risk. The "Nigerian Prince" recognition in her eyes flared up again, the allure of money and danger usually won out against an employee handbook.

Deep down, she still believed I was the Nigerian Prince. Well, she wasn't wrong, but I would never confirm my real identity.

"You are trouble," she murmured.

"I'm the best kind of trouble."

She hesitated for a split second longer, then made her move. She grabbed a small notepad. Keeping her hand low behind the high ridge of the computer monitor, shielded from the camera's angle and her colleague's line of sight, she quickly scribbled a sequence of digits.

She tore the slip off and slid it across the marble, tucked seamlessly underneath my room keycard.

"If anyone asks," she whispered, her eyes darting back to her computer screen as she began typing furiously, "I was just writing down the Wi-Fi password for you."

I slid the keycard and the paper into my pocket. "Understood. The Wi-Fi."

I winked at her. She fought back a blush and turned to answer a ringing phone. I walked toward the elevators, feeling the familiar rush of a small victory.

CHAPTER THIRTY-ONE

Safe in my room, I threw the deadbolt. I checked the window. I checked the bathroom. Paranoia was my new roommate.

I opened my burner laptop and connected via a VPN, routing my signal through three different countries before it touched the open web. I needed a new nationality. I needed a place that sold freedom.

I researched Authorized Agents for the Commonwealth of Dominica Citizenship by Investment Unit. Dominica was perfect; it was respectable, it offered visa-free travel to over a hundred countries, and most importantly, it was for sale.

I picked an agent listed on the official government website. I didn't email him.

Emails sit on servers forever. Emails get subpoenaed. I called him via an encrypted VoIP line. Voice data disappears into the ether.

"I want to apply for the Economic Diversification Fund," I told him when he answered. "Single applicant."

"Excellent choice," the agent said. He sounded British, efficient. "The contribution is $100,000."

"I have the capital," I said. "How fast can we do this?"

"It takes three months for the background check," he said. "You will need to send us the application forms, your medical report, and a police clearance certificate. Once those are submitted, you pay the $7,500 Due Diligence fee. You do not send the main $100,000 until you receive the Letter of Approval in Principle."

"Understood," I said.

"Is there anything that might flag the background check?" he asked. "Criminal records? Visa denials? Political exposure?"

I looked at my reflection in the dark window. I saw a felon. I saw a fraudster. I saw a fugitive.

"No," I lied. "I have a clean record."

If I applied as Josh Balogun, the due diligence firms like Thomson Reuters or Bishop's would find my US conviction in five minutes. Their databases ran deep.

I needed a ghost. I needed Chibuzor Okafor to become flesh and blood.

The next morning, the Lagos heat hit me like a physical blow. It was humid, smelling of exhaust and roadside dust.

I took a taxi to the Nigeria Immigration Service office in Ikoyi. The place was a madhouse. People were shouting, sweating, waving papers in the air. Louts were grabbing at arms, promising to expedite files for a fee.

This was the engine room of Nigerian bureaucracy, and it ran on chaos.

I didn't go to the public queue. I walked around the back, to the "Fast Track" office. In Nigeria, there is always a back door if your pockets are deep enough.

I found a senior officer. She was a woman with tired eyes and a uniform that was slightly too tight around the arms.

Her name tag read Mrs. Adebayo. I walked into her office and closed the door. After exchanging pleasantries, I went straight to the point.

"I need a fresh passport," I said, switching to Yoruba. "New name. New date of birth."

She didn't even look up from her paperwork. "That is impossible. The system is biometric now. One face, one record. It goes to the central server in Abuja."

I reached into my bag. I didn't pull out a form. I pulled out a thick, brown envelope. inside was two hundred thousand naira in cash.

Digital transfers leave trails. Cash is anonymous. Cash has no memory.

I placed the envelope on her desk. It made a heavy, solid sound.

She stopped writing. She looked at the envelope. Then she looked at me.

"The name?" she asked.

"Chibuzor Okafor," I said. "Date of birth: 1999."

She opened the envelope just enough to see the color of the notes. She nodded, satisfied.

"We can override the name," she whispered. "We can change the date of birth. But the fingerprints? If you scan your fingers, the AFIS system will link you to your old passport. It will flag a duplicate. The computer does not take bribes."

"Leave that to me," I said.

I had anticipated this. I knew the technology better than they did. Biometrics were the trap, but every trap has a release mechanism.

"I have a solution," I said.

I went outside to the car park. Sitting in the back of my rented Toyota was a young man named Tobi.

I had picked him up at Obalende bus stop an hour ago. He was a bus conductor, one of the yellow-bus boys who hung off the sides of moving vehicles shouting destinations.

He had rough hands and eyes that looked like they were always searching for the next meal.

I had promised him 10,000 *naira* for a "quick job." To him, 10,000 *naira* was a fortune. It was a week's wages.

"*Oga, we don reach?*" Tobi asked, looking nervous.

"Yes," I said. "Come with me. Don't say a word. Just do what I say."

He was my Fingerprint Mule.

But first, I needed to change my face. The facial recognition software was good, but it wasn't perfect. It relied on nodal points, the distance between the eyes, the shape of the jaw.

I had gone to a professional stylist earlier that morning. I cut my hair low, a skin fade that changed the silhouette of my head.

I couldn't wear glasses because the Nigerian Immigration Service, like the rest of the world, strictly banned them in photos to ensure biometric compliance. If I wore them, the central server in Abuja would auto-reject the application.

Instead, I used a method I learned from old Hollywood method actors. I placed two small, tightly rolled cotton balls between my molars and my cheeks. It was subtle, but it widened my jawline just enough to alter the triangulation of my face.

I also popped in a pair of honey-colored contact lenses. They didn't look fake, but they lightened my dark brown eyes, changing the contrast of my face. I looked in the rearview mirror. Josh Balogun was fading. Chibuzor Okafor was emerging.

I led Tobi into Mrs. Adebayo's office. "Sit," I told him.

Tobi sat in the capture chair. He looked terrified. He looked at the camera, then at the fingerprint scanner.

"Not you," Mrs. Adebayo said, confused. "I need your picture."

"Take my picture," I said, stepping in front of the white background.

I sat down. I kept the glasses on. I pushed my jaw forward slightly.

Click. The camera captured my altered face.

"Now, fingerprints," she said.

I stood up. "Tobi, sit."

Tobi sat down. Mrs. Adebayo looked at me, understanding dawning in her eyes. It was risky. It was highly irregular. But the envelope on her desk was thick.

"Put your hands on the scanner," she ordered Tobi.

Tobi pressed his rough, calloused thumbs onto the green glass.

Beep.

The machine whirred. It captured the ridges and whorls of a Lagos bus conductor. It bonded those prints to my photo.

In the digital brain of the Nigerian government, Chibuzor Okafor now had my face and Tobi's hands. If anyone ever ran a background check, they would search for Tobi's prints. The result would come back clean. Tobi had never applied for a passport. Tobi didn't exist in the system.

"Done," Mrs. Adebayo said. She looked at her screen. "Processing."

I handed Tobi his money. He took it with two hands, bowing slightly.

"Thank you, *sah*," he said. He ran out of the office before anyone could change their mind.

He had no idea he had just sold his identity to an international fugitive.

"Come back in a week," Mrs. Adebayo said. "It will be ready."

I walked out of the office into the blinding sun. The heat felt different now. It didn't feel oppressive. It felt like a blanket covering my tracks.

A week later, I held the new passport in my hands. It was green. It smelled of fresh laminate and glue. I opened it. There I was. Chibuzor Okafor. Nationality: Nigerian. Born: 1999.

I ran my thumb over the biodata page. It felt real. It was real. It was a legitimate document issued by a sovereign state, based on a lie.

I went back to the hotel. I scanned the biodata page. I logged into the secure portal the agent had given me.

I uploaded the scan. I uploaded the fake utility bill I had created for Chibuzor.

I uploaded the clean police report I had bought from a corrupt clerk at the police headquarters in Ikeja.

Then, I opened my burner laptop. I accessed my crypto wallet.

I converted $7,500 worth of Bitcoin into USDT. Then I used a third-party payment processor to wire the funds to the agent's escrow account.

Transaction Complete.

I sat back in the chair. The room was silent. Now, all I had to do was wait. I had to wait for the government of Dominica to vet a man who didn't exist. They would run Chibuzor Okafor through Interpol. They would check his fingerprints against the FBI database.

And they would find nothing. Because Chibuzor Okafor was a ghost with the hands of a bus conductor.

Once the approval came, I would wire the main one hundred thousand dollars. I would get the second passport. I would get the new citizenship.

Nneka wasn't on duty that night, so I booked a short-let apartment and invited her over. She wanted danger and I was trouble.

I put The Weeknd's "Often," Gesaffelstein & The Weeknd's "Lost in the Fire," Bruno Mars "Gorilla," Chris Brown's "Under the Influence," DJ Neptune & Kizz Daniel's "Wait," and Doja Cat's "Need to Know" in a playlist and put it on repeat.

I slid my rod right into her creamy wetness as The Weeknd's voice on "Lost in the Fire" blasted through the speaker. He said, **"Baby, you can bring a friend; she can ride on top your face while I fuck you straight."**

By the time DJ Neptune's track "Wait," with Kizz Daniel's voice singing, **"Nneka wait, open for daddy. Come on, open,"** was blasting through the speakers, Nneka was already straddling my face, grinding her wet love spot into my tongue as I lapped up her pussy like the dog I was. Her juices kept pouring down my cheeks and soaking my breath.

CHAPTER THIRTY-TWO

You don't think I spent those three months in Lagos just sitting in a hotel room, fucking Nneka, and waiting for a passport, do you? A hustler is like a shark. If he stops moving, he dies.

While I waited for the slow wheels of Caribbean bureaucracy to turn "Chibuzor Okafor" into a citizen of Dominica, I secured a retirement fund that most Fortune 500 CEOs wouldn't see in a lifetime.

I made $30 million. I had arrived in Nigeria during a very tense period. The Economic and Financial Crimes Commission (EFCC) had launched a brutal crackdown on Politically Exposed Persons.

The Federal Government had weaponized greed by introducing the Whistleblower Policy. The government offered snitches anywhere from two-and-a-half to five percent of the recovered loot. It turned the country into a surveillance state overnight.

Gardeners were snitching on bosses who buried cash in septic tanks. Drivers were recording conversations in the back of Rolls-Royces. Mistresses were calling the EFCC hotline on their sugar daddies.

Every corrupt Nigerian moved with an air of paranoia. Trust was a currency more valuable than the naira. And I walked right into the middle of it.

It started at the Eko Hotel swimming pool. I barely went out. Even with my new haircut and glasses, I was paranoid that someone might recognize "The Nigerian Prince."

I didn't swim. I sat on a lounge chair in the corner, wearing dark shades, nursing a glass of Pepsi.

"Are you planning to swim in denim jeans?"

I turned. Standing there was a girl who looked like she had just walked out of a music video. Taller than me, light-skinned, expensive Brazilian hair, and a Fendi swimsuit.

"No," I said, recovering my composure. "I am just chilling."

She eyed the bottle of Pepsi. "Is there *coco* in there?"

I looked confused. "*Coco?*"

She reached down, grabbed my glass, took a sip, and wrinkled her nose. "It is flat. I can't believe you are drinking raw Pepsi. You aren't mixing it with Codeine or *Refnol?*"

"I don't do drugs," I said. "Unless I am stressed."

Instead of drugs, alcohol, and smoking, I preferred sex. I would rather have a Latina sit on my face than smoke weed.

"Wow. A Lagos boy who doesn't do tramadol? Are you an *SU?*"

SU. *Scripture Union*. Slang for the overly religious people.

I laughed. "No. I just like to keep my head clear."

She sat on the lounger next to me, uninvited. "I am Seyi."

I hesitated. I couldn't use Josh Balogun. "I am Chibuzor."

She looked at me skeptically. "Chibuzor? You don't give Igbo boy vibes. You have a Yoruba accent."

I smiled. "My mom is Yoruba. I grew up in Lagos."

"Okay, Chibuzor," she said, testing the name.

Luckily, Seyi didn't recognize me. She was too busy talking about herself. She was a quintessential *Ajebutter*, a rich kid from the one percent who had never experienced a day of hardship. Her father was a powerful Senator in Abuja; her mother was in the House of Representatives.

"Most Nigerian guys are so boring," she complained, scrolling through her iPhone. "All they talk about is crypto, fraud, drugs, and sex. None of them can hold a conversation about... I don't know, geopolitics or climate change. Fucking dummies."

I chuckled. She was arrogant, entitled, and exactly the kind of shield I needed. A guy moving alone in Lagos is suspicious. A guy moving with a Senator's daughter is untouchable.

We exchanged numbers.

Over the next few days, Seyi dragged me into her world. She picked me up in a Mercedes G63 AMG, the official uniform of the Lagos elite. A Lamborghini would have been destroyed by potholes on the road, but the G-Wagon bullied the road, parting traffic like the Red Sea.

I enjoyed her company, but I kept my guard up. Melina had destroyed my ability to trust women, and Zendaya was the only one who had managed to crack that armor. Seyi was just a distraction.

Then, she dropped the bomb. "My dad is flying in from Abuja this weekend," she said. "He wants to meet you."

"Why?"

She rolled her eyes. "He wants to meet my boyfriend."

I choked on my drink. I hadn't asked her out. Yes, we had had sex ten or twenty times, but I had never asked her to be my girlfriend. I thought we were just friends with benefits. But in Seyi's world, if she decided she liked you, she owned you.

"Seyi, we are just hanging out," I said. "Going with the flow."

"Don't be shy," she laughed. "Just come for dinner. Banana Island."

Banana Island. The most expensive real estate in West Africa. An artificial island built for billionaires who wanted to separate themselves from the chaos of Lagos.

The driveway of her father's mansion looked like a luxury car dealership. Rolls-Royce Cullinan, Bentley Bentayga, Ferrari 488. There were more than thirty cars parked there.

"May God punish these thieves," I muttered in Yoruba under my breath.

My father, a civil servant, had died of hypertension because he couldn't afford better healthcare. This man had millions of dollars in metal sitting in his driveway, bought with public funds.

"Your parents do well for themselves," I commented dryly as we entered the mansion.

Seyi chuckled, oblivious to my disdain.

We walked into a living room that was larger than my entire hotel floor. Her father, Senator Adeyemi, was sitting on a gold-rimmed sofa, watching CNN. He was a large man with a heavy face and the weary eyes of someone who played dirty games for a living.

As a Yoruba man, I knew the protocol. I prostrated flat on the floor. In Yoruba, we call it *dobale*, a sign of total submission and respect.

"Good evening, sir," I said from the floor.

"Stand up," he grunted.

He stared at me. It was the same look the receptionist at Eko Hotel had given me. A flicker of recognition. It seemed like everyone in Lagos recognized me except Seyi.

Seyi chatted nervously for a few minutes, then went upstairs to change.

The moment she was gone, the air in the room changed.

The Senator leaned forward. "You introduced yourself as Chibuzor."

"Yes, sir."

"But you look exactly like that boy on Instagram," he said, his voice low and dangerous. "The Nigerian Prince."

My heart hammered against my ribs. I kept my face neutral.

"I get that a lot, sir."

He smiled. It wasn't a nice smile. "So, it is you. The fraudster. The boy who flaunted dollars while the EFCC was sleeping. You were so young then, not up to eighteen years old. Yet, you were living the life many people dreamt of. Flying in private jets, burning money, chilling with women most people only see on TV and magazines."

I didn't answer. Denying it now would insult his intelligence.

"Relax," he said, handing me a business card. "I didn't become a Senator by judging how men make their money. I like people like you. People who hate poverty and will do anything to escape from it. I need to talk to you. Alone. Call me tomorrow."

I took the card. "Yes, sir."

I met Senator Adeyemi the next day at a discreet, members-only cigar lounge in Ikoyi. He didn't waste time.

"I know you are into illicit finance," he said, cutting the tip of a Cuban cigar. "A boy with your lifestyle didn't make it selling pure water."

I remained silent.

"I didn't call you here to arrest you," he continued. "I need your help."

He lit the cigar, blowing smoke into the air. As he did that, a guy walked past who looked just like one of my mentors, Ray Hushpuppi.

"The government has gone mad," he said. "This Whistleblower Policy... it is a disaster. They are offering five percent to anyone who rats. My driver, my cook, even my own brother... they are all looking at me like I am a walking ATM."

"What do you need, sir?"

He leaned in. "The EFCC has flagged my passport. I can't fly to Dubai. I can't move funds through the banks because the NFIU tracks everything over five million naira. I am stuck with a significant amount of liquidity."

"How much?" I asked.

"I have cash," he said. "Stored in a reinforced strong room behind a false wall in my guest house. But I need to move it. I need to hide it before one of my staff gets brave enough to call the hotline."

"How much?" I repeated.

He looked around the empty lounge to ensure we were alone. "$100 million."

I froze. $100 million. In cash.

"Sir," I said, my mind racing. "Do you know the physical volume of that? Even in hundred-dollar bills, that weighs over two thousand pounds. It is a logistic nightmare."

"I know," he said. "That is why I called you. You are young. You understand the new ways. Crypto. Shell companies. Most of the people only know the archaic methods which is suicidal right now. I need you to make this money disappear from my house and reappear in a secure structure where the government cannot touch it."

"What is my cut?"

He looked at me. "Thirty percent."

$30 million.

I did the mental math instantly. With the $6 million I had from laundering money for The Professor, other cartel members, and my own personal contacts in the underworld, plus this $30 million... I wouldn't just be rich. I would be a king. I could take my Dominican passport, disappear to an island, and never touch a keyboard for crime again.

But I couldn't use the method I used for the cartel. I couldn't use art, not for this volume in Nigeria. I couldn't use Bitcoin ATMs; they didn't exist here in any significant capacity.

I needed a structural solution.

"I can do it," I said.

"But we can't use international transfers. The correspondent banks will block it. We have to keep the money in Nigeria but hide it in plain sight."

"How?"

"Shelf companies," I said.

"We don't register new companies; that raises flags. We buy existing, dormant companies, businesses registered ten, fifteen years ago that have 'died.' We revive them. We open corporate Domiciliary Accounts. We make it look like legitimate commercial revenue."

He nodded slowly. "And how do we get the cash into the bank without the sensors tripping?"

"Leave that to me," I said. "But Seyi must never know. If she finds out, the deal is off."

"Of course," he smiled, tapping ash into the tray. "She thinks money falls from heaven. Let's keep it that way. She doesn't understand that for every rich kid out there, there's someone who got their hands dirty on their behalf. She thinks it's my salary as a senator that's paying for her Paris shopping trips."

I left the lounge with my heart pounding. I had a plan. I wasn't going to use Ghana-Must-Go bags to deposit such a huge amount. That was amateur hour.

To move $100 million in Lagos, I needed two things: **A corrupt bank manager who sold "Ghost Accounts." And a Bullion Van.**

CHAPTER THIRTY-THREE

I spent the night scheming. Lagos was not Los Angeles. In America, money talks. In Nigeria, money screams. It opens doors that don't even have handles.

But I had a logistical nightmare. $100 million in physical cash is enormous. It weighs roughly two thousand, two hundred pounds. It occupies about fifty cubic feet. You don't put that in the trunk of a Corolla.

I needed structure. I needed to build a financial pipeline that looked legitimate from the outside but was hollow on the inside. The next morning, I took an Uber to the Corporate Affairs Commission office in Alausa.

The office was a monument to bureaucracy. Files were stacked in precarious towers that threatened to topple and crush the civil servants sleeping at their desks. The air conditioning was broken, and the room smelled of sweat and old paper.

"How can I help you?" an officer asked, barely looking up from his bowl of *amala*.

"I need to see your *oga*," I said.

He waved a dismissive hand. "See this stupid little boy. No respect. Do I look like your servant? Are you mad? Are you—"

I reached into my pocket. I slid a bundle of 20 thousand naira notes onto his desk, right next to his stew.

He stopped chewing. He looked at the money, then at me.

"My boss is busy," he said, the cash vanishing into his pocket like magic.

"But I can take you to him. You seem like a 'good customer.'"

He led me to a back office. The boss, Mr. Fasanmi, was a pot-bellied man that took up half the room.

"E ka san, sir," I greeted him, prostrating fully on the dusty carpet. I needed to create a good first impression.

He smiled. "A well-raised Yoruba boy. Rare these days. Stand up."

I went straight to the point after exchanging pleasantries. No need to beat around the bush.

"Sir, I need fifteen dormant companies," I said. "Registered at least ten years ago. Clean tax history, but inactive."

Buying existing companies, Shelf Companies, is a legal gray area. It gives the illusion of longevity. A company registered in 2008 looks trustworthy. A company registered yesterday looks like a scam.

"That is expensive," Fasanmi grunted, tapping a pen on his desk. "Finding clean files from ten years ago... it takes work."

"I will pay two million naira per company," I said.

His eyes widened. He did the math. "Thirty million naira?"

"Cash. Today."

An hour later, I was the proud owner of fifteen zombie companies. BlueSky Logistics, Apex Construction, GreenField Agro-Allied. They were hollow shells, but on paper, they were veterans of Nigerian industry.

Next, the bank. I went to Wema Bank in Victoria Island. I didn't take a number.

I walked straight to the executive wing and asked for the Branch Manager, Mr. Oni. I bribed the right people, and I was sitting in front of Mr. Oni in less than ten minutes.

He was a sharp man in a sharp suit, skeptical of a young man in jeans. I placed a bundle of one hundred thousand naira on his desk. "Just for the introduction."

He sat up straighter.

"I need to open fifteen corporate Domiciliary Accounts for these companies," I said, laying out the certificates of incorporation I had just bought. "And I need to deposit significant cash liquidity."

"How significant?"

"Seventy million dollars."

Mr. Oni choked on his coffee. He coughed, wiping his mouth with a handkerchief.

"Seventy million? The NFIU will flag that instantly. The sensors..."

"Not if we use Bullion Vans," I said calmly. "We structure the deposits as 'Cash-in-Transit' from legitimate business operations. Retail chains. Construction sites. We don't use the teller counter. We drive the van straight into your secure loading bay. You verify the cash in the vault, off-camera. No CCTV."

"And the KYC?" he asked, sweating now. "The directors?"

"I have the documents," I said. "But I need you to handle the BVN mapping. I need you to link these accounts to... let's say, less scrutinized profiles."

"You want me to risk my job? My pension?"

"I will pay you one percent," I said.

He froze. One percent of seventy million dollars was seven hundred thousand dollars. In Nigeria, that is generational wealth.

He licked his lips. He looked at the door.

"When do we start?"

The logistics were military-grade.

We couldn't move the money in cars. The risk of robbery, or police shakedowns, was too high. In Lagos, traffic is the great equalizer. A Rolls-Royce gets stuck in the same *go-slow* as a danfo bus.

I contacted a private security firm that operated Armored Bullion Vans. These are the heavy, bulletproof trucks used by banks to move cash. In Nigeria, money buys anything, including the police escort that comes with the van.

I rented a warehouse in Ikeja, posing as a logistics company.

We moved the cash from the Senator's bunker to the warehouse at night, using his personal convoy of Land Cruisers with tinted windows. It took three nights.

Once at the warehouse, we loaded the pallets of shrink-wrapped hundred-dollar bills into the Bullion Vans.

The next morning, the convoy rolled out. Two armored trucks, flanked by a police escort with sirens blazing. *Wee-ooo-wee-ooo.* The traffic parted. To any observer, it was just another bank transfer. Central Bank business.

We drove straight into the secure loading bay of Wema Bank. Mr. Oni met us there. We bypassed the banking hall entirely. The cash went straight into the vault.

Over the next two weeks, we moved the entire seventy million dollars. The money was now sitting in corporate accounts, ostensibly the earnings of fifteen established companies.

One evening, after a long day of logistics, I was walking back to my hotel in Ikeja. The sun was setting, casting a dusty orange glow over the chaos of the streets.

I saw a young boy, maybe ten years old, hawking bottled water in the traffic. He was skinny, his ribs showing through his torn shirt. He was weaving between cars, dodging okada riders who drove like they had a death wish.

I whistled. "*Wa!*" Come!

He ran over, breathless. "Water, sir? Cold water?"

"Why aren't you in school?" I asked in Yoruba.

He wiped sweat from his forehead with a dirty hand. "My parents can't afford it. My dad is sick. My mom is blind. I have to sell water to feed my siblings and take care of my parents."

It broke my heart. This was the reality of Nigeria. Politicians like Seyi's dad stole billions, hiding cash behind false walls, while kids like this drank gutter water.

I was once like this kid. Poor and helpless while my loved ones got sick and died because we couldn't afford to pay their medical bills. I felt sorry for the boy. I wanted to help him.

"What's your name?"

"Kayode, sir."

"What do you want to be when you grow up?" I asked.

The boy straightened up. His eyes shone. "*Mo fe sa se tin ba ti dagba. Mo fe ma se Yahoo.*"

I want to do Yahoo. I want to become a fraudster.

I felt a cold chill run through me. The system was so broken that crime was the only aspiration left. The only way out of the ghetto was a laptop and a lie.

"Don't say that," I said sharply. "Fraud destroys you. Look at me. Do I look like a *yahoo boy?*"

He looked at my clean clothes. My expensive watch. "Yes, sir."

No, kid. I don't scam people anymore. I launder money for drug cartels and corrupt politicians now.

I laughed sadly. "Kayode. I am going to help you. But you must promise me one thing. No Yahoo. You go to school. You must become a doctor, an engineer, a lawyer. Anything but a thief."

"Sir? That is impossible. My parents can't afford to send me to school. Even if I go to college, I won't get any job after graduation since I don't have any connections. In this country, you can't get a good job without knowing the right people."

He was right.

"Come with me," I said.

He hesitated.

"Don't worry," I said. "I want to give you something for your mother. But not here."

I led him down the street to the gated entrance of my short-let apartment complex. I had moved from Eko Hotels to the short-let apartment complex permanently. I couldn't be carrying cash around the hotel with lots of CCTVs.

I couldn't let him inside, I had sensitive documents and cash in there, but the gatehouse was secure.

"Wait here with the security guard," I told him. "Don't move."

I went inside. I opened the safe where I kept my personal "float." I counted out five million naira in 1,000-naira notes.

I stuffed the bricks into a black opaque nylon bag, the kind market women use, so no one could see the contents.

I walked back to the gate. Kayode was waiting, looking nervous. I handed him the heavy bag.

"Listen to me," I said, my voice low. "Do not open this on the street. Run straight home. Give this to your mother. Tell her to start a business. A proper business."

He felt the weight of the bag. His eyes widened in shock. "Sir...?"

"And you," I said, gripping his shoulder. "You go to school. You become a doctor, an engineer, a pilot. Anything but a thief. Do you hear me? Come back to where we met earlier tomorrow at 10 AM. I have something else for you."

He fell to his knees in the dust, grabbing my legs. "Thank you, sir! Thank you! *E se gan*!"

"Stand up," I said, pulling him up roughly. "A man does not beg."

I watched him run off into the night, clutching the bag to his chest like a lifeline.

The next day, I wanted to ensure the money lasted. I found him at the same spot, he wasn't hawking, he was waiting for me. I took him to a GTBank branch in Ikeja.

I sat down with the manager. I used my new "Chibuzor Okafor" ID.

"I want to open an Educational Trust Fund for this boy," I said.

I deposited fifty million naira.

The manager's jaw nearly hit the desk. He looked from me to the street kid in oversized clothes.

"You can't touch this until you are eighteen," I told Kayode, signing the deed. "And only if you finish secondary school with good grades. The bank manager here will receive your report cards every term. If you fail, the money freezes. Do you understand?"

Kayode nodded, tears streaming down his dusty face. "I understand, sir."

I walked out of the bank, leaving a crying boy and a confused manager behind. It was penance. I was laundering millions for a thief who stole from the country, but maybe, just maybe, I could save one soul from the fire I was burning in.

I spent the next month cleaning my own share, the thirty million dollars. I didn't use banks. I used the Hawala system. The Bureau De Change operators in Sabo.

I took my cash to the currency market. It is an open-air stock exchange of dusty men sitting on plastic chairs with bags of cash. I sold the dollars for naira at the black market rate, then used the naira to buy Bitcoin from OTC brokers.

It was slow, tedious work. I had to break it down into small chunks to avoid attention. But eventually, I had thirty million dollars in Bitcoin sitting on my Ledger Nano X.

I contacted my sister, Abisola.

"I am sending you something," I told her over an end-to-end encrypted WhatsApp call. "Create a wallet."

I sent her ten million dollars in Bitcoin.

"Josh?" she gasped. "Where did you get this?"

"Don't ask," I said. "Just live. Travel. Be free. You don't have to struggle anymore. And stay away from boys. You're not allowed to have boyfriends until you're thirty years old."

I didn't want anyone to break my sister's heart.

Eighty-four days later, an email arrived.

Subject: **Approval in Principle – Citizenship by Investment Unit, Commonwealth of Dominica.**

They had vetted Chibuzor Okafor.

They ran the fingerprints of the bus conductor. They ran the face of the man with the glasses.

Result: CLEAN.

I wired the $100,000 investment from my shell account.

Two weeks later, a courier package arrived at my hotel. I opened it. Inside was a blue passport with gold lettering. Commonwealth of Dominica.

Name: Chibuzor Okafor.

I laughed. It was a maniacal sound that startled the maid in the hallway.

I had done it. I had beaten the FBI. I had beaten the Nigerian government. I had beaten poverty. AGAIN.

I looked at the passport photo, the man with the glasses and the slight smirk. He didn't exist, but he was free.

"Hong Kong," I whispered. "Here I come."

CHAPTER THIRTY-FOUR

It would have been sheer folly to fly directly from Nigeria to Hong Kong. Direct flights from Lagos are red flags for drug enforcement agencies, and "Chibuzor Okafor" had no travel history. I needed to build a pattern of leisure travel first.

So, I utilized the Visa-on-Arrival policy of the Republic of Maldives.

I flew Qatar Airways from Lagos to Doha, then connected to Malé. At immigration, I presented my Nigerian passport and my booking for the *Gili Lankanfushi*. The officer stamped me in for thirty days.

I stayed in the Private Reserve, the largest overwater villa in the world. It cost $15,000 per night.

Multiply that by fourteen nights.

It was an obscene display of wealth, but for Chibuzor Okafor, a man with no criminal record and a "successful crypto trading" backstory, it was perfect cover.

The resort was isolationist heaven. But even in paradise, my demons followed me.

Two nights before my checkout, I was sitting on my private deck, staring at the turquoise water and listening to "Litty" by Meek Mill and Tory Lanez. I was at the part where Tory Lanez said, "They be making memes, I be making millions," when a staff member brought my lunch on a silver tray.

I lifted the cloche.

Lobster Thermidor.

I stared at the bright red shell, cracked open to reveal the white meat.

Something inside me snapped. Maybe it was the stress of the double life. Maybe it was the memory of the cage I had lived in. But seeing this creature, something that just wanted to live in the dark, dragged up and boiled alive for my amusement, triggered a violent rage.

I stood up and kicked the table.

The silver tray flew. The porcelain plates shattered against the teak deck. The lobster skidded across the floor.

"What is this crap?" I shouted.

The server, a young Maldivian woman, flinched, terrified. "Sir? I... I thought..."

"Is this how you treat your guests?" I screamed, pointing at the shattered remains. "I specifically stated in my booking preferences: no seafood."

"I am so sorry, sir, I will—"

"Do you know what that is?" I walked over and pointed at the lobster. "That is a sentient being. It lives in the deep. It minds its own business. And you dragged it up, boiled it alive, and put it on a plate with cheese? How can you hurt an innocent sea creature?"

"I will fix it, sir. I will bring the wagyu beef."

"I don't want beef!" I roared. "I want you to respect the order!"

My phone buzzed on the deck chair. It was Don Alberto. I took a deep breath, adjusting my silk robe. I picked up the phone, switching instantly from manic rage to professional calm.

"*Ciao*, Alberto."

"*Mio amico*," his voice rasped. "I hear shouting. Is everything okay?"

"Just the staff," I said, eyeing the terrified waitress. "They served me lobster. You know I don't eat anything from the sea."

"Nate," Alberto chuckled. "You launder money for murderers, but you cry over a fish's death? You eat chicken, no?"

"Chickens are bred for food," I said, my voice cold. "Sea creatures are different. They live in a different world. We should let them enjoy their habitat peacefully. It's about consent, Alberto. The ocean didn't consent to feed us."

I waved the waitress away. She scrambled to clean up the mess.

"Did chicken consent to be your dinner? You are a strange man, Nate Haliv," Alberto said. "But your brain works, so I tolerate the madness. Now, listen. We have a problem."

"Go on."

"I have the twenty million dollars liquid. But moving it from Italy to Hong Kong... the banks are watching the wire transfers too closely. If I send twenty million to a new company in Hong Kong, the Italian regulators will freeze it."

I walked to the edge of the deck, looking down at the sharks circling in the water below. They were honest predators. I respected them.

"Do not use the banks," I said. "Use the Chinese Underground Banking System, the *Fei-Chien*."

"Explain."

"There are brokers in Prato and Milan," I said. "They service the Chinese textile importers. You give them the physical Euro cash in Italy. They don't wire it. They settle the balance internally with their partners in China."

"And how do I get it?"

"You tell them you want the payout in USDT (Tether)," I said. "Not Bitcoin. Bitcoin is too volatile. If the price drops 5% while we are moving the funds, you lose a million dollars. USDT is stable."

"And then?"

"Then, you send the USDT to my cold storage wallet," I explained. "I will carry the hardware wallet to Hong Kong physically. Once I am there, I will go to an OTC (Over-The-Counter) Desk in Kowloon. I will swap the USDT for Hong Kong Dollars cash, and then I will deposit the cash into the corporate account of our new shell company, Apex Global Logistics."

"You make it sound easy," Alberto said.

"It is not easy. It is structured. Send the USDT in batches of five million to the address I generate. I will verify receipt on the blockchain."

"*Bene*," Alberto said. "The first batch moves tomorrow. Enjoy your... non-seafood lunch."

I hung up.

I sat back down, watching the sharks. The waitress returned with a plate of pasta. She placed it down with trembling hands.

"I'm sorry," I said softly. "I didn't mean to scare you. I just... I hate seeing things trapped."

She nodded and fled.

That night, I had to perform my other role. I FaceTimed Zendaya.

I turned off all the lights in the villa. I sat in the corner of the bathroom where the wall was plain plaster. I draped a black towel over my shoulders to hide the expensive robe.

"Hey baby," she said, her face lighting up my screen.

"Hey," I whispered.

"Why is it always so dark?" she asked.

"You know we don't have good electricity in Africa," I lied. "And the generator fuel is finished. I don't have money to buy fuel tonight."

"I'm sorry, babe. Should I send you some money via Western Union?"

"No!" I yelled.

"Josh, I know you're struggling right now, and I still love you. You don't need to pretend to be okay. Let me send $1,000 to you to buy some fuel and get groceries."

God damn it! Stop making me love you so much, woman!

"I'm fine, baby. I'll let you know whenever I need a loan from you."

"Okay. I miss you," she said. "Are you eating okay?"

"Yeah," I said, thinking of the $300 pasta I had just eaten. "I ate some roasted yams earlier. Village food."

"I'm proud of you, Josh. Working so hard. You're one of the rarest men we have on earth. No greed. Just pure hard work."

"I'm doing it for us," I said.

We talked for ten minutes until I feigned a bad connection and hung up. I felt sick. I hated lying to the only person who loved me apart from my sister.

The plan was set. But now came the most dangerous part of the trip: The Shake.

I had entered Maldives as Chibuzor Okafor (Nigerian). I needed to enter Hong Kong as Chibuzor Okafor (Dominican).

The name was the same, but the privileges were vastly different. A Nigerian passport holder needs a difficult-to-obtain visa to enter Hong Kong. A citizen of the Commonwealth of Dominica, however, can enter Hong Kong visa-free for 90 days.

I checked out of the resort and took a boat to Malé International Airport.

I checked in for a flight to Dubai using my Nigerian passport.

When I landed in Dubai, I did not go through immigration. I stayed in the transit zone.

I went to the bathroom and locked the stall door. I put away the green Nigerian passport. I pulled out the pristine blue Dominican passport.

I walked to the transfer desk for Cathay Pacific. I had booked the connecting flight to Hong Kong under the name Chibuzor Okafor, which matched both documents.

"I need to print my boarding pass for Hong Kong," I told the agent.

"Passport, please," she said.

I handed her the Dominican passport.

She scanned it. Since I was in the transit zone, she didn't care how I arrived in Dubai; she only cared if I had the right to enter Hong Kong. As a "Dominican citizen," I did.

She handed me the boarding pass.

"Have a safe flight, Mr. Okafor."

I smiled. The Nigerian national who needed a visa had vanished in a bathroom stall in Dubai. The Caribbean investor with visa-free access was now boarding a flight to Asia.

Six hours later, I landed at Hong Kong International Airport.

I walked toward the immigration line. I saw the automated Smart Gates. They were faster, scanning faces and fingerprints automatically.

I stopped. My Dominican passport had my face (with the subtle alterations), but the chip contained the fingerprints of the village boy in Lagos. If I used the automated gate, the facial recognition might pass, but if it asked for a thumbprint, I would trigger a mismatch alarm. The barriers would lock. The police would come.

I couldn't risk it. I shifted lanes, walking to the manual booth manned by a tired immigration officer.

I handed him the pristine blue passport. He opened it. He looked at the photo (me with the cotton in my cheeks and the glasses).

He looked at my face (me with the cotton in my cheeks and the glasses). He didn't ask for a fingerprint. He picked up his stamp.

Thump.

HONG KONG IMMIGRATION - PERMITTED TO REMAIN - 90 DAYS.

I walked through the sliding doors into the humid air of Chek Lap Kok.

I hailed a red taxi.

"The Peninsula Hotel," I said.

I patted the Ledger Nano X in my pocket. It held $20 million in encrypted USDT.

I had successfully turned Italian drug money into digital tokens, flown them across the Indian Ocean, and landed in the financial capital of Asia. Now, I just had to wash it clean.

CHAPTER THIRTY-FIVE

Hong Kong rendered me speechless. It was the nightmare of any socialist and the wet dream of every capitalist.

It is a city built on the concept of "Laissez-faire." Low tax, high speed, and absolute discretion. Hong Kong is among the top six locations with the highest number of billionaires globally, and for good reason. The territory prides itself on its capitalist nature.

In America, you are constantly looking over your shoulder for Uncle Sam. You pay up to 37% of your earnings in federal tax, plus state tax, plus sales tax. In Germany, if you earn a decent living, the government takes nearly half your gross income.

But here? In Hong Kong, the corporate tax rate caps at 16.5%. There is no capital gains tax, no dividend tax, and no inheritance tax. It is a jurisdiction designed to let money breathe.

I checked into the InterContinental Hong Kong. I booked the Presidential Suite at $12,628 a night. My trip was sponsored by the Camorra, so I burned their money with a smile. I lodged at the hotel for twenty days, spending over a quarter of a million dollars on accommodation alone.

I realized quickly that in this city, money has no color. In America, I was a Black ex-con. In Europe, I was an immigrant. But in Hong Kong, arriving in a hotel limousine and wearing a Patek Philippe, I was "Sir," a boss.

When you are rich and successful, people see you as a person irrespective of your skin color. But you are just a "normal Negro" to everyone when you are an average Black person.

I wasn't distracted by the luxury. I was there for the wash. I needed a local guide, not for tourism, but for bureaucracy. I hired a "translator" through the hotel concierge, requesting someone with business experience.

They sent Wing Chan. He was a quiet man in his fifties, wearing a suit that was ten years out of fashion.

He spoke perfect English, having lived in London before the handover.

"Whatever I say stays between us, right?" I asked as we sat in the hotel's tea lounge. "In my line of business, trust is crucial."

"Of course," Wing Chan replied in a professional tone. "I have worked for many people. I am an interpreter, not a rat."

I studied him. He looked tired. Worn down by a city that crushed anyone who didn't have capital.

"How old are you, Wing?"

He looked surprised. "I am fifty-two."

"And your children?"

"I have just one son." His face lit up with a mixture of pride and anxiety. "He will be eighteen very soon."

I nodded, leaning back in the plush chair. I decided to attack him psychologically. I had found the weak spot.

"Do you want your son to end up like you?"

He blinked. "I don't understand."

"Do you want your son to work as a translator, bowing to men young enough to be his children? Do you want him to serve people like me for the rest of his life?"

He stopped smiling. "Why are you insulting me? My job is honest."

I placed my hand on his shoulder. "There are only two types of people in this world, my friend: the rich and the poor. Unless you win a lottery, your son is destined for the same grind. Unless you change his trajectory."

Wing Chan remained quiet, staring at his tea.

"I can give you enough money to send him to Harvard. Or Stanford. Or Kingsley University."

He shifted uneasily.

"Kingsley University is the most expensive college in the world. It's not for people like me."

"It is expensive," I agreed. "But I am willing to pay you one million dollars if you follow my instructions."

He froze. One million dollars was twenty years of salary for him.

"What do you want me to do?" he asked with a sigh.

"I don't need a translator," I said. "I need a Nominee Director."

I explained the job. I wasn't going to ask him to open 3,000 bank accounts or carry bags of cash. I needed him to be the "Face."

In Hong Kong, you can legally hire a local resident to sit on the board of a company, so the real owner remains anonymous. It is a service offered by law firms every day.

"You sign the papers," I said. "You attend the meetings. But I hold the Power of Attorney. You take the administrative risk; you get the million. Your son goes to Harvard."

He looked at me, fear warring with greed. Greed won.

"I will do it."

Wing introduced me to a broker I will call Mr. M. I won't mention his real name due to personal reasons. Don't ask me why.

Mr. M operated out of a nondescript office in Central. He wasn't a retail stockbroker; he was a Private Equity Manager. He specialized in "Alternative Assets" and high-risk capital.

Unlike the big banks like HSBC that required mountains of paperwork and strict compliance checks, Mr. M operated in the gray zone. He accepted USDT (Tether).

In Hong Kong, Bitcoin and stablecoins are viewed as virtual commodities, not legal tender.

This regulatory gap allowed private funds to accept crypto as "in-kind contributions" without triggering banking alerts.

I transferred the $20 million in USDT from my Ledger wallet to Mr. M's cold storage.

"Clean or dirty?" Mr. M asked, checking the transaction on his iPad.

"Gray," I said. "Gambling proceeds. Unregulated."

He smirked. He knew it was narcotics or mafia money, but he didn't care. Mr. M was the Julian Schmitt of Asia.

"Here is the structure," I said. "We cannot open thousands of individual trading accounts. That is a logistical nightmare. Instead, we open a Private Investment Fund."

This was the fix.

If I tried to open 3,000 brokerage accounts using fake IDs, I would need 3,000 utility bills, 3,000 phone numbers, and 3,000 bank accounts to fund them. The compliance department would shut me down in a week.

But a Fund? A Fund is a single legal entity.

"We structure it as a Segregated Portfolio Company (SPC)," Mr. M suggested. "The Fund is the legal entity that buys the stocks. The Fund has one Director, Wing Chan. But the capital comes from the Limited Partners (LPs)."

"Exactly," I said. "And I have the LPs."

This was where the fake IDs came in.

OpSec (Operational Security) is religion in this business. You do not use an iPhone. You do not use a Samsung. And you never, ever use a standard Android device to ask incriminating questions.

Google is the Feds' official spy. Everything you do with a standard Google account is logged. Your location history, your search queries, your voice metadata.

Even if you turn off "Location Services," the standard Android OS still pings cell towers and Wi-Fi networks to triangulate you.

If you commit a crime with a factory-setting phone in your pocket, you are building your own prison cell. That is why I didn't buy a shady "encrypted phone" from a dealer. After the feds took down EncroChat and Sky ECC earlier, nobody trusted those pre-made devices anymore. They were all honeypots.

Instead, I built my own.

I bought a Google Pixel 6 Pro.

I know what you are thinking: *didn't you just say Google is the spy?*

Yes. But the Pixel hardware is the most secure on the market because of the Titan M2 security chip. The trick is to wipe the software.

I connected the phone to my laptop and flashed the operating system, replacing the standard Android with GrapheneOS.

GrapheneOS is a hardened, privacy-focused system. It completely de-Googles the phone. No Play Store, no tracking services, no backdoors. It looks like a normal phone, which is great for crossing borders without raising suspicion, but inside, it is a fortress.

I accessed the dark web using Tor Browser routed through a VPN and a bridge relay. I had visited a forum called Dread, a dark web version of Reddit. I liaised with a vendor named 0x981.

0x981 worked for a KYC (Know Your Customer) verification firm that contracted with major crypto exchanges and fintech apps. When people uploaded their passports and selfies to sign up for "Binance" or "Wise," 0x981 stole the data.

I bought 3,000 "Fullz"—complete identity packs including passports, utility bills, and selfies.

I handed the encrypted drive to Mr. M.

"These are your Limited Partners," I said. "Three thousand investors, contributing small amounts ranging from $5,000 to $10,000 each. They are passive investors. They don't vote. They just provide capital."

Mr. M nodded. "The Fund aggregates the capital. Wing Chan signs as the Director.

"The Fund buys $20 million worth of blue-chip stocks like Tencent, Alibaba, AIA. To the regulators, it looks like a standard retail investment vehicle pooling money from small overseas investors."

It was brilliant.

The $20 million flowed into the stock market. We bought shares in safe, stable giants. We weren't trying to beat the market; we were trying to store value.

Mr. M took a 4% commission. It was steep, but for washing $20 million without a single ID check on the real owner, it was a bargain.

Two days later, I called The Professor.

"The Italian funds are secure," I reported. "Invested in the Asian markets."

"Good work, Nate," she said. "But since you are there… I have been looking at the map."

"And?"

"Asia is a goldmine," she said. "The price of a kilo of cocaine in Los Angeles is $25,000. In Australia, it is $200,000. In Japan, it is $180,000."

"You want to expand," I said. "You want to set up a lab?"

"No," she said. "Manufacturing in Asia is suicide. Hong Kong and Taiwan are surveillance states. There are cameras on every corner. If you cook fentanyl there, they will hang you."

She paused. "I don't want to make drugs there. I want to move them. I want a pipeline. We need to ship product from Mexico to Australia. But we can't ship direct. The Australian Border Force scans everything coming from South America. They profile the ships."

"We need a transshipment hub," I realized.

"Exactly. Cargo coming from Hong Kong is considered 'low risk.' I want you to buy a logistics company. A freight forwarder. We will ship the product from Mexico to Hong Kong hidden in legitimate cargo like textiles and machinery. Once it clears customs in Hong Kong, it is 're-originated.' We repackage it as Chinese goods and ship it to Sydney and Tokyo."

It was a classic Transshipment Scheme. You wash the cargo's origin the same way you wash money.

"I'm on it," I said.

I went back to Wing Chan.

"I have another job for you," I said. "The Fund is going to acquire a subsidiary."

Using the capital in the Fund, we acquired a struggling Freight Forwarding Company in Kwai Chung Port.

We didn't manufacture a single gram of drugs in Hong Kong. We just managed the boxes.

The cocaine arrived from Manzanillo, Mexico, concealed inside industrial spools of copper wire. The copper shielded the organic density of the drugs from X-rays.

My team in the warehouse, hired by Wing Chan, unpacked it. They threw away the Mexican shipping manifests. They repackaged the bricks into crates labeled "Consumer Electronics" or "Precision Auto Parts."

We created fake invoices. Fake certificates of origin.

Then, we put the containers on ships bound for Melbourne and Osaka.

The profit margins were insanity. We were buying a brick for $3,000 in Sinaloa and selling it for $200,000 in Sydney. The arbitrage was nearly 6,000%.

Within three months, we had generated $50 million in pure profit.

Our problem wasn't making money; it was storing it. The Hong Kong stock market strategy was saturated. We couldn't pump $50 million more into Mr. M's fund without raising flags with the Securities and Futures Commission.

So, we went old school. We bought gold.

Hong Kong has one of the most active gold markets in the world. In the Sheung Wan district, there are dealers who sell kilogram bars of 99.9% pure gold and accept cash, no questions asked.

I took the cash proceeds from the logistics company. I bought gold bars.

Then, I rented safety deposit boxes in Private Vaults.

Unlike banks, private vaults in Hong Kong (like those operated by security firms) are not subject to the same CRS (Common Reporting Standard) data sharing. You pay cash for the box. You use a biometric key.

I walked into the vault room, the heavy steel door sealing behind me. I opened the box.

It was stacked with gold bars, glowing under the fluorescent light. Each bar was worth roughly $60,000.

I stood there, surrounded by silence and wealth.

I was Nate Haliv. The god of money laundering. I had a Dominican passport, a Nigerian passport, a Hong Kong logistics firm, and a vault full of gold.

I looked at my reflection in the polished surface of a gold bar. I looked successful. I looked untouchable.

I played Post Malone's "Motley Crew" on my phone and screamed alongside him, "I'm at the top of the pyramid."

I paid Wing Chan his million dollars. He wept with relief. He enrolled his son in a prep course for American universities.

"You saved my family," he told me, grasping my hand.

I looked at him with pity. I hadn't saved him. I had made him an accomplice to international drug trafficking. If the police ever kicked down the door of that warehouse, Wing Chan would be the one in handcuffs, not me.

"Just make sure the paperwork is clean, Wing," I said. "For your son's sake."

I left the vault and walked out into the neon-lit streets of Kowloon. My phone buzzed. It was a text from Zendaya.

"Hey," she said. "How is Benin?"

"Hot," I lied, looking up at the skyscrapers of Hong Kong. "Just working hard on the farm."

"I miss you, Josh."

"I miss you too."

I hung up and hailed a taxi.

CHAPTER THIRTY-SIX

I didn't fly back to Dominica. There was no need. My business in the Caribbean was done, and the passport was already in my pocket.

I flew from Hong Kong to Lagos using the Chibuzor Okafor passport. I spent two days in a hotel in Ikeja, shredding documents and wiping digital footprints.

Then, I made the crossing. I took a bush taxi to the Seme Border. This time, I was moving from Nigeria back into the Republic of Benin. I bribed the guards on the Nigerian side to let "Chibuzor" leave without a stamp, and I walked across the dusty No Man's Land.

Once I crossed into Cotonou, Chibuzor Okafor ceased to exist.

I went into a public restroom at a petrol station. I washed my face. I popped out the honey-colored contact lenses and flushed them. I reached into my mouth and removed the cotton balls I had used to widen my jawline for the past year. I took off the thick-rimmed glasses and crushed them in the trash.

I looked in the cracked mirror. Josh Balogun stared back.

I changed into a worn t-shirt and jeans. I slumped my shoulders, dropping the confident posture of an international financier and adopting the weary slouch of a contract worker.

I took a taxi to Cadjehoun Airport in Cotonou.

I approached the airline counter and slapped my blue American passport on the desk. The agent opened it. She saw the entry stamp from eleven months ago.

"You have been in Benin a long time, sir," she noted.

"The cocoa harvest ran long," I said, looking exhausted. "I just want to go home."

She stamped the exit visa.

COTONOU - DEPARTED.

The loop was closed. According to the US State Department and the Department of Homeland Security, Josh Balogun had entered Benin, stayed for eleven months working on a farm, and returned to Los Angeles. My trips to Nigeria, the Maldives, Hong Kong, and Italy had officially never happened.

Zendaya was waiting at LAX. She looked beautiful, but there was a tightness around her eyes. Eleven months is a long time to wait for a boyfriend you barely know.

"I thought you were never coming back," she whispered, burying her face in my chest.

"I promised, didn't I?" I held her tight. "The job just... it got complicated. But the pay was good."

She had moved into my apartment while I was gone—I had encouraged it to keep the place looked-after. It made OpSec difficult. I couldn't set up my "command center" in the living room anymore.

For the first week, I was radio silent. I kept my GrapheneOS Pixel powered down and hidden inside the hollow leg of my IKEA dining table.

But I couldn't stay away forever. I had entered the stratosphere of the underworld. Nate Haliv was no longer just a cleaner; he was a deity.

In the criminal world, reputation is everything. If you mention Heisenberg, people think of meth. If you mention Nate Haliv, criminals think of a ghost who can wash cash through walls.

I had $86 million in my cold storage wallets. My sister, Abisola, had over $40 million sitting in hers, traveling the world, oblivious to the fact that her luxury life was funded by fentanyl and extortion.

But greed is a fire that consumes you. I didn't stop at $100 million. I operated entirely through the dark web using PGP-encrypted emails and Session (a decentralized messaging app).

I never met clients in person anymore. They sent me crypto. Mostly dirty USDT, tainted Bitcoin from ransomware attacks, and hacked Ethereum.

I washed it. I moved it through mixers like Tornado Cash (before the sanctions), routed it through privacy coins like Monero (XMR), and layered it through shell companies in Hong Kong, Dubai, and Singapore.

I raised my fee. The industry standard was 10-12%. I started charging 20%.

"You are robbing us," a Russian arms dealer typed to me once.

"Then go to a bank and see if they take your money," I replied.

He paid the 20%. They always paid. They knew their money was safe with Nate Haliv.

My net worth climbed. $150 million. $220 million. $320 million.

It was enough to buy a small country. It was enough to disappear for a thousand lifetimes. I made up my mind. It was time to kill Nate Haliv.

The heat was getting too intense. I was browsing the FBI's Cyber Most Wanted list on my secure laptop one night while Zendaya slept.

There, between a North Korean hacker and a Russian botnet operator, was a new entry.

UNKNOWN SUBJECT. ALIAS: "NATE HALIV." CHARGES: Money Laundering, Conspiracy to Aid Racketeering, Unlicensed Money Transmitting.

There was no photo. Just a gray silhouette.

"The suspect operates a sophisticated global laundering network utilizing cryptocurrency and shell companies in Asia and the Caribbean. Identity unknown. Considered armed and dangerous."

I stared at the screen. They didn't know I was Josh Balogun. They didn't know I was a cleaner in LA. They didn't know I cleaned toilets for a living.

But they knew my name. And in the digital world, once they have a name, it's only a matter of time before they find the IP address that connects the ghost to the man.

I closed the laptop. I looked at Zendaya sleeping peacefully.

I had to get out. But you don't just hand in your resignation letter to the Cartel.

CHAPTER THIRTY-SEVEN

My love for Zendaya grew, but it was a love built on a foundation of rot. It was a terrifying, suffocating kind of love because I knew that every moment of happiness was stolen time.

She marveled at my humility. She constantly praised me for being a "good man" in a city of narcissists. She had no idea she was sleeping next to a monster. She would slip me a random $50 or $100 bill to buy new shirts because she thought I was struggling to make ends meet as a cleaner. There was even a month where she paid my share of the rent.

"It's the least I can do," she had said, kissing my cheek, her eyes full of that innocent, trusting light. "We're a team, Josh. I've got you."

Her kindness felt like a physical blow. It twisted in my gut like a knife.

I sat in my home office, a small corner of the bedroom Zendaya thought I used for "video games," and unlocked my GrapheneOS Pixel. I opened the hidden volume of my Ledger Live app.

I stared at the number on the screen. **$524,380,210.45**

Five hundred and twenty-four million dollars. *What the hell?*

I had half a billion dollars in liquid assets. I had gold bars sitting in a private vault in Kowloon. I had USDT staked in liquidity pools in the Cayman Islands. I had shell companies in Panama and Belize holding real estate deeds in London.

I could buy the entire apartment complex we lived in with cash and not even make a dent in my net worth. I could buy Zendaya a fleet of those Mercedes G-Wagons Seyi drove. I could buy her a private island in the Caribbean.

And yet, here I was, taking fifty dollars from a girl who worked double shifts at a diner, pretending to be grateful for the charity. The disparity was maddening. It was a psychological torture I hadn't anticipated.

When would it end?

I looked at the walls of the apartment. They felt like they were closing in. I had enough money to live like a king for ten lifetimes, but I couldn't sleep.

Every time a car idled too long outside, I was at the window, checking for unmarked vans. Every time my phone clicked during a call, I assumed it was a wiretap.

I was the King of Money Laundering. I was Nate Haliv. I was a god in the underworld.

But Josh Balogun was a nervous wreck on the verge of a breakdown. I made up my mind. I had to get out. I had to quit the cartel.

It wasn't a decision I made lightly. I knew the rules. Blood in, blood out. But I arrogantly assumed that I was different. I was the financial architect.

I held the keys to their Asian infrastructure. I wasn't some street soldier they could just dispose of; I was too valuable. Or so I thought.

I planned to approach The Professor. I would tell her that I had done my time, built her empire, and now I wanted to retire.

I would offer to consult from a distance, to train a replacement. I convinced myself she would listen to reason.

But before I approached her, I made a mistake. A rookie mistake born of fear. I tried to contact the DEA.

I didn't do it from my encrypted Pixel. That would have been suicide; The Professor likely monitored the traffic on the devices she knew about.

Instead, I went to a Walmart in Inglewood. I bought a cheap "burner" phone, a prepaid flip phone, and a Mint Mobile SIM card paid for with cash.

I waited until Zendaya was asleep. I drove three miles away to a strip mall parking lot.

I parked in the dark, my heart hammering against my ribs like a trapped bird. I dialed the number I had memorized: 1-877-RX-ABUSE.

The line rang.

"Drug Enforcement Administration, how may I direct your call?"

My throat closed up. My hand shook so badly the plastic phone rattled against my ear. I opened my mouth to speak, to say, "I have information on the Sinaloa-Camorra pipeline," but no sound came out.

Panic seized me. I saw images of what cartels did to snitches. The Funkytown gore videos. The bodies hanging from bridges in Juarez.

I hung up. I pulled the battery out of the phone. I crushed the SIM card.

I did this three times over the course of a week. Each time, I drove to a different location.

Each time, I lost my nerve. I tried accessing their anonymous tip portal via Tor on a library computer, but I couldn't bring myself to hit 'Submit'.

I was trapped in indecision.

That night, back in bed, I ran my fingers through Zendaya's hair. She stirred, murmuring in her sleep.

"Zendaya," I whispered into the darkness. "What would you do if you found out I wasn't... who you think I am?"

She sat up, rubbing her eyes, her hair a messy halo. "What do you mean? Are you a murderer or something? Are you secretly Batman?"

"No," I said, my voice tight. "Just... not a cleaner. What if I was someone bad?"

She shrugged, lying back down and draping an arm over my chest. "Well, you will always be my sweet little Josh no matter what. I know your heart. You're gentle. You couldn't hurt a fly."

She paused, her voice turning serious. "As long as you aren't involved in drugs, Josh. You know that. After what happened to my brother. After watching him die because of that poison, I could never forgive that. I would hate you."

Her words were absolute. They hit me with the force of a physical conviction. *I would hate you.* Fuck me!

I was the man moving the money that paid for the poison that killed her brother. I was the engine of her misery. I had to end it. Tomorrow.

The next morning was Sunday. The California sun was streaming through the blinds, mocking my internal darkness.

"Ain't you going to church today?" Zendaya asked, pulling on her floral dress. She looked radiant, pure.

I shook my head, pulling the covers up. "I feel under the weather. My stomach. Pray for me, babe."

She frowned, coming over to feel my forehead. Her hand was cool and soft. "You don't have a fever. Just rest. I'll bring you some soup when I get back."

She kissed me. "I love you, Josh."

"I love you too."

I waited until I heard the lock click and her footsteps fade down the hallway.

I threw off the covers. I didn't have time to be sick. I went to my safe. I took out my GrapheneOS Pixel. I didn't use the burner this time. If I was going to do this, I had to do it facing the music.

I called The Professor via Session, an encrypted messaging app that doesn't require a phone number, only a session ID.

She answered on the first ring. "Nate Haliv," her voice was smooth, cultured, and terrifyingly calm. "To what do I owe the pleasure on a Sunday morning?"

I took a deep breath. "We need to talk. In person."

"Oh?"

"I'm coming to the estate," I said. "It's urgent."

"Very well," she said. "Miguel will be waiting."

I dressed in black. I felt like I was dressing for a funeral. Maybe my own.

The drive to her estate in the Hidden Hills was a blur. My hands were slick with sweat on the steering wheel. I ran through my speech a thousand times. I've made you millions. I've been loyal. I just want out.

I pulled up to the massive iron gates. The camera buzzed, and the gates swung open slowly.

Miguel met me at the front door. He was a mountain of a man, ex-Mexican Special Forces. He patted me down, thoroughly and professionally.

He checked my ankles, my waistband. He took my phone and placed it in a Faraday bag to block signals.

"She's on the patio," Miguel grunted.

The Professor was sitting at a glass table overlooking the valley, sipping herbal tea.

"You look nervous, Josh," she said. She gestured to the empty chair. "Sit."

I sat. My knees were shaking.

"I want to quit," I blurted out. I couldn't hold it in. "I want to stop working for the cartel."

The Professor didn't blink. She didn't scream. She didn't look surprised. She just set her teacup down with a delicate clink.

I remembered when she used to sit on my face. Damn, I haven't slept with her for quite a while.

Focus, Josh, focus. You're here to quit the cartel. Keep your bloody cock to yourself.

"I see," she said softly.

"I've done everything you asked," I rushed on, desperate to fill the silence. "I set up the Asian pipeline. The Hong Kong accounts are self-sustaining. Wing Chan can handle the logistics. I just... I want to live a normal life. I want to be safe."

The Professor sighed, looking disappointed. "Safe. You think you can dip your hands in blood and then just... wash them off?"

"I haven't killed anyone," I said. "I just moved numbers."

"You facilitated the movement of three tons of fentanyl last year alone," she said. "How many overdoses is that? Ten thousand? Twenty thousand? You are a mass murderer, Josh. You just use a keyboard instead of a gun."

She reached under the table and pulled out a thick manila envelope. She slid it across the glass.

"Open it."

My hands trembled as I undid the clasp. I pulled out a stack of 8x10 photographs.

The first one was of me and Zendaya eating at KFC three days ago. Taken from a car across the street.

The next was of us entering her apartment. The next was of Zendaya sleeping in my bed. The angle was from the fire escape outside my window. They had been watching us while we slept.

My breath hitched.

Then came the others.

Abisola.

My sister walking to her lecture hall. My sister sitting in a restaurant, laughing with friends. My sister grocery shopping.

The photos were high-resolution, recent. Some were timestamped yesterday.

"How?" I whispered. "How did you find them?"

"You are a genius with numbers, Josh," The Professor said, her voice dripping with pity. "But you are an amateur at tradecraft."

She leaned forward.

"You bought a burner phone last week. You drove to a parking lot in Inglewood to dial the DEA hotline. Very dramatic."

I froze. "I... I didn't..."

"Don't lie to me," she snapped. "You made a fatal error, Josh. You brought your primary phone, the Pixel, with you in the car. You turned it off, yes. But modern batteries and GPS chips have passive logging. When you turned it back on at home, it uploaded the location history."

She tapped the table.

"Co-location Analysis. We correlated the movement of your burner phone's IMEI with your primary phone. They moved together. They stopped together. You led us right to your secrets."

I dropped the photos.

They scattered across the table. Images of the only two people I loved, targeted by the most dangerous woman in the hemisphere.

"Please," I begged, my voice breaking. "Don't hurt them. I'll stay. I'll do anything. Just leave them out of this."

"I know you will stay," she smiled. "But promises are cheap, Nate Haliv. You have gone soft. You have been flirting with the idea of being a rat. You think the DEA can save you? You think Witness Protection can hide a girl living in Nigeria? I could give someone $1 to end your sister's life in Nigeria, Josh."

She snapped her fingers and stood up.

"I need insurance. I need to know that you are bound to me not just by money, but by blood. I need to know you are one of us."

She signaled to Miguel.

"Take him downstairs."

Miguel grabbed my arm. His grip was like iron. He marched me through the house, past the beautiful living room, to a heavy oak door near the kitchen.

Behind the door were stairs leading down.

The air grew colder as we descended. The smell hit me first. It was a chemical cocktail of bleach, copper, and damp earth.

At the bottom of the stairs was a steel door, reinforced with acoustic foam. A soundproof door. Miguel unlocked it.

We stepped into a room that looked like a nightmare. The walls were lined with heavy plastic sheeting. The floor was concrete, sloping toward a central drain. Bright, clinical fluorescent lights buzzed overhead.

In the center of the room, a man was duct-taped to a metal chair.

He was unrecognizable. His face was a swollen ruin of purple and black bruises. His nose was smashed flat. One eye was swollen shut.

"This," The Professor said, stepping into the room behind us, "is Diego. You remember him? He handled our logistics in Sinaloa."

I stared at the broken man. He whimpered when he saw us.

"Diego is not Mexican," The Professor said. "My contacts in the Mexican Federal Police ran his biometrics. His name is Agent Michael Torres. He is DEA."

My knees almost gave out.

"He has been feeding his handlers information on our shipments for six months," she continued. "He is the reason we lost the cargo in Rotterdam. He is the reason I lost twelve million dollars. *Pendejo*."

Miguel stepped forward and ripped the duct tape off Diego's mouth.

"Please," Diego gasped, spitting blood and teeth. "I have a family. Just kill me. Don't touch them. Please."

The Professor ignored him. She nodded to Miguel.

Miguel walked to a side door, a closet I hadn't noticed. He opened it and dragged three people out. They were bound, blindfolded, and gagged.

A woman. A little boy. A little girl. The children couldn't have been older than five.

They were terrified, shaking, making muffled sounds of panic behind the gags.

Diego screamed. It was a raw, primal sound that tore at his throat.

"NO! NO! PLEASE! GOD NO! KILL ME! LEAVE THEM ALONE!"

The Professor looked at me. Her expression was bored.

"You betrayed me, Diego," she said to the agent. "There is a price for treason."

Her beautiful face was clouded with fury. Was this the same lady that was always letting me "finish on her face?" I couldn't recognize her anymore.

She turned to me. She pointed to a metal workbench in the corner of the room.

On it sat a chainsaw. It was a heavy-duty Stihl logging saw. The bar was long, the teeth sharp and gleaming with oil.

"Pick it up, Josh," she ordered.

I shook my head, stepping back. "No. No, I can't. They're children."

"If you don't," The Professor said, her voice devoid of all humanity, "Miguel will drive to your apartment right now. He will bring Zendaya here. And he will strap her to that chair. And he will peel her skin off while you watch."

I looked at Miguel. He stood by the door, arms crossed. His face was stone. He would do it. He would enjoy it.

"And after Zendaya," she continued, "we will tell our contact in Nigeria to end Abisola's life. Imagine your teenage sister dying because of you. Do you want that on your conscience?"

I couldn't breathe. The room was spinning.

"Pick up the saw."

I walked to the table. My legs felt like they were moving through molasses. I reached out and grabbed the handle. The saw was heavy. It smelled of gasoline.

"Start with the girl," The Professor said. "Let him watch."

Diego was thrashing against the chair, tearing his wrists open on the zip ties. "PLEASE! TAKE ME! NOT HER! PLEASE!"

"Do it!" The Professor barked. "Or Zendaya dies today!"

I pulled the starter cord.

Sputter. It didn't start.

"Start it!"

I pulled again, harder.

ROAR.

The engine screamed to life. The chain blurred, vibrating violently in my hands. The sound was deafening in the small, enclosed room. The exhaust fumes filled the air instantly.

The little girl heard the roar. She started to cry and scream behind her gag, thrashing on the floor.

I dissociated. I felt my mind leave my body. I floated up to the ceiling, looking down at the man in the black shirt holding the chainsaw. That wasn't me. That wasn't Josh Balogun. That was a demon.

I approached the girl. "I'm sorry," I whispered, though she couldn't hear me over the engine. "I'm so sorry."

I revved the engine. I swung the blade. The room turned red.

Movies don't show you the reality of a chainsaw. They don't show you the resistance. They don't show you how the machine bucks and kicks when it hits bone. They don't show you the hot spray that coats your face, tasting of copper and salt.

It was messy. It was brutal. It was long.

Diego's scream broke something in the universe. It was a sound I will hear until the day I die.

"The boy," The Professor commanded.

I moved mechanically. I was crying, blinding tears mixing with the blood on my face, but my hands obeyed the order.

I killed the boy.

Then the wife.

It was harder with the wife. She was stronger. She tried to roll away. I had to pin her down with my boot. The saw snarled and chewed.

By the time I turned to Diego, the room was a slaughterhouse. The floor was slick. I could barely stand.

"Finish it," The Professor said.

I walked over to the broken man. He wasn't screaming anymore. He was staring at the remains of his life. His mind shattered into a thousand pieces. He looked at me, and his eyes were empty. He was already dead.

I raised the saw.

When the silence finally returned to the room, my ears were ringing. The only sound was the drip, drip, drip of fluids running into the floor drain.

I dropped the chainsaw. It clattered on the concrete. I stood there, vibrating. My clothes were soaked. My skin was stained.

The Professor walked over, stepping carefully over the carnage in her expensive heels. She handed Miguel a video camera that had been recording the entire time.

"We have it all on tape," she said. "You just murdered a federal agent and his family. There is no witness protection for this. There is no plea deal. You are a cop killer now, Nate Haliv."

She reached out and grabbed my chin, forcing me to look at her. Her fingers dug into my jaw.

"If you ever try to leave me again... if you ever try to call the DEA... I send this tape to the FBI. And then I kill your girlfriend and sister."

I didn't speak. I couldn't. My tongue was heavy in my mouth.

"Clean him up, Miguel," she said, turning and walking out the door.

Miguel took me upstairs. He led me to a utility sink in the garage. He hosed me down like a dirty dog. The water ran pink into the drain. He gave me fresh clothes from a gym bag.

He drove me home in silence.

I unlocked my apartment door. The lights were off. Zendaya wasn't home yet.

I walked into the bathroom. I turned the shower to scalding hot. I stepped in, clothes and all, and slid down the wall until I hit the floor.

I scrubbed my skin until it bled. I scrubbed until the water ran clear. But I knew the stain would never come out.

Josh Balogun died in that basement. Only the monster remained.

CHAPTER THIRTY-EIGHT

Zendaya knocked on the door. It was a soft, rhythmic sound. To anyone else, it was the sound of a girlfriend checking on her partner. To me, it was the sound of the engine turning over.

Then the roar.

I was curled in the fetal position on the floor of the closet, sandwiched between a hamper of dirty laundry and the cold drywall.

My hands were clamped over my ears so tightly my fingernails were digging crescents into my scalp. But hands are flesh, and flesh cannot block out the frequency of hell.

The sound of the Stihl heavy-duty logging saw was not in the room. It was inside the architecture of my skull. It was reverberating against the parietal bone, bouncing off the frontal lobe, shredding the gray matter.

I squeezed my eyes shut, but the darkness was a canvas. In the blackness, I saw the basement in Hidden Hills. I saw the plastic sheeting shimmering under the fluorescent lights. I saw the red mist hanging in the air like a fine, iron-tasting humidity.

I saw the little girl. She was wearing a pink shirt with a cartoon unicorn on it. I saw the unicorn disintegrate.

"Josh?" Zendaya's voice came through the door, muffled and terrified. "Please, baby. Open up. You haven't eaten in two days. I can hear you breathing."

I didn't answer. I couldn't. If I opened my mouth, the sound of the chainsaw would escape and cut her in half, too. I was a vessel of containment.

I had to keep the horror inside or it would consume the world. I needed to reset. I needed to reboot the system.

I crawled out of the closet and slammed my forehead against the wall.

THUD.

A flash of white light. Good. Pain was grounding.

THUD.

"Josh!" she screamed from the hallway.

THUD.

I did it until the drywall cracked. I did it until a warm, sticky liquid trickled down my nose. But the chainsaw didn't stop. It just idled, a low, menacing growl in the back of my throat.

I scrambled to my feet, swaying like a drunkard on a ship deck. I stumbled to my desk. My hands, shaking violently, fumbled with the combination of the safe.

Left 40. Right 10. Left 80.

The door clicked open.

Inside lay the GrapheneOS Pixel. The black monolith that held the keys to the kingdom. I picked it up. My thumb ghosted over the screen, unlocking the hidden partition.

I opened the Ledger Live app. I needed to see it. I needed to know why I had done it.

The numbers glowed in the dark room, a string of white digits against a void of black.

524,380,210.45 USDT.

Five hundred and twenty-four million, three hundred and eighty thousand, two hundred and ten dollars. And forty-five cents.

The forty-five cents almost made me laugh.

It was so precise. So banal. I had slaughtered a family for a number on a screen.

I had severed the spinal cord of a five-year-old boy for a fluctuating balance of digital tokens.

"It's not real," I whispered. My voice sounded like grinding glass. "None of it is real."

I threw the phone. It hit the mirror above the dresser, shattering the glass. My reflection split into a thousand jagged pieces. A thousand monsters stared back.

I needed anesthesia.

I pushed the heavy oak dresser aside with a strength I didn't know I possessed. I didn't bother with shoes. I grabbed a wad of cash from the safe. I didn't count it, just grabbed a brick of hundred-dollar bills and unlocked the bedroom door.

Zendaya was standing there, her hand raised to knock again. She looked exhausted, her eyes rimmed with red. She was wearing her waitress uniform.

"Josh—"

I pushed past her. I didn't look at her. If I looked at her, I would see Diego's wife. I would see the way her head rolled.

"Josh, wait! Where are you going? You're bleeding!"

I ran down the hallway. I took the stairs two at a time. I burst out of the lobby into the cool Los Angeles night.

The pavement was gritty and cold.

I stepped on a piece of broken glass, feeling it slice into my heel, but the pain was distant, a signal from a planet I no longer inhabited. I looked like a wraith. I was shirtless, ribs showing through my skin, blood smearing my forehead, and barefoot.

I walked to the liquor store on the corner. The neon sign buzzed. OPEN.

I shoved the door open. The bell chimed.

To me, it sounded like the elevator dinger in the basement.

I marched to the premium shelf. I grabbed three bottles of Grey Goose. The glass clinked together, a sharp, piercing sound.

"Sir?" the cashier asked. He was a young kid, maybe twenty. His eyes went wide when he saw the blood on my face. His hand drifted toward the panic button under the counter. "Sir, are you okay? You can't be in here without shoes."

I stared at him. The fluorescent lights of the store were too bright. They were X-rays. They were exposing the rot inside me.

"I need it quiet," I whispered. My voice was a croak. "The engine. It's too loud."

"Sir, I'm going to have to ask you to—"

"The total," I snapped. "Give me the total."

"It's... it's $115. "

I reached into my pocket and pulled out the brick of cash. It was definitely more than $5,000. I threw it on the counter. The bills fluttered like dead leaves.

"Keep it," I rasped. "Just keep it. And turn off the lights."

I turned and ran.

Back in the apartment, Zendaya was on the phone, her voice high and frantic. She hung up when I kicked the door shut.

I didn't speak. I uncapped the first bottle and drank. I didn't sip; I swallowed the vodka in great, heaving gulps. It burned my throat, a cleansing fire. I drank until I choked, coughing up clear liquid and bile onto the carpet.

"Josh, please," Zendaya sobbed. She tried to approach me. "Let me help you. Talk to me."

"Don't come near me!" I screamed, backing into the corner. I hurled the bottle at the wall. It shattered, spraying glass and alcohol everywhere. The smell of ethanol filled the room.

It smelled like the solvent Miguel used to clean the chainsaw.

"You made me!" I yelled at the empty air above Zendaya's head. "I didn't want to! You made me pick it up!"

"Who made you?" Zendaya cried. "Josh, there's no one here!"

"The children!" I roared, tearing at my own hair. "They're here! Can't you hear them? They're screaming! Oh God! No!"

I lunged at the wall, punching the drywall until my knuckles split. I needed to get them out. I needed to silence them.

"Josh!"

Zendaya grabbed my arm. That was the breaking point. The contact sent a jolt of electricity through me. I spun around, eyes wide, pupils dilated to black saucers. I didn't see my girlfriend.

I saw The Professor. I saw the woman who held the gun to my head.

"You witch!" I snarled.

I grabbed her shoulders and shoved her back. She tripped over the ottoman and fell hard, hitting her elbow.

She screamed. The sound of the woman I loved in pain flipped a switch in my mind.

I collapsed to my knees, rocking back and forth, clutching my head.

"I cut them," I moaned, the words bubbling up like black tar. "I cut the boy. I cut the girl. The machine... it bucked in my hands. It was slippery. There was so much red."

The door burst open. Mr. Henderson, the neighbor, stood there with a baseball bat, looking terrified.

"I called 911!" he shouted. "Back away from her, son!"

I looked up at him. I smiled. It was a broken, jagged smile.

"It doesn't matter," I whispered. "You can't clean the drain. The DNA is in the concrete."

Then the sirens came.

CHAPTER THIRTY-NINE

The next seven days were a blur of chemical restraint. I was in the secure ward of Los Angeles County-USC Medical Center. Time didn't exist here.

There was only the white ceiling, the leather straps binding my wrists and ankles to the bed, and the IV drip feeding Haldol and Ativan into my veins.

The drugs dampened the noise. The chainsaw faded from a roar to a distant idle. When I finally woke up and stayed awake, the manic energy was gone. I felt hollowed out. Scraped clean. I was a husk of a human being.

I was sitting in a small, white interrogation room within the hospital. My wrists were cuffed to the table.

Zendaya was there. She sat in the corner, wrapped in a blanket. She looked like she had aged ten years in a week.

"Josh," she whispered. Her voice was trembling. "The doctors said you had a psychotic break. They said it was stress."

I looked at her. I loved her so much it physically hurt. And because I loved her, I had to destroy her.

"It wasn't stress," I said. My voice was dead. Flat. "It was memory."

"You said... you said you killed children," she said, tears spilling over. "That was a delusion, right? Tell me it was a delusion."

I looked at the two police officers standing by the door.

"Agent Michael Torres," I said clearly. "He was DEA. His wife, Elena. His son, Mateo. His daughter, Sofia."

The room temperature seemed to drop ten degrees.

"I killed them," I continued. "Two weeks ago. In a soundproof basement in Hidden Hills. I used a Stihl MS 880 chainsaw. I started with the girl."

Zendaya let out a sound I will never forget. It was a choked, horrified gasp. She put her hand over her mouth and turned away, sickened.

The taller officer stepped forward, his hand resting on his holster. "Torres? There's a federal bolo out for an Agent Torres."

"Get the DEA," I said, closing my eyes. "I'm done running."

It took three hours for the suits to arrive.

They cleared the room. Even the doctors were pushed out. The air in the room was heavy, charged with the static of high-stakes federal jurisdiction.

Two men walked in.

One was older, with gray hair and a face carved from granite, Special Agent Miller. The other was younger, sharp-eyed, Agent Chen.

"You're the guy claiming to know about Torres," Miller said. He didn't sit. He loomed.

"I don't claim," I said. "I know."

I looked at Zendaya. She was still in the corner, paralyzed by shock. "First," I said. "Her." I nodded at Zendaya.

"She is innocent. She thinks I'm a cleaner. She doesn't know anything. But The Professor will kill her the moment I start talking. I need her in protective custody. Right now. Or I don't say a word."

Miller looked at Zendaya, assessing her. Then he looked back at me. "If you give us Torres, we can put her in a safe house tonight. Pending WITSEC evaluation."

"And my sister," I added. "Abisola Balogun. She's in Nigeria. Obafemi Awolowo University. Help me save her. Reach out to contacts in Nigeria. Put her somewhere safe."

Miller nodded to Chen. Chen stepped out, phone already to his ear.

"You have our attention," Miller said, pulling out a chair and sitting down. "But if you're wasting my time, I will make sure you never see the sun again."

I leaned forward as far as the cuffs would allow. The bruise on my forehead throbbed.

"Agent Miller," I said softly. "How would it feel to be the man who took down The Professor, the Hell Hound, and Nate Haliv all in one day?"

Miller froze. His eyes widened slightly. It was the reaction I expected.

These weren't just names. These were myths. The Professor was a rumor, a cartel head no one had ever seen. The Hell Hound was the Camorra's grim reaper. And Nate Haliv... I was the ghost in the machine. I was the reason they couldn't trace the money.

"You know Nate Haliv?" Miller asked, his voice low.

"I am Nate Haliv."

Miller stared at me. He looked at the hospital gown. He looked at the handcuffs. He looked at the terrified girl in the corner.

"You?" Miller scoffed. "You're the architect? The guy who laundered half a billion dollars through the Asian markets? The one who laundered money for almost all the drug lords we've arrested in the last six months?"

"Three hundred and twenty million last year alone," I corrected. "Check the blockchain. The wallet address ends in x9F4. It hasn't moved since last Tuesday."

Miller pulled a tape recorder from his jacket. He clicked it on. The little red light blinked. "Start talking."

I talked for eight hours. I vomited the truth. I gave them the structure.

I explained how I used the Segregated Portfolio Companies in the Cayman Islands to mask the ownership of the Hong Kong funds.

I explained the Trade-Based Money Laundering scheme using the logistics firm in Kwai Chung Port, how we over-invoiced copper wire to move value across borders.

I gave them Don Alberto Rossi. I gave them his safe house in Naples. I gave them the encrypted messaging handles he used.

Then, I gave them The Professor.

"Her name is Camilla," I said. "She lives in an estate on Saddle Creek Road in Hidden Hills. You're looking for a scar-faced cartel boss. You're wrong. She is twenty-one years old."

"Twenty-one?" Miller asked, incredulous.

"She inherited the throne when she was nineteen," I said. "She's a prodigy. And she is a psychopath."

I grabbed a notepad and a pen with my cuffed hands. I drew the basement.

"There's a hidden door behind the wine rack," I said, sketching the lines. "Soundproofed. Steel core. Inside, there's a floor drain. You'll find traces of Agent Torres's blood in the trap. And you'll find the camera."

"Camera?"

"She filmed it," I said, my voice shaking. "She made me do it, and she filmed it for leverage. It's on an SD card in her safe. That's your evidence."

Miller looked sick. He looked at me with a mixture of disgust and awe.

"And the money?" Miller asked. "Nate Haliv is sitting on a fortune. Where are the keys?"

The room went quiet. This was the moment.

"It's gone," I lied.

"Don't bullshit me," Miller snapped. "You laundered millions. You don't just lose the keys."

"I destroyed them," I said, meeting his gaze. "When I cracked... when I started hearing the voices... I realized the money was cursed. I wiped the Ledger. I burned the seed phrase paper. I formatted the drive."

"We can subpoena the exchanges," Miller threatened.

"It's in cold storage," I said calmly. "It's Monero. It's mixed USDT on the TRON network. It's sitting on the blockchain, encrypted by a 256-bit key that no longer exists.

"You can subpoena God himself, Agent Miller, but you won't find that money."

Miller stared at me for a long time. He was looking for the tic, the tell. But I didn't blink.

I hadn't destroyed them. The seed phrase was burned into the neurons of my hippocampus. Twenty-four words. A poem of wealth and damnation.

Lantern. Echo. Gravity. Solar. Ridge. Harbor. Winter. Asset. Blue. Timber. Ghost. Iron...

I recited them in my head while he stared at me.

"You know what happens now," Miller said, leaning back. "You confessed to the murder of a federal agent. And his family. That's a capital crime. The death penalty is mandatory."

"I know," I said.

Miller looked at the stack of notes he had taken. He looked at the map of the basement. "But," he said, rubbing his temples. "You just gave us the entire Sinaloa-Camorra connection. You gave us the hierarchy. You gave us closure for the Torres family. If this intel is good... if we catch her..."

He paused. "We take death off the table. You plead guilty to all counts. Life without the possibility of parole. You die in prison, but you die of old age."

I looked at the observation window. Zendaya was being led away by two marshals. She looked back at me one last time. Her eyes were empty. The love was gone, replaced by a horror that would never heal. "Deal," I said.

CHAPTER FORTY

The raid happened at 0300 hours. They hit the Hidden Hills estate with three SWAT teams and a helicopter.

Camilla didn't surrender. She was twenty-one, and she believed she was immortal. She engaged the federal agents from the top of her marble staircase with a gold-plated AK-47.

She took two rounds to the chest and one to the head. She died on the foyer floor, bleeding out onto her imported Italian tile. They found the basement. They found the drain. They found the SD card.

Don Alberto was arrested in Naples by the *Carabinieri*. He will die in an Italian 41-bis prison cell.

And me?

I stood in federal court a month later. I refused a defense attorney. I stood before the judge in my orange jumpsuit and shackles.

"How do you plead?"

"Guilty," I said.

The judge sentenced me to Life Imprisonment Without the Possibility of Parole, plus one hundred and forty years.

ADX Florence. Supermax. The Alcatraz of the Rockies.

I sit in my cell. It is seven feet by twelve feet. The walls are poured concrete. The bed is a concrete slab with a thin mattress. The desk is concrete. The stool is concrete.

There is a window. It is four inches wide and forty inches high.

It is angled upward so I can only see the sky. I don't know where I am in the complex. I don't know if there are mountains or plains outside. I only know the gray of the Colorado sky.

I have been here for two years.

I am in solitary confinement for twenty-three hours a day. I have no contact with other prisoners. I have no phone calls.

The silence here is absolute. It is a tomb for the living.

I don't hear the chainsaw anymore. The medication helps, but the silence helps more. There is no stimulation here to feed the demons.

I think about Zendaya. She is in Witness Protection. She has a new name. A new history. She lives in a small town in Montana or maybe Nebraska. She will find a good man—a man who works with his hands, a man who sleeps through the night.

She will have children, and she will love them fiercely, and she will never tell them about the boy who cleaned toilets in Los Angeles.

I think about Abisola, my sister. I haven't heard from her since I was locked up.

And me?

I close my eyes. I sit on my concrete stool.

Lantern. Echo. Gravity. Solar. Ridge. Harbor. Winter. Asset. Blue. Timber. Ghost. Iron...

I recite the words. Over and over. A mantra. A prayer.

$524,380,210.45

It is floating in the digital ether. It is sitting on a ledger distributed across a thousand computers around the world.

It is one of the greatest fortunes ever amassed by a single criminal, and it is locked behind the door of my memory.

I am the poorest man in the world. I own a toothbrush and a jumpsuit. Yet, I had half a billion dollars hidden in a crypto wallet.

The buzzer sounds. *BUZZ.*

It is time for the one hour of recreation in the solitary cage.

I stand up. I walk to the heavy steel door. I wait for the slot to open for the handcuffs.

I am Josh Balogun. Inmate Number 49201-018.

THE BEGINNING

Other Books by Nate Haliv

- Lucy Far: The Untold Story of Child Trafficking
- Seeing the World Through a Black Woman's Eyes
- The Girl Who Ran Without Legs
- A Letter to Feminists

Made in the USA
Coppell, TX
05 February 2026

70240986R00194